Souls of malapace: Book 1

The Book of Taba

Malapace, Mutants, and Misfits

By seon jung

CONTENTS

To Diana

Couldn't have gotten this far without you, thanks :)

"Leadership is the least coveted role to the most qualified of leaders."

-The Overseer, Babs

CHAPTER 1

The three of them silently walked down the cracked dirt path, the morning mist kissing their cheeks. Stepping over the encroaching roots, rusted fences, and misshapen rotting carcass, Taba, Queenie, and Hush all stared up at the dusty brick tower.

Queenie raised an eyebrow at the crumbly wall. "Look. I *know* I'm not supposed to doubt you...but uh, are you *certain* this is safe to climb?"

"Nope," Taba responded. "The wrong step or turn, and your feet'll give out to rotted wood. Step *exactly* where I step."

Hush pursed his lips and silently nodded. Queenie opened her mouth to protest before her brother smacked her back. She scowled before giving him a slight shove, but kept her focus on Taba's cautious steps.

Is it safe for us to step here? **O**
Is it safe for us to grab that handle? **X**
Is it safe for us to jump onto that step? **O**
Is...

Taba quietly and efficiently climbed around the withered clock-tower, avoiding seemingly safe spots while jumping onto what looked like hollow, rotten wood. He couldn't see their faces, but he was sure that the siblings behind them were flinching with each of his steps. From the timid echoes, they were reluctantly mimicking his movements, trying to avoid putting as much pressure on their feet as possible.

After about fifteen minutes of stressful clambering, the trio reached the top of the clocktower. From this height, they could briefly see the damned city's grand walls, along with the creeping path that led to it.

Queenie flopped onto the more solid roof with a groan. "Look. Why couldn't we have climbed this with chains? I have plenty of them in storage, and it would've been *way* less nerve-wracking."

Hush sat down, a slight bead of sweat tricking down his neck as he did. "Is it in regards to the soul used? Would it have caught their attention?" he asked.

Taba nodded, a flicker of uncertainty in his pupils. "Well...yeah. I don't know why, but apparently climbing with Queenie's chains would be wrong."

She let out a sigh of exasperation as she unstored her weapon, laying flat on her stomach as she calmed her breathing. Setting up its stand, her brash aura vanished as she steadily peeked through her scope. Without removing her eye from the lens, she calmly chambered a bullet and rolled her shoulder. "You know, for as cool as your blessing is...it makes *no* sense sometimes," she muttered.

Taba leaned against the rickety tile as he stretched his back. "Yeah, join the club," he said. "Get comfy, we're gonna be here for a few hours."

...

The three of them silently lay against the roof until the sun stretched into the heavens, with birds slowly ruffling their feathers in song. Occasionally, a bird's song would end abruptly, with silence quickly following the area the chirps originated from. However, as quickly as it vanished, their song erupted once more in desperation to find a partner. It was probably a mutant. Taba checked with his blessing: it would clear way of the tower and wouldn't interfere with their task. So, it wasn't worth stressing about.

Hush's eyes quickly widened as he calmly placed a hand on his sister's shoulder. She took a soft exhale as their targets slowly emerged into view over the hill. An ageless woman wearing a white dress, suge-gasa, and sandals. A buff, shirtless bald man wearing only breezy dark green pants, held up with a purple rope belt. A slouching scraggly man with unkempt grey hair wearing a brown leather coat with grey pants. The three targets all looked fairly unremarkable...but they were the Gatekeepers for the grand city of Malapace. If they were taken out of the picture...then...

"That's them," Taba said. "When they enter range, take the shot."

Queenly quietly thumbed the safety. "You sure it's them?"

He rolled his eyes. "You know my blessing. Of course it's them."

"Both of you, shut up." Hush said with a frown, watching as the Gatekeepers slowed their walking pace. "She's saying some-thing...nevermind, it's just a cough."

Taba wrinkled his brow. "Why are they stopping? It's the middle of th-"

The teenager felt his blood run cold and quickly tapped into his soul.

3

Do they know we're here?

O

As his soul drained slightly, Taba cursed. They *knew*? Furthermore, the amount of soul drained meant that this question was *heavy*, and that meant the answer was something not obvious.

He flicked his head to Queenie, who lay prone. "They *know*. **Shoot.**"

Queenie pulled the trigger, and the sniper snapped with a scream, its bullet flying towards the target known as G. Her shot hit true, and G's body was thrown back as he crumpled to the ground. Queenie quickly unscoped, her eyes shining with confusion and fear.

Hush's eyes widened. "I...I know they were out of range....but you *missed* the head?"

Queenie slowly shook her head, her hands trembling. "Who the hell do you think I am? I don't miss. The *bullet* missed."

"Yeah, that sounds like you mi-"

Suddenly, the trio froze up as they heard the crunch of cracked tile behind them. Not daring to turn, they stayed motionless as a man yawned behind them, followed by the sound of fingers scratching skin.

"I mean, got to hand it to ya. It's been a while since someone pulled a sniper on us."

If I turn now, will this stab connect?

X

If I surrender, could I survive?

O

If we fought, could we wi-

Suddenly, Queenie screamed, her sniper vanishing as it was placed in storage as she pulled out a dagger. Before Taba could stop her,

Hush also chose to turn and face their target, his fingers flexed to activate his blessing, blinding their assailant. The man standing behind them raised his eyebrows in mild surprise as his sight vanished ever so suddenly.

Queenie's first slice brushed over the man's head as he quickly ducked her attack. Hush threw a kick, to which their target caught with relative ease. Hush's eyes widened in confusion.

"How? You're bli-"

The target known as Patchy rolled his neck, before slamming down on Hush's knee. A sickening crack rang in the air as Hush screamed bloody murder. He flexed his fingers, and Patchy blinked his eyes.

"Whoa, I can see again. You got the *weirdest* blessing, man." Patchy said.

Sweat dripped from Hush's face, but he stayed suspiciously calm for a person whose leg just broke. Taba closed his eyes, blew out a breath, and slowly turned to face Patchy. Patchy stared back with glowing lazy eyes, slouched posture, and a carefree stance that was full of openings. However, as Taba's eyes gazes at numerous possibilities, every single one was apparently impossible.

Hush raised his arms, sweat dripping down his back. "Forgive my friends. Let them go. I'll take their place."

Hush and Queenie both looked at their friend with bewilderment. "Taba?"

Patchy frowned and scratched his face. "I mean, you shot G. That isn't something that can just be *forgiven*, you feel?"

Taba grimaced, but nodded. "Fair."

He nodded to Queenie. "Give me your dagger for a sec...and trust me."

Queenie blinked but handed over her weapon with confusion. Taba took the blade with appreciation, sweat dripping down his forehead as he proceeded to plunge the weapon deep into his left pec. As he twisted the handle and dragged the weapon downwards, he could hear the screams of siblings. Taba looked back, exhaustion suddenly overtaking his body.

Though he struggled to inhale with half a lung, he nodded to his friends. "Run."

Before the energy left his body, he dove off the watchtower, placing all his bets on the pathway his blessing revealed to him.

As the whistling of wind brushed past his hair, the last thing he remembered was someone firmly gripping his body.

...

Taba took a deep inhale and immediately vomited as he sat up.

"Dude, what the *hell*?" The man standing beside him snapped with a scowl.

Taba felt his chest as he looked down, baffled that his chest was intact. He looked up at the people surrounding him, even more baffled to find his targets staring at him. He was surrounded by the Gatekeepers. Patchy (his eyes no longer glowing), Sana, and a now vomit-covered G.

G grumbled as he nodded to Patchy. "Could you...?"

Patchy sighed and suddenly the vomit that was on G splattered to the floor. As G rubbed his face in discomfort, Sana knelt down and stared at Taba with soft eyes.

Though holding a kind expression, her brow was stern. "Could you explain why you and your friends tried to kill us?"

Taba rolled his arms, still confused how he felt no soreness or pain whatsoever. For some reason, he felt no reason to lie.

"Dad. I didn't want to let him down."

Sana furrowed her brow. "Who's your Dad?"

Taba hesitated and refused to speak any further. Dad would kill him if he did. Sana stared at him, a concerned expression listed on her face. She stood up, brushed her dress with her hands, then walked to Patchy and exchanged quiet whispers.

Meanwhile, Taba slowly glanced around, looking for Queenie and Hush. They both seemed to be missing, so perhaps they had managed to escape. He closed his eyes and tapped into his soul. Though he didn't have much in his well (on the account that he nearly died), he whispered his questions in his mind.

Are they safe?

O

Did they run away?

X

Taba grit his teeth as his eyes opened, only to see Sana staring at him with a blank expression. Taba struggled up to his feet, and bowed.

"I'm sorry, but I need to go."

"Wait, nonono," Patchy said with a frown. "You're sticking with us. We can't just let you go now, can we?"

Taba was running dangerously low on soul, but he could probably ask a few questions before he was fully tapped out. If he could just take out *one* of the targets, he could use the chaos to flee. Of course, it was ridiculous to assume he could take one of the Gatekeepers on his own...but he had to try.

Two questions, thats all he could afford himself to ask. Which Gatekeeper could fall in two questions? Taba darted his eyes to G. No, G somehow got up from a sniper bullet. It was safe to assume he was immortal or untouchable. Taba then glanced at Patchy, before immediately dismissing the thought. If he and his friends couldn't take down Patchy in a 3v1, it was completely improbable to take him down in a 1v1. So that left...

Taba balled his fists and turned to Sana. He bolted to the calm woman, and quickly asked a question.

Would a leg sweep work?

ϴ X

Taba blinked, completely caught off guard by the response. He had never had his questioning change answers before. Out of desperation, he went for the leg sweep regardless, but Sana stepped back with relative ease. Not easing up, he put pressure on his knees and pushed up to slam his palm into her chin. In response, Sana grabbed Taba's wrist and flung him over her shoulder and onto his back in a swift motion.

As he groaned in pain, Sana stared down at the boy with mild confusion. While staring at him, she walked over to Patchy and whispered a few phrases in his ear. He looked up and took a small breath, his eyes glowing once more. Before Taba could realize what was happening, Queenie and Hush suddenly appeared by his side, both of his friends looking stunned at their sudden appearance.

Sana nodded to the trio. "We're taking you into Malapace. Please don't try anything funny, I don't want to hurt you any more than needed."

...

There wasn't a being around that wasn't at least *aware* of the grand city of Malapace. Even with the dismantling of the internet, the rumors of Malapace's glory was spoken in hushed whispers.

"I heard that it was the first soulbearer to construct its walls."

"You know that bald Gatekeeper? I heard he's immortal!"

"They say that Malapace's citizens can eat every day."

"Have you seen the cattle? The Overseer was able to donate a few cows to our village!"

Very few humans had the opportunity to visit Malapace...because everyone was too busy trying to survive and protect what little they had. The only ones who could afford to travel out were the merchants and soulbearers.

So for Taba and his friends to be taken into the city? It was baffling, to say the least. Usually, enemies were dispatched of immediately.

After making a splint for Hush's leg, the trio began to slowly make their way to Malapace by foot. Though they could see the looming stone walls, the entire walk took about an hour and a half. Every time the *idea* of fleeing flashed in Taba's mind, Sana turned her head back with a frown. No words were exchanged on the entire journey, so Taba took the time to take in a more detailed examination of the Gatekeepers.

Patchy, the one who couldnt have been older than twenty-five and had somehow teleported behind them, walked while scratching the inside of his ear with a pinky. Though it wasn't obvious from afar, the man had grey, shoulder length, scraggily hair with his face littered with uneven stubble. With his slouched posture, his eyes were half-opened and one hand always fiddling with *something*, be it scratching his skin or rubbing his fingers.

G looked to be in his late twenties, and for some reason, wore no shirt and shoes. As impressive as his physique was, the most notable thing was his lack of blemishes whatsoever. He had smooth skin, no pimples, and, most curiously, no scars. Maybe the rumors of him being immortal were true. Taba would tap into his soul to ask...but his soul was drained.

And then...there was Sana. He wasn't sure what to make of her. The female Gatekeeper could've been anywhere between fifteen and fourty years old. The simple, long, white dress that flowed in the wind put her in an odd limbo between a young girl dancing in the wind and a mature woman who had seen the seconds of time take away everything she had loved. Balanced on top of her silky, long black hair was a sugegasa with a string around her neck, straw sandals laced around her feet. Apart from that, she had no adornments, jewelry, or makeup...similar to Queenie.

While Taba stared at her, Sana looked back with a puzzled look on her face, causing him to flinch and turn his gaze elsewhere. There were rumors of an omnipotent Gatekeeper who knew everything. Though Taba had dismissed such rumors out of impossibility...he began to suspect that perhaps the hushed whispers had some basis.

In time, the party stood in front of the looming walls of the enemy. From inside, the muffled chatter of merchants, families, and soulbearers could be heard. Though the tops of the walls were far out of reach, small dots could be seen talking as they patrolled the magnificent walls. Basic footsoldiers nodded upon seeing the Gatekeepers, pounding their chest in respectful salute. Only Sana returned their greeting with a warm bow, with G and Patchy ignoring the gesture.

Before Taba could properly think of a plan, G gripped his shoulder with enough force to make him wince. "Hey. Don't piss around in the city, ok buddy?"

A bead of sweat dripped down his neck, but Taba closed his eyes and slowly nodded. G huffed and let go of the shoulder. Sana frowned at the action, and whispered a scolding into G's ear. The man pursed his lips, but looked down with a slow nod.

Just before entering the city, Sana flinched and held up her hand to the others. Everyone trained their eyes on her as the female Gatekeeper held up three fingers and coughed five times. Once she put her fingers down, G immediately turned from the city and sprinted at a shocking speed down the road. Not ten steps down, and a man emerged from behind a tree and stabbed G squarely in the neck. He choked...before reaching out and grabbing the stabber's neck. The bandit's eyes widened in surprise, before a sickening *snap* rang out across the field. G unplugged the dagger from his neck, then yelled loudly.

"To the remaining fourteen of you: come on out."

At first, nothing happened. Then, the bandits slowly lumbered out of the trees with confusion and anger. A bigger man stepped out from further down the road, a snarl plastered on his face.

"All your belongings. Now." the bandit demanded.

G rubbed his chin, contemplating the order. After a few seconds, he looked down with a wild grin.

"Nah."

He then ran full sprint towards the bandit leader, not even sparing a glance towards the men surrounding him. The other bandits roared in a declaration of war, pulling out their weapons to face the sole Gatekeeper. To Taba's amazement, G didn't stop. He ran through slashes, stabs, and even bullets. Despite it all, he continued running as though nothing happened, his body sustaining zero wounds. The lead bandit's eyes widened as he screamed in rage, raising two stilettos. Before Taba could process the current events, the aggressor drove both daggers through the bottom of G's head and through the top of his skull.

That should have been a finishing blow to anyone...but G reeled back his right arm and threw a jab that landed squarely on the leader's head. The leader collapsed immediately, his skull somehow caved in with a single punch. All the other bandits looked at G in horror as he slowly plucked the daggers from his head, groaning as he rolled his neck.

The bald man rubbed his mouth in annoyance. "Damn, that's the third time people were aiming for my head today."

He looked at the remaining thirteen bandits with bloodshot eyes.

"...Next."

...

Taba, Queenie, Hush and the city guards all stared in amazement as G disposed of the remaining thirteen bandits with a single hit each. As the man shook the blood off his knuckles, Taba desperately wished he had some soul leftover. G's blessing was a mystery to the entire nation. Was it immortality? Was it super strength? Intangibility? There were too many possibilities to consider.

G flicked blood off his arms and scowled as he looked at his pants, now riddled with tears and holes. "Crap. These were my last clean pair. I guess I gotta do laundry when we get back."

Taba didn't need to look, but he *knew* that Queenie was eyeing the weaponry that lay on the floor. Furthermore, Taba *also* knew that

Hush was scowling as he grabbed Queenie's arm. Queenie always lacked self-control when it came to weapons, so it was up to her brother to reel the girl in. Taba imagined that the Gatekeepers wouldn't take too kindly if their captive ran towards guns and daggers that were scattered across the floor.

Sana frowned as she dabbed at G's face with a handkerchief, to which G scowled and pulled his face away. Patchy chuckled, and the remaining gunk that was smeared on G's face suddenly splashed on the floor. Though Taba said nothing, his mind raced wildly. Was Patchy's blessing the ability to repel? No, but that wouldn't explain how Patchy got the jump on them. Furthermore, how did he *know* where they lay prone? Too many questions.

Sana pocketed her handkerchief and adjusted her hat's strings mildly before turning to her captors with a small smile. "Shall we continue?"

The party entered the grand city, the city guards pounding their chest with refreshed respect as they passed. Upon entering the city, Taba's mind was a flurry of questions. Before he could decide whether or not to speak, a raspy voice spoke out from behind them all.

"Hey...why aren't you killing us?"

The five members turned to the weary Hush, whose eyes now had heavier bags. The Gatekeepers stared in silence, before Patchy sighed and scratched his head furiously.

"Honestly? If it were up to me, you'd all be..." Patchy then ran a finger across his neck. "Still, Sana wants to bring you in for questioning. Don't ask me why, man."

Queenie frowned. "Questioning? What questions would you have for us? If you're trying to interrogate us, we aren't snitches."

Sana shook her head. "I imagine you wouldn't share any close-guarded secrets, no. Regardless, I want to talk to you all. We're simply holding it in Malapace because I trust you all to be kind souls."

Taba frowned. "...and what if you're wrong? What if we have plans to overthrow Malapace?"

G laughed. "If you did, I'd gut you all, don't worry."

Sana frowned and elbowed G's gut, who reeled back with a scowl. The female Gatekeeper sighed and gave a slight bow. "Sorry about G, he's a bit...crude. I hope you'll forgive him."

"An hour ago, they shot a sniper rifle at me. I think I have every damn right to be 'crude'."

Sana looked back at the bald man with a smudge of discontent before shaking her head. "Well...I *suppose* you have a fair point. Anyhow, we're almost there. Once we're in, do try to be on your best behavior. If you act up, then G will dispose of you...and I will unfortunately be able to do nothing but watch on the sidelines."

As they passed through the city gates, the captives could do nothing but gaze around in slight awe. There were stone roads, stone-sculpted buildings, and stone as far as the eye could see. In a normal village, perhaps one or two buildings could be adorned with parts of stone to fortify a house's base, but apart from that, many buildings used alternative materials. Stone was seen as too tricky and time consuming to sculpt, so stone projects were usually reserved for the most important or specific pieces.

As they walked deeper into town, the citizens of Malapace turned and cheered at the sight of the Gatekeepers. Sana smiled and gave polite waves and bows. Patchy yawned and walked as he waved them off. G flipped the bird and spat on the road.

After turning a few blocks, the party reached a grand building that wasn't *just* stone...but also had metal? Queenie instinctively touched the corner of the building with mild awe as she recognized the natural texture of the base.

"Is this...?"

Patchy looked at Queenie with mild curiosity. "Oh, the metal? Yeah, we're trying to see if we can create a fully natural metal building. Well, as it turns out, that's *so* much more difficult than we expected...but we do try to use natural metal to fortify more important buildings."

Queenie looked at Patchy with awe. "You're able to sculpt *natural stone* and you're attaching *natural metal*? *How*??? Are you finding bigger pieces of stone? What about winter or summer? Is it a blessing? What do you do wh-"

Hush cleared his throat and placed his hand on her shoulder. "Queenie."

The light quickly faded from her eyes and she took a step back as she averted her gaze. "...Nevermind."

Patchy looked at the siblings with an amused chuckle, and nodded to the building. "Well? Get in. Questioning time."

The inside of the interrogation building had smooth stone walls with numerous rooms. Sana and G both ushered Taba into the first room as Patchy waited outside with Queenie and Hush. The siblings looked at their friend with a worried look, but he waved them off.

"I'll be fine...probably. Be right back."

The inside of the room had a table that was built into the floor. G stood in the corner as Sana and Taba took a seat. The interrogation room was a bit chilly, but overall nothing was too uncomfortable. Hell, compared to the caves, this was comfy.

She cleared her throat, causing Taba to flinch and focus in. She smiled and folded her arms on the table.

"Now, I'm sure you're aware of who I am. My name is Sana, and I'm one of the Gatekeepers of Malapace. I just wanted to ask a few questions. Try to be honest with each one, alright?"

Taba hesitated, but nodded. He guessed that Sana would use her blessing as a sort of "lie detector". If possible, he would try to tell half-truths whenever possible. No point in giving information to the enemy if he could help it.

G cleared his throat from the corner of the room. "If you lie two times, Patchy kills your friends."

Sana whipped around with a scowl, but the small statement was enough to make Taba's blood run cold. She shot a warning glare at the bald Gatekeeper, who looked at his toes in silence.

She turned back with a sigh, pinching the brow of her nose. "Don't...don't listen to him. He's just trying to get into your head. Just answer truthfully, and we won't have any issues. Ok?"

The captive nodded silently. Sana cleared her throat. "What is your name?"

"...Toukie."

Taba wanted to test the extent of the Gatekeeper's blessing and see how minor of a lie it could detect. When she raised her eyebrow, Taba bit his tongue as a bead of sweat dripped down his neck.

"I lied. Sorry. It's Taba."

"I see. How old are you, Taba?"

"...Nineteen."

16

"Mhm. Now, can I assume you have a blessing? I can't imagine you try pulling off such a risky attack without one."

Taba *desperately* wanted to hide his blessing: Dad warned him of the dangers of exposing it's capabilities. However, it wasn't worth his friend's lives. Sana seemed to be a kind person, but he couldn't trust G. He could very well go out and kill the siblings on a whim.

So, he grit his teeth and nodded. "Yeah, I have one. It isn't much though."

"I see. Could you describe it's abilities to me?" Sana asked.

"...Only on one condition. Keep quiet about it. Don't tell anyone." Taba said.

Sana raised an eyebrow. "Oh? You do understand your current position? Would you really make a demand of me?"

He nodded. The female Gatekeeper rubbed her cheeks in intrigue as she stared at him. After a few seconds, she nodded.

"I can't *promise* anything, but I'll try to keep silent about it. If I were to tell anyone else, it would be Patchy... and maybe a friend of mine. I'll hold G to the same standard as well."

G scowled but turned away. Taba chewed his lips, but nodded. "I...can ask yes or no questions regarding people."

Sana leaned in with a furrowed brow. "Could you elaborate?"

He scratched his head. "I...can ask a question in my mind. The amount of soul used is depending on how accurate or unique that question is. If it's a question that's inconsequential or vague, it doesn't take much soul."

Taba nodded to Sana. "I can show you an example. Do you have a coin?"

She frowned and ruffled into her dress's pockets, pulling out a dull circle. He nodded. "Place it into your hands. I promise I'll guess which hand it's in ten times in a row."

Sana palmed the coin in her hands and rattled it around. Taba didn't have much soul in his well, but a simple "cointoss" question wouldn't require much soul.

Is the coin in her right hand?

O

Is the coin in her right hand?

X

Is the coin in her right hand?

O

Is the coin in her right hand?

O

Sana watched with amazement as Taba correctly guessed the location of the coin seven times in a row. After that, he had to hold a hand up, his head pulsing madly from exhaustion. The fight had drained him more than he thought.

She pocketed the coin, her mind seemingly processing many things. "Are there any restrictions to this blessing?"

He lifted his head with great effort, wincing as he did. "Well, there's a few. For the most part, my questions are restricted to living beings. Secondly, I need to be "aware" of that being. Lastly, I need to be within proximity of that said being. But-"

G spoke out from the corner of the room. "...you can find workarounds to those restrictions if you change the wording of your questions, right? Changing the question from 'Is G going to sneak attack me' to 'Is someone about to attack me' would work, right?"

Taba lowered his gaze. "...Yeah."

The female interrogator rubbed her chin with fascination. "That's fairly close to omnipotence, huh?"

He shook his head. "It's nowhere near your level, no. I need to constantly be asking questions, and those questions can't be meaningless. It doesn't take too much soul to ask questions, but I don't want to spend soul or energy when I don't have to. Plus, there are times where my question is 'answered', but I'm still left in the dark. Say my target has a blessing to...I dunno, split the earth. What would a question do in that case? It's an awful blessing. "

Sana raised an eyebrow and pondered his words. After a moment, she smiled and looked into his eyes with warmth.

"I've seen tons of blessings. Blessings to control the elements, blessings to change physics, so on. However, I find that the strongest blessings are also the weakest. Weak blessings need to be creative to be on the same level as strong blessings. That creativity is quite flexible, and ends up being quite unpredictable in numerous scenarios. Today, you were more threatening than those bandits that ambushed us earlier, so take pride in your ability."

Though he was a captive, he couldn't help but shake his head in frustration. "No, that was Queenie with her sniper and Hush with his-"

Taba caught himself, but not before Sana took note. "Could you tell me their blessings?"

"No."

G unfolded his arms and stepped out from the corner. Taba turned to face the bald Gatekeeper. "I didn't lie. I can't tell you their blessing.

19

You'll need to get that answer from their mouth. If they want to hide their blessing, I'll happily die to keep that secret."

The man tilted his head with an unreadable expression sprawled across his face, but Taba stared with strong conviction. After a few seconds of silence, Sana clapped, causing both men to flinch.

"Fair enough, I suppose that *is* their business, right? I'll ask them during their interrogation. Could you tell me who hired you, or what organization you're from?"

The cold silence that took the room was immediate. Taba had no soul, an exhausted body, and a tired mind. Still, the presence he held by simply standing up was enough to put the two Gatekeepers of Malapace on edge. Both Sana and G took defensive stances as Taba rose and glowered over the two Gatekeepers.

"I'd rather die than sell out my Father, and I know Queenie and Hush feel the same."

After a minute of silence, he flinched as common sense flooded back. He had just provoked two Gatekeepers while utterly exhausted. He hesitated, but held his ground with trembling feet. He wasn't prepared to die, nor did he want his friends to perish, but his statement held true. Sana quietly stood up, causing Taba to tense up. She raised her right arm, causing him to close his eyes and prepare for the worst.

Nothing could've prepared the bafflement that filled his body as he felt Sana's surprisingly calloused hand ruffle his hair.

"I see. Sorry about that. It seems that this man is quite dear to you, hm?"

Blood rushed to Taba's ears as he opened his eyes in confusion. The Gatekeeper smiled warmly as she rubbed his shoulder. She walked away from the desk and opened the door.

"You can head out to the lobby. We're done with the questioning."

...

Queenie was next, then it was Hush. The entire time, Patchy read a book in the corner of the room without even glancing at the captives. Despite this, Taba didn't dare run or fight back. After about an hour, the trio sat in the lobby as they shared confused glances. It was clear they all wanted to talk about the interrogation, but didn't want to discuss it while Patchy was in their presence.

Sana walked up while stifling a yawn, then nodded to the captives with a smile. "Well, let's go see the Overseer for the final verdict."

The Gatekeepers escorted the trio down winding alleyways until they approached a grand town hall adorned with white stone red carpentry. Workers in the front were quietly cleaning the shrubbery with hedge trimmers and carpets with soap and combs. The inside of the town hall bustled with life as merchants made deals with officials and office workers made deals with business owners.

The front desk receptionist nodded to the Gatekeepers as they approached. "Sana! Patchy! G! Welcome back! Thanks for all the hard work."

"Bah. Did you expect us to struggle or not come back?" G said while rolling his eyes.

Sana elbowed the bald man in the ribs before slightly bowing to the receptionist. "Sorry about that. Thanks for the welcomes, Tabitha. Could we go see the Overseer? We have a question regarding our scouting."

Tabitha looked at the various paperwork scattered on her desk. "Mmm...it seems she's currently overseeing, but you can host a meeting after that."

"Eh, she'll be fine." Patchy said with a yawn.

Before Tabitha could protest, Patchy walked ahead with wide steps. Sana hesitated, bowed in apology to the receptionist, then chased after the nonchalant man. G nodded to the trio, and they followed in turn. Patchy turned down a hallway and walked until they approached a door that was painted red, white, and gold. Instead of knocking, Patchy kicked the door open, leaving a dirty sandal print in the middle of the white door frame.

"Yo, Babs. We're back."

As the trio entered the room, they stared in amazement. The room had white curtains draped from its tall ceiling. The floor was built with smooth white marble, a circular pattern focusing in on a single woman wearing a blindfold in the middle of the room. She looked elderly and wore a draping robe with a red belt, its sleeves rolled down to reveal withered arms and uncut fingernails. She wore gold earrings with a green stone in its center, along with a simple gold necklace. Her grey and stringy hair was tied into a tight bun, wrinkles adorning her sharp cheekbones. After a minute, she raised her arms to untie the blindfold to reveal white irises and baggy eyelids.

"First off," the elderly woman scowled, "I'm the Overseer, *not* 'Babs'. Secondly, I'm working. Why'd Tabitha let you in?"

Patchy scratched his hair. "She...didn't. We walked in."

Sana slapped the back of Patchy's head, causing him to wince. She ducked her head apologetically. "Sorry about that, Babs. Patchy kind of...walked ahead of us and did what he wanted."

The Overseer's scowl deepened. "I'm not *Babs*. Call me by my title."

G cleared his throat and gave a surprisingly polite bow to the elderly woman. "Babs, give us the order and we'll kill these guys."

Babs seemed torn behind confusion and exasperation, eventually choosing to focus on the former emotion. "Hmph. Who are these guys?"

Taba opened his mouth to speak but Sana cut him off. "We found them outside. They have blessings, and they seem to be quite proficient in their abilities. I would love to fortify our forces with their aid."

Babs looked at the trio with a sharp glare before focusing on Hush's knee. "Why is his leg broken?"

Hush bit his lip and looked down. G spoke up after clearing his throat. "I broke it."

"Why?" Babs asked, squinting at the bald man.

"He tried to kill us."

Babs raised an eyebrow as Sana glared at G. The Overseer stared at the trio with a cold stare, before getting up and slowly walking up to the trio. She stared at the three of them, before speaking with a crackled voice.

"Who's the leader?"

Hush flinched and averted his gaze. Sweat rolled down Queenie's brow, but she refused to look away.

Not wanting her to take the brunt of the trouble, Taba cleared his throat. "I'll take responsibility."

Babs swiveled to him, took three wide strides, then slapped him with enough force to throw him to the ground. Granted, Taba was already weakened, but the impact still stung to high hell.

Queenie roared and pulled a gun out of her storage, pointing it to Babs. Hush glowered as he flexed his fingers, tremendous bullets of sweat suddenly dripping down his neck as the Overseer's vision was robbed. In an instant, Patchy's eyes glowed as he suddenly appeared behind Queenie and held her in a headlock and G slammed Hush into the ground with tremendous force, immediately knocking him out. Queenie choked as her grip on her pistol slowly weakened.

However, the only thought coursing through Taba's mind was on how Sana said or did nothing. If she truly *was* omnipotent, why didn't she stop Queenie before she pulled out the gun? Babs took notice of Taba's stare and looked upon the boy with a silent expression. The elderly Overseer knelt down and grabbed Taba's face, forcing him to make eye contact.

"That's for harming my children, you bastard."

He swallowed, but nodded as much as he could. "Ish shorry."

Babs scowled and let him go. She stood up and rolled her wrist with a grimace. She snapped at Patchy and G. "Let the damn brats go before they *actually* die."

Patchy raised his arms and Queenie collapsed to the ground as she sucked in desperate breaths between coughs. G rolled his eyes and got off Hush's unmoving body.

Babs turned to Sana, who quietly stood off to the side. "What do you want to do with them?"

Sana cleared her throat. "I want to spare them, Babs."

The elderly woman closed her eyes and rubbed her temple. She let out an exasperated sigh. "You damn brats will be the death of me. I'll see if I can get Juliette to supervise them."

The female Gatekeeper frowned. "Isn't she out?"

"She returns tomorrow, I saw her on the road." the Overseer responded.

24

"Ah, guess we should check the pub tomorrow."

Babs nodded. "Mhm. For now, check them into...ah, the guestrooms."

Patchy frowned. "Woah, Babs. Is that safe? That's pretty close."

The Overseer waved him off. "It'll be fine. If they try anything, then I die. Big whup, I'll finally be allowed to rest."

G creased his brow with...worry? As Taba blinked with mild surprise, the bald Gatekeeper nodded. "Babs, take better care of yourself, damn. Who else is gonna run all this?"

"It'll sort itself out. Now get out, I need to continue my work."

The Gatekeepers all nodded with respect. Patchy lifted Queenie up to her feet and G hoisted Hush over his shoulder as if he were carrying a bag of flour. Sana extended an arm to Taba and helped him stand.

The party exited Babs's room and turned two corners, approaching four doors. Sana nodded to the rooms. "You three will be living here for now. Tomorrow, we'll meet with Juliette, your supervisor. For now, rest up."

Taba hesitated and turned to her. "Could you, uh...is it possible to heal Hush like you did to me?"

G rolled his eyes, then nodded to Patchy. "Give me the spare I gave you earlier."

Patchy nodded and handed over a white pill from his pockets. G took it, opened up Hush's mouth, and stuffed it inside. After the unconscious boy swallowed the mysterious medicine, Hush roused with a groan.

"You up? Cool. Get off me then." G said.

He dropped the boy, who collapsed to the ground with a thud, causing Taba to wince. Hush slowly clambered to his feet, obviously disoriented. Though she was still recovering, Queenie quickly dashed over to her brother and checked on his face with notable concern. As she did that, Sana opened the first guest room with a nod.

"Get some rest, ok? Welcome to Malapace, you guys."

CHAPTER 2

"*So, Queenie, how old are you?*"

"*...17.*"

Sana nodded while Queenie nervously tapped her fingers. She didn't like how the Gatekeeper was just... staring at her. It made her feel fidgety. She would've loved it if she could twirl a dagger around her fingers, but the Gatekeepers probably wouldn't like it if she suddenly whipped out a weapon.

Sana continued her interrogation. "Could you tell me about your blessing?"

Queenie chuckled, pleased to finally have an excuse to pull a weapon out, and pulled out a knife from her storage. G stepped forwards, but Sana held her hand up to the bald, hulking man.

Queenie began twirling the dagger around her fingers to calm her nerves. "It's just a portable storage room. Nothing much."

"I see. Can you store anything?"

She shrugged as she slowly peeled and rewrapped the bandage around the dagger's handle. "Well...kinda? It takes soul to pull out and store things. I can technically store other people, but that gets exhausting quickly...so it isn't the most useful. So, I try to only store inanimate objects into my storage room. The more complicated or large the thing, the more soul it takes to drag out and store. There are more specifications...but you get the idea."

The gatekeeper nodded as she chewed the inside of her cheek. "Who knows about this blessing?"

Queenie shrugged. "Eh. Taba. My brother. Dad. Not too many, but that's mostly because I don't know many people."

"Your brother? Your dad?" asked Sana.

"Yeah. Hush is my brother. You don't need to know about Dad."

Sana hesitated and seemingly chose her next words carefully. "Do you...not care if others know about your blessing?"

Queenie laughed as she stored her dagger. Sana flinched and jumped away from the table as chains suddenly whipped around the air, just barely missing the female gatekeeper. As she raised her head, Sana stared down the barrel of a small hand pistol.

She grinned a mad smile. "It doesn't matter if someone knows about my blessing: that won't stop me from getting what I want."

...

Queenie woke up with a small groan. The beds...sucked. She had more comfort sleeping in treetops than she did sleeping on this cold slab of a mattress. She rolled out of bed as she massaged her neck, grabbing clothes from her storage.

Once changed and washed up, she peeked outside of her window. As expected, Taba was outside, his black hair bouncing as his toned body did small laps around the town hall. He always seemed to despise his blessing as it didn't give a direct boost in combat ability, so he did whatever he could to close the supposed 'gap' that lay between him and others. However, if you asked Queenie? Very few could best Taba in a one-on-one. She could count the number of times Taba lost a fight on one hand. Hell, if you exclude the times that Taba took the fall for the sake of her or Hush, Taba was nearly undefeated.

She chucked her pajamas into her storage and headed out into the hallway. Queenie needed to check in on her brother. However, as she exited her room, she saw Hush quietly standing off to the side, staring at her.

She swallowed her anxiety and walked up with a calm demeanor. "Hey. You feeling ok?"

Her brother flexed his leg. "Honestly? The only pain I feel right now is from how crappy that bed was. I've slept in trees more comfortable than that."

"I *know*, ri-wait, no. I mean, is your leg ok? Your face?"

She quickly poked at his cheek as Hush scowled. "Relax, I'm fine. I have no idea what they fed me, but I'm genuinely fine. I don't feel sluggish and my soul is normal. No drawbacks."

"Weird. I wanna store that medicine."

"No." said a third voice.

The siblings turned to face the voice that responded. Patchy walked down the hallway with a wide yawn, scratching his stomach as he did so. "You kids wake up *wayyyy* too early."

Queenie scowled. "First off, I turn eighteen in four months, I don't think that qualifies me as a '*kid*'. Secondly, blame your damn beds for being uncomfortable. Lastly? You aren't old enough to be calling us *kids*."

Patchy's eyebrows raised as he gave an odd smile. "Well...you aren't wrong. We're actually pretty close in age."

"You're eighteen?" Hush asked.

Patchy waved him off. "You wouldn't believe me even if I said I was. Well, I'm also lying. I should be...twenty-six? I can't remember, but I *feel* eighteen. Age is weird for me." He shook his head as he slightly nodded to the window. "Eh, we're getting off topic. Let's go grab the lunatic who decided to start running laps two hours before the sun rose. We need to go see Julie."

...

The trio walked throughout the surprisingly quiet city. Sure, it was morning, but there should've been tons of merchants who rose to set up shop or make deals. As Queenie took small glances here and there,

Patchy noticed and gave a small grin. "You're probably wondering why it's so empty. Most of our merchants do business at night over dinner and drinks, so they're all sleeping or hungover. You'll see a few merchants here and there, but this is all fairly normal for the most part."

Queenie frowned. Shame. She would've loved to nick a few weapons from various stalls. Hush seemed to read her mind and elbowed her side, frowning as he did. Taba cleared his throat.

"So...where are we going?"

Patchy scratched his left ear as he stifled another yawn. "Babs wants to assign a supervisor to you guys, and this supervisor is probably..."

The party turned a corner and came face-to-face to a bar. "...there."

Taba stared at the bar. "Uh...is she a bartender...?"

"Nope. She's a drinker."

"...but it's like, what? 9 AM?"

"Yep."

Patchy swung open the front door as the trio followed his lanky back with perplexed footsteps. The bar had wooden floors, wooden tables, and dim candle lights hanging from the ceiling. The bar, as expected, was mostly empty. The only patron was a woman in the corner, taking large swigs from a bottle.

Patchy cleared his throat as he walked forward. "Yo, Julie. Whatsup."

The woman faced the party of four. She had on half of a festival mask in the shape of a fox, with bright red lips standing out on pale white skin. She donned a hooded kimono with the sleeves rolled down to reveal clean, pale arms. Next to her was a long, thin box tied to a string, obviously for carrying on one's back. Her bare feet flapped against thin sandals as she tapped her red fingernails on the crusted bottle in her hand.

She took another swig and then placed her drink on the bar counter. "...Patchy. What brings you here? Who're the brats?"

"Babs wants you to supervise them."

"Nah."

Patchy scratched his head and sighed. "Sana wants you to supervise them, too."

The masked woman stared back, her vibrant red lips piercing their eyes. "Oh?"

"Yep."

Juliette took another swig of her drink, rinsing it in her mouth as she carefully pondered the request. She then grabbed her bottle and dragged herself over to a booth, stretching widely in one of the seats, gesturing the others to her spot. Patchy shrugged and sauntered to drag a stool over, whereas the trio exchanged glances before scooting into the slightly sticky booth. Shortly after sitting down, a burly man came out of the back with a nod.

Juliette, with the hand holding her alcohol, extended two fingers. "Snacks."

The bartender silently nodded before retreating, returning within a few minutes with a plate of various munchies, placing it in front of Queenie. Juliette gave an appreciative bow before continuing to take swigs from her bottle, pushing the plate closer to the trio. "All yours. I don't eat well in the mornings."

While Taba and Hush exchanged glances, Queenie grabbed a small handful of salted peanuts and chucked them in her mouth. While chewing, she wrinkled her nose. "Ugh. Slightly stale. Still, you can't eat but you'll daydrink? Sounds like you got your priorities mixed up, lady."

Hush elbowed his sister, but Juliette waved her hand dismissively. "Eh. You aren't wrong."

She hissed as she slammed down her bottle, dabbing her lips with a napkin. She looked up, sharp blue pupils staring at Queenie from within the day drinker's fox mask. "So. Why does the Overseer want me to look over you ragtag Misfits?"

Before Queenie could open her mouth, Taba cleared his throat. "She sees us as a valuable asset. That's all."

"Mm. And how did she find you all? It isn't everyday that the Overseer pesters me to tutor someone."

Taba hesitated, seemingly trying to choose his next words carefully. Before he could formulate the ideal sentence, Queenie shrugged and leaned back into her seat. "Tried to kill the gatekeepers. Failed. Guess the dumbasses liked our balls."

32

Juliette's hand stopped mid-reach to the snack plate, an odd expression of surprise plastered on her monotone face. "Huh."

She turned to Patchy, who was cleaning the inside of his finger with a pinky. "And you say it was *Sana* who wanted me to look over the brats? *Her?*"

He sighed, wiping his pinky on his pants. "My thoughts exactly. I sometimes wish I could see the world like she does."

The woman slowly nibbled on a cracker subconsciously, her expressionless mask staring holes into her drink. After she swallowed, she stood up, slung the box over her shoulder, slapped a few coins on the table, and slowly began to walk out the bar. Patchy gestured to the trio and the party slowly followed the masked woman.

After silently walking for twenty minutes, the party reached a nearby park. Juliette unslung her box, and stretched. She then drew a small circle on the dirt around her with her foot and turned back to the party with a limp neck.

"Let's make a deal then. If they're able to make me step outside of this circle within two minutes, I'll supervise the brats, train them, whatever. If they can't, then they're on their own. I'm not gonna be weighed down by those who can't carry their own weight."

She nodded to Patchy. "Keep track of the time. Don't stop counting until they either give up, or until they push me out."

He sighed and slapped his pockets, pulling out an antique pocket watch. "Yeah, yeah. But man, you're seriously evil."

Queenie raised her hand, to which Juliette nodded. "Mm?"

"Can we aim to kill?"

The silence in the morning air was palpable. Still, the masked woman tilted her head as she pondered the request, then shrugged.

33

"Eh, doesn't matter. Do what you want: the result will be the same."

Before Queenie could act, Taba stepped up and raised his hand. "We'll need a bit of time to strategize, is that ok?"

"Yeah, yeah. Whatever."

Taba walked over and asked a few questions to Patchy in hushed whispers. The Gatekeeper seemed slightly surprised, but answered him with an amused expression. After a moment, he returned to the siblings with a hesitant expression.

"...Well?"

Taba pursed his lips. "I...asked Patchy if he thought he could win a one-on-one against the lady. He said he *could* win...but she would win nine times out of ten. He also said that Sana had the best chance in beating her, and even then it would be an even fifty-fifty."

Queenie and Hush stayed silent. Taba only asked important questions when formulating strategies. If he seemed grim, that was something to be genuinely concerned about.

Hush shrugged. "I mean...what's to stop us from blinding her and pushing her out?"

Taba rubbed his eyes. "I thought of that. For some reason...it wouldn't work. She has no barrier. She has no foresight. I *think* she's a weapons user of some sorts. However...Queenie's bullets won't connect."

Queenie scowled. "That's a load of crap. I don't miss."

Taba stared back with concerned eyes. "You 'missed' yesterday. We should consider her to be on the same level of a Gatekeeper."

Queenie bit her lip. He got her there. "Chains? Guns? Swords? Nothing?"

Taba's eyes were closed as he calculated everything. Suddenly, his eyes flung open with hesitation. "I...we need to see her weapon. I need to see how she counters our advances. Once I see it..."

...

The trio stood around the masked woman as she took a sip from a portable clay flask. She dabbed at her lips as she glanced over at them. "You finally ready?"

Queenie grinned. "You sure you wanna be drinking? You might die today."

Juliette tied her flask to her waist as she opened the box she carried around, revealing what appeared to be a massive paintbrush with silver bristles, the length of the tool equivalent to the size of her entire body. "If I were to die to you with only *this* much alcohol in my blood, I deserve death."

Patchy coughed as he waved his hand. "We start in ten...nine..."

The silence of the air was deafening as the trio slowly prepared their blessings. Taba's strategy seemed to almost bank on a *gamble*...something he never based a strategy around. Still, it seemed as though it was their best bet, and the trio agreed to go for it. She glanced at the teenager and noticed his pupils flickering wildly as he muttered to himself. Seems as though he was already asking questions and formulating a plan.

"Two...one...**go**."

Queenie immediately pulled two semi-automatic guns from her storage and sprayed at the woman. Hush flexed his fingers, blinding Juliette. With the cover, Taba ran sideways, his eyes focused on the opening.

Then, Juliette slashed with her paintbrush. Then she did it again. And again. As Taba had stated, each bullet disintegrated before they reached their target, despite Juliette's slashes seemingly slashing randomly. As her guns clicked empty, Queenie cursed and dropped her guns, pulling out more from the storage.

Once confirming that Queenie's bullets proved ineffective, Hush and Taba rushed the blinded woman in a pincer move. Suddenly, Taba flinched and screamed a phrase at Hush as a line of red appeared across his friend's chest. Queenie's blood ran cold as she manifested chains to yank her brother and friend away to safety. Her soul took a massive toll in pulling out multiple items at once, and she hunched over with a wild gasp.

The blinded woman stood up from her stance as she wielded the paintbrush. She tilted her head as she flicked the brush once more. "What? You asked if you could aim to kill. I'm simply returning the respect you've shown me."

Queenie swallowed slowly. Forty seconds had passed, and this random woman had completely nullified their advances. They had obtained no information and had actually *lost* ground against her.

Suddenly, Queenie, Hush, and Julliete flinched as Taba quietly raised his hands and cupped his ears. Hush understood the request immediately. He flexed his fingers, and the woman's sight returned. However, she flinched as she wildly flung her head around at the trio.

Taba sucked in his breath and screamed. **"Queenie. Don't stop firing."**

She bit her lip, but grabbed a rifle from her storage. She grit her teeth and let loose a flurry of bullets. Juliette noticed, and began to swing once more. Just like it had prior, each bullet was obliterated.

Meanwhile, Taba barked orders at a bleeding Hush. Her brother, sweat beading down his face, nodded. As Queenie drew Juliette's attention, Taba dove and grabbed the masked woman's arm, stopping her swings. Hush then swung his legs at her feet in a rapid maneuver.

Anyone would've been able to easily sidestep such an assault. Even more so, someone on par with a Gatekeeper. However...Juliette had lost her sense of hearing. She could not hear the two men advance. Furthermore, She couldn't afford to turn her head to look for them, not with the barrage of bullets raining down at her. Queenie grinned. They had won.

The Drunken Fox stared a void into their bodies. "...Did you think the conditions of my blessing were the slashes? Well...you aren't wrong, I suppose."

Suddenly, splashes of red scattered along Taba and Hush's bodies, causing Queenie's smile to drop as blood drained from her cheeks. She screamed as Julliete's fox mask stared back with cold eyes. Though her soul felt as if it were already tearing, Queenie grit her teeth and manifested more chains around Juliette. Without the masked woman even swinging, the chains shattered.

Queenie fell to a knee, her heart pumping at a rapid pace. She was reaching her limit. As she lifted her head in desperation, she noticed Taba stare at her with reassured eyes. She watched as his eyes stared at Juliette's ankle.

In an instant, Queenie understood what needed to be done.

She manifested fourteen chains all above Juliette. She gazed at each one, and they all shattered.

She missed the chain that wrapped around her left ankle. The fox lady looked down with shock.

Queenie let out a guttural yell as she tugged at the chain.

Then, she collapsed as the world around her went dark.

...

When Queenie roused, she threw up. The man standing next to her yelled in anger. "*Again?*"

G wiped the vomit off his face in disgust. Patchy walked up with a chuckle, then the puke splashed off of the bald man. Queenie tried to sit up, but her head throbbed deeply, causing her to groan as she lay back down on the grass. Hush knelt over her and laid his hand on her forehead.

"You *idiot*. You need to keep track of your soulwell more. You were *insanely* close to dying."

She forced her groggy eyelids open and stared at her brother. Though his clothes were tattered, he had no scars or injuries.

Her mind was foggy. "D...did you get one of those pills?"

"Yeah. So did Taba."

"Did you get any extra? I want to store one."

"You nearly died by overusing your blessing, then you *immediately* want to reuse the blessing? I don't know what Sana sees in you." scoffed G.

She wanted to flip the bald man off, but her body ached to all hell, so she just frowned as deeply as should could at the Gatekeeper. Laying back down, she noticed a familiar fox mask staring down at her, blocking out Queenie's view of the sky.

The tired girl coughed. "Did we...do it?"

"No." said Juliette as she shook her head.

Tears stung at the corners of Queenie's eyes, and she grit her teeth as she turned her head away in frustration. It was always *her* fault. Taba would make a plan. Hush would follow up. However...whenever it was Queenie's turn to pull the weight, she would always falter. It was *her* fault that they had failed.

A small tear trickled out of her eye as bitter feelings clogged up her throat. She looked down at the dirt that her cheek rested on. "Sorry, Taba. Sorry, Hush."

From the shade of the tree, Patchy coughed. "Julie..."

Juliette sighed. "Yes, Patchy?"

Though she couldn't see him, Queenie could hear the mischievous grin in his voice. "Why did you change the test *specifically* for these guys?"

Taba sat up with confusion. "What?"

Patchy turned to him with a grin. "Yeah. Babs would always ask her to supervise someone and Julie would always turn her down. She would always hold these tiny tests with the excuse of 'wahhh I don't want goobers to hold me back wahhh'. Except... the test wasn't 'Push me out of the circle'. It's normally 'Enter this circle with either your body or blessing."

The trio silently digested the information as their tired minds came to understand the meaning of Patchy's words. Suddenly, they all turned their heads to the masked woman in confusion and shock.

Hush struggled up to his feet and stared at the woman with wild anger in his normally calm eyes. "Explain yourself. **Now.**"

Juliette took a sip of her flask. "I don't nee-"

Queenie watched in shock as her brother slapped the flask out of the fox woman's hands. The clay jug clattered to the floor as alcohol glugged out onto the soil. The woman quietly turned around to face her brother with calm anger.

"My sister nearly *died trying* to fulfill your stupid test. A test, mind you, that we *nearly* passed. So, care to explain *why* you decided to crank your requirements all the way up for us. **Please**, enlighten us." Hush said through clenched teeth.

The woman slowly lifted up her hands and quietly removed her fox mask, revealing startling blue eyes. She wasn't even focusing on Queenie, but she could feel Juliette's eyes pierce her heart with controlled wrath.

Then, her eyes began to calmly glow.

Patchy and G suddenly flung to action. The trio all vanished from the area within a blink of an eye as the entire park suddenly rang out in a symphony of screeches. Trees were obliterated. The ground was razed. The air itself was wiped out.

Suddenly, the screeching stopped. The trio returned to the same spot that they normally lay where Juliette stood. Quietly, she picked up the flask that lay unchipped on the floor, tied it to her waist, and then readjusted the mask onto her face. She took small, controlled steps to a trembling Hush.

Her red lips leaned into his ear. "Could you survive *that*?"

Hush said nothing, failing to even meet her eyes. She leaned back as she stood with her head high. "Where I go? This is commonplace. Whom I fight? This is expected. *Why* I fight? Sometimes it's for the most trivial of reasons. I do commend you for not only touching me, but also nearly dragging me out of the circle. Truly, I tell you: not a single one of the Overseer's 'requests' has done that feat. However, this test is solely to see where you stand on the grand scale of those whose blessings can reap the sky. You have *barely* jumped, and you have the audacity to try and cleave the moon?"

She nodded to G and Patchy, who stared back at her with a careful gaze. "Those two? They can not only perform *similar* feats to what I showed, but they could very well *best* me in combat while protecting hundreds of civilians. How could I expect brats like yourselves to move onto a bigger playing field when you would die such meaningless deaths? No, it's better for you to quietly grow and live a simple life. You don't deserve the hell I live through."

Taba took a shaky step towards the now-masked woman. She turned to him with a curious gaze. In turn, he bowed. "On behalf of Hush, I'm sorry. He's a good guy but, well, he's a bit protective of his sister. I hope you'll forgive his outburst, no matter how justified it was."

Queenie hesitated, struggling to sit up to say a word of protest, but the throbbing in her head caused her to wince as she leaned on G's shoulder.

Juliette considered Taba's words, then took a soft breath. "You're...Taba, yes? Your leadership was excellent. The coordination you had with the other two is what held them together. I could see you being on the same level as the Gatekeepers, given enough time."

Taba kept his head low as he hesitated. Queenie understood his thoughts. He was being praised by an enemy, stating that he was weaker than them. However, the praise was something that was also true. With mixed emotions, Taba simply kept his head low as he pressed his lips together.

Juliette pressed a finger to her lip. "However...you made mistakes. Anyone else, you would be dead. Not just that, but the blood of your friends would be on your hands: on your *failures*. That potential

41

would be useless if you were to be snipped right here and now, no? Surely, you can see where I come from."

Taba stayed silent. Juliette then turned to Hush, who flinched and looked to the ground. Her thin sandals flapped against the floor as she walked closer to the trembling man.

She repositioned the box on her back as she rolled her shoulder. "You're... tenacious. You've learned to maximize your blessings to its fullest, and take advantage of small openings when you can. Commendable, truly. Still...what are you without leadership? You're just a waste of space: a sheep nodding at whatever order comes your way. Your blessing alone could've taken me out, if you knew how to use it."

Then, Juliette turned her head to Queenie. She walked over, then knelt to the ground, her black fox eyes staring coldly into Queenie's soul. "You...are a disappointing failure. No way about it."

Queenie bit her lip, but refused to look away. She took a shaky breath and forced a question out with a raspy voice.

"...Why?"

The fox mask tilted. "You know why. You only listen to orders. You don't think of plans yourself. You don't know your own limits. Due to your numerous shortcomings, your partners nearly died today. Their blood would be on *your* hands as well, simply because you could not fulfill your responsibilities."

Taba lifted his head and voiced a protest. "With all due respect...my plan wouldn't have ever worked without Queenie. She played the biggest role in this execution."

Juliette didn't bother looking at the voice behind her. "She played the *simplest* role. Any monkey with a gun could've done what she did, except a monkey would know its limits. She has paint and an easel...yet she draws simple lines. She has wings...yet walks."

The black fox eyes stared silently as Queenie let out a tear of frustration. "She has an ability that could not just rival, but even *surpass* the Gatekeepers, and she listens to orders. What a waste."

Queenie grit her teeth. Her well was empty, her body dead. And yet, her spirit roared in defiance. She forced her essence to reach into her storage and pulled out a small pair of safety scissors. As she did, her entire body lurched, but she forced herself to stay conscious. Her eyes glazed over, but she stabbed her arm to force adrenaline.

Her near-dead eyes stared at the drunkard. "Then you can stay there, and watch as I surpass this entire damn city. Not because my Dad demanded it. Not because you're my enemy. I *will* surpass you all, just to *piss you off.*"

Juliette tilted her head. "Oh? Are you declaring war on the entire city of Malapace out of *spite*? Even though that includes me *and* the Gatekeepers?"

Queenie could no longer muster the energy to speak or raise her pathetic pair of scissors. Her body collapsed onto the floor, her head rolled to the heavens. However, her glazed eyes held conviction as they stared up towards the fox mask.

Juliette stood up and tilted her head to the sky. Then, to everyone's shock, she laughed. It was not a sound of malice, nor was it mocking. It was a laugh of pure joy and amusement.

After thirty seconds of glee, Juliette kneeled down and touched Queenie's chin. Though her consciousness was already fading, she forced her eyes open a crack.

The last thing she remembered as black slowly crept around her vision were Juliette's red lips smiling. "I like you."

CHAPTER 3

"*Now...Hush, was it? How old are you?*"

"*...Twenty-one.*"

Sana quietly nodded. "And what's your relation with the others?"

Taba tightened his lips. He flat out didn't trust these guys...especially the bald one in the corner. If they knew that Queenie was his younger sister, they could use that as leverage against him.

Sana stared quietly into his eyes, slowly nodding as she did. Then, she turned to G and waved her arm to him.

The bald gatekeeper scowled. "No."

Sana glared with stern eyes. G took a sudden interest to the floor and walked out.

The female gatekeeper adjusted her hat's strap with a smile. "G is a nice guy, but he...isn't the best at expressing it. I felt as though you weren't comfortable around him, so could you open up with me? Taba and Queenie told me matching testimonies, so I just need to hear it from you."

Hush narrowed his eyes. What did she know? What testimonies have they said? Was she bluffing? Could he quickly take her down in this room? After all, Hush was pretty good in a one-on-one. Well...he never beat Taba, but...

Sana raised her hand, cutting off his thoughts. "Before you try, no. You wouldn't be able to beat me in a fight...especially with that broken leg. I'm not trying to trick you, really. The only information the others divulged to me is that you're Queenie's older brother. I don't know anything else about you apart from that. I promise."

Hush blinked, mildly surprised. Could she read minds? No one knew of Sana's blessing, but there were tons of speculations that she was an omnipotent god. Father sent out a few soulbearers to take her down, and she had quite easily survived every attempt. It seemed impossible to get the jump on her.

Well...if she already knew... "Yeah. I'm Queenie's older brother. Our parents aren't around anymore, so I'm watching over her now. Well, me and Taba I guess."

"Are you all close? This isn't part of the interview or anything, I'm just...curious about your bonds."

Hush kept quiet. Sana frowned. "Fair enough. I guess you wouldn't want to share information with your 'enemy'. Well, could you tell me about your blessing? The others already told me their blessings: Taba with his questioning, and Queenie with her storage. Neither one wanted to tell me your blessing."

Hush raised his eyebrows in surprise. Taba gave away his blessing? His friend never told others his blessing. The Gatekeepers must have threatened...something.

Suddenly, he narrowed his eyes as a thought ran through his mind. "...Did you threaten Taba?"

Sana hesitated, then sighed in defeat. "I didn't, no...but G did. I swear I didn't tell him to. He just...did it. On his behalf, I'm sorry."

Hush felt conflicted. On one hand, he felt anger on Taba's behalf. On the other? Sana seemed genuinely regretful. Oddly enough, he believed her to be telling the truth.

The captive sighed as he scratched his hair. "...I can either nullify or amplify a sense. That's my blessing."

"Is that why you're so calm...despite the broken leg? Could you tell me the qualifications or limitations of your blessing?" Sana asked.

Hush hesitated but nodded. " I activate it by flexing certain fingers. It only works on someone within a certain range. I can only augment one sense at a time. So, if I were to blind you...I would feel pain again. Nullifying a sense doesn't ignore the effects it has on the body, though. For example, nullifying the pain does nothing in energizing my body: I'll still feel tired, or I'll move more sluggish as a response to my broken leg."

She said nothing, and quietly listened to Hush's explanation. After he finished speaking about the details, she nodded with raised eyebrows. "That's...incredible. Small activation requirement, super flexible...wow. I imagine that blessing alone would be a nightmare to face."

Hush scowled. "Blindness does nothing against higher skilled targets: for example, Patchy sidestepped a blind kick earlier. Plus, if I have to nullify my pain just to focus, then I'm already fighting someone without my blessing. The ability to impact senses does nothing to those who can instantly kill me. My blessing is useless the stronger my opponents are. The fact that you're all alive is proof of it."

...

The blood drained from Hush's body as his sister's eyes slowly dulled.

He dove to her feet, shoving aside the woman who once terrified him, and tapped his sister's cheek.

"Hey. Queenie? Queenie? Stay awake. Queenie. **Queenie.**"

G watched silently as Hush desperately tried to wake his sister up. She was growing colder and colder. Her lips were slowly turning blue. Her damn pride could *actually* kill her. Unlike physical wounds...soul was near impossible to replenish rapidly. Still, he refused to give up while there was even a grain of chance to save her.

He whipped around to G. "Give me one of those *damn* pills."

Patchy sighed as he reached into his pocket to hand on to the distraught brother. He snatched it up and forced it down his sister's gullet.

She couldn't even swallow. Her chest stopped taking breaths. Hush choked, his body stiffening up. What...what could he do?

He turned to Juliette and immediately bowed, his forehead touching the floor. "Please, give my sister some of that alcohol. I need her to swallow this pill. *Please.*" Hush begged.

"Raise your head."

Hush flinched as the bald Gatekeeper grabbed Hush by the hair and yanked him onto his feet. Once he stood up, G punched Hush sharply in the cheek, causing the brother to stumble a few feet backwards as he tumbled into Taba.

G's jaw was flexed in...anger? "What kind of man **bows** to the enemy? Do you not have pride?"

"What else can I do? I...I..."

G tightened his lips, closing his eyes. After four seconds, he opened them and stared at the grey-haired Gatekeeper. Patchy nodded quietly, his eyes glowing once more.

The scenery changed, and everyone blinked into the town center. The men stared at Patchy, whose lips were tightened as he stared at the ground.

"That man is *seriously* too kind." said Juliette with a sigh.

After a few seconds, they shifted back to the now decimated park. G stood over Queenie's body as it now took quiet breaths, color returned to her lips. Hush let out a shaky breath of relief, and knelt to his sister's body, quickly hugging it.

After twenty seconds of silent hugging, he then turned to G. "I owe you my life."

G's eyes flickered slightly. "You don't owe me squat."

The bald Gatekeeper lifted the unconscious girl up and over his shoulders. "I'm taking her back. She needs rest. Last thing she needs is to randomly wake up, see Juliette, and decide to deplete her soul again."

Patchy nodded. "You want me to...?"

"Nah. You're overusing your ability. I'll walk: need the steps anyhow."

As G walked away, the soft sashaying of sandals crept up behind Hush. Hush turned around, staring face to face with the fox mask of Juliette.

"What did we learn today?" she asked.

Hush hesitated, but said nothing. What did she want to hear? What was she expecting?

Juliette stared silently for a few seconds before sighing and shaking her head. "Nothing? Really?"

"What do you want me to say?"

"Well, let me ask another question: why didn't you forcefully take my flask? Why did you kneel?"

Blood rushed to his ears as he quietly stared at the ground. Juliette nodded. "There you go. Now you get it. So, let me ask again: what did we learn today?"

Hush could feel his friend staring at his back. Shame burned through his entire body, but he sputtered out his lesson. "I'm...weak. I couldn't do anything."

Juliette placed her hand under Hush's chin and lifted it. Hush raised his head and found himself staring into the black eyes of the fox. There was no malice in her expression, nor was there mockery. Instead, there was something similar to respect. "Not really the answer I expected, but good. Many dig themselves into denial, refusing to acknowledge their situation, thus they never grow. The ones that reach extraordinary heights are those who've been humbled and can acknowledge that shame. Remember this day. Remember what actions you took. Remember what you almost lost. Do that, and you'll never need to kneel again."

She took a step back and untied the flask from her waist. As she lifted it, Juliette frowned as she softly shook it. The masked woman sighed. "...I'm out. I guess I need a refill."

She turned and slowly began to walk towards town. Behind him, Taba called out in a hesitant voice. "So...what happens now? Did we pass?"

Juliette stopped walking, then tilted her head back, a hint of blue eyes glinting through the black eyeholes. "Why do you care if you passed or not? What does it matter if I'm your supervisor? Aren't we your enemies? Why would you want to willingly be watched?"

Hush turned back to stare at Taba's stunned expression, obviously unsure of what to say. This surprised the older brother. Normally, his friend was composed and knew what to say in every scenario: Taba was *never* stunned in silence.

As Juliette turned her head back and began to walk again, a pull of Hush's heart compelled him to speak. He blurted out his thoughts before he could regret it, a trait very much unlike him. "You're stronger than us. If you help us grow stronger, we'll be better opponents for you to face. Train us, *please.*"

The fox woman continued walking. As Hush amplified his hearing, he could hear her soft chuckles. Then, a whisper that was surely only meant for his ears.

"*I'll give it some thought. Tomorrow, Patchy will let you know my decision.*"

...

Hush woke up, his entire body sore. As he rolled out of bed, an agonizing groan escaped his lips. Was it due to yesterday's test or due to the crappy quality of the bed? Who knew?

He glanced out the window and saw Taba doing crunches on the stone pavement. From the amount of sweat glistening on his neck...he had been out for at *least* an hour. Hush wasn't sure how Taba was able to do such extreme exercises every day with such little sleep. The older brother had once tried to follow Taba's training regiment but had thrown in the towel on day four.

Hush washed up and threw on his usual outfit, a navy t-shirt, jeans, and an olive green jacket. As he tied up the tiny bit of loose hair at the back of his head, he walked out of his room...only to stare at his sister waiting in the hallway. She wore her usual outfit of baggy brown hoodie, black pants, and worn boots. Her brown hair was tied up in the usual ponytail.

Before he could step up to check in on her, she quickly walked up and poked his face, seemingly checking for any scars from yesterday's scuffle. "You ok? Do you feel hurt? Any injuries?"

Hush pulled away and grabbed his shoulders, rage and worry causing his arms to tremble. "*Never* overuse your soul like that again, *understood*?"

Queenie flinched at the strong grip of her older brother, but she lowered her head in genuine apology. "I...I just wanted to be useful."

"You aren't *useful* to anyone if you *die*. Don't push yourself like that *ever* again, *ok*?"

The younger sister hunched her shoulders slightly. Her response was very quiet. "Sorry. Yeah. Ok. Sorry. Sorry."

The older brother sighed in frustrated relief and hugged his sister tightly. Queenie hesitated, but lifted her arms for a small hug. Their embrace was interrupted by a cough.

"Look, that's like...*really* cute and all, but we gotta move."

Hush yanked away from his sister and looked down the hall to see Patchy standing there with his arms stiffly in his jacket pockets. He removed one arm to cough into his hand.

"Yeahhhh. Grab your friend: Babs wants to see you guys. Let's go, and *please* don't pull a gun on her this time, ok?"

...

When Patchy kicked the door open, the party stared at the Overseer as she sat on the floor, slurping up noodles. Upon seeing them, the Overseer stopped slurping and stared at them with a blank expression.

After a few seconds of awkward staring, Patchy waved his hand. "Hi, Babs. We're here."

Babs chewed her noodles and swallowed with obvious annoyance. "You couldn't wait five minutes for me to finish lunch?"

"I didn't know you were eating. Really."

She scowled. "Mhm. Did Tabitha not say anything?"

Patchy shrugged. "Eh. She said something, but I kept walking. I have no idea what she was trying to say."

The Overseer placed her bowl down and dabbed her lips with a sigh. "I just wanted to call you all in to say...Juliette is considering you guys. Honestly, I'm surprised she's interested: that child has turned me down far too many times."

Patchy whistled. "Ol' Julie is softening up? Who woulda thunk?"

Babs scoffed. "Bah. She wants these misfits to enroll in the mentorship program first. She's willing to put forth a recommendation to the kids to allow them to try out."

Taba's eyebrows raised in surprise. Queenie and Hush stared at each other in confusion. The older brother cleared his throat. "So...uh, what does that mean? Why is that important?"

Patchy stared at Taba with curiosity. "He seems to understand why this is such a big deal. You wanna explain it?"

"I'm...not too certain, but from what I've heard? Mentorship is like having a personalized teacher. However, because the ratio of mentors to students is so vast, the requirements to even *apply* for the program is steep. I think it's...a few years of...something." Taba said as he scrunched his brow.

The Gatekeeper nodded. "Yeah, you got the gist of it. Essentially, Julie, who has *never* taken anyone under her wing, is allowing you to cut hundreds of other applicants and not study for years. You realize why this is such a big deal now, right?"

"Why would she do that?" Hush asked.

Babs let out a light chuckle. "Great question. Bigger question, why would Juliette apply for mentorship before you even *sign up* for the application process? It's as though she knows you'll pass the thing."

Queenie raised her hand. "So, uh...what's the actual application procedure? Why is it so difficult?"

"We want the strongest talents to fully utilize each mentor. How do you think we procure the strongest of hundreds of applicants? How would *you* determine the strongest?" Patchy asked with a smile.

Hush hesitated. "Is it...a bracket tournament?"

"Bingo."

The older brother sighed in mild relief. "Oh, that's it? We should be fine then. When's sign ups?"

Babs picked up her bowl of soup and took a big gulp. After she finished downing the bowl, she popped it down on the floor with a big content sigh. "Ahh...oh, the sign ups? Today is the last day. Preliminary brackets start in two hours from now. Get going."

...

The four of them quickly sprinted over to the city's mini stadium. A lady sitting behind a wooden foldable desk took note of the trio running with the disgruntled Gatekeeper with surprise.

"Oh..! Sir Patchy! An honor to meet you. How can I help you?"

"I...yeah. Sign these goobers up, please."

The lady hesitated, checking her clipboard. "I'm sorry, but everyone has already checked in. We aren't missing any-"

The Gatekeeper dug into his coat and pulled out a crumpled envelope, handing it over to the receptionist. She took it with mild confusion and unfolded/uncrinkled the letter. After scanning the contents of the message, her eyes widened.

She peeked over the letter and stared at the trio with curiosity. "...Really?"

Patchy sighed. "I *know*, right? Anyways, can we scoot em in?"

The lady cleared her throat. "Of course, sir."

She scribbled some numbers on some pieces of paper attached to rope and handed them to the new participants. "Wear this around your neck and head in. Once inside, please choose one of the eight lines to stand in. The winner of each line moves onto the finals. Good luck, contestants!"

"I'm gonna watch from the stands to eat popcorn. Good luck, or something." Patchy said with a nod.

As he walked to the stands, the trio stared at each other with a shrug and headed indoors. As they followed the stairs and walked deeper and deeper, the party gazed in mild awe at the vast open underground space filled with numerous soulbearers. They stood in a tall, hollowed out cave with its ceiling coated in grey stone. Scattered around were sixteen long, winding lines that led to dirt fields. Some lines were obviously longer than others, as contestants snuck to lines where they thought they could fight more easier opponents. The echoing chamber filled the cave with screams, roars, and referees yelling out numbers.

Taba turned to the siblings with a nod. "We should stand in separate lines. I'll see you guys at the finals."

They all tapped fists and walked into their respective lines. After an hour of hearing grunts, screams, and the various sound effects of differing blessings,

The man standing in front of him hesitated, then turned to nod towards Hush. "You wanna go ahead?"

Hush shrugged and stepped ahead. In front of him stood a teenager who looked to be the same age as Queenie. He wore a tight black tank top and black shorts, revealing a fairly thin frame. He was littered in piercings, and had a snooty look about him.

He grinned upon seeing Hush, nodding at his new opponent. "So...you're my next fight?"

Hush turned back to his opponents, who all stared nervously at this fighter. He sighed. Apparently they were all scared of this...teenager.

He turned back and stared at his foe with baggy eyes. "I guess I am. So do we start, or...?"

He flinched as he quickly took a quick step back, the wind slicing the space between him and his opponent. Hush's opponent grinned. "I'm not gonna kill you, relax: I'm just gonna make you bow and *beg* me to end the fight."

Hush nodded in silence. He then flexed his fingers. Darkness overtook the arrogant boy, and fear suddenly flashed across his face. In a frenzy, sharp wind whipped around the arena, causing the older brother to step back with rapid movement. The quiet man took note of the patterns of wind, and noted the time between each slash. Deciding that blindness wasn't the way about this, he returned the sight of the arrogant teenager.

Sweat dripped down the arrogant boy's tank top, but he grinned nervously. "Reached your blessing's time limit? I guess I was worried for nothing."

Hush simply closed his own eyes and flexed his fingers to enhance his hearing. Right before each slash was a directional *woosh* of wind. So, he ran forward and silently dodged each invisible slash.

His opponent's face began to waver with each approached step, until he screamed in frustration. "You...*you*...**Stop**."

He frantically waved his scrawny arms in a horizontal line to send out a wide wave of sharp air, to which Hush jumped over with relative ease. After leaping over the boy's desperate attack, the older brother closed the gap in a near instant by sprinting full speed. Once up close with his opponent, Hush slammed his fist into the boy's throat, causing him to kneel over, choking. As he gasped for breath, Hush calmly grabbed the back of the boy's tank top and threw him out the ring.

The referee was silent. Both lines surrounding the sparring field stood silently. Hush looked around confused, nervously pointing at the once-arrogant boy. "He...uh...isn't dead. He's just out. Do I move on, or...?"

The referee blinked and coughed. "Ahem, my apologies. Contestant nine-hundred eighty seven wins. Next participant, please step up."

...

The rest of the fights were boring.

Nearly every contestant leaned heavily on their blessing and would crumble when their blessing failed to touch Hush. Some contestants saw the fights and simply walked out of line. After nineteen consecutive fights, both lines murmured as they all stared quietly at the man. Hush wasn't even out of breath: his momentary training with Taba was *much* more difficult than this.

Both Hush and the referee stared around. No one stepped up. The referee cleared his throat.

"If no other participant steps up, then contestant nine-hundred eighty seven will be crowned the victor of ring six. Going once...twice..."

Not a single participant made an effort to move. The referee hesitated, looking around in confusion.

"And...uh...three! Participant nine-hundred eighty seven moves on to the finals!"

Hush stretched and stepped off his podium, peering over to the other rings. The referee approached Hush with mild awe.

He held up a red ticket with a number scribbled onto it. "Participant nine-hundred eighty seven? Please take this ticket to the receptionist as soon as possible."

Hush pocketed the ticket, dismissed the referee without as much as a greeting, then walked around. He shortly found Queenie, looking bored as she dispatched foe after foe. Many foes seemed to be determined to take down this petite girl, but the older brother knew that Queenie wasn't even *trying*. She seemed to be drastically handicapping herself by only using a yardstick. She sidestepped obvious fireballs, desperate lunges, and telegraphed stabs. She slapped each contestant with a yardstick and then proceeded to throw them out of the ring with relative ease. After ten minutes, the other contestants seemed to give up, and Queenie was crowned the victor.

She stepped off her ring and noticed her older brother. "How long were you standing there?"

He shrugged. "A few minutes, maybe. Hey... these guys kinda..."

"Bro, they *suck*."

"Yeah. Weird. Where do you think Taba is?"

The siblings walked around until they reached the longest line. They peeked at the front, and surely enough, there stood Taba. Taba's opponents all seemed baffled and frustrated that none of their blessings were hitting. To add salt to their wounds, the black-haired boy seemed to be dispatching every contestant with sheer physical prowess. Of course, Taba was almost certainly using his blessing...but to these guys, it seemed as though their life's efforts were being effortlessly mocked.

After an hour of fighting, Taba didn't even seem exhausted. His forehead stayed dry as he rolled his shoulders, looking around in curiosity. He noticed the siblings and waved, in which the siblings cheerfully gave a thumbs-up in return.

After a few minutes, Taba sighed and checked the clock mounted on the wall. He turned to the referee to ask a question. The referee hesitated, unsure of the correct procedure, but nodded. He turned to the remaining ten participants in line.

"Contestant nine-hundred eighty five wishes to fight you ten at once."

The remaining contestants were stunned silent. Then, raged morphed on all their faces as they stepped into the ring. The ten contestants surrounded the teenager, who quietly faced forward with an unreadable expression. Then, the first soulbearer screamed as a rock shot out of the ground. Following this projectile, the other nine soulbearers threw their blessings at Taba.

The next three minutes were simply mesmerizing.

Taba ducked under the rock and rolled to avoid another soulbearer's burst of sludge. He jumped to grab the soulbearer on his right to block the burst of pressurized water that came from his left, causing the soulbearer to sputter as he was easily thrown out. A soulbearer with the ability to alter his size roared as his bodysize doubled, charging at the teenager. Taba pursed his lips, sidestepped his lunge, grabbed his arm, then flung him into two other soulbearers, knocking them out. The soulbearer who sent out the sticky sludge then threw two balls of goop towards Taba's back, who leaped blindly into the air to avoid the surprise attack. The goop then slapped onto another soulbearer, causing her to cry out as her enchantment suddenly stopped. Taba prepared his hands and caught a rock that came from beneath his feet, using the momentum to throw it at the bound girl, throwing her out of bounds. The water soulbearer roared as he spat out another gush of water. However, Taba didn't even bother sidestepping this one, and tanked the weakened burst of water as he focused his attention to seemingly nothing on his right. He suddenly thrust his arm forward and a now visible girl appeared with a startled squeal. He chucked her towards the stream of pattering water, throwing the two soulbearers out.

Taba took a deep breath and turned his groggy eyes to the remaining soulbearers. They all nervously shifted their feet. Suddenly, the teenager bolted towards the nearest boy, who flinched and held his arms up to manifest a green barrier. Taba threw two quick punches at the wall, shattering the feeble shield. He then grabbed the boy's shirt, then threw him towards the furthest girl, who lowered her bow and arrow in shock as they both tumbled out of the ring. The last boy screamed in fear, his voice seemingly carrying pressure in the arena. Taba, however, leapt to the ground and began to crawl at frightening speed towards the last participant. He then used his arms as a springboard to slam his heel into the remaining boy's chin, propelling him out the ring.

The entire room became quiet as everyone stared at this soaked, but overall unfazed, teenager. Even the referee held his breath upon the spectacle, not even trying to step in to interfere.

Soon, a solitary clap rang out from the corner of the room, to which Taba turned to address with a frown. "I thought you were in the stands?"

Patchy stepped up with a mad grin. "*Seriously?* That was brilliant. Well done."

"You can be honest," Taba said with a frown as he wrung his shirt out, "That was nothing compared to what you could do."

"Nah, what makes you think I can do anything like that?"

"Yo, ref," Patchy said, "Can he get a ticket and get a move on to the finals? I wanna see his first match."

The referee wrote out a stub with trembling fingers. "Uh...I...um...Participants have a day to rest and then they'll meet up tomorrow to fight."

Taba frowned. "Why would we need to rest? We can just fight now and get this over with."

Everyone stared at the teenager's nonchalant comment, causing him to flinch and stare at everyone else in confusion.

Patchy roared in amusement. "Man, I'm starting to like you. Shame that'll make it harder to kill you when the time calls for it."

The referee coughed into his hand. "I'm sorry, contestant, but, uh, things are set up to allow rest for the finalists...even if some may not need the rest."

"Yeah, fine. Sure." sighed Taba.

He stepped out of the ring and walked towards the siblings. Hush nodded as he held out a fist. "Took you long enough. The two of us finished *way* sooner than you."

Taba ruffled his hair to shake out water. "Not my fault. People all just wanted to fight." Queenie flinched as a fleck of water splashed onto her cheek. She scowled and reached into her storage to hand the teenager a towel, who accepted it with appreciation.

Queenie rolled her eyes. "Fight, shmight. This was lame. Let's head back and eat, I'm hungry."

...

As they quietly drank soup, Patchy explained the rules of the brackets. The fights were mainly for the mentors to see the skills and faults of each finalist. Winning or losing didn't necessarily mean acceptance or failure. The Gatekeeper reached into his pocket and pulled out a crumpled chart.

He pointed to the brackets. "Here's the matchings."

Hush scanned at the pairings, raising an eyebrow. "Huh. We aren't fighting in the first fight."

"Well, *we're* fighting in round two. No hard feelings, right?" asked Taba.

"Don't hold back," Hush said with a grin. "It's been a while since we sparred. I want to see how far I've come."

Taba stared back with a twinkle in his eyes. "Don't speak as though you're weaker than me. You could very easily win if you outsmart me."

Queenie groaned as she looked at her pairings. "Aw. I'm fighting these nobodies? Boo. Least I'll fight one of you guys in the end."

"Are you assuming you'll win both your fights?" Patchy asked.

"How could I lose?" Queenie scoffed. "If the skill level of my opponents are what I've seen in the preliminaries, I could beat them *without* my blessing."

Patchy chuckled. "Well, now you see why Julie doesn't mentor others, right?"

It was obvious. If *this* was the skill level of the average applicant, they would flat out *die* on missions. Hush turned to Patchy, mildly chewing on his lip as he hesitated on asking his potentially rude question.

The scraggly man noticed. "Mm?"

Hush frowned. "Why are they...uh...so *weak*?"

Patchy chuckled, a soft sadness filling his face. "They grew up peacefully. You guys didn't. Simple as that."

Taba stared at the Gatekeeper. "Aren't you one of the strongest in the city? W-"

"Well, look at the time, time for me to hit the hay." Patchy threw a few dollars on the table and nodded at the trio. "Use that to pay. I'll see you guys tomorrow."

...

The trio stood in front of the stadium, all checking their tickets. The same lady from yesterday stared at them in surprise, darting her eyes down at her clipboard to reconfirm the participants. "Huh. I guess she wasn't going insane after all." She scratched down some notes on the clipboard and then nodded to them. "Do you guys want me to call you by any specific name, or...?"

The trio looked at each other, then looked back at the receptionist. Taba cleared his throat. "Could we just go by our participant numbers?"

The receptionist raised her eyebrow. "You want to go by nine-hundreds? You know the announcer will be calling out these names, right?"

"Yeah. It's fine."

She shrugged. "Alright, sure. Head down the hall and wait in the room with the white curtains."

The trio all walked into the stadium, quietly glancing at the building. The building itself seemed fairly outdated compared to the buildings surrounding it, with dirty red carpentry draped between random wood pillars. While other buildings were made with stone, this one was build with furnished wood. Some sections were blocked off, seemingly going under repairs from the damage of previous fights. The trio walked down the narrow hallway until they reached a room blocked off by a white partition. They stepped in and looked around. The others all looked up and stared at the trio.

One of the boys called out to them: "Which one of you is nine eight five?"

Taba stared silently. The boy grinned and stood up, extending an arm. "You looked up first. I'm guessing you. Nice to meetcha, I'm Gary, your first opponent. Heard how you wiped everyone out: here's hoping that was just a fluke."

The teenager stared at the extended hand, not bothering to extend his own. Gary frowned, clasped his own hand, then nodded. "Well then, aren't *you* friendly. Good luck in the ring: I'm not holding back."

Gary sat back down and continued to fiddle with the dagger in his hand. Hush leaned in and whispered to Queenie. "Remember. *No* guns. Only handheld weapons."

She rolled her eyes. "Yeah, yeah. Whatever. You act like I'll need them."

After a few minutes, a referee entered the room to verify everyone's presence, then refreshed the participants of the rules. No killing, no malicious maiming, no ranged machinery (but hand-drawn bows were ok), no outside support, and first to force the other outside the ring *or* render the opponent unconscious would win. Once everyone nodded in agreement, the referee walked around to collect tickets then left the waiting room. Shortly after, a loud boom rang out from the speaker's box and the crowd roared in delight. The announcer declared the first match and Gary stood up with a yawn. Taba rolled his shoulder and walked out with him. Queenie and Hush stared from the sidelines with interest. Gary seemed to know about Taba's overwhelming victory, yet was still confident. Hush couldn't help but be curious in that pride. So, he flexed his fingers inside his jacket pockets to listen to the humming air around the combatants.

When the referee blew his whistle, the arena silenced awkwardly as the two fighters stood still for a minute. To any spectator, they were staring into each other's eyes as the wind rustled their clothes. Even Queenie wouldn't be able to tell a significant difference: after all, she couldn't *hear* the vibration of the air dampen tremendously like Hush did.

He stopped flexing his ring finger and began to flex his pinky to enhance his sensations. Just as he had predicted: the ground was softly thumping, tremors quietly shaking the stadium. Gary and Taba were locked into place due to a blessing. Whether that was increased gravity or pressure, Hush didn't know. Still, judging from the bulging veins from his friend's neck...it was no light burden.

Gary, seemingly used to the effects of his blessing, strained his arm to detach a baton from his leg. He raised a trembling arm with gleaming eyes, taking shaky steps to what he believed was certain victory.

...Hush couldn't blame the guy for crumpling backwards in surprise as Taba broke out into a sprint.

He quickly kicked Gary's weapon away, using a free arm to half-drag, half throw the combatant out of the ring. Gary stumbled awkwardly against the floor, just barely managing to grip to the floor and stay in bounds. The boy huffed with desperation, struggling to his feet as he failed to notice Taba's kick being thrown towards his chest.

After a direct hit, Gary tumbled out of the arena with ragged breaths. Once his bottom touched the floor, the subtle humming of the arena seized as Taba exhaled a shaky breath. The stadium, unsure of what exactly had just transpired, gave awkward claps as the announcer declared Taba as the winner. His friend groaned as he rolled his neck, light jogging back to the breakroom.

Hush and Queenie met him and tapped knuckles. "Good job."

Taba winced. "It's been a while since I felt that kind of weight, but it wasn't anything too bad."

"Oh, so it *was* gravity?" Hush asked.

Taba shook his head. "Eh. Something similar I think. Doesn't matter, he lost."

"Fair. Well, you're up: the announcer is calling your name."

The two nodded at each other, and Hush stepped up to fight.

CHAPTER 4

Taba leaned against the wall with a groan, rolling his shoulder. Queenie looked over at him with mild concern. "You alright, Taba?"

He squeezed his shoulder. "I wasn't expecting the sudden pressure. Shoulder cramped because of it. Massage it?"

She shrugged and started rubbing/punching his back. Taba curved his back with a mild sigh, his face warping into a small wince the longer Queenie punched. "Yeah, yea-*ow,* that's good. Thanks, Queenie."

The girl grinned as she slammed her elbow into his shoulder for good measure, causing Taba to lurch forwards. He looked back with mild annoyance but sighed. Queenie shot a thumbs up and nodded to the next matchup. Hush stood in the arena with an armless girl who was introduced to the stands as Alexandria. She couldn't have been any taller than five feet tall, yet she stared at Hush as though she were looking down at him.

"What do you think her blessing is?" asked Queenie.

Taba frowned as he began to ask questions. *Is her blessing physicality focused?* **O** *Does her blessing allow her to alter her brawn?* **O** *Does her blessing have anything to do with her missing arms?* **O** *Does...*

He scratched his head as he continued to shoot off seemingly random questions to reverse-engineer her blessing. Sure, part of it was strategic...but Taba just did it because he had fun asking the questions. The little sparks that shot between his synapses with each everyday occurrence just tickled his fancy. Taba couldn't help but light that spark with random questioning whenever he saw the opportunity.

After a minute of silent questions, his eyes slightly widened as he softly smiled. Queenie took notice and tugged at his shirt. "Tell me."

Taba shook his head and nodded to the arena. "You'll see soon. She got unlucky in facing Hush."

She scowled as she poked his gut and turned to face her brother. Hush had his hands in his jacket pockets as he quietly observed his opponent. Alexandria wore a sleeveless gown with the arm straps criss-crossed over her neck. Though she had no arms, her waist and legs seemed fairly built. Furthermore, she wore goggles over her head to shield her eyes, with short scruffy hair adorning her head.

The referee cleared his throat and blew the whistle, to which the audience erupted in ecstatic excitement. Alexandria stomped into the ground and small chunks of the arena began to lift and wrap around her shoulders, forming long flexible poles until they settled as stretchy stone arms. She took a deep breath, then lurched her upper body, causing one of her created arms to stretch forward at a frightening speed towards Hush. His eyes slightly widened as he took a small hop over the swing, then flinched as he looked upwards as Alexandria's second arm came crashing down from the skies. Hush swung his left leg upward and tapped his foot on the descending woman's stone arm *just* as it was moments away from crushing his ribs, then pushed off with his leg to swivel his body midair and dodge her attack.

It was a small maneuver, but the audience roared in delight as Hush did all this without removing his hands from his pockets. As disrespectful as a gesture it seemed, Taba knew that his friend was doing it to hide which fingers were being flexed...though Alexandria most likely would never get to know his blessing. She scowled as her arms slowly retracted towards her in preparation for her next attacks.

Then, her eyes widened as her arms suddenly went limp.

Alexandria stared at her arms with a horrified expression, struggling to even rotate her shoulder forwards due to the weight of the stone. Hush quietly walked towards the panicking girl, hands still in pockets. After a few strides, he stood directly in front of her. His opponent looked back with confused eyes, before those same eyes bugged out from the force of Hush's kick to her abdomen. For anyone else, this kick would've thrown them outside the arena. However, Alexandria was weighed down by her stone arms. As such, she was only sprung back a few inches, struggling to stand on her feet as she gasped for air.

Hush took one stride and landed another kick, squarely in her ribs. A sickening *crack* rang from the arena. The stands slowly stopped their cheering and stared in mild horror as Hush continued to land strong kicks in the same spot, over and over, shifting her towards the "out of bounds" zone inch by inch.

By the seventh kick, Alexandria was coughing up blood...yet she refused to stand down or surrender, simply staring back with confused but angry eyes. Hush kept a monotone expression, as did Taba and

Queenie. Malapace was the enemy, what sympathy was there to spare for them?

By the tenth kick, the stands began to boo at Hush. He paid them no mind as his opponent now collapsed to the ground, wheezing in a puddle of her own saliva, snot, and blood. From how she lay hunched, it was clear that one of her lungs had either been deeply injured or possibly collapsed. Hush knelt down in the small puddle of sticky gore and whispered something to his foe. She snarled and spat at him. Hush stood up, wiped his spit off, then slammed his foot squarely into her head. As he did, the rocks surrounding Alexandria's arms crumbled away into normal earth as the crowd fell into hushed silence.

The referee ran over and felt her neck for a pulse. After a few seconds to check for a response, he confirmed that she was unconscious and declared Hush the winner. Taba's friend walked off the arena with a massive boo from the audience, screams of rage raining down from the stands. Hush rejoined Queenie and Taba, who bumped fists in return.

Taba nodded. "Did you...?"

"Yeah. Took a gamble, hoped that her blessing was linked to her sensation and got lucky. She wasn't thrown around much because the stones were tied to her soul, like an anchor to a ship. Kicks should've been painless because I nullified her pain." said Hush.

His sister frowned as she looked up at the stands. "Yeah, but *they* don't know that. They all hate you."

"Eh. I don't care." said Hush.

"If you insist."

Queenie turned on her heel and walked towards the lounge room. Taba turned to her and frowned. "Not gonna watch the next fight?"

71

She shook her head. "Nah. I want a challenge."

The two guys looked at each other and shrugged. As Taba walked back to the break room, Hush stood still. He nodded to the unconscious opponent. "My blessing is still on her. I don't want her to feel the pain of the fight, so I'll wait until she's healed."

"You're too kind of a person. We'll be inside." said Taba.

When he returned to the waiting room, he saw Queenie yawning as a big man laughed at her, slapping his firm stomach.

The man grinned widely. "...*Why*! Ain't you a small one! You sure you wanna go through this kerfuffle? No shame in backing out!"

Queenie scratched the inside of her ear, completely disinterested. "I'm sorry, who are you again?"

The big man looked taken aback as she stared at him lazily. "Why...haven't ya seen the brackets? I'm Harrison! I'm ya opponent!"

Queenie chewed the inside of her cheek slowly as her eyes glazed across the room. "Wow, I see. Well, Harrison...I, uh, *really* don't care about you."

Harrison grinned, pulling up his arms to proudly flex his biceps. After a few seconds of one-sided boasting, he jutted a thumb to his gi with a a hearty laugh. "By the end of our fight, ya *will* remember me."

She waved him off. "Whatever. Now, if you'll excuse me...I'm gonna take a piss. Later."

Queenie squeezed past Taba and walked down the dusty hallway, leaving Harrison mildly upset as he sat in his chair with a big grumble. To pass time, Taba decided to ask questions to reverse-engineer Harrison's blessing.

After a few minutes, he had fully understood the limitations of the big man's abilities and acknowledged that this man had, at least, a basis for his confidence. Queenie still wasn't back from the bathroom, which led Taba to believe that Queenie was just hiding in a stall to avoid small talk with the other combatants. Surely enough, the second the third round concluded, Queenie waltzed in the room without a care in the world.

Harrison leapt out of his chair and ran onto the arena, letting out a guttural yell. The audience, obviously recognizing him, cheered in response. Harrison grinned wildly as he nodded towards the break room, causing Queenie to groan as she slumped over to the center of the coliseum, giving small fist bumps to Taba and Hush on the way.

The referee announced the combatants, then blew his whistle. Taba blinked then poked Hush. the older brother looked over in intrigue.

"Remind her to not use guns." said Taba.

Hush nodded and enhanced his voice, letting out a small whisper. Queenie flinched and looked over at the two guys, frowning as she did. She flipped them off, then turned to face Harrison, who stood with crossed arms and a big grin. "Go on, little girly! Give it ya best shot!"

Queenie stretched her back...then bolted forward in a blitz. She quickly grabbed a knife from her storage and slashed his chest four times in two seconds. She kicked off his shoulders and over his body, looking at his back with mild surprise.

Harrison grinned as he faced her once more. All he wore was a white gi with a black belt and a sweatband over his forehead. As for his chest...there were no signs of any damage. He roared loudly as he slammed his chest, causing the audience to cheer.

The big man grinned as he boasted. "My blessing is 'impenetrable skin'! My skin can't be damaged! Your attacks are all null against me!"

Queenie blinked. "Wait...that's it?"

He frowned. "Huh?"

Queenie stored her dagger as she stared at the man with confusion. "Wait...that's *it*? **That's** why you're so confident? Impenetrable skin?"

Harrison stayed silent as he stared at her with a confused smile. The girl rubbed her face in exasperation. "I...I thought you'd at least be...*gah*. Whatever."

She bolted at him once more. Harrison grinned as he lifted his arms, ready to intercept her with a grab. Right as he lunged, Queenie slid underneath his legs, released a chain from her storage to fly upwards, then manifested a sledgehammer from her storage. Harrison barely had time to look upwards as a giant slab smashed into his shoulder, causing him to tumble down to the ground.

The second her toes touched the ground, Queenie then dashed to Harrison's left, storing the sledgehammer and manifesting a chain wrapped around a bit of rubble that remained from her brother's fight with Alexandria. She swung around a few times before releasing, sending a giant stone flying towards the big man. He looked up in time for a giant stone to slam into his chest, flooring him once more.

Not letting up, she used another chain to yank her forwards, propelling her at frightening speeds towards her foe. Harrison couldn't even raise his head in time before Queenie propped herself on her arms and slammed her heel directly into his chin, causing the man to fall onto his back. Once the big man lay on the arena floor, groaning in agony, Queenie manifested some steel knuckles from her storage, slipped them on, then proceeded to slam into Harrison's face over and over.

After a minute of this beatdown, Harrison slowly swatted away at the girl. She jumped backwards and stored the knuckles, pulling out another dagger and twirling it between her fingers, laughing as she did. The big man climbed to his feet, struggling to stay upright.

"Impenetrable doesn't mean invincible. Your insides are still *super* vulnerable: I just need the right weapon to hurt you." Queenie said with a grin.

Harrison stood tall with his head staring upwards to the clouds. After a few seconds, he roared, causing the audience to cheer. When he looked down at his challenger, Queenie stared in mild surprise as her foe donned a wide, bloodstained, grin.

He clapped proudly. "Excellent! You are wonderful!"

Queenie frowned. "The hell is wrong with you?"

The man took a step...and stumbled, falling to one knee as he caught his breath. After a few deep breaths, he chuckled. "Ah, drats. I can't stand. I concede, girly."

The crowd roared in delight as the juggernaut threw in the towel. Though he lost, he pumped his fist up to the crowd and walked to the medical office with a limp, his massive frame requiring the support of two assistants to aid his walk.

Queenie stared at his back, shrugged, then hopped off the arena, nodding to her companions. "Whaddya think?"

"You won, right?" Taba chuckled.

"Man, coulda fooled me, the way he walked off the stage with that cheer." Queenie said with a frown, rubbing her elbows.

Hush shrugged and lifted his fist. "End of the day, you're moving on. You're fighting either me or Taba, who are you betting on?"

Queenie tapped her brother's fist. "Taba, duh."

"Damn. Not even a second of hesitation?" Hush looked at his sister with a slightly amused, slightly hurt look.

"You can't even keep up with Taba in his morning workouts. How do you plan to beat him?" Queenie said as she rolled her eyes.

Her brother opened his mouth...then closed it, obviously stumped. Taba shrugged and nodded to the arena as the referees waved them on. "Let's go, man. They're calling us on."

She nodded and gave them both quick, excited, hugs. "Good luck, both of you guys!"

As the two friends stepped onto the arena, the crowd's reaction seemed...mixed. On one hand, the person who had anticlimactically won due to a forfeit. On the other, the man who had seemingly mocked and tortured an armless girl. Though no one knew what to feel, the crowd was at least certain in their *boos* towards Hush, who paid them no mind.

The referee blew his whistle and the two men stood still. Taba walked forward and raised his hand, grinning as he did. Hush blinked, grinned with amusement, and clasped his friend in a firm handshake. After a second of camaraderie, Taba turned around and walked back to his post. To the crowd's surprise...Hush didn't strike at this obvious opening. Though Taba was a bit disappointed at this lack of initiative, he understood: his friend wanted a *fair* fight, one where both parties were at their best.

Once he reached his starting spot, he nodded to his friend. Hush nodded back. His voice reached Taba's blessing enhanced ears in a soft whisper. "*You ready?*"

Taba nodded...and his world went dark. As he heard rapidly approaching footsteps, the now-blind boy began to ask a rapid series of questions.

Is it a kick? **X** *Is it a punch?* **O** *Is it with his left hand?* **X** *Is it towards my upper body?* **O** *Can I dodge it with a sidestep?* **O** *Will he follow-up with a legsweep?* **O** *Will he headbutt?* **X** *Will I stay blind for the next minute?* **X** *Will he nullify my hearing within the next three minutes?* **O** *Will a right jab connect to him?* **O** *Will it connect with his chest?* **X** *Will it connect to his arms?* **O** *Will a forwards kick land?* **X** *Will an uppercut catch him off guard?* **X** *Will...*

Taba continued to ask these numerous questions as he quickly sidestepped and dodged the flurry of moves that Hush threw at him. Hush threw a quick left swing, to which Taba sidestepped. As he did, Hush lowered to the ground to sweep at his friend's legs, to which Taba leaped over and translated his midair momentum into a direct dropkick. The move landed squarely into Hush's chest, causing him to stumble a few feet backwards. Before he could recover, Taba bolted forwards blindly...and his vision returned. For a split second, Hush nullified Taba's hearing...before *amplifying* it.

As Taba's next jab landed squarely into Hush's jaw, the older brother grabbed the jab and yanked the black-haired boy abruptly towards him and screamed into his ears. The attack proved effective as Taba winced and stumbled backwards, subconsciously clasping his ears in pain. Hush took the opportunity to run forward and jumped into Taba's face with a knee. The blow landed sharply, and his face stung with a *crack* as a flurry of red spewed from Taba's nose. Hush then returned Taba's sense of hearing back to normal...only to amplify Taba's sense of feeling. The small ache of the broken nose now throbbed in massive waves across his whole face, the ripples of pain disrupting the questioner's concentration even further. With his face distorted in pain, Hush grinned as he sprinted to land a solid blow to his friend's eyes...

...being completely caught off guard as Taba fell backwards. The questioner caught himself with his arms and pushed upwards with a locked leg, uppercutting the older brother with a full-force kick. Hush's eyes rolled to the back of his skull, but he caught himself as he slammed his leg into the ground. He wheezed as he stumbled backwards, trying to orient himself once more.

To the crowd, this looked like a simple martial arts fight, and even so, they roared in surprise at the sharp snaps of each combatant's moves. Ignoring the cheers of the crowd, Taba noted that his face still throbbed to an unnatural degree, letting him know that his friend hadn't nullified his own sense of pain. Before his foe could orient himself, Taba noted their positions and asked a quick question to his soul.

If I were to ... would it work? **O**

Taba grinned and bolted to his friend. Right as he began to orient himself, Taba dove at Hush, knocking him off his feet. He scowled and lifted his elbow to strike...interrupted by the shrill of a whistle. Hush looked down in surprise and noticed that Taba had tackled the two of them out of bounds. However, because Hush had landed first...

As the referee declared Taba the winner, the crowd let out a cheer. It wasn't as loud as some of the other fights, due to the anticlimactic finish, but the audience seemed pleased that the boy who kicked the armless girl had lost. Taba rolled over to the ground, laughing as he stared up to the sky. Hush groaned and lay on the dirt floor in return.

"You improved. First time you hit me with that one." said Taba with a grin.

"*Man*, I could've *sworn* that this was the day that I beat you," groaned Hush. "Damn. How far ahead did you ask?"

"Honestly? I didn't expect you to amplify my hearing. I had to ask a new batch of questions because of it."

"Hm. I guess it kinda worked then."

Queenie ran over and knelt to the ground, her eyes twinkling. "Holycrapthatwasamazingbroyouactuallylandedahitontohimandthenheslammedyouinthechinwithakickand**damn**yougotrocke-da-"

The referee blew his whistle, cutting off Queenie's rambling. She sighed, flipped off the referee, then stood up. "Go heal up, I guess. I'll try to wrap this up quickly."

"You sure? The next girl-"

"...is just as boring as Harrison. I'll be fine, and you won't be missing anything."

The two male contestants shrugged as they got up and brushed the dust off their butts, then hobbled over to the medical office. Similar to the break room, the hallway leading to the medical office had dirt floors and curtains in place of doors. Sweeping aside the gray curtain of their destination, the two men stared in mild surprise upon seeing G sitting in a chair with a scowl.

Seeing the two contestants, he raised an eyebrow. "Oh? You guys actually got injured? Really?"

Taba shrugged. "Well, Hush is a strong opponent: hard to not get injured. Bigger question is, why are *you* here?"

The bald Gatekeeper huffed as he reached into his pockets, pulling out the white pills that were distributed earlier. "Honestly, I don't want to be here either...but Babs insists that I need to directly distribute these things since they're super valuable. Here."

Taba took the pill, his eyebrows furrowed as he tried to examine the contents of the cure. He tapped into his soul to try and reverse engineer it.

Will I be fully healed after consuming this? **O** *Would I consider the materials of this tablet 'rare'?* **X** *Does Father know the materials to make this tablet?* **O** *Is it possible for me to easily craft this tablet?* **O**

The teenager hesitated. How was such an incredible cure also not rare? Furthermore, if it wasn't rare and father knew about it...why was it not replicated back at home? Before he could ask more questions, G noticed Taba's stalling and scowled, squeezing the shoulders of both injured contestants.

"Hey. I know what you're doing. Stop it. Take the damn pill and get out, *now*."

The two contestants quickly dry swallowed the pill and immediately both felt better. G sighed and let them go, pushing them towards the exit as he did. "Alright, now shoo. I want my alone time."

As they walked down the dark hallway, Hush noticed Taba's quiet murmuring. "Trying to understand the medicine?"

"The pill is common. It heals. Father knows about its material. Plus...it's replicable. All of this doesn't make sense. Is it a monopolized drug? I...hm." Taba muttered.

Hush said nothing, nodding as they continued down the hallway. Taba appreciated that his friend gave space to allow him to think. So many would try to fill the silence with awkward small talk which would only serve to distract any questioning...but Hush knew the value of quiet company. It was a rare trait that Taba cherished.

As the two squinted at the bright sun that invaded their eyes upon stepping out of the dark tunnel, they looked up to the sky to see Queenie laughing maniacally as she flew circles around her foe. Her opponent was a slender girl who was equipped with a soul-created bow, arrows, and wings. Despite the seeming aerial advantage she had, the winged opponent whipped her head around frantically as Hush's sister used "half-summoned chains" from her storage to seemingly grapple onto nothing but the air itself. The winged combatant would desperately try to fire arrow after arrow, but Queenie would easily evade each shot. After a few arrows, the archer's eyes fluttered slightly as her weapon unmanifested and her wings vanished, falling out of the sky. Queenie sighed as she summoned a chain to catch her foe before the foe slammed onto the dirt arena. Once landing, she then grabbed her unconscious opponent and threw her out of the ring for good measure. The crowd erupted in delighted screams, to which Queenie sighed and turned her attention to the male duo watching her.

"She was fun...kinda." Queenie said as she walked over. "I wish she stuck around longer, though: I *never* get the opportunity to swoop around with chains."

Hush ruffled his sister's hair with a grin. "Look at you. Five years ago, you were struggling to manifest chains partially and now you're swinging around mid-air. So proud of you."

Queenie's ears flushed red as she swatted her brother's hand away with an embarrassed face. "Shut up." She turned to Taba with a nod. "You good to go?"

He stretched his shoulders as he tilted his head. "I mean...yeah, but are good? You just used some soul last round for fun."

"Eh, you used some soul in your fight too. Doesn't matter, it'll all work out. Let's just have some fun with this, yeah?"

Taba frowned as he followed her. Before they could take their stations, the referee walked over to Queenie and whispered into her ear. At first, she frowned...then she tilted her head in amused confusion. After hearing the referee's relayed message, she held a finger up to Taba and dashed off to somewhere in the coliseum, her brown ponytail bobbing away in the wind with each step.

He frowned and walked up to the referee. "What's happened?"

"I'm not too sure," said the referee, "but the Dancing Painter herself requested an audience with finalist nine-hundred eighty six, and I don't want to be the one to say 'no' to her."

"Wait, the Dancing Painter? Isn't she just a children's fable? Is it a nickname or does she *actually* exist?" asked Taba.

The referee looked back with a slightly confused facial expression. "What, you don't know about her? She's super famous in Malapace. Rumor has it that she's mentoring this year, which is why there were so many participants this time around."

The questioner's mind flew at sharp speeds. There was no way this was all just a coincidence. He tapped into his soul to confirm his thought, but even upon hearing the answer, Taba looked up to ask the question that would leave no room for doubt. "Do you know her name?"

The referee rubbed his whistle as he thought for a second. "You mean *names*? She has a few. Dancing Painter is her most famous one. There's also the Drunken Fox. If you're asking for her *actual* name... I think it was Juliette."

CHAPTER 5

Hop! Hop! Hop goes the Dancing Painter!
There she goes, painting the sky!
She may come now! She may come later!
Don't view her portraits: you may just die!

Dance, Dance, Dance! She strokes the air!
Her silver paintbrush, foes beware!
Her lips are bright, her skin is fair!
Run, Run, Run! You're in her lair!

Her laugh is mad, her dance is captivating.
Stay or run, both are devastating.
The Drunken Fox cries, she mourns her lover.
Red ribbons cover you in an instant flutter.

As her mind recited the famous nursery song, Queenie sprinted towards the judge's stands. Juliette was the Dancing Painter? Really? No way. But...no. No way.

She barged into the small conference room to witness a startled Sana holding a teacup as Juliette sat across from her, sipping from her jug. Queenie blinked at the two powerful women in the room, unsure of what to say.

After a second, she cleared her throat and blurted out her thoughts. "So *you're* the Dancing Painter? That isn't *just* a nursery rhyme?"

Juliette lowered her jug and dabbed at her lips with a sigh. "I never asked for the damn rhyme to be made. People just kept seeing me, stories got around, and now I'm an urban legend. Surprised you never pieced it together during your test."

"Look. I was fighting for my life and nearly died *twice*. I think you can forgive me if I wasn't focused on nursery rhymes in the midst of it. Speaking of which, I've heard your song since I was a kid. You aren't that old...are you?"

Sana stifled a laugh as Juliette sloshed her drink in her hands. "I'm pretty up there in age. How old did you think I was?"

"You aren't supposed to ask a lady her age. So... forty?" Queenie guessed.

Sana choked on her tea as even the monotone Juliette looked mildly offended. "Do I really look that old?"

"No, but now I know you're younger than forty."

The black eyes of the fox stared back at her. "Well, you aren't wrong."

"Well to be fair Jules, you really haven't changed since we first met." said Sana with a smile. "How do you do it?"

Juliette shrugged as she tied her jug to her waist. "Beats me. I just drink and set my blessing up." She then nodded to the chair in front of her. "Sit."

84

Queenie stayed standing with a frown. "Why?"

"Fine. Don't sit. I just wanted to talk to you about your blessing."

"What's there to talk about? It's pretty straight forward."

Juliette's lips twitched as she stopped drinking, corking her jug. "That's the issue. You only *see* it as 'straight forward'. You don't even see the tremendous potential your blessing has. I wasn't kidding when I said you could overwhelm me and the Gatekeepers. From spectating your two matches, it's obvious that you've obtained fair mastery over numerous weapons. You even compensate for any physical weaknesses with your surroundings or weaponry. In that, I have no complaints."

"Then what's the problem? I'm good. I'm winning. Why are we talking?"

"Have you ever beaten Taba in a fight?"

Queenie frowned. "No, but Taba is amazing. He doesn't count."

The Drunken Fox tilted her head as she pondered the statement. "I wouldn't call him 'amazing', but he certainly works hard to make up for his shortcomings. However, don't you think it's weird? You can summon guns, chains, daggers, and so on...yet you can't beat one *boy*."

"He isn't just some *boy*," Queenie snapped as she pulled a pistol out from her storage. "How would you know anything about Taba?"

"His blessing is nothing on the same level as those he's fought, yet he's dispatched them with ease." Sana quietly spoke from the corner, causing Queenie to flinch and dart her eyes to the new voice. "He is creatively pushing his power to the utmost limit in every aspect, and then some. Jules and I both understand how much one has to work to get to Taba's level. I would imagine you worked quite hard yourself.'

The female Gatekeeper's voice seemed to dissipate Queenie's anger as she clenched her gun. "If you know that, then it's understandable why I would lo-"

Suddenly, pain flared in the girl's left hand. Queenie winced as she looked down to see a small scratch suddenly appear on her left pinky. She looked up to see Sana staring daggers into a monotone Juliette.

"You make no sense. Do *you* understand how hard that boy works? No matter how incredible he is, at the end of the day, he's a boy and you have a gun. There's no excuse for being outclassed." the Dancing Fox said.

Queenie scowled. "You think I haven't tried to shoot at him? Bullets don't work: he dodges them all."

"Oh? I didn't realize all it took to dodge a bullet was routine exercise."

"Of course not, Taba has his ble-"

The Drunken Fox glared back at her. "His blessing is to ask *questions*. It isn't foreshadowing, omnipotence, or time warping. That boy is constantly considering every single possibility and the counter to each one. To you, he dodged a full magazine. To him? He's most likely constantly asking a hundred to two hundred questions a minute while planning for every single outcome: when you'll be firing, where you'll be firing, how to counterattack, so on. Do you understand how taxing that is on his mind, body, and most importantly, soul?"

The girl grit her teeth in frustration. Of course she knew that. She's been on countless missions with him. Queenie saw Taba when a plan didn't work out. She also saw him knock out, exhausted at day's end. No one worked harder than him. How could anyone compare her to that insurmountable hurdle?

The stoic lady leaned back into her chair. "I called you in here to say this: if you don't impress me this round, I refuse to mentor you."

"I don't give a damn if you tutor me. Why should I?"

"Fair enough. I'll give you two reasons." replied Juliette.

She reached into her sleeves and pulled out a paper that had been furled into a cylinder. Upon opening the container, she flashed its contents to the suddenly awestricken girl.

The Dancing Painter traced her finger under the title. "Blueprints for a cannon."

Ever since World War III, humans had struggled to fully rebuild what they had lost. However, when blacksmiths and inventors slowly began to obtain blessings, it suddenly became possible to create certain things...if one had the blueprints to accurately make it *and* if the creator had enough soul to make it. It was shockingly difficult to find blueprints, even more so for weapons that Queenie could actively store and use. The idea of adding that much firepower to her arsenal made Queenie's mouth water in anticipation.

Once she had confirmed that Queenie understood the parchment, she wrapped it up once more and stuck it in her sleeves. "The second reason? I'm interested in mentoring Taba and Hush."

"That...isn't a reason." Queenie said with a frown.

Sana hesitated, but spoke up. "Queenie...your *brother* is the one that requested that Jules mentor you all. He wanted to grow stronger and saw her as the best way to that goal."

Queenie stared at Sana in disbelief, but the Gatekeeper's eyes held no lies: only sorrow and truth.

Juliette cleared her throat. "I am more than willing to mentor those two alone, but that would not only separate you trio more and more, it would also widen the strength gap between you Misfits. You would end up being a bigger burden, and soon enough? Well...you can guess."

The excitement for the blueprint had faded into harsh silence. Queenie stared at her dirty boots, unsure of what emotion she should be feeling. Fear of being left behind? Anger at admitting she was weaker? Longing to be useful to Taba and Hush? No...Queenie just didn't want to be someone that others would need to *protect*.

"I just need to impress you?" Queenie asked with a steeled jaw.

The Drunken Fox nodded, her black eyes staring a void into Queenie's challenging eyes.

"Fine. Just know, I'm not doing this for you."

"I know."

Queenie stormed out of the room, thinking as she made her way back to the arena. How could she impress someone who seemingly hated her? What weapon could she summon that could "wow" that woman?

Her mind was lost as she quietly stepped onto the arena, kicking aside pebbles as she did. Taba noticed her lost in thought and ran up to her. "Yo. You ok? What did she say?"

Queenie stayed silent. If she told him...Juliette would most likely see through it. So, Queenie slapped her cheeks and looked up at her friend with strong eyes.

"Just don't hold back, alright?"

Taba raised an eyebrow in intrigue, but nodded. "Ok."

The duo tapped knuckles and walked to their starting points. The two took their place and the referee blew his whistle. Queenie immediately opened up by pulling out daggers and dashing to Taba. Taba read her move and shifted his weight on his backfoot, preparing to leap away depending on her actions. Right as she was ten feet away from the boy, she stored one of her daggers and used a suddenly manifested chain to immediately change direction and snap to Taba's left. The black haired boy was not caught off guard, snapping his foot into her right wrist as she stepped in to slash. Queenie winced as the dagger clattered out of her hand.

Deciding to leave the dagger on the floor, she immediately threw two swift jabs at her opponent, who ducked one and parried the other, flipping Queenie over his back. Before she could slam onto the ground, she manifested scattered kunai to fly at Taba from random directions. The boy barely flinched as his grip on her strengthened and pulled upwards, suddenly using her as a shield against her own attack. In response, Queenie stored her kunai and slammed the weight of her elbow towards Taba's cheek. In response, he simply leaned back and threw her towards the edge of the arena. Queenie yelped, manifesting a chain to catch and pull her towards safety...

...only to meet Taba midair as he rammed his knee into her side.

Granted, he had performed the attack midair, so his attack didn't *nearly* have his usual power. Still, Queenie bounced and slipped off the floor, gasping in pain as she clutched her ribcage. Nothing *felt* broken, but Taba had landed a crucial hit. As she lay writhing on the floor, she tried desperately to turn her attention to her opponent. When she finally looked up at the calmly approaching boy, he grabbed her by the arm and slowly began dragging her to the edge of the arena.

Fear struck Queenie. She had done *nothing* impressive. All her attacks had easily been shut down, all while her opponent hadn't even broken a sweat. He had read through every plan, and now moved to take her out. At this rate, Juliette wouldn't be impressed, Taba and Hush would go on without her, and...and she would...

Queenie sucked in air as she grit her teeth. No. She refused to lose on anyone's terms but her *own*. She pulled out bags of flour from her storage, flinging them at Taba's face. The boy, surprisingly caught off guard, began sputtering as he let go of the weakened girl.

The last time she had done something similar was when she was a kid. That was when...it didn't matter. Regardless, she grit her teeth and opened her storage to "store" herself, vanishing from the world around her.

The best way to describe her storage was...infinity. It was a plain blank space, with various things scattered about. Miscellaneous items were wrapped in her soul, making it impossible to even interact with these objects without Queenie's blessing. Her belongings scattered for an eternity, making the entire space seem...blank.

However, this was *not* the time to be fascinated by the storage room. The moment she had entered her space, her soul began to deplete at a horrifyingly rapid rate. She quickly took two steps forward, grabbed a claymore (which took even *more* soul from her soulwell), then "pulled" herself out of her storage.

When she reappeared, she had slapped her claymore into the ground, completely missing the stunned Taba who stood seven feet away. The exhaustion of overexertion kicked in all at once as her claymore and disarmed dagger automatically crumbled back into her storage. Queenie fell to a knee, coughing in bitter frustration as her eyes began to spin.

Her last memory before passing out were a pair of bright red lips, smiling at her.

When she woke up, the girl lay in bed as her head was throbbing. Queenie groaned as she struggled to sit up, coughing up saliva as she tried. Her fuzzy head heard cursing as she struggled to understand her surroundings.

As her eyes focused, she found herself staring at an angry G, thick saliva splattered across his face. Behind him stood Taba, G, Sana, and...Juliette, who sipped away at her flask. Queenie opened her mouth to speak, but her throat cracked and she coughed openly to her right, unintentionally coughing directly into G's face once more. He swore even *more* loudly, wiping his face on Queenie's bedsheets.

After a few seconds, she squinted at her audience. "...Did I win?"

Taba frowned and looked at Sana. "Did she? I mean..."

"Though it may *appear* as though Taba won...the final match was declared a 'draw' because Jules decided to step onto the arena, kind of rendering the entire match null." Sana said with a chuckle. "The judges are discussing what to do."

Hush scowled as he knelt next to his sister. "Didn't I *tell* you to manage your soul better? Why did you try doing that?"

Queenie hesitated, unsure of what to say. Juliette took a long swig from her flask, then tied the jug to her waist. "Because I wanted to be impressed."

Her brother grit his teeth as he turned to face the Drunken Fox. "*Pardon?*"

Taba placed his hand on his friend's shoulder and stared at Juliette. "So...did Queenie impress you?"

"On one hand...she wasn't cautious of her limits: something I *heavily* critiqued her on last time. On the other? She tried something:

91

a possibility that has infinite potential. She's expanded the definition of her blessing in a split second of determination." said Juliette.

Queenie stared in surprise as the fox's red lips smiled once more. "Yes. I'm *very* impressed. I will mentor her."

The girl grinned wildly, pumping her fist in the air weakly. "Hell yeah. I want my blueprint."

The Dancing Painter softly smiled as she shook her head. "I'll give it over, once you've regained your soul. I don't want a repeat of last time. Good job today, all of you."

As she slowly walked out of the room, the female Gatekeeper turned to the rest of the trio with a wide grin on her face, doing small jumps of excitement. " 'Good job'!!! Jules *never* praises others! Well done, all of you!"

While Sana was still a target for elimination, Queenie found it difficult to not be infected by the lady's bubbling energy. Turning to face the other men in the room, it appears they also felt her overflowing excitement as their ears turned red and they all looked to the ground. Though no one said anything, Sana squealed and hugged G, who scowled but didn't shoo her away.

After a minute of small celebration, G pushed her off and stared at the trio. "We need to think of a name for you guys. I'm getting tired of just 'referring' to you all."

Taba and Hush shuffled their feet in awkward silence. Those two weren't ones for "team names" or whatnot, so their sudden silence made sense. For Queenie, her head was throbbing so she couldn't care less about a 'team name', so she said the one thing that stuck out to her.

"Uh...how about 'Misfits'? I think that has a good ring to it." proposed Queenie.

G raised an eyebrow. "Misfits?"

"Yeah. Juliette called us that, and it stuck in my mind. We all cool with it?"

The two guys shrugged. They seemed overall indifferent to team names, just as Queenie expected. She gave a weak nod to G as her exhaustion kicked in once more. "Misfits it is. Can I go to sleep now?"

G sighed, pinching the bridge of his nose. "Yeah, sure. Whatever. Go knock out. Everyone, leave."

Hush looked at his sister with concern, but Queenie just nodded. "Relax. I'm just sleepy. I'll be fine."

He nodded, coming in to give a small fist bump. She grinned as she softly tapped his knuckles, sleepiness slowly overtaking the dark room. Sana quietly touched Hush's shoulders to guide him out the room. The remaining members in the room were now Queenie, G, and Taba.

"You held back, huh?" G said to Taba.

Taba flinched but kept a monotone face. "If you're talking about the finals, I tried, I don't know what you mean,

G rolled his eyes as he nodded to Queenie. "She needs to hear this too. I get *why*, but at the end of the day, you *did* hold back. If you want her to learn, you gotta be ruthless."

"Overwhelming her won't teach her squat." Taba said as he crossed his arms.

"She isn't *that* weak. The gap between you two isn't as big as you imagine: stop inflating your ego."

Taba opened his mouth to protest...but closed it with a small nod. He turned to her with an unreadable face expression. "He isn't wrong. Rest up, you did well today."

Queenie gave a small grin and thumbs up as he exited the room. G turned to her with a sigh as he checked a clipboard on a nearby nightstand. "Yeah, go to sleep. I just need to double check something before heading out: don't mind me."

Though she disliked sleeping in front of others, the weariness that began to overtake her spoke otherwise. Without a word of protest, her eyelids drifted shut with her soft breathing slowly filling the hollow room.

...

It hurt to breathe. It hurt to think. It hurt to stand. It hurt. It hurt. It hurt. Where was Hush? Why wasn't he here, helping? Why did he leave her alone?

There was a massive block in her heart, threatening to tear everything to shreds if she pulled it out. However, the same block also kept draining at her strength. The sun hadn't moved at all, but it felt as though she had been crumpled on the floor for years.

After whimpering in a puddle of her own snot, bile, and tears for what felt like an eternity, a shadow fell over her. She peaked upwards with a painful look, staring at the man who was soon to be her savior.

His grey eyes pierced her very being as he crouched down, kneeling in the mulch of vomit without much care. He used his calloused thumb to wipe away a tear from her slightly glowing eyes.

"You poor thing. Let me help you."

She opened her mouth...only to cough up some chunks of canned peaches. The man wiped her mouth with his own shirt sleeve, shaking

94

his head. "Don't try to speak: I can't imagine that life was easy for you. Worry not, I will set things right."

As he placed his hand on her head, a soothing whisper caressed her brain as the block in her heart vanished. Suddenly, Hush appeared, next to her, his eyes closed and his body much *more withered than Queenie remembered. She lifted her arm to touch him, but an excruciating pain caused her to yelp and stop any movement. The stranger said nothing, instead placing his hand on her brother's head as well. Almost immediately, color returned to his cheeks, his slightly glowing eyelids dimming in the process.*

The man said nothing as he stroked their hair, humming a soft tune. After thirty minutes of this, he lifted both children under each arm and began to walk. The woozy girl turned to her savior with curiosity, awe, and fear.

The stranger in return, smiled. "Don't worry: I'm not your enemy. In fact, I'm a friend! You can call me...uh...hm...'Father'."

...

Queenie woke up with a deep inhale, sweat drenching her brown hoodie. She peeked out the window, only to discover that it was now night time. Her body was still a bit sore, but a decent amount of her soul had returned. Sick of lying down, she got up and stretched her limbs, getting the jitters out as she did. Afterwards, she took off her drenched hoodie, revealing an equally drenched white t-shirt. Though she would have loved to take her damp clothes off, strutting around Malapace, the *enemy's territory*, in nothing but baggy pants and a sports bra? Probably not the best idea. So, she scanned around the room to look for outfits to wear. To her surprise, a small pile of clothes lay neatly on a stool with a small note on top of it. She unfolded the note to see the contents, her nose wrinkling in mild disgust as she did.

Hey Queenie!

I know that you probably wouldn't like it, but here's one of my dresses! I think you would look so cute in one! Of course, you don't need to wear it...but it'd be wonderful if you did. Hope it fits! :)

-Sana

The sweaty girl unfolded the dress, her face morphing into one of repulsion. It was a flowy white sundress with built in shorts. She stared at the outfit and her drenched hoodie, determining which one was the less condemning choice. After a minute of contemplation, she let out a defeated sigh as she threw on the 'gift'. Surprisingly, the dress was easy to move in and seemed to cover her up fairly. Though Queenie adored baggier clothes, this dress wasn't... *that* bad.

Needless to say, she would take it off the moment she got back to her dorm room.

She peeked out into the hall of the dark colosseum. Once confirming the coast was clear, she scampered down the hall with swift legs, her dress fluttering in the wind as she did. As she dashed back to the town hall, a constant swishing sound caught Queenie's attention. She turned to the direction of the sound, hesitating on whether to sate her curiosity or change out of the ridiculous outfit as soon as possible. Her former decision won as she tiptoed towards the city's park. She peeked around the corner and *immediately* became captivated at the sight she beheld.

There was Juliette in her usual attire of a hooded kimono, wielding her paintbrush. She danced in a wide motion, moonlight bouncing off the fox mask and her pale skin. The Dancing Painter took careful steps, ranging from tiny hops to wide leaps, her arms outstretched in an animated motion as her paintbrush whirled into the midnight sky as its bristles twinkled with each flick. The Drunken Fox's head tilted back with exaggerated motion, her red lips piercing the dark night, like the glowing eyes of a beast in a blackened cave.

To call it 'graceful' would be an insult, like calling an unmatched fighter a loner. No, this was something *beyond* grace. She couldn't be touched. It was impossible to approach her. How could one live up to this beauty? Just like how a rose does not "try" to sway in the wind, Juliette did not "try" to appear elegant. She simply moved, and the crickets silenced themselves to watch. The trees stopped their rustling to witness this performance. The stars dared not twinkle, in fear that it would disrupt her performance. Witnessing these movements made the world, and everything Queenie knew, appear dull, solely by comparison. How could *anyone* call *anything* beautiful, when this existed?

The awestruck girl was so captivated, she didn't even notice the small bit of drool that escaped her lips...nor did she notice the Gatekeeper approaching her from behind. Finching *hard* upon feeling the tap on her shoulder,

Queenie whirled around to meet the warm smile of Sana, staring at the moonlit dancer. "Beautiful, isn't it?"

Queenie struggled to respond. "I...I can't say it is, but yeah."

Sana held a hand to her mouth as she chuckled. "I get what you mean. It's *more* than beautiful, but how could one go beyond the peak? What a pleasant problem, hm?"

"...absolutely *not* what I meant."

The female Gatekeeper removed her hat and watched with a long gaze. "This is how I first met her, by the way. I found her randomly dancing in a meadow. She eventually stopped dancing, but I wasn't sure how long I stayed there. Jules stared at me and I didn't know what to do...so I just...*clapped*. Then, *she* didn't know what to do, so she stiffly bowed and walked away. I still tease her about it to this day."

Sana poked Queenie's cheek with a grin. "By the way, I'm glad my dress fits you. You look *gorgeous* in it."

Queenie flinched and blood rushed to her entire face. "I...didn't really have a choice. Rest of my clothes were soaked. I'm taking it off as soon as I can."

"Aw..."

Suddenly, Sana flinched as her head turned to the field. Queenie followed her gaze to see Juliette staring at them, the black fox 's eyes sending chills down her spine. Sana chuckled as she repositioned the hat on her head. "Ah, beans. She caught us: let's go say hi to her."

The two of them approached the still fox. Oddly enough, it seemed as though the world suddenly sprung into motion once more the *second* she stopped her dance. Crickets resumed their song, trees stopped holding their breath, and the stars cheered in uproarious applause.

After walking up to the performer, Sana grinned as she gave a small wave. Juliette's face betrayed no emotion. "Hey, Jules. Great performance once again."

Juliette's nose twitched as she slightly grimaced. "I told you to stop coming by. I hate being watched."

Sana chuckled as she shook her head. "Not going to happen. Plus, I'm not the only one who thinks so, isn't that right Queenie?"

The girl hesitated, unsure if she should compliment the enemy. However, she couldn't lie in good conscience. "It was...ok. I guess."

"High words of praise from Miss 'piss you off'." noted Juliette.

Queenie scowled and flipped her off. Sana stifled a laugh and did her best to frown at the gesture. The masked woman waved her off without much thought. "Whatever. Anyways, why are you here? Aren't you supposed to be resting?"

The girl opened and closed her hand, feeling the soreness with caution. "Well...I'm recovering, but I'm much better. How long was I knocked out?"

Sana tilted her head, her eyes turned to the sky. "Mmm, a day and a half? Taba and Hush have just been doing their own things, waiting for your recovery, so you didn't miss much."

The female Misfit winced. She disliked "holding back" her team, but Queenie wasn't even fully recovered. "Can't you guys just...give me the white pill thingy?"

"That cure doesn't work to regenerate soul, no." Sana said with a soft smile.

Queenie frowned. "How did you 'cure' me that one time during the test, then?"

The female Gatekeeper winked as she held a finger to her lips. "Gatekeeper trade secret, sorry."

The girl scowled. As a breeze blew by and flowed through her dress, her scowl deepened as she lowered her arms to prevent the outfit from flapping uncontrollably. "I'm heading back, I want to take this thing off."

The other two women nodded, with Sana giving a cheerful wave. "Got it. I need to stay here to talk to Jules about something, but go get some rest! Wait, did you need us to walk you back?"

"Uh...I'll be fine. Bye."

She turned on her heel and jogged back to the dormitory. Surprisingly, the town hall was unlocked with no one manning the front desk. Queenie would've loved to rifle through the supplies to "store" some objects for future use, but her soul was recovering. So, she headed to her room to change out of her dress, then promptly collapsed on her bed to try and fall asleep once more.

However, whenever she closed her eyes, all she could see was a flower fluttering through the wind, her red lips and fox mask shining in the moonlit sky. As she replayed the animation in her head over and over, the girl lost track of time and suddenly sat up witnessing the shimmer of the morning sun. However, she couldn't help but notice that even the sunrise seemed dull compared to the beautiful performance in the park yesterday.

How odd, she thought. The nursery rhyme didn't do the performance justice. Furthermore, it failed to capture how truly lonely and sad the solo waltz was. As Queenie arose and slowly washed up, she was left wondering if others should witness such divine beauty...or if they were better off turning their eyes away from such a sorrowful dance.

CHAPTER 6

*I*t was...well, it wasn't white. *It was clear, transparent.*

As Hush struggled up to his feet, he took a glance around the vast empty space. There was the occasional doll or bracelet, but it was the equivalent of seeing a tiny piece of trash in a canyon. Sure, it was there...but it was overwhelmed by the sheer mass of everything else.

He took a step forward and instantly collapsed. The beating that Jin had given him was especially rough today. Hell, if it weren't for Queenie, he might've actually killed him this time around. As he lay wheezing on the ground, the ground around him began to tremble. The teenager looked up with horror to witness what could only be described as "infinity becoming finite". The space around him simultaneously folded and dissolved. Former objects that were previously stored shattered and vanished in an instant. As it all slowly began to collapse onto him, the older brother understood what was happening: Queenie could not handle the pressure of "storing" him. Queenie needed to eject him, quickly.

And yet, as the unfathomable became fathomable, Hush stayed in the storage.

His mind raced. Why was she not spitting him out? Was there danger outside? Was something compromising her? Was she unable *to spit him out? Panic slowly began to bubble up his body as a horrifying realization kicked in: if Queenie's blessing kept sucking up her soul because of Hush, then Queenie could very well* **die***.*

*He ignored the pain and soreness he felt as he raspily roared in fear, slamming on the floor. "****Queenie. You need to spit me out, now****."*

He remained. Maybe she couldn't hear him. Maybe she refused. He didn't know why, but as the world around him collapsed, he began to curl up into a tighter and tighter ball. It was fine if he died, but he wouldn't be able to live with himself if he was the reason for her death.

In a last ditch effort, he placed his palms on the ground and flexed all his fingers. She needed soul to maintain the storage. Hush had no idea on how to give his younger sister soul, nor did he have any left in his soulwell. However, he would be **damned** *if he couldn't help her. So, he pushed and forcefully activated his blessing with no target in mind, doing anything he could to try and give his sister some more soul.*

The rumbling that coursed through his body was an agony that he had never felt before. It felt as though his blood threatened to explode through every centimeter of his skin. Organs were crushed, veins popped, bones crumbled. It felt as though a hundred men grabbed a bit of him and pulled in opposite directions, threatening to obliterate his existence in a malicious competition. Hush couldn't even harness the energy to scream in pain: the teenager just lay there, trembling. His instincts screamed at him to stop, yet the trembling of the storage around him began to stabilize. That was enough for him to keep going.

Hush was not sure how long he pumped out soul that his body did not have, partially because it was impossible to tell time in the storage and partially because his brain couldn't properly form thoughts. His body had stopped autonomous commands and he was now actively choosing which organs functioned. He prioritized his heartbeat for one minute, then his lungs the next. It felt as though he stood in a burning building and was using a water gun to put out the smallest of embers around him as the incinerated debris crashed down around him.

Right as his soulwell was about to collapse onto itself...he felt his body touch solid ground. None of his organs worked. Though his eyelids lacked the strength to open, he knew that his sight was gone. He could not hear anything. Even the sensation of the floor began to fade. Just as it was all about to end, he felt what could only described as a "warm coolness" seep into his brain. This feeling spread throughout his body slowly until his entire body's functions resumed back to normal.

Hush desperately *wished to open his eyes to check on his sister, but his body was* long *past its limits. So, just as his body was fished from the brink of obliteration, he passed out.*

...

Hush woke up, rubbing his eyes as he squinted at the sunrise. Though the skyline was beautiful, the worry he felt for his sister was greater. So, he quickly washed up and slipped on his olive green jacket, white shirt, and jeans. Once he tapped his shoes on, the older brother quickly stepped out to the hallway. To his surprise, Queenie stood there, hands in her hoodie, nodding to him.

"Hiya."

Worry bubbled up Hush's throat as he briskly walked up, quickly giving her a rough checkup. "You feel-"

Queenie scowled as she brushed his hand aside. "I'm good. I woke up last night with most of my soul. I'm back to normal now."

He opened his mouth to lecture her but she cut him off. "...and yes, I won't do it again. I just needed to impress the daydrinker because she had a blueprint I wanted."

Hush grit his teeth, but sighed. "Fine. As long as you understand."

The siblings heard a cough from down the hallway and turned to see Patchy standing there with a quizzical eyebrow. "No hug this time?"

"What do you want?" Hush asked with annoyance.

The Gatekeeper shrugged. "Babs wants to see you before she sends you off with Julie. Let's go, go grab Taba for me."

...

The Misfits followed Patchy as he kicked down the Overseer's door. This time, she sat in the middle of the white marble, her black blindfold over her eyes as she quietly murmured to herself. She wore her usual garment, adorned with the usual gold jewelry. Her withered and untrimmed fingers clacked as they seemed to be mentally counting something, her head tilting every seven of eight clicks.

After a minute of this, the older woman took off her covering with irritation. "Knock, damn it."

"Eh. You knew we were coming." Patchy said with a shrug.

The Overseer looked at the group and nodded at her guests. "You three, sit."

Hush raised an eyebrow as Taba sat. If he was sitting, then that meant he had good reason to follow her orders. Queenie seemed to understand this as well, so the siblings followed suit and sat as well. Patchy chose to stay standing, yawning as he picked his ear.

Babs stared at the trio, not with annoyance, but curiosity. "Do you know my blessing?"

The older brother had an idea of her ability, but stayed silent. After all, better to let the enemy assume that they were clueless.

...So it baffled Hush when Taba spoke up. "You're blessing is some form of continental omnipotence, right? You can quite literally over-see different villages and towns all at once."

The old woman cracked an unintentionally terrifying grin. "Hah! Omnipotence! I guess it *looks* that way, but it's much weaker than you give it credit for. With permission, I can simply look at someone's actions. That's all. The conditions for this is that I have to be relatively still, so it's useless in combat or invasions. Furthermore, even *if* I could move around while using this blessing, the other condition requires permission. If the other party takes away their permission, I'm sud-denly blind to their actions."

"Why are you telling us this?" Hush asked with a frown.

"What do you mean? You guys seemed like you wanted clarity on my blessing."

Taba shook his head, the confusion showing on his face as well. "No, like...we're your *enemies*. Why tell us info?"

The woman rolled her eyes as she waved him off. "If you wanted to kill me, you could do so: I don't give a damn. You aren't an enemy, just a lost child throwing a tantrum."

Patchy frowned. "Ok, I'm gonna have to step in for *just* a bit. Don't try to kill her, please and thank you."

"Let them try," the Overseer chuckled. "One more excuse for me to finally pass on the mantle. I'm *so* over this job."

Queenie cleared her throat. "Ok, sure. We're kiddos in your eyes. Whatever. Even so, why tell us all this? Even from a 'logical' stance, its a random topic to start babbling about."

"Hmph. My *point* is, I see tons of places all at once. These places trust me to give aid and assistance as I see fit. Our numbers are small, so I have to make decisions on who need what help the most. So what I may ask of you may seem completely random, but trust me when I say it's needed for the sake of peace."

Hush raised an eyebrow. "And why should we help?"

"Sana trusts you all to be good kids," Babs said as she leaned in. "That's all I need to know that you would absolutely help us out. *Especially* if the requests I give help struggling people without 'strengthening' Malapace, right?"

He pursed his lips. There was always a catch with these kind of things, but the Overseer seemed to be speaking with blunt honesty.

Taba spoke up with an unwavering voice. "What else did you want to ask us?"

The white-eyed elder raised her eyebrow. "Oh? How did you know?"

The questioner blinked. "Did...did Sana not tell you about my blessing?"

"No, should she have?"

The siblings locked eyes with each other. Though they didn't know *why* Sana kept this information hidden from who was essentially the ruler of Malapace, they knew that Taba's surprise meant that he expected to have been exposed. If they had to guess, Taba made a deal with the female Gatekeeper...and she had surprisingly kept her promise.

Taba quickly regained composure. "Nevermind. You wanted to ask us something else, right?"

"Mhm. Do you know about 'Ascension'?" asked Babs.

"No, never heard of it."

Babs actually seemed taken aback by this. "*Really*? Now that's a shock, but good. Let's keep it that way. Anyways, I have an ability that lets me read the mind and history of a person...if they give me permission. I imagine it's pointless, but I wanted to ask if you would let me-"

"No."

The older woman sighed with understanding. "Yep, figured. Worth a shot. Alright, that's all I wanted to ask. Go to the bar and meet up with Juliette. She wanted to start mentorship today."

...

The Misfits and Patchy found her sipping away at a jug in the corner of the alley bar. When she heard the doorbell jingle, the woman turned her head nonchalantly.

"Morning."

Taba frowned. "It's like, 9 A.M.. Why are you drinking?"

Juliette downed the rest of her glass before hissing with satisfaction as she dabbed at her lips with a napkin. After reslinging her wooden box, she unfurled some bills from within her sleeves, placing it on the counter.

"Thanks, Hutch."

The burly barkeeper grunted in approval, nodding in respect as she walked out. The Misfits and Patchy followed the tipsy woman as she strolled over to the park, stretching her arms as she did. Once they reached the usual spot, Juliette turned around as she rested her arm on the top of the wooden box. Patchy quietly sat on a stump of a nearby tree to watch from afar.

"So, what do you guys know about soul?" asked Juliette.

The trio blinked and stared at each other. Queenie frowned. "Big ol' energy bar. Use it for your blessing. Pew pew. Runs out, you die. Did I miss anything?"

Juliette sighed. "Sadly, that's the extent of what the mass majority knows. They aren't *wrong* in that, but we learn soul 'backwards', in a sense. In an ideal world, soulbearers grasp the idea of soul *before* using their blessing. However, we can't grasp the soul until we unconsciously use it for our blessings. We take it at face value, then never try exploring further than that."

Hush crossed his arms as he tilted his head. "You make it sound like there's more use for soul."

"There is. Not much, but there is." The Drunken Fox nodded at Queenie. "Pull out a gun and shoot me."

Queenie, though mildly surprised, did not waste this sudden opportunity as she immediately pulled out a pistol and fired three rounds at her mentor. The bullets whistled through the air, yet Juliette seemed to be able to easily sidestep each bullet. Queenie scowled, seemingly more frustrated than baffled that none of her shots landed.

"You probably can't see anything, since you aren't accustomed to seeing soul." Juliette said as she straightened her attire. "You'll get there with time, but for now it probably looks as though I just sidestepped your bullets. However, what I did was envelope myself in a little bubble of soul, while also using soul to amplify my movements. The end result is me being more protected *and* more agile against your attack."

Taba scratched his head. "Ok...but if this is so useful, why haven't we ever seen it before? Why haven't *we* been able to unlock it naturally?"

Juliette strummed her delicate fingers on her wooden box, pondering slightly on the question. Then she held up a finger. "Show me your index finger."

Taba extended it as instructed. Juliette nodded. "Good. Now bend it."

The teenager bent it, obviously confused. The woman nodded. "Good. How did you do that?"

The questioner blinked, caught off guard by the question, "I...just bent it? What do you mean?"

"How did you bend your finger?"

"I...just did. I bent it because you told me to."

The Dancing Painter nodded at the Misfits. "And that right there is the answer to why you haven't been able to unlock the idea of using soul more 'freely'."

"...Huh?"

Juliette tapped her temple. "Your brain sent neurons to a part of your body. Your body pulled tendons. Muscles contracted. A ton of different cogs just moved to produce a single action, and you weren't aware of it. Likewise, that's how you use your soul. You just 'use' it. You don't know how it works, why it works, or how to command it. It's so natural that you don't know how to utilize it in a way that isn't your blessing."

Hush frowned as he shuffled his feet. "You want us to do automatic commands...with intention? That's like demanding us to control our own heartbeat or to force our stomach to digest. We don't 'control' that."

Their mentor nodded. "That's exactly what I want you to do. The first thing I want you guys to master before *anything* is to understand

109

the concept of soul and how to utilize it for various things. Furthermore, you all need to see the strengths and limitations of this."

"Why should we?" Hush asked.

"You want to surpass me?" responded Juliette. "You want to kill me, right? Then this is the first step."

Queenie stored her pistol and pulled out a dagger, slowly unpeeling and resticking the tape on the handle. "Ok, whatever. Do we get any pointers, or..."

"Nope. This isn't something I can easily teach. It has to be something you manually discover. If I were to tell you how to do this, your growth would be stunted." The woman picked up her box and began to walk towards the stump where Patchy sat. "This lesson *alone* might take a while to master. Don't feel bad if it feels like you aren't making progress. Keep at it. Good luck."

...

The Misfits sat in a circle, the siblings staring at Taba as his eyes were closed and his brow furrowed. He had been asking questions for the past twenty minutes with very little success, something insanely rare for him. The only things he had gathered were that it *was* possible to utilize soul like Juliette had mentioned. Furthermore, this "boost" would allow heightened strength, agility, and defense against soul-based attacks and even soulbased weapons. That would explain how Queenie's gun and bullets, created using a blacksmith's blessing, were easily evaded. From his questioning, Taba deduced that this "defensive soul bubble" wasn't the most effective against physical attacks, which explained how the two guys were able to dive onto Juliette during their test. If anything, it would alert the person about an oncoming person, making it useless if the user had low reaction speed.

"This is dumb," Queenie groaned as she lay down in the dirt, repeatedly throwing her dagger into the air and catching it before it pierced her face. "What does it matter if bullets won't work? I have other weapons too."

"Man, I have no idea," Taba groaned as he rubbed his face in frustration, no closer to the solution than he was twenty minutes ago. "I only know how to use soul in questioning. That's all. This is like trying to force an apple to be an orange."

Hush crossed his arms as he closed his eyes. For the past few minutes, he was hesitatingly contemplating what Juliette and Taba had said.

'That's like demanding us to control our own heartbeat or to force our stomach to digest. We don't 'control' that.' 'That's exactly what I want you to do'

As the older brother's mind flashed back to his dream from this morning, he tightened his lips. Back then...had he already 'grasped' the idea of using soul for other purposes? Hush never tried to replicate it again, partially because of trama, but what if he was wrong? Hell, could he even repeat it if he wanted? How would he go about it? *That* time only worked due to the storage being hungry for soul, so he was able to give it the small bits of soul from his body, like a dehydrated plant desperately sucking any moisture out of the soil.

What if...what if he could do it again? Instead *this* time, keep the soul regulated in his own body? Hush hesitated, but extended his arms as he concentrated. His sister and friend stopped brainstorming to stare at him in curiosity. The older brother grit his teeth and tried to replicate the sensation of his very essence being...*purged* from his body. Nothing happened. Maybe he could try to remember the "feeling" of his soul being used. So, he flexed his fingers as he heightened his hearing.

In that instance, he felt everything tense up and his brain shuttered. It was nowhere near as intense as it was during *that* event, but the feeling was similar enough. He immediately flinched as his fell to his side, sucking in what little air his body allowed as his vision and various senses flickered in and out. It felt as though each individual cell in his arms and chest were scattering into tiny pieces, as though his skin and bones were melting, merging, and splitting all at once. Patchy suddenly appeared next to him, checking on his body. After a small nod, the Gatekeeper's eyes glowed as they suddenly appeared next to G. The bald man stood in his apartment wearing nothing but boxers.

At first, he snapped at the grey man, but stopped upon seeing Hush. G instinctively slapped at his sides, forgetting he didn't have his pants on. He briskly walked over to a nightstand to grab a white pill and covered the Misfit's eyes as he jammed the medicine down his throat. After a while, he could feel his soul return and his body's functionality restored. Hush coughed directly into G's face, to which the bald man roared in disgust.

Suddenly, they appeared back at the park with Hush being gently placed next to his friends. They crawled over to him with worry, poking at his face. Hush, surprisingly no longer feeling fatigued, stared back at them.

Juliette stood up from her tree stump and walked over, surprise showing through her mask. "Well then. How did you grasp it so quickly?"

Hush stared at the mentor. "What do you mean? I don't think I..."

He stared at the compact dirt where he once sat, revealing the shattered ground. Juliette cleared her throat. "You did it. Granted, *far* from perfect, but that's the equivalent of going '100%'. You just need to focus on control, but what you did? That's the hard part that some mentors spend *years* on. How did you do it?"

"It was a sensation I had experienced once a few years ago," Hush said nervously as he stared at the ground. "I thought about replicating it. That's all."

Juliette tilted her head. "You grasped the concept of soul manipulation as a teenager?"

"I...yeah? I guess? I don't know if I did, or if I got lucky."

Patchy cleared his throat, a bit of curiosity in his eyes. "How did it feel? Describe the sensation."

Hush crossed his arms as he closed his eyes, trying to recall the agony. "Well...like tons of people were pulling at me from different directions, or like my blood started leaking through my skin. I don't know how else to describe it apart from 'being forcefully spread thin'."

The grey-haired man looked back at the woman with a shrug. "Sounds about right."

Juliette leaned on her wooden box as she pondered something. After a while, she nodded. "Good. Now try to limit how much soul you 'output' throughout your body."

She nodded to the other Misfits. "As for you guys...keep at it. Hush, don't tell them how to do what you did."

Taba stared at him, his eyes narrowed in confusion. Queenie looked to her feet, probably familiar with what 'sensation' Hush had experienced years ago. She probably felt guilty still. He wanted to tell Taba tips and comfort his sister, but Juliette was right: giving them tips on this would only make it more difficult to grasp. If he had told them to 'imagine your soul bursting out of every cell of your body', they would *never* understand.

So, he simply nodded at the others and quietly resumed his training. The others nodded in confused hesitation and worked to attain similar results.

...

Since then, three weeks had passed. Every morning, the Misfits would eat with Babs a light breakfast of steamed vegetables and mystery meat (Taba eventually deduced it as pork). After a silent meal, they would saunter over to the park and sit in a circle. Hush would try to focus on "controlling" his soul manipulation, whereas the other Misfits would scowl as they tried to grasp the idea of soul. Taba would go about this by asking numerous questions in meditation. Queenie took a more physical approach and would try to use various weapons in differing ways in an attempt to "feel" what her soul felt like. After two to five hours, Juliette would stroll in while sipping her jug with Patchy following her (with the exception of one day, where Sana visited for fun). G seemed to be preoccupied with other tasks and wouldn't stop by the field.

Hush couldn't seem to find a middle ground. He would either only be able to use his soul for his blessing *or* exert all of it in soul manipulation. It seemed impossible to limit how much soul he output, like trying to have the clock strike A.M. and P.M. at the same time. How was Juliette able to seemingly use her blessing simultaneously with soul manipulation? It just didn't click. What was he missing?

He closed his eyes and tried to recall what it felt like. The feeling didn't originate from his core. It was almost as though each individual cell were activated. Was that even possible? If so...

Hush opened his eyes and quietly stared at his pinky finger. He tugged at his depths of his being, but instead of tugging from his chest he tried to tug through his pinky. It was a ridiculous thought, but worth an attempt nonetheless. After nothing happened, he imagined trying to activate his blessing without flexing his fingers.

Suddenly, he felt a tiny tingle in his first pinky's knuckle. It was painful, but the sensation was *much* smaller than his previous attempts. He winced and clutched his finger, peeking to reveal that his fingernail had slightly split open with a droplet of blood dribbling down his hand.

"You're grasping this at a shocking fast rate," Juliette said as she peered over his shoulder. "Shame you're an enemy."

Blood rushed to his ears as he leaned away from her. "A split fingernail is 'good'? *Really?*"

"Yep. You've went from using 100% throughout your entire body to using 80% in a tiny part of your finger. That's honestly remarkable."

Hush sucked his pinky. "How do you know the percentages? Are you just making up numbers?"

She shrugged. "Partially? I'm just going off my experience and what I've seen other mentors go through. Some mentors flat out blow parts of their body up due to having a high volume of soul. You're lucky in that sense."

"Lucky me, thank goodness I'm so weak." Hush said as he rolled his eyes.

"Unironically, yeah. You're lucky. Now, there are two ways you can go about this: you can try to lower the soul used in your pinky...or you can try to increase that feeling throughout not just your pinky, but your entire hand. Both aren't bad."

She slowly raised her hand, her lips hesitating. After a moment, she ruffled his hair. "Well done."

Before he could blink and process what had just occurred, she turned on her heel and had walked over to the other Misfits to check in on them. Hush frowned, shaking off her praise before his heart felt any more fuzzy. He then stared at his index finger, determined to channel soul through it without breaking the nail.

After two hours and ten broken fingernails and six broken toenails, his first success shown through his intact right middle toe. To his surprise...it didn't feel that much different from not using soul manipulation. His toe didn't feel much more sturdy or agile. It still felt like his toe. His second shock was how much soul he had to use in order for this weak soul manipulation. It was like blowing up a mountain for a single stone. All in all...this didn't feel worth it.

When he stood up and hobbled over to Juliette to ask her about it, she nodded. "You got it. Well done. Keep practicing to make it consistent while your friends try to grasp it."

"But...why? What's the point of doing all this? It doesn't seem worth it. Wouldn't it be better to hone my blessing?" asked Hush.

"You're partially right. Nine times out of ten, you won't need this. However, that one time? It'll be crucial and will save your life," the Drunken Fox responded as she sipped from her jug.

"I guess? But even then, wouldn't expanding the definition of my soul be better?"

She shook her head, an air of sadness somehow shining from her monotone face. "This *is* the better alternative, trust me. Plus, let's say your opponent has a blessing that's able to send a wall of unavoidable fire your way. How will deafening him help?"

She tied her jug to her waist before dabbing her lips with a napkin. "Soul manipulation is a tool that will strengthen you as a side effect. Your control of your blessing will be expanded. You will have more options against every opponent. Your soulwell will grow. There's a reason so many mentors spend years on this training, even though they may never *need* to use it." Juliette glanced at the other Misfits. "What makes this tricky to teach is that there's no actual way to 'teach' soul manipulation. It's all innate and varies from person to person. I know one mentor who said it felt like his limbs shattered simultaneously. Another mentor said it felt like he was being crumpled into a tiny ball. Then there's someone who said it was as though their organs just turned 'black'. The general consensus is that the first time one uses soul manipulation is quite unpleasant. Apart from that, there's very little connection in each case."

"What was it like for you then?" asked Hush as he squeezed his fingers.

To his surprise, she softly chuckled before her mask's hollow eyes stared icicles into his heart. "Time stopped. I was alone for thousands of years in a silver room. I couldn't move or scream, all I could do was try not to go insane until I woke up."

"That...sounds harsh."

"Mhm. On the plus side, it made me much more patient and collected. So, it wasn't a *complete* loss."

Suddenly, the silence of the air was shattered as a roar echoed through the park. Hush and Juliette turned to see Taba clutching his head as he lay writhing on his side. The pair ran towards the teenager in a hurry, only to discover that he was frothing at the mouth. Furthermore, his eyes were rolled to his skull and his sclera was bloodshot in a deep crimson hue. Patchy appeared next to Taba in an instant, but to everyone's surprise, Taba flung a blurred backhand at the Gatekeeper. Patchy took a swift step back, but Hush noticed that there was a small scratch on the man's cheek with a trickle of blood flowing down to the ground.

Before anyone could recover, Taba had jumped to his feet and thrown an elbow to the Gatekeeper. Patchy's eyes were alert yet calm, catching the blow as he clenched his fist to counterattack. As he threw his punch, Taba flung his legs into the air and used one of his arms to rotate on Patchy's shoulder, his leg swinging full force into the Gatekeeper's Achilles tendon. The teenager suddenly fell to the floor as Patchy vanished and reappeared two feet from his previous position, staring at the Misfit with intrigue. Right before he crashed into the floor, Taba took a handstand and swung both his legs at his target, both swings causing their own individual breeze. Despite the attack's speed and force, both kicks were effortlessly dodged.

When he stood up, everyone stared at the blood trickling down from the corners of Taba's eyes. His arms and legs glowed light blue as his limbs trembled crookedly. His face suddenly twitched as he took a fighter's stance.

Then, his body seemed to vibrate as another...*entity* began to emerge from his body. Right before the...*thing* split away, a hollow roar echoed from Taba's throat that caused Juliette to flinch and grab her mask, her paintbrush already unsheathed. The roar slowly gained foundation before Taba's voice screamed in defiance. Veins pulsated across his entire body as he grit his teeth, tremors appeared in the light blue shimmer that shone from him.

Then...the entity slammed back into Taba's body, causing him to jolt with a cough. He took a deep breath as his eyes rolled back to normal. Though they were still crimson, the teenager grinned wildly as he took deep breaths.

"I...I think I...got..."

Before he could finish his sentence, he groaned and fell to the floor.

CHAPTER 7

As Taba dashed at Patchy, he felt euphoric. Normally, his mind felt extremely cluttered as he asked multiple questions to prepare for every possible outcome in a fight. However...his mind was oddly empty as every single one of his attacks landed predictably. As his body moved naturally to move the most optimally, Taba felt...*free*.

And yet...he hated it. These weren't *his* actions. It was as though he were forcibly put in the backseat of his own body and watched as another person gloated, taunting him that all his efforts were so pathetically far from what he *could* be doing. As Patchy blinked away from him, he felt the limit of what he could do. His body *yearned* for more. It *needed* to evolve. In its current state it would be impossible to overwhelm the Gatekeeper. So, his body subconsciously asked questions and came to the conclusion of what needed to be done to secure victory.

His mind suddenly split as his vision vibrated. For a few seconds...it felt as though he were seeing from two different positions at once. His body existed...twice. This was not normal. Taba understood that this was *correct*, and the *only* way he would be able to beat Patchy in a fight.

And yet...for the first time in many years, Taba was horrified and scared of the uncertainty that lay before him.

So, he screamed as he forced his body to merge once more. It was hard to describe, but it felt like the equivalent of shoving two trees onto the same stump without breaking either tree *or* the stump. As his mind felt like it was about to shatter from impossibilities, something just...clicked. He suddenly understood a way to evolve his blessing. If he could expand his soul throughout his entire body, each body part? If they could all "think"...then he could move more efficiently and *act* more decisively.

His body slammed into itself as he grinned. His vision was gray with tinges of red at the edges, yet as he stared at his arms, all he could do was feel excited. Taba's blessing had suddenly unlocked, and *so* much more was possible.

This was a way to kill the Gatekeepers and overthrow Malapace.

He stared up at his horrified friends, his mentor, and the Gatekeeper. "I...I think I...got..."

Then, his entire body popped as his legs crumpled. Taba groaned as he took choppy breaths, sudden soreness creaking throughout his entire body. His arms, legs, abs, but most of all his *head* was exhausted. Well, that was to be expected, he supposed. Taba's body had been pushed beyond his normal limits. If it weren't for his daily training, the teenager probably would have been unconscious.

Queenie hesitantly walked up and pulled out a yardstick from her storage, poking him with it. "You, uh...you alright?"

"I..." Taba stopped and began to cough harshly, cracks spreading through his lips. "...kinda? I'm suddenly super tired, but it makes sense."

Patchy rubbed his cheek and stared at his hand with mild surprise. "Not gonna lie, kiddo: it's been a hot minute since I last got hurt. I don't know if I'm supposed to congratulate you or execute you."

Juliette sighed as she packed away her paintbrush. She then walked up to the teenager and knelt down to stare at him closely. "How do you feel?"

"I...man. Sore. Excited. *Really* tired. I could go for a nap."

The Drunken Fox nodded as she strummed her wooden box. "Most soulbearers nearly die upon unlocking soul manipulation. The fact that you're conscious alone is...borderline unfathomable. Check in with G so he can do a quick checkup on you before passing out. Patchy, could you take him there?"

Before the Gatekeeper could step forward, Hush's quiet voice surprisingly spoke up. "Actually, I can take him there."

"Oh? How do you know where he is?"

Hush shrugged. "Patchy took me to his place last time. Is he still there?"

"Eh...he *should* be, but who knows?" said Patchy.

The older brother lent him a shoulder, to which Taba graciously accepted. It was all he could do to not fall asleep. "Well, see you guys tomorrow."

As they hobbled out of the park, Taba suddenly turned to his friend with tired excitement. "I think I can take out the Gatekeepers with this."

Hush raised an eyebrow, yet said nothing for a minute. After turning the block, he muttered under his breath a phrase that only Taba's suddenly enhanced hearing could hear. "*If it isn't a certainty...you probably can't take them out. Not yet, anyways.*"

Taba scowled, but Hush had a point. If something wasn't a certainty, then it wasn't worth doing. *Especially* against someone as strong as the Gatekeepers. The teenager nodded in quiet acknowledgement as the duo limped over to G's place.

...

Despite Hush's confidence, it took them a solid twenty minutes of scouring the area and knocking on incorrect doors before they accidentally stumbled on G muttering to himself as he stared a book in front of a cafe. Despite the buff shirtless man sticking out like a sore thumb, the other patrons seemed to pay him no mind as they each focused on their own individual tasks.

As the two Misfits hobbled over to the Gatekeeper, G casually looked up at the guys before groaning. He placed his book down before searching his pockets for the pill. Taba took notice of the book with mild curiosity: '*The Human Heart, sixth edition*'.

Before shoving the pill down the teenager's throat, G stopped and stared at him with mild confusion. "Wait. Did you grasp soul manipulation?"

"I...think so?"

"How are you conscious?"

"I dunno."

G nodded to the tired boy. "Open your mouth."

Taba listened and slightly recoiled as G shoved the pill in his open mouth, causing some head turns at the cafe. Almost instantly, a decent amount of the questioner's fatigue vanished. Though he was still tired, Taba no longer needed to use Hush's support to stand upright. Confusingly, his soulwell was still utterly depleted.

"I don't get how that pill works. Why am I still depleted of soul?" he asked as he stretched.

G rolled his eyes as he picked up his book again. "Don't worry about it. Now piss off."

"Why is it that you're the only one with the pills?" Hush asked. "Why not trust them with Sana or Patchy?"

The bald man kept his eyes on the book as he waved his hands. "'GaTeKeEpEr SeCrEt', or whatever Sana says. Now, shoo."

Though Hush shrugged, Taba raised an eyebrow. The older brother had a point. Surely the other Gatekeepers were more than qualified to carry around such potent medicine. There must be a reason as to why only G held the pills. If he had the soul, Taba would've asked questions to try and figure out more of the pill's secrets. For now, he wanted sleep.

So, the two Misfits nodded as they walked to the town hall. They quietly nodded to the waving Tabitha and bumped fists before turning into their respective rooms. Once alone, the teenager took his shoes off and collapsed into his bed.

...

Father stroked his chin quietly as Taba yawned. Father's question had drained much more soul then what he was used to. It was the equivalent of overturning a rock in the woods, but instead of finding a few tiny bugs, three rabbits had bolted out from a hidden burrow.

"And your blessing...is it ever incorrect?" Father asked.

"No. It's always correct." Taba said through a stifled yawn. Sometimes its more hard to reach certain 'answers', but it'll technically be possible."

"Hm...ok. Got it. If that's the case, I will trust you wholeheartedly."

"Why? We just met."

Father chuckled as he ruffled the boy's hair. "You are my son. What reason would I have to distrust my son?"

"What if I were lying? What if I were wrong?" asked Taba.

"Doesn't matter. You're my son. I'll trust you with everything, so trust me with everything." The man turned to face him, his gray eyes causing Taba to flinch. "Don't tell others of your blessing. In the wrong hands, many will abuse it for their own personal gain."

The boy hesitated. "Uh...like...like you?"

Father winced as he rubbed his neck. "I...huh. Yeah, I guess. You got me there. Well, don't trust others. Only trust those who you would die for."

"Die for? Why would I die for others? Any particular traits or characteristics that define them?"

He shrugged with a small smile. "I can't say what to look out for, but trust your gut."

"What if my 'guts' tell me to not trust you?" Taba asked with a frown.

Father nodded. "Even then, trust your gut. Prioritize yourself. If you're correct, you will win no matter what. If you're wrong, you will inevitably lose. Do whatever you want: I'm not going to force you to stay with me."

The boy hesitated. "I...I'll stick with you. For now, anyways."

The man grinned, his gray eyes twinkling. "Sounds good. If that's the case, come with me: there's somewhere I want to go."

...

The teenager woke up, still slightly sore. His soul was mostly replenished, but he stretched with a big yawn as he stared out the window. The sun was setting as the sky lit on fire. Feeling bored, he slipped on his shoes and stepped out to stroll around Malapace, trying to memorize the little nooks and crannies of the massive city.

As he did, he heard faint gunshots and *woosh*es from the park. Raising an eye, he walked over to see Queenie and Juliette locked in fierce combat. Well, 'fierce' was the wrong word: it was completely one-sided. Queenie was flying around with agile steps and strung chains, her brown hair being flung everywhere as sweat dripped from her brow. Meanwhile, Juliette stayed calm as her paintbrush casually deflected bullets, taking brisk strides to sidestep Queenie's 'unpredictability', and counterattacking at every available chance.

Surprisingly, Queenie seemed to be accurately...'foretelling' the slashes. No...from the way her eyes were darting around the park...could she *see* them? It would explain the sudden and random movements that she would suddenly make. After a few minutes, Taba decided to step up once Queenie's movements slowed down considerably. The women noticed his approach and stopped their fighting.

Queenie wiped her face with the front of her hoodie, looking annoyed and slightly embarrassed. "You're...up."

"Mhm. Whatcha guys doing?"

Juliette flicked her brush then rested it across her shoulders. "Application training. Queenie can't use soul manipulation. Well, to put it better, her blessing changes how it works. She can use her eyes to slightly see soul traces from other blessings, but it requires tons of focus."

"What do you mean she can't 'use' soul manipulation?"

Queenie sat on the dirt floor with a sigh. "My soul is tied to my storage, and all the things inside of it. So, it's impossible for me to channel my soul through my body in the usual sense, according to her. However..."

"-since her soul is tied to her storage, it *is* possible to wrap her soul around whatever she pulls from her storage," Juliette cut in. "It changes certain aspects of whatever she uses, be it lethality or durability."

"Wait..." Taba frowned. "So that one time we baked bread from the flour with your storage..."

Queenie's ears flushed as she stayed silent. Juliette tilted her head back as she took a huge gulp from her jug. After swallowing and dabbing her lips, she nodded. "Yep. *Technically*, you guys were eating bits of her soul. It wasn't much, but it was absolutely there."

The teenager winced as he rubbed his neck. "Is that, uh...is that safe to eat?"

Juliette shrugged. "You aren't dead, so yes. Plus, tons of things use soul on a daily basis, be it weaponry or even daily living. It isn't uncommon to be unconsciously exposed to someone's soul. You guys will be fine: keep eating your soul bread."

"Oh, like *hell*," Queenie scowled. "It feels weird to know y'all have been chomping on my soul."

"Did you feel your soul being eaten?" Taba asked with a small grin.

"No, but it's still weird."

"What if we were starving in a forest or something?"

"What a shame we wouldn't be able to use raw flour in the forest."

"I know for a *fact* you have a furnace in storage."

"Oh piss *off*."

Juliette chuckled as she tied her drink to her waist, stopping the Misfits from any further bickering as they stared at her with mild embarrassment. "You all are adorable. The sun is setting, go get rest. We can continue training tomorrow once your soul has recovered."

...

The Misfits spent about two more weeks sitting in the park, simply focusing on soul manipulation. Hush huddled away next to a tree stump, spending the days seemingly focused on his fingers. Queenie continued physical training with Juliette, sounds of gunfire and chains whipping around the area as the teenage girl fought with intention to kill. Juliette seemingly seemed to nonchalantly evade all of her moves, further frustrating Queenie with each passing minute.

Taba spent his days pushing his blessing, seeing what qualified for a "question". Before, he had assumed that since only his brain could "think", that only his brain could ask questions. However, if he treated each individual cell as it's own living organism with it's own ability to "ask"? Suddenly, he could have his body move on near *instinct*.

Of course, the biggest issues with this lay in both the required soul for such a feat and the fact that he wasn't fully *sure* on how to automate each limb, not to mention the physical toll such a task would have on his body. To focus on this, Taba decided that it would be for the best if he spent his time in physical training while continuously asking questions. The endgoal was to either minimize the amount of soul used *or* increase his soulwell, all while ensuring his body was able to grow to greater heights.

One thing still bugged him, however. He wasn't sure *how* to reach the state that Juliette had displayed. Making a defensive soul bubble, enhancing his body with his soul, or seeing soul with his eyes were all so out of reach. He had *tried* to "see" soul, but all he had succeeded in doing was creeping out Patchy with a sharp glare.

Each day ended nearly the same. Hush walked home with bleeding fingers and toes, lending a shoulder to an exhausted Taba. Queenie trudged home while littered in tiny cuts, cussing up a storm. Juliette and Patchy staying behind to talk about...something. For all of their efforts, the Misfits bore minimal fruit.

At the end of the second week, Juliette cleared her throat as she called out to the Misfits leaving the park. "Before you leave...the Overseer wants to see you guys."

Queenie sighed and glanced over her shoulder. "Like...tomorrow morning? Why?"

"No," an elderly voice rang out from behind them. "Today, and because I have a task for you guys."

The trio flinched as the Overseer herself shuffled out from behind a wall in her white garb, nodding at them. "I would have preferred if you mastered soul manipulation, but there's a town that needs help."

"Why should we?" Taba asked with a weary look.

Babs nodded with a raised eyebrow. "Figured you would ask. It's for a small village, disconnected from Malapace for the most part. The last time we gave them any help was two years ago. They've recently been ransacked by a mutant."

"You still aren't providing a good reason as to why we should help out." he frowned.

Babs rolled her eyes as she held up a finger. "One, because it'll split sources away from Malapace. These villagers provide zero benefit to us, so you fulfilling this task would weaken the city, your biggest end-goal." She held up another finger. "Two, these are innocent villagers. I understand why you dislike this city, but these are good working people who just want to make an honest living. I would like to protect them, and I imagine that anyone Sana would actively choose to rescue would wish the same." She held up a final finger. "If you don't do it, we have Juliette execute you as prisoners. I would've *preferred* to not use threats, but sometimes it's a necessity. If you don't like it...bite me."

Queenie scowled at the threat, but when she tapped into her storage all she was able to pull out was a slingshot. Still, she held it up to Babs with clear intention to fire. Juliette used her blessing to snap the strings of Queenie's weapon with ease, causing the girl to scowl even further.

The old woman stared at the display of resistance without flinching, her white eyes staring the girl down. "I'm glad we're in agreeance. We'll see you off tomorrow."

...

The trio stood by Malapace's front entrance the next day accompanied by Juliette and Sana. The female Gatekeeper gave them all paper baggies containing small goodies, to which everyone accepted with awkward hesitation. Sana gave a quick hug to Juliette and gave a grand sendoff as the party departed down the road. Queenie peeked into her bag and pulled out some taffy, popping it into her mouth.

Taba stared at their silent mentor as they walked down the dirt road. "I thought we were 'splitting resources' from Malapace? Why are we traveling by foot?"

Juliette peeked into her goody bag and pulled out a rice cracker, crunching it as she took her time in providing a response. "The village we're going to is under attack. No point in sending well groomed merchants if they're just going to either die or get in our way. So, we go first, clear out the threat, *then* send in the merchants."

"Guess that makes sense. So, we're dealing with a mutant?"

130

"Mhm," Juliette said as she washed down her rice cracker with a swig from her jug. "Have you guys every fought one?"

"Like...*fought?* Only twice. The first time, we were *severely* underprepared and had to retreat. The second, we were caught off guard and barely won."

Juliette nodded and the party walked down the dirt road in silence for an hour, nodding to any passing merchant along the way. After a while, the Dancing Painter broke the silence with an odd question. "Do you know how blessings came about?"

The Misfits stared at each other, a bit confused at both the randomness of the question and in thinking of a response. Hush cleared his throat. "After the third world war, right? When the majority of the world died, the remaining handful suddenly got their blessings."

Their mentor tilted her head as she pondered the answer. "Mmm...you aren't wrong, but not what I'm looking for. That's the history of the blessing's origins, but what about the *cause* of the creation of blessings?"

"I thought some nutjobs said that some God took pity and gave us power...or something. Cheebus? Jerrus? I can't remember." Queenie said.

"That's *one* popular theory," said Juliette. "The other one is that the radiation that settled into the air and caused humans to mutate. Then, people gained blessings when hitting puberty, due to their desires running rampant. Well, the link between blessing manifestation and puberty is still a bit inconsistent: it just might be a coincidence."

"Ok, but where did this all come from?" asked Taba.

The Drunken Fox glanced back with a monotone expression. "The big emphasis I want to make is that no matter which theory you believe, there's a definite correlation on the blessing *and* the strongest desire of a person. However, if we're going on radiation theory, then that means it wouldn't just be humans that are affected, but the wildlife. The key difference is that-"

The realization dawned on the questioner. "...wildlife have very basic desires. If those are enhanced..."

"Bingo. Suddenly, you have creatures running around who are *very* efficient at doing basic things like 'hunting' or 'survival'. So, it makes sense why you guys struggled so hard against the mutant." said Juliette.

"Huh. Never saw it like that." Queenie said as she chewed on a mini pretzel.

Juliette faced forward, a small chuckle escaping her lips. "Funnily enough, do you know who came up with the theory of animal radiation blessings? G."

Taba raised an eyebrow. "Oh? The same dude who runs around shirtless and cusses up a storm? *That* guy?"

"Mhm. *That* guy. Despite how he seems, he's surprisingly smart: just doesn't seem like it because it's hard to detect intelligence between cuss words."

Queenie stopped chewing and squinted at her mentor. "Is...is that a jab at me?"

"No, because that would imply you're smart."

Before Queenie could throw a wrapper at Juliette, Hush grabbed his sister's hoodie to stop her movements. Once securing the flailing girl, he looked to his mentor's back. "Do we know anything about the mutant that's attacking this village?"

Juliette answered without looking back. "Not much. All we know is that there was slime everywhere *and* some villagers were suddenly dragged away from afar. You do what you will with that information until we reach the village."

...

After two days, they reached the village. It was only a handful of slime-covered log cabin houses surrounding a stone well in the center. However, as Taba ran his fingers across the slightly squishy texture of the water well, he knew it was made by an amateur smithy who was unable to properly materialize stone. To the left of the houses lay a wide carving of the dry stream only showing a pathetic trickle of water with massive craters periodically dented into the ground. From the amount of tree stumps to the quantity of wooden cabins, it was evident that each home was made with a combination of natural wood and soul-created wood.

Juliette walked over to the first house on her left and knocked on the door. After a few seconds, a hesitant voice whispered out. "*H...Hello?*"

She cleared her throat. "Good day. My name is Juliette. We were sent from Malapace an-"

The door suddenly flung in and a man with a bushy grey moustache dragged the entire party in with surprising speed, startling even the stoic mentor.

Once they were inside, the small man stared up at the party with cautious hope. "Has...has the Overseer heard our call?"

Juliette hesitated, but nodded. "She has. We are here to help."

The man fell to his knees, hugging his shoulders. "Oh, praise the Overseer. Praise him."

Queenie opened her mouth in hesitation, but was cut off with a harsh stare from Juliette. Taba's mind was swirling with multiple questions. They had called her? They didn't know Babs was a female? Why were they worshiping her? Was she a god to them?

O X - O

Taba grimaced. It was very likely that Babs was elevated to a godly status without her consent. The poor woman was being idolized by various villages, but ignoring such praise could lead to the fall of many villagers. It seemed like a lose-lose situation, and suddenly Taba found himself pitying the Overseer *much* more.

Juliette rolled her shoulder. "Could you tell us about the mutant? Whether the species or the quantity?"

The man nodded quickly, standing up once more...right before the backwall of his cabin shattered. The trio stood in shock as they stared at the man's horrified face, his arm suddenly yanked to its side.

Sparing no time, Juliette unsheathed her paintbrush and slashed downwards, a red splash suddenly decorating the living room. The man was thrown a few feet to his left from the force of being yanked, but remained within the damaged cabin. However, his scream suddenly echoed out to the cabin. As he writhed in pain, the Misfits stared as the man turned on the floor, his arm now severed with splashes of blood spilling across the floor.

Juliette glared at Hush and barked an order. "Mute him. ***Now.***"

Hush grit his teeth and flexed his fingers, silencing the man. Though the thumps of his writhing could still be heard, his screams of agony were deafened. Taba's mind raced wildly, asking numerous questions as he tried to understand the sudden turn of events.

Are we under attack from the mutant? **O** *Does it know we're here?* **O** *Is it alone?* **O** *Are we in range of it's attack?* **O** *Are we in danger of dying?* **O**

Can we kill it with our current abilities? **O**

Juliette quickly pulled out some bandages from her sleeves, hastily wrapping them around the now crippled man's elbow. Laying low to the ground, she quickly flicked her head about, seemingly looking for something.

After a few seconds, she nodded to the Misfits who had all crouched on instinct. "Give it your best shot: *where* is the mutant?"

Taba's mind flew wildly as he considered everything he had seen upon the village. The slime. The craters. The fact that it was the *back* wall that had shattered. All this led him to believe...

He peeked outside. "The mutant is blocking the flow of the stream. If we follow the trickle, it should lead to the damned thing."

Juliette nodded. "Good job. Fortunately, I've been here before so we have a small advantage. We need to approach *it* without *it* snagging us. How do you reckon we do that?"

Queenie raised her hand a few inches, catching Taba's attention. "Question. Is that 'grapple' thing it uses, like, lethal? Like, will I die if it touches me?"

Taba hesitated but tapped into his soul. *Is the grapple lethal to the touch?* **X** *Does the grapple lead to eventual death?* **O**

He shook his head. "No, but I think its a way for the mutant to drag you in and eat you. I wouldn't risk anything rash."

Queenie tilted her head. "Is its 'grapple' invincible? Like, would I be able to cut through it?"

Taba asked the question and shook his head. "No, but I think it can, like, regenerate it. Why?"

The rash girl grinned wildly, the gears clearly clicking in her mind. She summoned a long rope from her storage and quietly tied it to her waist, then slid the other end over to Hush.

"What's this for?" Hush asked with confusion.

Queenie cackled as she suddenly leapt up and ran towards the shattered wall. Both the guys *and* Juliette flinched at this sudden movement, everyone yelling in protest. Unfortunately, they were too late to realize her idea as she was suddenly snagged and yanked away in an instance, her holler of joy echoing as she was dragged towards the deep forest.

Without sharing a word, the party jumped up and immediately sprinted full force as they followed the quickly tightening rope. Hush's face was pale as he stared at the rope growing more and more taut, with Taba's clammy mind asking the same two questions over and over, fearing a different result with one.

Is Queenie dead? **X** *Is Queenie hurt?* **X** *Is Queenie dead?* **X** *Is Queenie hurt?* **X** *Is Queenie dead?* **X** *Is Queenie hurt?* **X** *Is Queenie dead?* **X** *Is Queenie hurt?* **X** *Is Queenie dead?* **X** *Is Queenie hurt?* **O** *Is Queenie dead?* **X** *Is Queenie hurt?* **O**

After a minute of full sprinting, the party arrived to stare at Queenie being pinned down by a...blob, the weight of the creature obviously making it impossible for her to move around. To their worry, her face was red as she continuously stabbed at the mutant. However, her dagger proved to be ineffective as it only pierced a slimy coating of the being. It had three heads that seemed to all emerge from the center of its body, with each mouth being accompanied by watery eyes. However, each eye seemed to have numerous *other* eyes within each pupil, with each little circle twitching in their own individual directions. The giant ball of slimy fat had massive warts that bubbled and hissed, spitting out sludge that was a different color from what coated its body. It had six legs, all equidistant from each other. When it inhaled, its massive body jiggled, slightly pulling in its surroundings, growing even more bloated, before letting out a massive *croak* that exuded a tremendous amount of pressure and force to its surroundings.

Taba, keeping his eyes on it's target, shot a question to both Juliette and his soul.

"Is that a...frog?"

Both his soul and his mentor answered in unison. "Yes. That's our mutant. Don't let your guard down."

CHAPTER 8

As she was dragged away at blinding speeds, she *should* have been terrified. However, as her hair whipped through the wind, all she could do was laugh with joy as she manifested daggers in her hands. After a few seconds, she decided she had risked enough and stabbed one of her weapons through the slimy appendage that had stuck itself to her hoodie and used her other knife to cut away at the mutant's tendril. Blood splattered towards her face, but she blocked the spray with her baggy hoodie's sleeve.

As the mutant's "whip" quickly retracted into the woods, she stripped the mutant's severed appendage from her hoodie and looked up. Though the thing had *long* vanished from her sight, she could still feel her soul resonating within her dagger. After a few seconds, it stopped and rested. Deciding to act on the opportunity, she cackled and bolted towards the action.

As she broke through the clearing, she wasn't too sure as to what she was staring at. It was big, fat, slimy, and had multiple heads, eyes, and legs. Still, it was alive...so it could die.

She stored her dagger and pulled out a revolver. Against a creature this big, there was *no* way this would kill. However, Queenie wanted to test the mutant's durability. She fired two powerful rounds into the creature, raising an eyebrow as the bullets were stopped by the slime covering the beast.

Its numerous pupils suddenly fixated towards her, a bit of blood dripping from one of it's mouths. Most likely, the creature had whipped out its tongue at her, the same tongue she had cut off. If that were the case, that would explain the blood. If not...then the creature just drooled blood. It was one or the other, she supposed.

She shrugged and stored her revolver. She was barely learning how to incorporate soul into her weapons with aggression. She found that while she struggled to enhance small bullets, she could load up melee weapons with tons of soul. So, she pulled out a simple one-handed sword with a chipped guard as she stared her opponent down.

The *thing* blinked hundreds of times at her. In response, she blew a kiss. Apparently, that was the wrong response.

One of the mutant's heads bubbled before shooting out it's tongue at blinding speeds to her. It was all Queenie could do to quickly raise her weapon and barely deflect the being's attack. Due to her unprepared grip, her sword left a notable gash in the creature's tongue before flying off into the woods. The girl swore, making the mistake of tracking her weapon instead of watching the creature's other heads. The mutant's second head bubbled and shot out its second tongue. Queenie flinched and instinctively withdrew a shield from her storage. Though the defense protected her from being grabbed and eaten, the force of the tongue punched the shield towards the girl, slamming into her stomach as the air was sucked out of her lungs. She flew backward with a wheeze, slamming into a nearby tree.

She scrambled to her feet through blurred vision to see a wave of sludge flying towards her. Alarmed, Queenie instinctively manifested a chain from her storage to wrap around her arm and yank her to the right, dodging the mutant's attack. As she rolled into the shallow creak, it was all Queenie could do to summon another chain to propel herself further before the mutant moved with shocking power and speed towards her. Though she was able to mostly dodge the creature's charge, her elbow was clipped by its leg with a sickening *pop*. Immediately, sweat beaded from her face as the small graze had enough momentum to send her flying deeper down the creek. She rolled onto her back, eyes closed as she clutched her elbow in agony.

Because she closed her eyes, she was unable to see the creature using its numerous legs to bounce off the treetops, slamming into the girl's body and pinning her into the ground. Had it not been for the mutant's fatty and slimy mutation, Queenie would have been dead. Still, the weight of the mutant slowly pushed the air out of her lungs, and soon the pain in her elbow was dulled as she slowly began to suffocate. With resilience, she grit her teeth as she pulled out a dagger, loading it with soul, and began to stab into the being. Unfortunately, her weapon was too short, barely nicking the creature's fat through the layer of slime on it's skin.

Soon, her friends and Juliette burst through the woods and began to stare at her. She wanted to warn them of the mutant's abilities, but the lack of oxygen in her lungs made it impossible to even utter a sound. The party was exchanging words that didn't reach her ears. From their concerned eyes flickering from the mutant to her reddening face, it was clear that her allies were all concerned with rescuing her. They were idiots: they could focus on taking the creature down, and that would free her. If they killed the damned mutant too late...well, at least her death wouldn't be in vain. On the other hand, Hush probably wouldn't want her to die. Probably.

If she could somehow escape, that would free up so much possibilities for her team. There were two ways she could do that. The first one was summoning a weapon (or tool) from her storage to push the mutant off of her body. The only thing she could think of that had enough force to do that was her cannon, which she had commissioned from Malapace's blacksmith a few days ago. However, that solution required tons of setup, and though the cannonball would certainly pierce the mutant's slime armor, it wasn't guaranteed to assume that the cannonball would carry enough force to push it off her. Not to mention, the required soul to remotely withdraw her cannon and activate it from afar was impossible.

So...it was plan B.

Queenie grit her teeth, tensing up her entire body before "storing" herself, entering a white void immediately. Not sparing any time, she quickly rolled over twice and "withdrew" herself from her storage, effectively blinking four feet to the right. Because she hadn't brang anything else out of the storage this time, she still had a small amount of soul left. However, factoring in her injuries, it was very clear that she could no longer summon bigger weapons for the time being.

Her allies flinched at her sudden disappearance and reappearance, but spent no time staring at her in awe as they immediately refocused back to the mutant. Half of the creatures pupils glanced downwards, staring at it's escaped prey. The other half flickered back towards the entire party, blood tricking from two mouths now.

The mutant's mouths suddenly bubbled, causing both Queenie and Taba to flinch. As he turned to yell a command to Queenie, she had already summoned four chains to whisk her allies away to safety, each chain flying away to the treetops with its member in tow. As quick as her response was, it was only *barely* enough to dodge the mutant. Had she reacted any less slowly, there would at the very least be three eaten allies in the mutant's belly. Even the emotionless Juliette seemed on edge from the creature's attack. As the thing's eyes suddenly flicked upward in unison, Queenie noticed it's legs slowly growing more..."full".

Queenie immediately summoned eight chains to frantically drag her party in various directions. Though the thing had only one body, the speed in which it moved put every single member at risk as it bounced between the treetops. Had it not been for the girl, each of the Misfits would have been taken out. Taba's eyes were darting wildly as his mind asked hundreds of questions. Hush's fingers flexed as his hearing enhanced to listen for any sound ques of the mutant's moves. Juliette, however, simply raised her paintbrush.

Then, she lowered it.

In an instant, the Dancing Painter's chain snapped without any input from Queenie. Invisible cuts rained upon the mutant, but the mutant seemed unphased as its body bubbled in random spots. The Misfits, while suspended in the air, stared in awe as their mentor darted around the woods, painting brushstrokes into the air. The way she gracefully painted into the sky as she nimbly dodged each of the mutant's attacks made each of them unintentionally slow their breathing, completely forgetting the danger that lay before them. Juliette, betraying no emotion, turned her back as she suddenly gripped her paintbrush with both her arms, suddenly slamming it into the air in a two-handed attack. In response, the mutant bubbled and shot out its uninjured tongue to the Drunken Fox. As it did, the being's tongue was suddenly cut into ribbons as she elegantly flipped over the thing's now crumbling tongue. To the Misfit's surprise, their mentor suddenly began to climb the trees until she was within earshot of her students.

Though her face remained calm, the urgency in the tone of her voice was clear. "Do you remember where I did that big slash? *Do you?*"

Queenie and Hush flinched, but Taba nodded with confidence. The Drunken Fox nodded. "Your task is to not only bring him to that spot, but to *hold* him there. Now, *go.*"

She jumped off the tree and began to continue her dance, each of her attack doing minimal damage to the creature.

Taba turned to the siblings and spoke with controlled resolution. "Hush, blind it. Queenie, use a cannon at..." The leader pointed to a spot. "...*that* spot. Once you do, withstrain it with chains for two seconds. That'll defeat the frog."

Wait. That's *what a mutant frog looks like?* Shaking the thought from her head, she hesitated. "I...don't have enough soul to summon the cannon. Me storing myself drained my soul, the chains aren't helping either. Plus, even if I *did* have enough soul, there's no way I could summon enough chains to restrain it."

Taba stared at the girl with confidence. "My blessing is never wrong. You *can* summon the cannon. I don't know how, but you *can*. I promise you. You have twenty-six seconds to figure it out: *go.*"

143

As Queenie dropped the Misfits to the ground, her mind began to race. This wasn't just faith: there was a way for her to summon the cannon that she wasn't aware of, and she had a little over twenty seconds to figure out how. As her entire party began to play their part effortlessly, Queenie stood in the spot that Taba had pointed at. She knew the limits of her soul: it was *impossible* for her to summon the damn cannon. What could she d-

The girl blinked as she stared at Juliette. Though they were in danger, a single question formed in her mind: how was her mentor able to use so many attacks? If slashing was the activation requirement for Juliette's blessing, she should've been drained. And yet, the Drunken Fox didn't seem fatigued whatsoever. Sure, their mentor had a bigger soulwell than the Misfits, but it still made no sense. Did her blessing use *that* little soul, or was she just...was she just choosing which parts of her blessing to activate?

On *sheer* whim, Queenie donned a monotone expression as she "grabbed" her storage as she dragged her hand through the air, essentially "opening" a window to her storage, *right* in front of where her cannon was stored. The gears in her mind clicked as she removed bits of her soul that enveloped her weapon, unblocking parts to only expose the fuse and the mouth. She "moved" the gunpowder from one part of the storage to inside the cannon, then unblocked the powder as well. She did the same to a lighter she had stored away to light the weapon's fuse.

Then, she fired the cannon, all without "withdrawing" it.

The cannon's recoil caused her body and mind to shudder, the projectile flying at blinding speeds towards the mutant. The blind mutant, being so used to its superior vision, was caught off guard by the sudden blow as it was sent flying towards Juliette's marked spot. As it flew over the designated area, Queenie summoned six chains to quickly tie the mutant down. Her entire body and soul strained from such an effort.

Though Queenie couldn't have held the mutant down for more than a second, it was enough for the Dancing Painter. Without even swinging her brush, a red line suddenly appeared horizontally across the frog. Its multiple blind pupils darted frantically right before it split in two, splattering the entire area in blood, slime, and guts. The Drunken Fox elegantly dove behind a tree and dodged the gorey confetti. The Misfits, however, were all exhausted and took the frog's finale head on, being doused head to toe with blood. Groaning in weariness and disgust, the trio shook off what they could as their mentor stepped out of the woods, her head tilted slightly as she flicked tiny bits of blood off her paintbrush.

Juliette walked up to the trio, nodding to them all. "Well done. Let's return to the village." After the boys nodded and turned to walk back, Queenie's mentor leaned into her ear with a seemingly pleased whisper. "Well done to *you*, especially."

Queenie stiffened up. Though she was drained in every aspect, her face was flush with embarrassed pride in receiving such a complement from such a meticulous woman. She said nothing, not even acknowledging her, and walked back to the village with a small limp.

...

Though the threat was disposed of, the party stayed in the village for a few days to help around with various tasks. Hush was essentially given the task to stay by the small man whose arm had been severed, just to numb his pain. Taba was on patrol duty to ease the minds of the

145

villagers. Queenie, though she was still recovering, would activate her blessing here and there to pull out tools that the villagers would need to rebuild. Juliette would be seen around various houses, having small conversations and essentially maintaining the "trust" of the people to ensure that they wouldn't cut off their connection with the Overseer. Other times, she would seemingly vanish from the village.

Queenie muttered from her bed, pulling out yet another hammer for the village kids. They insisted that they were sent to her on an errand, but after the seventh "missing" hammer? It was more likely that they were just fascinated by her ability and just wanted to keep seeing her activate it (not to mention...she could *feel* the hammers being piled in the corner of a house). The children the hammer with an awestruck face, whispering in excitement as they bolted out of her room. The girl muttered as she rubbed her elbow. The mutant frog may have dislocated it, but Juliette and quickly popped it back into its socket with no warning once they had returned to the village a week ago. Hurt like *hell*, but their mentor promised that she would be ok to freely move it around after they returned to Malapace.

The girl scowled as she restlessly paced her room, wincing slightly with each step. She hated waiting and doing nothing. Every day was so damn *boring*. Plus, because she was responsible for handing out respiration tools to the villagers, she couldn't even afford to practice the whole "pocket" technique she had randomly attempted. So, every passing second, every passing minute, every passing hour, every passing *day* was agonizing boredom.

Her ears perked up upon hearing a quiet knock at the front door. She turned her head to the wood door opening, and to the girl's surprise, in stepped Juliette.

146

"Time to change your bandages," said Juliette. "Get on the bed and roll up your hoodie."

Queenie grunted as she followed the orders. Though they weren't life threatening, the female Misfit had gotten fairly bruised up when the mutant sat on her. As the bandages on her stomach were unwrapped, it revealed horribly swollen purple skin. There were a few scrapes where her skin had split, revealing scabbing wounds. Juliette, not flinching at the gruesome sight, nodded as she rubbed some ointment on her porcelain hands. With no warning, the emotionless woman slapped her cold hands onto the girl's feverish skin, causing her to flinch and audibly yelp. The damn medicine stung to high hell, but it seemed to be slowly working. She woke up each day with less soreness and was able to stretch a bit more before the stinging kicked in. She wanted to ask what the ointment was made of, but everything Queenie tried to pry the information out of her, Juliette simply stared at her with her black fox eyes in silence until Queenie looked away.

Once new ointment was spread on her upper body, Juliette got to quietly rewrapping fresh bandages. Oddly enough, neither the ointment nor the bandages were supplied by Queenie, so she wasn't sure as to where Juliette had gotten either. After finishing the procedure, the mentor lowered the girl's hoodie but stayed seated on the bed. Queenie turned around in mild confusion.

"So, how did you do it?" asked the Drunken Fox.

"You mean, the hammers? I dunno, I just have a crap ton of things just lying around my storage. It isn't a big deal."

"No, I'm talking about the cannon. How did you use it without summoning it?"

"Oh."

The girl grabbed a piece of bandage that had been unwrapped from her body, and nervously wrapped and unwrapped it around her arm. "I just...copied what you probably do, I guess."

"Elaborate." said Juliette.

Queenie began to rub the dirty bandage between her fingers. "Well, your blessing. I originally thought it was ranged attacks, but that can't be it: you've shown that you can attack without swinging the brush. So, I thought...maybe...just *maybe*...you were using a sort of 'token' system of sorts for your blessing."

The woman said nothing as Queenie quickened her speech as did her wrapping and unwrapping. "Even if it *wasn't*, that got me thinking: what if it *was*? How would one continuously deal with the soul being drained while the blessing was being used?"

Juliette leaned slightly forward. "And how would one deal with such an issue?"

The Misfit hesitated, unsure if her answer would result in mockery. "The...the blessing wasn't used. It was put on *hold*. If that were the case, the only soul one would need is to 'place' the ability, nothing more. Like...like preordering a hamburger, but only paying for the buns.

"A bit of a flawed analogy, but go on."

Queenie tugged at the dirty bandage, cutting off blood circulation to her index finger. "So...uh...my blessing 'stores' things by wrapping my soul around objects. I wondered if it would be possible to remove my soul from certain parts of certain things, so summon 'half' of my cannon without actually moving it from my storage. Since it hadn't moved from my storage and was technically 'stored', I could move gunpowder into the cannon with no effort. Furthermore, by heavily restricting what was 'unblocked', I was able to save tons of soul in exchange for inflexibility."

Juliette crossed her arms as she appeared to be pondering the explanation. "So...your cannon was in a 'limbo' of sorts, being stored and summoned at the same time? Plus, you locked its 'direction' to make it cheaper?"

"Yeah. All that was left to do was to open a window to my storage. So, I imagined summoning a chain, but with a *much* bigger opening. Then, all I needed to do was not summon the chain...and presto."

Juliette's face betrayed no emotion. "And you did all this off instinct, for the first time, while injured, within *seconds*?"

Queenie threw up her hands, frustrated, wincing as she forgot the state of her elbow. "Ow. Well, I want to experiment with it more to see how practical it is in combat, but I *can't*. It's pissing me off. I just wanna get back hom-to Malapace."

"Well, good news," Juliette said with a tint of a smile as she got up from the bed. "We're about done and the supplies should be here within a day. We can go 'home' soon."

...

Queenie woke up to the rumbling of wheels on a rickety road. As she peeked out of her window, she stared as two wagons and three cows rolled up to the villagers, who cheered upon the sight.

Juliette stepped forward and gestured to the wagon on her left and right. "To my left is a few seeds of various crops, as well as a few bushels of wheat. To my right include a few things of textiles, soaps, tools, and so on. The cows can be placed in the woods within line of sight from here. You may either slaughter them for food or keep them around for milk. We thank you for your patience."

The masked woman walked over to the left wagon, pulling out something wrapped in cloth. She then walked over to the short man, who had a bittersweet look on his face as he clutched his arm's stump.

"I apologize for being unable to fully protect you," Juliette said as she bowed at the waist level, handing the package over to the man. "The Overseer has seen your loss and has offered a small compensation."

The man curiously unwrapped the cloth, revealing an odd cylinder of metal and wood, with leather straps sticking out on various ends. Though Queenie was unsure of what the instrument was supposed to be, the man flinched as small tears formed at the edges of his eyes.

The Dancing Painter kept her head down. "Once your wound has fully healed, this prosthetic should comfortably slip over your missing limb. It should aid in simple things. I once again, apologize for my failures."

The short man used the cloth that was used to wrap the prosthetic to dab away his eyes. "No...no. You...saving this village was more than enough. You didn't need to do this. Thank you, truly."

Juliette raised her head and nodded to her students. The Misfits walked over to her side. The mentor bowed once more to the villagers. "If no one has any more questions or complaints, I will take my leave now. Stay strong, and just know that the Overseer will do whatever is possible to ensure your survival."

The villagers cheered as the party slowly began to return to their city. Though she could walk, each step made Queenie grit her teeth ever so slightly. It didn't *hurt*, but it felt like her entire body was carrying a heavy backpack, lurching with every step. The others seemed to notice her discomfort and they slowed their walking speed in quiet consideration. Though the girl said nothing, she felt mildly insulted and made it a point to walk faster than normal, which added to her irritation.

After an hour of silent walking, Taba cleared his throat. "So...Juliette."

Their mentor turned her head with mild curiosity. "Mm?"

He nodded towards her. "Your blessing. How many know its specifics?"

The wind stopped blowing and the party halted their movement. The siblings darted their eyes back and forth between the expressionless woman and the inquisitive teenager. Though there was no murderous intention displayed, the tension in the air was palpable.

Juliette turned her entire body to face the questioner. "So...you understand how it works through your blessing?"

Taba shrugged. "I mean, to your credit, it *usually* doesn't take this long for me to discover someone's blessing. The entire time I was training to use soul manipulation, I was also trying to discover your ability, and even then, I only *recently* discovered your ability's activation requirements. So...I can't imagine that many others know about its specifics, right?"

The Drunken Fox unslung her wooden box and unsheathed her paintbrush. The Misfits all took a defensive stance in preparation. However, to their surprise, the woman's gaze stared past Taba. As they turned to see what had caught her attention, they found themselves staring at a man wearing a fine suit, straightening out his necktie. He had trimmed hair and wore dark shades, a single scar stretched over one of his eyes.

He straightened out his jacket and nodded. "Taba. Queenie. Hush."

The Misfits stared, a bit taken back by the man. How had he tracked them down? The only way was if...if *Father* had told him where to go.

Taba spoke up first, nodding in return. "Geralt. Glad to see you're doing well."

The man huffed as he removed his glasses, revealing one sharp brown eye and one pale eye. "'Well' is subjective. It's hot, and this suit does nothing for the heat."

"No one is forcing you to wear the suit." Queenie muttered as she squeezed her arms.

Geralt raised an eyebrow in her direction. "And misrepresent Father? Hah. Never took you for a jokester. Anyhow, come on, I'm here to pick you guys up."

The man raised his arm, but the trio didn't budge. Geralt raised an eyebrow, but didn't seem too surprised. He nodded to their mentor. "Is it because she's holding you hostage or something?"

Juliette finally spoke up, her cold voice piercing the air. "I'm afraid I'm in charge of these brats. I can't let you take them."

Geralt chuckled as he straightened his cuffs, shaking his head as he did. "'Take'? Lady, they're part of *our* family. *You* kidnapped our siblings, and you think you're in the right?" Suddenly, the smile died from his face as he quietly pocketed his shades. "I'm really not in the mood to ruin this suit. Can't we settle this peacefully? Just say you got overwhelmed and they got away. I won't tell if you won't."

Juliette said nothing, but she lowered her stance. In one arm, she held her brush, cradling it between the crook of her elbow and her side. With her free hand, she slowly reached up to her mask. Geralt, in response, reached into his pocket to pull out a single marble. He placed it in the center of his palm and held it to the Dancing Painter, as though he were offering her a gift.

The two adults held their respective stances for ten, long, silent, minutes. Not a word was exchanged. Not a movement was spared. The Misfits began to sweat nervously, unsure of who to watch. Juliette was an incredible fighter, some would call her unmatched. On the other...Queenie had never even *landed* a blow on Geralt. It was a confrontation where two infallible champions could collapse, and, barring Taba, no one would know how such a fight would unfold.

Once a cloud creeped over the sun, Geralt made the first move by sighing and pocketing his marble. "Man, they said you were strong. I guess they were right for once. If you don't want to return my Family, that's fine...for now. However, I *am* here on behalf of Father to declare war on Malapace."

Juliette removed her hand from her mask, but still held her stance. "Would your 'Father' start a war over these three idiots?"

The man shook his head. "No, he wouldn't: they were just the tipping point. I was sent as a messenger to see if there was any hope of collaboration between us...but today proves that this is impossible. Neither of us can exist in harmony. So, we will tear you down." Geralt nodded to the Misfits. "Stay put. Don't die. We'll come get you guys." He then addressed Juliette with a stern jab. "There will be no date on when we attack. Be anxious. Be afraid. This confrontation is the only warning you'll get. May the more correct side win."

After that, he turned on his heel and began to casually stroll away. Until he was clearly out of sight, Juliette held her pose. Once he was, she sighed and stored her weapon once more, slinging it on her back.

She nodded to the Misfits. "So, guessing you know him?" The trio stayed silent. "Guess you do," muttered Juliette. "Let's continue back to Malapace."

The party trudged back to Malapace in silence. Due to Queenie's injuries, they took longer to return to the city, camping out for an extra day. On the final day of travel, Taba finally broke the silence by continuing his conversation before they had met Geralt.

The teenager cleared his throat. "So, how are you able to use your blessing?"

Juliette sighed and turned her head. "I activate it."

"You know what I mean." said Taba.

"No, I don't."

He opened his mouth to say something, but stopped. He glanced at his friends and then nodded to the woman. "Are you really ok with me sharing your blessing in front of them? Isn't it private?"

"What does it matter? You'll probably tell them the first chance you get, anyways."

Taba shrugged. "Fair point. Anyways, how are you able to...'activate' the slashes? Your blessing only allows you to 'trace' an action once, right? How are you able to use slashes in places where you've never, well, cut?"

"You haven't fully gotten my blessing, if that's what you think it is." Juliette said, adding to Queenie's confusion what did it mean to 'trace' an action?

"Whatever, it's close enough. How are you activating your blessing in places you haven't been before?" asked Taba.

The woman stopped walking, turning to properly face the Misfits. "Who says I haven't been to those places?"

"I'm not too sure on what's going on...I got lost four sentences back," said Queenie. "Could someone explain?"

Hush nodded. "She's 'retracing' her attacks. So, if she were to swing an axe at a tree, she could 'retrace' that cut to produce another 'chop'. Make sense?"

Queenie's mouth slowly opened in understanding. "Oh, so like...when you're activating your slashes, you're just...'cashing in' on attacks you've made before?"

"Yes...and no." Juliette said with a sigh as she turned around and continued to walk.

"Could you explain, or..."

"No."

Queenie scoffed. "Why? Scared?"

Suddenly, she felt a small prick on her cheek. When Queenie put a finger to her face, she stared in surprise at the small bit of blood on her fingertip.

Juliette continued to walk without facing the Misfits. "What does it matter if you know my blessing? It won't give you an edge when fighting me. I'm not saying anything, solely because you guys are the enemy. That's all."

The trio took the hint. Though they weren't sure how, they were already surrounded by their mentor's ability. The only reason they were alive was because she had no reason to kill them. So, they all closed their mouths and continued to trek on home. Though not a word was spoken, the Misfits spent the rest of the return trip exchanging glances as they tried to make sense of the impossibility that was the Drunken Fox's blessing.

CHAPTER 9

As they walked up to Malapace, they saw a woman in a white dress excitedly waving at them. Though she had already known about their arrival, Sana's massive smile seemed genuinely thrilled at their return. When they arrived to the front gates, the Gatekeeper squealed as she hugged each of the Misfits, each member unsure of the emotion they should be evoking. When she finally let go of Hush, Sana turned and dove towards Juliette, who chose not to sidestep the telegraphed lunge. With a laugh, the ecstatic woman hugged the fox, who sighed as she was rattled around.

After a minute of this, Sana let go and took a step back with a big grin. "Welcome back! How was your first assignment?"

Taba hesitated. Queenie averted her eyes. Hush muttered a phrase. The Gatekeeper noted their reaction and frowned, quizzically staring at Juliette. Their mentor untied the jug on her hip and tipped it to her mouth, scowling when not a single drop poured out. She sighed as she retied it to her hip. "A villager lost an arm and Queenie almost died. Not the best start."

Sana chewed the inside of her cheek slowly, nodding as she did. "...but you're all alive! Isn't that worth celebrating?"

"San-san, you're too positive." Juliette said with a frown.

"Not my fault that there's light everywhere I look. Come on, I'm sure Babs wants to see you guys!"

The tired party exchanged glances, a bit unsure of what to do. Sana noticed and pulled their sleeves. "Relax, it won't take long. Plus, she'll provide you guys dinner!"

So, the Drunken Fox and her tired students trudged through the city, catching stray glances from passerbyers. The occasional citizen would murmur an excited whisper upon seeing Juliette. The others would scowl upon seeing Hush, probably due to his performance in the mentorship tournament. Well, that was fine: Hush had no intention of being friendly with the city. So, he ignored their glares and walked along his way.

On the way to the town hall, they noticed an armless girl walking in the opposite direction from them, a bag of groceries hung around her neck and goggles around her eyes. Upon seeing the Misfits, her eyes narrowed and she tightened her lips, but walked up to the party. To everyone's shock, she walked past the Gatekeeper and the Dancing Painter, and stood face-to-face with Hush.

Though she was a foot shorter than him, the girl glared at the boy. Hush frowned, a bit uncomfortable at the situation. He rubbed his neck nervously. "Uh...Alexandria, was it? Can I...help you?"

His former opponent glared at him, her jaw clenched. After a few silent seconds, she bowed slightly, carefully to ensure that her groceries wouldn't spill out. When she looked back up, her eyes had an odd mixture of anger and respect. "First off," she said raspily, "Did you really need to toy with me during the fight? Seriously? Uncool."

Hush flinched, hesitating. He wasn't used to this level of direct confrontation. After trying to avoid eye contact for an awkward five seconds, he hung his head with embarrassment. "Uh...sorry. I guess."

"Still, I should thank you for not taking pity on me. So...thanks." The girl said as she huffed with mild satisfaction.

The quiet man awkwardly turned to face his friends, completely unsure of what to say or do. They all shrugged with muffled grins as they watched the entire situation unfold. After his silent plea for help went unanswered, he turned his eyes to the haughty girl. "Uh...you're...welcome? I'm sorry, I don't know what to really say right now."

Alexandria shrugged, a weird sight to see an armless girl do. "Same. I just felt like ignoring you would be the worst thing to do, so here I am. Still, I guess I just wanted to say...don't be a stranger? You seem cool, so it'd be a shame to hold a petty grudge over a single fight." She nodded to the party to say farewell, then "pointed" to her groceries with her eyes. "Well, I gotta go drop these off, or mom's gonna kill me. Later, and say hi if you ever spot me."

The armless girl walked away with a small spring in her step and Hush couldn't help but stare at her backside as she did. Sana cleared her throat, a smile in her voice. "She passed the examination too, by the way. The judges were impressed by her blessing's control, as well as her tenacity. So, you'll probably see more of her if you continue to do missions."

Hush turned around and continued their walk. "She wasn't strong...but I guess she wasn't weak at all."

Sana smiled as she followed along. "No, she certainly isn't."

...

The Misfits all sat at a table with Babs, each member offered some tea. Taba took polite sips. Queenie gagged after the first taste and pushed the cup away. Hush didn't touch the drink at all.

After a few minutes of drinking, Babs finished her cup and poured out another cup. "So...what did you brats think?"

Queenie scoffed. "About the tea? It's bitter and disgusting."

Hush elbowed the girl, who scowled in response. Taba frowned at the exchange. The teenager had always made it a point to show respect to hospitality, and it seemed as though this leaked to even his enemies.

"This tea is nice, thank you." Taba said politely.

The old woman rolled her pale eyes. "Bah. I don't mean the *tea*, you numbskulls. How was your first mission?"

Taba seemed slightly taken aback, turning to Juliette to allow her to speak on their behalf. However, as Hush turned to look at their mentor, she was busy downing a freshly refilled jug of spirits, so it was highly unlikely that she would speak anytime soon. Taba seemed hesitant to speak on Queenie's failures, so Hush took it upon himself to speak for his sister. "We didn't do so hot. Queenie got hurt. We didn't protect a villager."

Babs nodded, but still looked dissatisfied. "Mhm. And...?"

"What do you mean, 'and'? That's it."

The Overseer sighed as she put her cup down, then leaned in to stare at him. "Do you feel as though this mission was an overall success...or do you feel as though you failed?"

"Well...we disposed of the mutant. So..."

"...so did you succeed or fail?"

Hush pursed his lips. They did what was expected for them. Hell, these people weren't even their allies. And yet...

Taba spoke his thoughts perfectly. "Feels like we failed."

Babs nodded, completely satisfied with the answer. She poured herself another cup of tea and sipped it in silence, not asking anymore questions. There was no mockery, no scorning, nothing. The older woman simply continued to drink tea as though she hadn't asked a question at all. A few minutes later, a humble dinner of rice and steamed vegetables came out, accompanied by small chunks of lumpy meat. After watching the Overseer take her first bite of food, the other Misfits seemed convinced that the food wasn't tainted and dug into the food as well. As he ate, all Hush could think was how bland the meal was prepared for the supposed head of Malapace.

After they ate, Babs reached into a bag that lay by her side and pulled out three goodie bags, handing it out to each Misfit member. They all took the gift with confusion, peering inside with curiosity. The bag simply had small snacks and candy.

When they looked up at the Overseer, she nodded with a sad gaze. "Though I can't do much, I at least wanted to prepare something small as a congratulations for your first mission. I doubt money would mean much for you guys, since you could simply take what you want with force. So...I do hope you enjoy these snacks." The Misfits shifted uncomfortably in their seats as Babs continued to speak. "I saw the confrontation Juliette had with that man...Geralt, was it? When the war comes, I won't hold it against you guys for fighting for your 'Father'. Do as you wish." To their surprise, the elderly woman suddenly lowered her head till her forehead touched the ground. "However...until then, *please* help these villagers. They're innocent people and don't deserve such misfortune. Please."

The trio hesitated, unsure of what to do or feel. The sudden shuffle of sandals caught their attention as their mentor slowly squatted by the Overseer's bowing figure. "Raise your head, Overseer. A person of your position shouldn't bow to anyone."

The elder raised her head with moist eyes and a scowl. "I'm only doing what I think is correct, and *I* think that it's only right to ask a favor from your enemy with the utmost humility, no?"

"Why the hell should we do as you ask?" Queenie asked with forced anger. "I mean, you already have soulbearers, right? What difference do we make?"

Juliette stared at her students with silence, her expressionless face having a surprising hint of guilt upon her lips.

Babs answered the girl's question with blunt honesty. "Very few can actually survive an encounter with a mutant. Even *less* can assist in taking one down. So, your ability to survive and assist in the takedown of the mutant frog is undeniably valuable."

The siblings said nothing, but Taba's glare suddenly turned sharp. Though initially confused, Hush slowly began to understand the root of the teenager's anger as he said his piece.

Taba spoke through clenched teeth. "So, our first mission, the one where you divulged no information about, was a mission in which the majority of soulbearers would be useless and, most likely, *die* in attempting?"

"Yes, I won't sugarcoat it: I sent you all on a suicide mission."

The air was thick and loud. Time stood still. The only emotion that rang out clear through the room was nothing short of barely controlled rage. Taba quietly stood up and slowly unsheathed a knife strapped on his thigh. Juliette did nothing to stop the teenager. The siblings stared at the old woman, who did nothing to try and defend her body or her actions.

Hush wasn't sure how much time had passed. It could have been a minute. Maybe it was thirty. However, the older brother couldn't help but secretly wish for Taba to sink his knife into the Overseer. It was a well-deserved action that was not only justified, but also would *drastically* aid Father's cause. In short, there was no downside to taking her out.

And yet, Taba sheathed his knife with gritted teeth, a vein bulging in his neck. "You...of all the people I've met, you are perhaps the most loathsome of them all."

"You are not wrong," Babs whispered. "I am despicable."

The teenager took a deep inhale as he closed his eyes, and slowly exhaled all his rage away. When he reopened them, his gaze was stern, but understanding. "How frequent are the attacks in the surrounding villages?"

"Not too frequent. It isn't too frequent that we have mutants harass the people. Mostly it's those with blessings who are power tripping and choose to become terrorists for kicks and giggles. Other times, its just normal criminals. Hell, sometimes its just a basic landslide that causes the damage." responded the Overseer.

"Will we receive compensation for our work?"

"No, you're just a glorified prisoner."

"Fine. We'll do as you ask. That all?" asked Taba.

The Overseer closed her eyes, and gave a soft nod. "Yes, that's all. Thank you."

The teenager stormed out of the room, the siblings trailing close behind. Once they reached their rooms, they followed Taba into his room and stared at the questioner in disbelief.

The girl scowled at the teenager. "Why didn't you kill her? Was Juliette preventing it?"

"No," said Taba. "If I chose to kill her then and there, she would've died. Juliette would have allowed my attack to connect."

Queenie began to yell obscenities at the teenager, but Hush calmly thought to himself. Why would Taba not attack? Why did he ask all those questions at the end? Why did...

Suddenly, it clicked. The older brother flexed his fingers to mute his sister, who stared at him with wrathful frustration. Hush stared at his friend, a soft look slowly appearing on his face. Taba stared at the ground.

Hush spoke his friend's reasonings into the air. "You're doing it for the villagers? Really?"

Taba couldn't lift his head. "...Father wouldn't know. We're just prisoners being forced to do this. He would understand."

"Taba...you do realize what you're doing, right? We could have won this war."

"Well...yeah. I know. It's just...I'm just going with what I think is right."

Though Queenie was muted, her mouth shut as she stared at the conversation in mild disbelief. Hush was frustrated...but he understood where Taba was coming from. "I don't need to tell you that your choice may have damned some of our family to death in the upcoming war, right?"

"...Yeah."

"And you understand that their blood will be on your hands, solely because you wished to save some strangers?"

"...Yeah."

Hush nodded...and softly held up his fist. Taba hesitated, but weakly held his arm up as well. Queenie, though obviously frustrated, did the same. The trio tapped hands in silence, with Hush nodding as they did so.

"If you say you understand, then I'm with you all the way." Hush said.

Taba blinked rapidly, but nodded. "...Thanks, man."

Hush grabbed his sister's hoodie and dragged her out of his friend's room to give him some privacy. Once in the hallway, he undid his blessing and returned his sister's vocal cords to her. However, she said nothing and simply stared at Taba's room with concern.

She glanced at her brother with worry in his eyes. "Is he going to be ok? He looked..."

Hush hesitated, but shook his head. "He won't be ok, but he needs alone time. All we can do is be here for him as he gets back up. Until then...don't be too hard on him, alright?"

The girl pulled away from her brother and stared at the teenager's door. "You don't need to tell me twice."

The siblings nodded to each other and went off to rest in their respective rooms, the weight of Taba's decision weighing heavily on all their shoulders as they did.

...

The Hush clan, though massive, were scattered throughout the country. However, they allowed themselves to be spread out so thinly due to their tremendous efficiency in highway robberies. They hid out in caves next to roadways and would ambush merchants, usually "silencing" them quickly before taking their loot. On the off chance that they were accompanied by soulbearer bodyguards, the bandits would simply stay low and let them pass. These criminals did all they could to steal anything possible while giving no information to any authorities. There were times when someone decided to investigate the caves...but the clan was good with dealing with intruders as well.

The teenager who would be eventually known as Hush grew up in these conditions. His younger sister, Queenie, was promptly given a name due to her blessing's early manifestation. Furthermore, it was a blessing that proved to be extraordinarily valuable to thieves. So, she was given high treatment and favor by the entire clan.

The teenager who would be known as Hush, however, did not manifest his blessing for the longest time. This meant he was usually designated to the roles that no one wanted. Acting as an injured pedestrian on the side of the road, lugging whatever luggage that Queenie had no soul to store, or being the punching bag to vent out the frustrations of other member's failures. Particularly, Queenie's failures. After all, the clan couldn't afford to seem disfavorable to such a valuable asset. So, she was coddled even after numerous favors...and the teenager was beat in punishment behind the scenes.

Their logic was that he would dislike the beatings and teach his sister to not mess up as much. However, the teenager refused to let his sister get even a hint of the idea of what they were doing to him. So, he clamped his mouth shut and endured each of his sister's failures.

Queenie failed to catch dinner? Clench your jaw.
Queenie failed to take the merchant down in one hit? Grit your teeth.
Queenie failed to store three wagons worth of loot? Bite your arm.

Some would expect that the boy would develop some form of hatred from all of her failures, be it to her weakness or to his oppressors. However, no such anger existed to him. All he felt was worry and concern: worried that she might find out or that he may accidentally take irrecoverable damage.

So, when the boy obtained his blessing, he was thrilled. Within weeks, however, he began to realize that the nullification of pain didn't account for involuntary grunts or gasps. Rather than ease his suffering, the boy chose to silence his vocals in fears of any unintentional eavesdropping that might've happened.

Within a few months, the boy quickly discovered his control of his other senses after his sister chewed on a bland baked potato, complaining how she could barely taste the butter. All he had to do was flex different fingers and suddenly his sister's mediocre meal was bursting with flavor. Suddenly, Queenie was eagerly looking forward to each meal, unaware why the clan's tasteless food suddenly became delectable overnight.

Within years, the boy learned the absolute limits of both his blessing and other's blessings. The subtle sounds that were emitted upon activations. The movements of the soulbearer. How silent observation betrayed the openings of others. The physical limits and pain tolerance of his body. What he could recover from. How to properly curl up to minimize damage.

One day, Queenie pointed out the numerous white streaks throughout his hair. He wasn't even sure when they came about: he was too tired to notice. When his sister asked about it, he simply grinned and said it was fashion and genetics.

A few days later, when asked about his random bruises that never really faded, he claimed he tripped in the dark caves.

One month later, when she asked why he wasn't allowed to come on the raiding trips, the older brother lied and said he was in charge of other tasks.

After two months, she asked what his name was, saying she was "tired of calling him brother". He quickly proclaimed his name to be Hush, stating he was named after the clan.

However, like dominos, events occurred that led to the dismantling of their clan. On the run, the few survivors agreed to split up and regroup in the caves. The first ones to rendezvous were Hush and the head of the clan/his biological father, Jin. He decided to vent out his frustrations onto the boy with physical force.

The boy wasn't sure how much time had passed, but Queenie eventually stumbled into the cave with a stunned look. Hush's head rested on the cold floor as he spat up sticky blood. Jin looked up to his daughter's horrified face.

The man quickly shoved his disgraceful son behind him with a sweep of a leg and gave a wide smile to Queenie. "Hey, princess. How are y-"

Queenie, as rash as she was, had a brain. She wasn't stupid. She had her doubts, but always swallowed them because of her brother's reassuring smile. So, when the younger sister saw her older brother hunched over on the floor, covered in open wounds as he spat up vomit and blood? She put two and two together. Queenie screamed, her eyes glowing...and then Hush vanished.

...

Hush woke up with damp pajamas. Same nightmare. Same regret. He hated that day. Well, he had mixed feelings about it all. Had Queenie not discovered Jin's actions, they wouldn't have met Father or Taba.

Speaking of Taba, the sun hadn't come up but Hush could tell that his friend was already doing sprints around the city. Unable to go back to sleep, he stripped off his sweaty clothes and wore normal workout clothes to join his friend.

The questioner noticed his friend's unexpected arrival and stopped jogging to offer a fistbump. "You're up early."

"Couldn't sleep. Let me join you."

"Alright."

The duo then began their quiet morning jog around the town hall. After a few laps, Hush decided to break the silence with small conversation between pants. "So...you feeling better?"

"To be honest?" responded Taba. "No, not really. I'm just running to get my mind off of what I just did."

Hush nodded, saying nothing. There was nothing he could say to soothe his friend's mind. All he could do was solely keep him company as his friend struggled through his personal turmoil, and help him up if he were to stumble.

So the two men jogged until the sun rose. By the time day kissed the sky, Hush was hunched over, winded. Taba, on the other hand, continued his stretches without being too out of breath. Because he was so sweaty, the older brother tapped fists with his friend and headed in to take a quick morning shower.

When he headed into the town hall, he saw that Queenie had been staring at them through a window. Frowning, he walked up to his sister to tap fists. She met his gesture, but kept her eyes trained out the window.

She nodded to the stretching teenager. "He ok?"

"No, but he's honest about it."

Queenie bit her lip with worry. "...I...I guess that's all we can ask for, right?"

He patted his sister's shoulder and headed in to take a quick cold shower. After he had freshened up, he walked out to see his sister making small talk with Patchy. From the expressions of both members, it appeared that she was pestering him for information.

She groaned and crossed her arms. "Please? Just one?"

Patchy shook his head. "No. Sorry, I don't make the rules."

"But you're a Gatekeeper. Surely you could bend the rules, right?"

"...and you're technically the enemy. I don't really 'owe' you anything."

Queenie scowled and shoved her hands into her hoodie's pockets with annoyance. Patchy noticed the older brother with a nod. "Hey, hot stuff. You guys have free time today: Juliette is doing her own thing for a while."

"Is she drinking at the bar?" Hush asked.

"Surprisingly?" Patchy answered, "No. She's out setting up her-she's busy, alright? So, do what you want today." The Gatekeeper waved and walked away without looking back. The siblings looked at each other with a bit of confusion.

Queenie leaned in. "So...free time. With no supervision. What's stopping us from just leaving?"

Hush rubbed his neck. "Tempting, but I don't think they'd let us leave so easily. With the Overseer and Sana looking over the city *and* Patchy's teleportation, I'd imagine that escape is impossible. So, let's not risk it and look for another opportunity."

"I hate when you're logical."

Hush reached into his pocket to pull out a small hair tie, tying the loose ends of his hair. "Mhm. Now, did you want to do anything?"

Queenie took one arm out of her hoodie and grabbed something from her storage. Upon unfurling it, Hush raised an eyebrow. "Blueprints?"

"Yeah. Well...it's one I've had to make bullets. I was hoping to restock on ammo today since I really haven't had the chance to. Wanna tag along?"

"Eh, sure. Why not. Wanna grab Taba?"

The girl pursed her lips and shook her head. "Nah. Let's...let's leave him be for a little bit. I think he would prefer the quiet time."

Hush nodded, and they headed out. As they passed the front desk, Tabitha gave a cheerful wave. The siblings awkwardly nodded in acknowledgement. As they pushed open the front doors, the morning mist tickled their warm cheeks as they headed out to the blacksmith.

Though the merchants didn't set up shop early in the day, it was a different story for blacksmiths. Since blacksmiths were in high demand by soulbearers and militia alike, they were constantly open and *always* busy. The blacksmiths of today were different from the blacksmiths of old: ever since the birth of soulbearers, modern smithies would craft things out of soul, as long as the buyer had a detailed blueprint of the object. Of course, the buyer could ask for common items to be created using the smithies' personal blueprints...but that was usually extra.

The familiar crackling sound of items being forged slowly grew in volume as they turned the corner. The blacksmith's shop was honestly closer to a cage than an actual shop, with the smithies "locking" themselves inside the massive shop's metallic bars. This was due to the unpredictability of soulbearers, the design of the shop served as minor protection against more dishonest patrons. A multitude of smithies stood at their workbenches, staring quietly at blueprints as they poured their soul into making a mold for each request *and* to make the proper material for each item. One smithy was quickly churning out soul-made wooden handles for various tools, such as ladles or pencils. Another smithy was taking his time in properly forging a metalic hammer head. Though soulcreated materials were lacking compared to the original's material (like how soulcreated iron was far inferior to natural iron), smithies needed tremendous concentration when crafting certain items, lest the entire project be created with defects.

As they walked up to the shop, Hush frowned. "You know, I never understood something. What's stopping a smithy from just...making a weak tool?"

Queenie scoffed at she punched her brother in the arm, causing his eye to twitch in annoyance. "*So* many reasons. Specialized weapon dealers or users would be able to tell quality just by grabbing it, the smithy would lose both reputation *and* a customer if they sold a faulty tool, there are *tons* of smithies who want your business, so on. Are you dumb?"

He rolled his eyes and shoved his sister in retaliation. "I don't use smithies, chill. Sorry for not knowing something I don't use, damn."

Queenie continued her assault, stabbing her brother's gut with her fingers, grinning with each of his flinches. "Apology accepted."

The siblings continued their pathetic slap-fight all the way until they reached the blacksmith shop. Upon reaching the metalic bars, a big man with a potbelly and bulging muscles wiped his beard as he walked up to them.

He reached into his front overall pocket to pull out a handkerchief to wipe his shiny forehead. "Can I do for ya?"

Queenie nodded as she slipped her blueprints through the bars of the shop. "Just want some ammo."

The man tucked his handkerchief away and grabbed the blueprints, stroking his scruffily beard as he examined each parchment. "Mm. How many?"

She tapped her fingers, rolling her eyes to her skull as she muttered incoherent phrases. "Ehhhh...two-thousand each? May as well stock up."

The man lowered the papers and stared at the tiny girl, raising an eyebrow. "You have payment? For that many, it's gonna be 70% upfront *and* it's gonna take some time to whip out."

Queenie shrugged, pulling out two bags of coins from her storage, showing the bag's contents to the large smithy. "I promise I have enough."

The man peered inside each bag with a small whistle. He opened a small slot in the bars and slid a tray through. "Put 'em here."

Queenie plopped the bags down and slid them through. The smithy took the tray and gently rustled through each bag, quietly nodding as he did. After a few moments, the siblings flinched as he roared out a name. "***Oui, Harrison.***"

A familiar man came stumbling out from the storage room, carrying a box. "Yeah, pops?"

"Place 'at down and go count these."

As Harrison walked up to grab the moneybags, he looked up at the siblings, his eyes noticing Queenie. Upon recognition, the big man grinned.

"Girly!"

"Hoo boy." Queenie groaned.

The smithy raised his eyebrow and stared at the interaction. "Acquainted, I presume?"

"More than that, pops. She's the one that beat me!" Harrison said with a grin.

The smithy blinked and turned to stare at Queenie. She quietly pulled out a dagger and began to peel and wrap its handle nervously. After a few seconds of tense silence, the smithy roared in laughter, snatching a moneybag from his son's hands and gave it back to her through the window in the shop. Queenie blinked and confusedly took the coins back.

Harrison's father grinned. "You get a discount today."

Queenie grabbed the coins with hesitation. "Wait. What? Why?"

"My son spoke highly of you. No other reason."

Hush quietly observed all this unfold and stared at Harrison. The impenetrable man simply grinned in response. "That I did! It's been a while since someone overwhelmed me *that* easily! How could I *not* speak highly of you?"

Queenie sighed as she stored her partially refunded money away. "Y...yeah. Sure. Whatever. How long is all this gonna take to make?"

The smithy ruffled his beard with one hand and tapped his workbench with another. "Eh...I'll have it done by the end of the day. Sound good?"

Hush was mildly surprised. Normally, these large orders took three to four days to complete. "Wait...seriously? How?"

"Pops has been in this business for a while, brother! He'll get it done." grinned Harrison.

Queenie shuffled her feet as she twirled her dagger between her fingers. "Well...if you say so. I'll be here at sunset." The siblings politely waved their farewells at the father and son then began to walk away. Upon reaching the city's plaza, they took a small look around at the surrounding community. Naive toddlers waddling around. Mothers arguing with vendors about prices. A man reading the local paper as he took a smoke break. A barista accidentally dropping a dirty cup on the stone floor. A few boys cackling as they chased a tiny bird. It was a world so...average. So normal. Despite that simple fact, he noticed his sister's eyes carrying a soft sense of sadness as she stared at the crowd of citizens going about their blandly, boring, day.

A day she had never experienced, and one she most likely would *never* be a part of.

So without exchanging a word, the siblings walked over to a nearby bench...and sat. They simply bore witness to a world that they were robbed from, and a lifestyle of those that the duo were quietly envious of.

CHAPTER 10

As Taba completed his twentieth lap, his mind raced with worry. Father, Geralt, Zanshin, Nancy, Little Stuart, and many more. Had...had he damned them by not killing the Overseer? No, his family could take care of themselves. They would be fine. And yet, a tiny voice nagged at the back of his mind, the same one that loved to consider every possibility. *"You've seen how strong the soldiers of Malapace are. Can you imagine them losing?"* Taba shook his head, trying to shake the thought away. He didn't even know *where* to begin organizing his thoughts. When Juliette had faced off against Geralt...their former mentor would have won: Taba's blessing confirmed it. However, the Misfits would have died in the crossfire by their new mentor's hand.

Despite that...Juliette's statements when she apologized with remorse to the injured villager? They were all genuine, from the bottom of her heart. Taba wasn't sure what to feel. Yes, she was their enemy...but she wasn't a *villain*. She was just a person doing what she thought was best. The same went for all the Gatekeepers *and* the Overseer. They weren't evil overlords who ran a dystopia: they were just...human.

After his twenty-third lap, he leaned against the townhall's wall and stared up at the sky. He had finally grasped what his heart had been struggling with: these "enemies" were good people. He didn't want them to die. However, his family were all good people as well. Both sides seemed to have conflicting interests. Neither side could survive as the other did. By not choosing to kill Babs, many good people would die. And yet...despite this knowledge, Taba could not take it upon himself to kill such a selfless leader who put her people first.

Taba grit his teeth, frustrated at...everything. His choice, the inevitable war, the impending deaths, so on. Oh, how he wanted to run from it all and to curl up into a ball. But...but Father had always stated how important it was to be firm with your choices. So, the teenager took a deep breath and slapped his cheeks. If someone had to shoulder this burden, he would rather it be him than his friends. He chewed his lips with more sturdy determination and noticed the slowly increasing foot traffic of the town hall. It would be more and more difficult to continue doing laps. Still, the teenager had many thoughts to organize. So, he jogged over to the agriculture fields. From his time in the city, Taba took note at how there were little farmers in that area in this time of day, which would make it a perfect spot to simply jog his last few laps.

The fields were small dirt strips with various plants. The more important the plant was, the more strips they would receive. For example, while an eggplant patch might be a few rows, the tomato patch stretched on for quite a while. As he reached the dirt path that surrounded the fields, he noticed two people busy at work. One seemed to be a boy wearing dirty clothes as he planted crops, while the other was harvesting bushels of wheat with a sugegasa to block out the sun. The boy wearing the slimy tank top noticed the sudden visitor and looked up, his eyes widening in surprise as he did, quickly averting his gaze once recognizing him.

Taba frowned as he jogged over to the boy. "Huh. Gary, right?"

The boy flinched and sheepishly looked up. "Y-yeah. Hi. Didn't expect to see you here."

"Eh. Same, Alright, have fun." Taba said.

"Wait wait wait. Really? You...don't have anything to say?"

"What's the issue?" Taba asked. "You're obviously busy, don't let me get in the way of your work."

"I'm not *working*. I'm training." Gary said with a scowl.

Taba raised an eyebrow as he looked at Gary's basket. "By...planting potatoes?"

"...Yeah."

Taba crossed his arms and considered the exercise method. As odd as it seemed, agriculture was strenuous work. With the sun beating down on your back and constantly moving to dig and plant crops, it was a task that required surprising stamina. Still, it wasn't a regiment that the questioner would partake in himself, but that was fine. If it worked for Gary, so be it.

The potato planter stood up, stretching his back as he did. He then stared at the boy with determined eyes. "I promise I'll beat you next time."

It was an innocent declaration with zero malice. Taba felt oddly honored that this stranger had declared him as a worthy benchmark to surpass, and strangely enough? The Misfit encouraged such behavior. "You'll beat me? Well...you can try, I guess. Good luck."

"Ah...thanks?"

The Misfit glanced over at the other harvester in curiosity. The moment he looked at her, she turned and faced him, lifting her hat as she did. As they locked eyes, the teenager could only blink as the woman grinned.

"...Sana?"

The Gatekeeper waved at him widely, a metal sickle in her hand. Taba turned to Gary and nodded to her. "I should probably talk to her. See you."

"Yep."

The teenager trotted over to the woman, who spun the sickles in her hand as she waited. Once he got face to face, he politely nodded to the Gatekeeper. "Didn't take you as a farmer."

"Someone's gotta do it, right?" Sana said with a smile. "Wanna help a bit?"

"I..." hesitated Taba.

She nodded to a work shed by the field. "Go grab a sickle from in there. It's soulmade, but it'll get the job done."

The teenager only had intentions to simply greet the woman. He had no desire to harvest grains. Sana nodded with understanding. "It's a good way to keep your mind off of things. Plus, I could use the company."

Taba flinched. *Man*, he didn't like how she could just seemingly peek into his mind like that. After a few seconds of deliberation, he pursed his lips and walked over to the shed slowly, grabbed a sickle, and returned to her.

"You ever harvest wheat before?"

"No."

The woman nodded to the harvest in front of her, grabbing a handful as she did. "First, grab the top." She yanked it slightly. "Pull a bit, but not enough to uproot it. Then..." She raked her tool through the bottom of the plant, cutting it free from the ground. "Voila. After that, just chuck it in that wheelbarrow."

Taba turned to his pile and attempted to replicate her actions, wincing at how sore it made his hand after only a few small tugs. Though he felt as though his physical strength was *much* higher than the Gatekeeper, he found himself falling behind the woman's steady pace.

After a few silent minutes of struggled grunting, he took a small break and stared in amazement as the Gatekeeper continued her work. "How are you so good at this? I don't think you're that much stronger than me, if you even *are* physically stronger than me."

"Experience," chuckled Sana as she continued harvesting. "You get used to the technique after a while. So, what's on your mind?"

"Wish you'd stop using your blessing for petty things like this." said Taba.

"I wasn't. Well, not on purpose. Even if I weren't, it's sprawled all over your face. So, what's on your mind?"

Taba had no reason to tell her anything. She was the enemy who had captured him and his friends, after all. Hell, he was *still* looking for opportunities to take her down. Despite it all, he sat down with a deep sigh, planting his own harvester in the ground. "The upcoming war. A lot of good people are about to die and I can't help but feel it's going to be because of me."

"Are *you* specifically killing people?" asked Sana with a frown.

"No. Well, maybe? I...I don't know."

The woman chuckled, causing a mild bit of anger to flare up in the boy. "What's so funny?" asked Taba.

She waved her hand, flecks of dirt flying off as she did. "Ah. It's just...the questioner is unsure of a question? A bit ironic, no?"

He pursed his lips. She had a point. The Gatekeeper then leaned on her hands and stared at the sky. "Well, can't help you with that, I guess."

"Huh?"

Sana shrugged as she gazed at the clouds. "I'm not some omnipotent god. I don't know the correct answer to everything. I'm just a girl trying her best in life. Sometimes I do good, sometimes I mess up. I can't tell you what's correct, but sounds like that's a pretty big burden on your heart."

"Big help you were." muttered Taba. He stared at the ground in frustration, unsure of anything. Suddenly, a clod of dirt hit his leg. The boy looked up in annoyance to see Sana kindly staring at him.

"Don't stare at every single problem and assume responsibility for each one," said Sana. "Do what you can. Do what you think is correct. It may take a while, but it'll work itself out."

He grit his teeth. "That won't just magically make the problems go away."

"You're... not wrong. Still, you aren't responsible for the actions of others." Sana said as she yanked out a weed. "If I get into a fight with someone and die, that's because I got into a fight...*not* because you didn't step in and stop the fight."

"So...just...don't protect my friends and family? Don't prevent their deaths?"

"No, you can protect them." Sana said over her shoulder.

"What you're saying is all contradictory," snapped Taba, letting his blade fall to the ground. "The *hell* are you talking about?"

Sana stopped harvesting and stared at the boy directly into his eyes, causing him to flinch. "I'm saying there's no 'one' correct answer. There's always numerous correct options. Just as how I want to protect my city, you may want to protect your family. Doesn't mean either of us are wrong for doing it, right?"

Taba curled his fists into the dirt, packing soil into his hands as he did. "No matter *what* option I pick...people *die*. I couldn't give a damn if someone scummy dies...but...***good*** people will die. If I act, someone dies. If I don't act, someone dies." The teenager grabbed his head, dirt slowly crumbling down his head as he did. "I...I don't...what do...what..."

Suddenly, Sana reached over and tightly hugged the boy in silence. Though his breathing slowed, his mind continued to race frantically as he tried to search for an option that could spare *everyone*. There *had* to be something he could do. Something. *Something.*

The Gatekeeper eventually pulled away from the boy with sorrowful eyes. "It's a tragedy, but...there is *no* absolute answer. Just know, we won't hate you if your choice ends up making you our enemies. Do what you think is correct."

"But-"

She brushed off the dirt on the boy's face. "You aren't a villain, nor are you a hero. You are simply...Taba. So, do what you can. That is all. Ok?"

He said nothing, softly pushed the Gatekeeper away, picked up his sickle, and continued to harvest wheat. Sana slowly stood up and did the same. They continued to quietly work for an hour before Taba put his tool down and walked away. Sana did not call after him, nor did she look in his direction.

He appreciated that kindness.

...

After washing up, he stood in front of the doors of the Overseer once more, hesitating as he did. After a few minutes of quiet deliberation, a soft but raspy voice echoed out from inside the room.

"You don't need to stay waiting outside. Come in."

Taba took a deep inhale and opened the doors with purpose. As usual, the Overseer sat in the middle of the room, completely blindfolded as she tapped her fingers at seemingly random intervals. With each small movement, her robes rippled with shimmering light. He wasn't sure of his decision just yet...so he simply stood there, stalling for as long as he could.

Some time passed before Babs took her blindfold off with a sigh. "Ironically, you're more considerate than my own damn children. Sit."

He glanced behind himself once more to ensure the doors were locked and sat down. The elderly woman didn't falter as she rolled up her sleeves with a nod. "State your mind."

Before he could lose his nerve, Taba quickly unsheathed his knife and pointed it at Malapace's leader. She didn't flinch and her pale eyes met the boy's gaze. "Is that your final decision?" asked the Overseer.

"If...if I don't do this, Dad might die. If not him, my Family, the Gatekeepers, and Juliette. This is the choice that provides the least amount of deaths." Taba said.

To his surprise, the old woman chuckled. "You aren't wrong. My head on a silver platter would surely reduce the amount of meaningless deaths. Still, is that your final decision?"

182

"...Yeah."

"Oh? If my death is all you wanted, then why not just stab me while I was 'overseeing'?" the Overseer said with a twinkle in her eye. "Surely, less work and risk, right? So, why do this?"

The boy said nothing, simply focusing on holding his knife firmly.

"Perhaps...you *wanted* me to resist? You wanted to be overpowered and lose your opportunity to kill me?" asked the Overseer.

Taba flinched. The small twitch caught her eye, causing her to sigh. "You poor thing. You aren't here to kill me. You're here to get rid of your burdens."

"Wh-"

The woman simply leaned forward until the bridge of her nose was an inch away from the knife's blade. "Unfortunately, that won't happen. The ball will remain in your court. I will not resist. Heck, I'm a blind elderly woman whose blessing allows her to watch others. How strong would I be in a fight?"

The Misfit blinked, slightly lowering his dagger as he did. "Wait. You're blind?"

She raised a finger and snapped it in front of her eye, not flinching as she did. "As blind as you are dense, yes. Surprised you couldn't deduce that yourself. So...what's your decision?"

Taba clenched his blade tightly...and dropped to the floor. "I...don't know. Objectively, the correct answer is to kill you...but I can't. You aren't bad. My gut is telling me that I would regret it if I were to kill you."

Babs scooched to the corner of her room and returned with a pot of cheap tea, pouring two cups out. She handed some of the tasteless water to the conflicted questioner. "Drink."

He took small sips with glazed eyes. The Overseer did the same. The only sounds that filled the room were careful puffs to cool off the drink, cautious sips, and sighs of relief upon drinking some.

After their cups were empty, Babs spoke softly. "Leadership is the least coveted role to the most qualified of leaders. Being in charge of the fate of so many. Planning for the unplannable. Coerced into weighing the lives of two different good people. Turning a blind eye to those who actively need help. It's torture...and I'm sorry you've been placed in such a position."

"What should I do?" Taba asked as he blankly stared at his teacup. "I'm nineteen, why am I responsible for so many lives? Why do good people have to die do to my decision?"

The old woman's eyes gained another wrinkle. "Well...if not you, then who? If *you're* struggling this much, could you imagine others in your shoes? How would they act? How would they feel?"

To his own surprise, the boy chuckled. "I wouldn't dare want my friends to be responsible for this."

"And that makes you a quality leader. So...will you kill me? I won't hate you if you do." asked Babs.

"It's the objectively right answer..." Taba said as he sheathed his weapon. "...But I'm absolutely certain that killing you would be a mistake: it goes against everything Dad has taught me."

"Then...what will you do? Will you side with your...'Dad'?"

He closed his eyes tightly...then opened them with conviction. "As of right now, yes. Me and my friends are. When the war rolls around, we will side with them."

"Even if that means the death of many good people?"

The Misfit clenched his fists but held his chin up high. "Their deaths will be on my name. Their blood on my hands. No one will wear the label of 'murderer' but me."

Babs smiled with an upturned nose. "You are more of a man than the majority of whelps I've seen. I look forward to the day when you kill me."

He tightened his lips and got up to leave. Just as he was about to exit the doors, Babs called out in a nearly taunting manner. "By the way... you said 'as of right now'. Does that mean there's a chance that you'll be swayed to fight for us in the upcoming war?"

Taba said nothing and left the room.

...

Sana looked up with a smile. "You look...better."

Taba said nothing but simply held the sickle in his hand, holding a defensive position. Despite this clear stance of aggravation, Sana simply continued to harvest her grains with a hum. He already knew that it was impossible to kill her: his questioning proved it. However, he wanted to know the *gap* in their powers. How much stronger was she? How far did he have to grow?

With that in mind, he ran full sprint towards her.

Will she dodge my blow? **O** *Will an overhead stab connect?* **Ө X** *Will a leg sweep connect?* **Ө X** *Will an elbow to her right ear connect?* **X** *Will she counter attack?* **O** *Will she attack with a kick?* **X** *Will...*

The Gatekeeper was seamlessly dodging all of his blows without too much of a worry, humming a merry tune as she did. It was, well, frustrating to say the least. Every time his blessing said something *should* connect...it would change in real time. Attacks that were unpredictable were dodged casually as she reaped more wheat. What

185

would have killed many soulbearers was being casually sidestepped by a woman in a dress. How the *hell* was she so mobile? What was her blessing? What...

Taba blinked, a moment of brilliance suddenly striking him. He quickly turned and tossed his sickle in the direction of Gary. In a split second, the calm joy on Sana's face vanished in unexpected fear as she channeled soul into her legs and blew past Taba at frightening speeds. Though his sickle was thrown with no murderous intent and would have missed the boy, Sana quickly caught the thrown weapon before he had even turned around.

She took a soft exhale and turned to the questioner with a disapproving frown, as though to say '*Not cool*'. Almost immediately, Taba felt guilty and stared at the ground. However, as he stared at his dusty shoes, he couldn't help but feel his mind racing wildly. She *hadn't* been able to read that move. The omnipotent Gatekeeper was caught off-guard. There *had* to be a rea-

Suddenly, he felt a hand lightly smack the top of his head. "Don't go throwing your weapons at others. If you have a problem, fight *me*. Ok?"

"Sorry, sorry. I was just...sorry." winced Taba.

She huffed and handed the sickle back to the teenager. "If you're *really* sorry, help me harvest the rest of this field. Keep me company."

The Misfit quietly took the sickle and turned to the field, quietly noting the distance that Sana had essentially closed within only a few seconds. It was inhuman: she had essentially closed the distance of around fifty meters within *two* seconds. Making up his mind, he quickly turned to where Sana had left off and began to cut the wheat patch next to hers.

"Would be more efficient if you split up on the other side of the field, no?" said Sana.

"Eh, you said you wanted company."

"That I did," she said with a smile. "Let's get to it."

As they quietly harvested wheat, the boy hesitated as he was unsure of how to properly word his questioning. After a minute, Sana cleared her throat. "You can just...ask, y'know?"

"Ok...what *exactly* is your blessing?"

"That's a fun little secret for you to discover, hm?" Sana said with a light chuckle.

Taba sighed as he chucked his handful of wheat into the wheelbarrow. "Figured you wouldn't answer that, but I really want to know about that speed you just produced. How did you close that distance in *that* short of a time?"

"Mmm...you need to be able to properly move soul all around your body, first. Once you do, it's only a matter of using your soul in various ways." Sana then began to count on her fingers as she looked absentmindedly into the sky. "You can bottle up your soul and then use the pressure to blast off, you can 'move' the soul with such force that your entire body is thrown as a result, the list goes on."

"But...how?" Taba asked. "Just using soul manipulation is draining. Hell, I flat out don't think it's worth using due to how much soul it uses and requires."

"You aren't wrong! So, that begs the question: how can one easily use soul manipulation to the extent I did?"

"Well...you could either find a way to reduce the amount of soul used in soul manipulation...or..."

The Gatekeeper stopped her harvest and stared at the boy with a encouraging grin. "Hmm?"

"...or...if the soulbearer had an *insane* amount of soul in their soulwell...I supposed they could afford to just...*use* soul manipulation whenever. Still, that seems improbable."

"Why is that?"

The boy scratched his head with sweaty hands, slightly dismissing his idiotic thought. "Well...because you can't exactly *increase* the amount of soul you have. Sure, you gain a bit of soul with each passing year as you mature and you also gain a bit from training...but the amount you gain isn't drastic enough to the point where you'd be able to casually use soul manipulation. Those are the only two methods I could think of to increase your soul: I don't think there are other ways."

Sana opened her mouth as to say something, but closed it. She then turned to her field once more. "You're right."

Taba stared at her backside.

Was that a lie?

O

So...she was hiding something. Guess it was because he was still her enemy. The boy shrugged and dropped the topic, continuing his harvest as well.

As the sun slowly set, Taba got up and stretched. His hands, though not blistered, were red and sticky. His back was sore. As he got up, his knees cracked with a concerningly loud snap. Sweat had covered his entire body and exhaustion suddenly overtook the Misfit. Following his queue, Sana got up with a wide stretch as well.

The Gatekeeper yawned with a hand over her mouth, the other hand securing her sickle to her waistband. She then nodded to Gary, who continued to plant crops. "Lets call it a day. Go grab Gary, I'll treat you guys to some good ol' soba."

Taba shrugged. Free food was free food. He lightly jogged over to the other boy and tapped his shoulder. Gary turned around with exhaustion sprawled on his face.

"She's calling it a day and wants to buy us food. Let's go."

Gary groaned as he plopped down in the dirt. "I'm...ugh. *Man.* How the hell does she do this every day?"

Taba blinked. "Pardon? *Every* day? I thought she was just doing this today to pass time?"

"Nope." Gary said. "Hell, she upkeeps a solid thirty percent of the fields by herself. I don't even know how or *why*. Figured that it was the big secret behind why she was so strong, so I wanted to give it a shot. From how tired I am...it honestly might just be it."

"The secret to omnipotence is planting peanuts, hm?" Taba said, stifling a laugh,

"Hell, it might just be. Help me up, I want food."

...

The three of them entered the half empty shop with its only patrons being elderly citizens. Once they sat down, an older server came to greet them with shaky hands and a warm smile. Sana returned his greeting and held up three fingers. The man nodded, jotted something on his notepad, then headed into the kitchen. Sana gestured the boys to a booth and the party scooted in, sitting on thin cushions that lay on the hard wooden benches. The old man returned with iced water and then with their soba noodles.

189

As they silently slurped their noodles with exhaustion, Taba took quiet note on how the others ate. Gary was hastily devouring the noodles while Sana took small, calm bites. As Gary was finishing up his meal, Sana raised her hand and quietly ordered another meal for the famished boy. As the old man gently placed the extra meal in front of him, Gary slowed his eating speed with sheepishness.

"Eat, before the soup...soup? Sauce? Broth? Well, eat before it gets warm."

Taba began to quietly slurp his noodles as Gary choked down his last bite. After drinking a glass of water, Gary hesitated between staring at his next bowl and looking up at the Gatekeeper.

Sana nodded. "You can ask."

Gary cleared his throat. "Right. Uh...this is just out of sheer curiosity, but in your opinion, who's the strongest Gatekeeper?"

"Oh?"

He reached into his back pocket and pulled out a small notebook with a pencil attached. "Like, there's *tons* of discussion surrounding you guys. The immortal, the untouchable, and the omnipotent. I mean, you guys have *so* many fans and there are so many theories about your bles-"

Sana held up a hand, cutting off Gary's words instantly. She smiled with sad eyes. "You flatter us...but we're just humans. We aren't some 'unfathomable gods': don't put us on pedestals."

Gary's face was aghast. He flipped a few pages into his notebook, pointed at a line, slightly turned his notebook as to show the Gatekeeper...but stopped. With seemingly great difficulty, he nodded and closed his notebook. Sana smiled and quietly slurped her noodles.

While chewing, she stared at the ceiling in deep thought. She swallowed her food and spoke with curiosity. "I can't really *say* which of us is the strongest. I think that the others are stronger, but I also imagine they would say the same about me. I can say what *traits* are stronger among my friends though."

Gary paused for a split second before excitedly gripping his pencil and flipping to a blank page. "Yeah???"

"For example...between me, G, and Patchy...G is the smartest and the most emotional." Sana said. "Patchy is the most level headed and the best cook. I don't know what I would excel in, if I'm being honest...but I'm glad that those two consider me their friend."

Gary frowned as he flipped through his notes, scanning the pages. After a few seconds, he tapped his notepad with raised eyebrows. "Honestly, from my notes? I think you're the most popular, at least. Tons of people seem to like you for varying reasons, and even more find you approachable. It's hard to find someone who hates you: the few who do just seem to be jealous."

"I...see. Thank you." Sana said, her ears slightly pink.

Taba continued chewing his noodles while observing the conversation. Even *then*, Sana seemed surprised. She wasn't omnipotent, there were obvious gaps in her blessing's abilities. The question was...what was her blessing?

The Gatekeeper took note of his observation and nodded mid-slurp. "You have a question too?"

"Ah...no, it's nothing."

"If you say so." Sana shrugged. A few minutes passed before Sana suddenly perked up with excitement. "She's back."

Taba looked up with confusion. "Who?"

Sana got up and nodded to the boys. "Let's go greet her." She then waved to the old server who had given them soba. "Add it to my tab, Suga."

The old man shook his head. "Nonsense, I wouldn't ask payment from such a youngin'."

"No, I'm paying you back. If you don't remember, I'm doubling how much I give you." said Sana.

"You're the same old child. Go." he chuckled.

The Gatekeeper excitedly waved over the boys and they quickly jogged over to the front gate. Upon approaching, they stared at an empty road.

"So...why did we run?" asked Taba.

"Well...sometimes, you get to *see* it." Sana responded.

Gary hunched over, winded. "No...no one's here. Why...couldn't we walk?"

She elbowed the tired boy, nodding to a small figure way off into the field. "There she is. Shush."

And so...the boys stared quietly as they saw a silver line flicker around a form. As it approached the city, their breaths grew more silent as their eyes widened, fearing they might miss a single step. A soft sashay, a twirling staff, graceful leaps, and the setting sun reflecting rays of light off of her brush's bristles. Soon, her rustling kimono and bright lipstick came into view, her fox mask's hollow eyes staring into the void.

Both boys were captivated, but only Taba's mind quietly whispered calculated thoughts. *She isn't* just *dancing...she's setting up her blessing in advance. If that's the case...* He stared at Sana, who stopped watching her friend's performance to quizzically stare at the teenager. However, after seeing his stern gaze...she immediately understood and smiled softly, turning back to Juliette's dance.

Seeing her reaction, he quickly asked two questions. *Did...is she coming back from setting up her blessing? O Does her blessing last indefinitely in the air? O*

Taba blinked and stared at his mentor with amazement. She wasn't making random visits to various towns: she was setting up her blessing for any future endeavors. But...that was...

"...so *dumb*."

Sana's ears perked up upon hearing the phrase, but did not defend her friend. Instead, she nodded. "Yeah, she's a bit dumb. However, she works harder than *all* of the Gatekeepers combined. I don't think that fool knows the definition of rest."

After a few more steps, Juliette stopped her performance and packed away her brush. She then walked up to the trio with dainty steps. "I wish you'd stop watching me like that, San-san."

Sana grinned. "But it's so *pretty*."

His mentor looked at Taba with a tilted head. "Surprised to see you here, though."

He blinked moisture back into his eyes, clearing his throat before speaking. "...I was dragged along."

"Mm. Well, I guess you now understand more on how my blessing works." said Juliette.

"Yeah. You're...man," Taba said while shaking his head. "Why?"

Gary stared back and forth at the exchange, awe and confusion plastered on his weary face. Sana said nothing and quietly observed as well.

Juliette rubbed her neck and rolled her shoulder. After a moment, she spoke softly:

"I don't think I could forgive myself if I didn't. That's all."

With those words, she walked into the city as the sun died behind her.

CHAPTER 11

"Once more."

Hush groaned as he stanced up for the ninth time in a row, preparing to "dodge" yet again. With sweat beaded on her face, Queenie put pressure into her arm, trying to visualize opening a window in her storage. She firmly grabbed the "windowsill"...yet when she pulled, the storage simply "moved" with her arm. No space opened up. To any outsider, it looked as though a girl were sweating buckets while straining her arm through the air. Queenie scowled as she flopped to the floor, pulling at the grass as she did. Why couldn't she do it? What was she doing wrong? What was so different now, as opposed to when she was exhausted during the mutant frog? Why wasn't the window opening anymore?

"Let's call it a day," Hush sighed. "It's nearly time to pick up your order at the smithy, anyhow."

She grumbled as she threw a clod of grass. "Yeah, yeah. This is dumb. Why can't I do it again? I'm more energized and prepared. The hell am I doing wrong?"

"I dunno. Worry about that after picking up your stuff."

Queenie's eye twitched with irritation as she punched her brother in the shoulder. He rolled his eyes, got up, and lent a hand to his sister. She accepted with annoyance and the two set off to the smithy's.

Once they got there, they saw Harrison's father chewing a bit of jerky as he adjusted his glasses, staring at a blueprint. Not saying anything, they watched as the big man quickly crafted a chair. What would have taken the average smithy an hour took the man mere minutes.

He noticed his audience and looked up, removing his glasses as he did. "Oui, you lot are here? 'Bout time." The man reached below the counter and pulled up a box, the ammunition clattering inside as it slammed on the bench. He nodded to them as he slid the box through the shop's window slit. "Aighty, y'all are set. Get home safe, ya hear?"

Queenie frowned, the bag of coins in her hand slightly slinking. "Uh...don't I need to-?"

"Pah! I gave you my word, you get a discount."

"With all due respect, sir...this is closer to a robbery than a discount. You sure?" Hush asked. "We won't return this even if you ask."

"Oh dear, I guess I got robbed. Guess I'll have to cut me losses tonight. Not much I can do, eh?" Harrison's father grinned.

Queenie opened the crate and peered inside. She then ran her fingers through the shells, feeling the weight between all of them. She quickly pulled a gun out of her storage, loaded a bullet, then lifted the gun to the smithy. He simply raised an eyebrow as he stared down the gun's barrel. Before she realized what she was doing, Hush smacked her arm with a *bit* more force than normal. He then turned to the man and gave a small bow. "*So* sorry about that. My sister is a bit of an idiot."

She stared at her brother with confusion until it clicked. Though she had intended to simply feel the weight of the bullet in the gun, to spectators, she had pointed a loaded gun to the man who crafted her bullets. Whoops.

"Well...guess it really *is* a robbery now, eh? Hah!" The smithy said with a grin.

Queenie stored her gun and the bullets with mild embarrassment. Before her pride got the best of her, she muttered to her shoes. "Sorry, force of habit."

"You normally pull loaded guns on yer smithies?"

"No, I try to get a feel for the we-"

The man roared with laughter as he waved them off. "Oh, girly! You ain't the first one, relax. I saw no ill intent in yer eyes, yer good in me book. Now, go on home, shoo."

Hush held his sister's head down in a forceful bow before they melted off into the night. Once they were out of sight, he smacked his sister's shoulder with a harsh stare. "What did I say? Stop feeling for bullet weight in front of the smithies."

"And risk getting ripped? Hell no."

"You're an idiot." Hush said.

Queenie rolled her eyes. "I'm only an idiot if *all* smithies are trustworthy. Half of them are scammers, so I would say I'm valid in what I do."

"Whatever. What do you want to eat?"

Only after he had asked that did Queenie realize how hollow her stomach felt. She frowned as she rubbed her stomach. "I dunno. What's in the area?"

"No idea, but why don't we just walk around? Something will catch our eye eventually, right?"

The two of them walked around for a few minutes, peering at the candlelit and electric lights of varying stores, each one having different themes to them. Some were obviously more successful than others, but even these less fortunate restaurants seemed to have their niche customer base.

After a while, the siblings gave up and walked into the bar they had initially met Juliette in, curious if the place also carried decent food. As the bell clinked dully as they walked into the gloomy atmosphere, the place was fairly empty with only a few patrons tucked away in a few booths. Upon their entry, the stern bartender looked with a nod.

Seeing Queenie, he tilted his head, his frown covered by his moustache. "No alcohol, got it?"

She scowled, not because Queenie was looking to get drunk, but because the girl despised restrictions of any kind. Hush nodded in acknowledgement, and they sat in a booth that was tucked away at the back.

Shortly after sitting down, a familiar girl walked over. The straps of her work apron were crisscrossed over her neck, her scruffily hair doing nothing to hide the mild surprise on her face. "Oh, you guys?"

Queenie stared at her sides, revealing sleeves that led to nothing. She raised an eyebrow to the girl as Hush choked on his saliva. After taking a few seconds to compose himself, he took a slow inhale to nod to the girl. "A...Alexandria, right? Uh...hi?"

"Cool, cool," she grinned. "You remembered to say hi. What can I get yall?"

"Wait, you work here? I thought you were doing grocery shopping for your mom?" Queenie asked.

The waitress tilted her head to the pub's kitchen. "Mom's in the back as the chef. Dad's in the front as the bartender. I'm over here as the waitress. We ran out of ingredients so they sent me on an errand. Now, what do yall want? Any drinks for now? Beer?"

Before Queenie could speak, Hush frowned. "Your dad said no to alcohol."

"Dad's boring. He can't say 'no' to me, so if yall want it...just ask." said Alexandria.

Feeling pleased in having the restriction lifted, Queenie triumphantly stuck out her chest. Her brother noticed and rolled his eyes. "Just some iced water for us two, thanks for the offer though. What do you guys have for food?"

"Chicken wings." shrugged Alexandria.

"Normal or mutant chicken?" asked Queenie.

Alexandria stared at the younger sister with a judgmental glare. "Like we could afford mutant chicken. It's just normal chicken wings lathered in some sauce."

"You suck at marketing your food."

"You suck at common sense."

"What the he-"

Hush cleared his throat *loudly*, cutting off the two girls. "Just some wings, then. Twenty-four pieces, or whatever your largest serving size is. Thanks."

Alexandria nodded and headed back to the kitchen. Once she was out of earshot, Queenie ducked in and let out a loud whisper. "How do you think she's gonna carry the food and drinks?"

"*Dude*! You can't *ask* that."

"It's a fair question, and I'll be *damned* if I see her waddle back with my water cup in between her toes."

Their question was answered a minute later as the armless woman walked back with a little tray set up against her apron, with the sheet being firmly attached to some string that draped around her neck. She carefully made her way to the table, being careful to not spill any water as she did. Once she reached the table, she lifted her neck and leaned forward, causing the tray to gently slide the water cups onto the table.

She gestured to her armless sleeves. "Can't really 'place' the glasses in front of y'all, sorry. Be back in a few with the wings."

Queenie frowned. Before her brother could stop her, she asked a blunt question. "Why don't you use your blessing to make arms?"

Hush glared at his sister as Alexandria sighed, obviously used to the question. "Eh. I don't wanna. That's all."

"That's it? Sounds needlessly dumb."

"Yeah, you're not wrong," Alexandria responded. "Still, if I'm able to do what *you* guys can do *without* arms? I dunno...but that thought just tickles me funny."

Hush looked down at his lap with embarrassment from his sister's crude wording. However, Queenie was stunned with a shocking amount of respect, unconsciously nodding as she stared in awe. "You're...kinda cool, y'know that?"

Alexandria blinked, taken aback by the complement. Her face flushed slightly upon hearing the words, a mix of emotions on her face. After a few seconds, she stammered out unintelligible words and shuffled back to the kitchen.

Once she was gone, it was *Hush's* turn to lean in with a harsh whisper. "What the *hell* is wrong with you? Where's your sense of decency?"

Queenie stuck out her tongue. "It's paired right next to your sense of social awareness, shut up. She's cool. Plus, it isn't every day I can talk to an armless chick, so you know *damn* well I'm gonna."

"Show some sensitivity. It isn't polite to constantly jab at the fact that she has no arms." Hush said.

Queenie tilted her head with confusion. "That's how you see it? For *me,* I think its rude to pretend that she *has* arms. May as well get out of the way that she doesn't have arms and then act normal, right? I think that's better than faking that her being armless is a normal occurrence."

Hush sighed. "I'm not gonna be able to change your mind about this, but still. It wouldn't kill you to hold your tongue every once and a while."

"And it wouldn't kill *you* to show boldness here and there, dingle weed."

The siblings argued their petty fight for a few minutes, with Queenie occasionally pulling out randomly stored trash from her storage to chuck at her brother. Right before he could retaliate, the duo saw Alexandria take slow steps from behind the bar to slowly bring over their plate of chicken. She carefully extended her neck and tilted it downwards, the sizzling, battered meat crunching as it slightly rolled with her movements. The siblings brought the plate closer to the center, taking a small whiff as they did. Queenie grabbed a wing and abruptly bit into it, huffing hot air as she forcefully ate the piping hot wing. Her brother rolled his eyes and gave small thanks to their waitress. Before the armless woman could return to the bar, Queenie swallowed her bite and grabbed the hem of Alexandria's apron. She turned back with mild annoyance, staring in confusion at the sudden action.

Queenie pointed at the wing. "This is damn good. That's all."

"Uh...thanks? Not gonna lie, didn't take you to be the complementing type." said Alexandria.

The younger sister put the wing down on her plate. "So...food's good. Drinks are good. Atmosphere is good. Why is this place not thriving?"

The waitress shuffled her feet as Hush choked on his food. "Uh...that's a bit...y'know?"

Queenie leaned back in her chair with a raised eyebrow. "If you aren't comfy admitting your mistakes to others, y'all aren't ever gonna improve. Seri-"

Hush coughed loudly, cutting his sister off. He then turned to Alexandria with sheepishness. "Sorry about her, she's a bit...dull when it comes to decency. I hope you can forgive her."

"Uh...I'm...gonna go to the back. Yeah."

Alexandria hurried off and Hush glared at his sister. "First you mock how she doesn't have arms, then you ask why her family's business is failing? *Queenie.*"

Queenie sulked, tearing into her chicken as she did. Oddly enough, though she felt as though she had done nothing wrong...the younger sister felt *bad* for what she had done. She had asked average questions with no malice in enemy territory, it made no sense. So, why did she feel guilt?

Hush sighed as he calmly chewed a wing. After swallowing, he nodded to his sister. "Did you mean to hurt her?"

"...How could she have gotten hurt? It...isn't my fault."

"Cool, so you didn't mean to hurt her. Go apologize then."

"Bu-"

"Go apologize. Doesn't matter if you think you did nothing wrong," said Hush. "You hurt her feelings, right? So, apologize for *that*, then try to explain your side of things when the time is right."

"Why does it matter?" Queenie sulked. "She's an enemy, right?"

Hush stared at his sister with tired, but understanding eyes. "I get it. If that's the excuse you want to use, fine. Do whatever you want."

Queenie silently chewed, the delightful wings suddenly having lost their flavor. It wasn't like her to feel regret like this. The more she chewed, the more the pit in her stomach grew. After a while, she started to uncomfortably shift in her seat. The girl then pulled out a dagger and began to fiddle with it to calm her nerves. Hush, noticing all this, said nothing and just sipped his water.

When Alexandria returned in a few minutes to refill their waters, the younger sister blurted out a surprisingly sudden apology. "Sorry. I...didn't mean to offend...I guess."

"Oh. Didn't take you to be the type to apologize." Alexandria said with mild surprise.

Hush slowly sipped his water, a small twinkle of pride in his eyes. "Neither did I."

Her face flush with embarrassment, Queenie stared at her plate. Still, the pit of guilt had shrunk. Guess it was worth it. Before she could second guess herself, Queenie blurted out an invitation. "Wanna sit down?"

Alexandria blinked, taking a slight step back as she did. She cleared her throat, hesitated, glanced around the restaurant, then jogged back to the bar counter. After talking with her dad for a few minutes, the father huffed and placed three drinks on her tray. The armless woman then powerwalked back to the booth, slid the drinks back onto the table, then scooted in next to Queenie. As she did, the tray around her beck folded up into a surprisingly compact necklace.

Oddly enough, *she* seemed embarrassed too. "I...uh, dad said he would watch the tables for now, so I...can sit for a bit. Yeah."

Hush stared at the bottles that she had brought over. "...Beer?"

"Y-yeah."

"Haven't seen this brand before," Queenie said as she stared at the brand. "Is it good?"

"I dunno, but it sells out well." said Alexandria. She suddenly blinked and swore under her breath. "Crap, didn't bring a bottle opener. My bad, I'll be right back."

Before Alexandria could get up, Queenie grabbed a bottle opener from her storage and then popped the tops off of all the bottles. The armless woman stared in mild surprise. "Huh? What...huh?"

Though initially confused, the younger sister's mouth slightly opened in realization. "Oh...you were unconscious during the remainder of the bracket fight. This is your first time seeing my blessing, right? Well, don't worry about it. More importantly..."

She gestured to the opened bottle. "How are you, uh...how are you gonna drink it?"

In response, Alexandria grabbed the bottle in her mouth, tilted her head upwards, then put the bottle down, licking her lips after she had done so.

204

"Like that."

Queenie whistled slightly, then nodded to the chicken. "How do you eat that?"

"Same as the beer."

"Man, just make arms."

"Nah."

The trio slowly ate and drank their meal. Hush tried his best to pay no mind to Alexandria's eating pace, while Queenie poked fun at the girl here and there. Surprisingly, the armless woman didn't seem to mind, instead taking jabs at Queenie in return. After a few awkward minutes, the girls began to share laughs as the alcohol slowly began to work it's way in their system. It wasn't enough for them to be drunk, but the girls loosened up any tension that had existed prior.

Alexandria leaned back into her booth, staring at the ceiling. "Earlier, you asked why we aren't doing so hot. Well, mom and dad refuse to tell me...but I think it's my fault."

Hush leaned in. Between the three of them, he was the only one who hadn't touched his beer. "Why?"

With her neck, she gestured to her stubs. "I'm a slow server. Last thing people want is slow service when they're hungry...especially when there are other alternatives."

"Then grow arms." Queenie said as she sipped her beer.

"I should...but I'm just being stubborn," Alexandria hollowly chuckled. "I feel like if I did, I 'lose'. I don't know how to explain it."

"I kinda get you, weirdly enough. So, what are you gonna do about it?" asked Queenie.

"No idea."

Hush shrugged, sipping water. "Do what you can, that's all you can do."

Alexandria scoffed as she picked up a bit of chicken with her teeth, speaking through huffs and chews. "Thanks, genius."

As Queenie nibbled a bone, she suddenly took note of a lanky figure scratching something on a clipboard. Darting her eyes to the man, she immediately "recognized" the dark cloak with the drooped hood, accompanied by the thin, bony hand with uncut fingernails. He got up from his table to leave, not bothering to leave a payment as usual, and began to walk out the door.

Queenie's blood ran cold, quickly withdrawing a slimy bead from her storage before he could turn the corner.

Suddenly, the female Misfit blinked. What happened? Her answers were answered when she felt the palm of her hand feel slimy. Double checking her pockets, she took note of the dreaded swamp-green pellet that rest in her hand. She looked at her brother with serious eyes. Though he had no idea what was happening, he met her sternness and nodded.

Queenie pulled out a bag of coins from her storage and plopped it in front of Alexandria. "Thanks. Something came up. We need to go. Keep the change."

Alexandria blinked, staring at the bag. "Huh? Wh-"

The siblings abruptly scooted out of the booth (with Queenie climbing over Alexandria's body), and the duo hastily exited the bar. Once they did, Queenie's eyes darted around to look for the cloaked figure, frustrated in finding nothing.

Hush firmly grabbed her shoulder. "What happened."

She grimly pulled out the bead from her pocket. His eyes widened. "...Zanshin?"

"Yeah. He was here."

"When? How long? Why?"

"You know I don't know the answer to those questions."

Hush cursed, rubbing his hand through his hair as he closed his eyes. After a few moments, he opened his eyes with a nod. "Let's reconvene with Taba. We need to talk."

...

The teenager sat on his bed, rubbing his face with his hands. "...C ripes. *Zanshin?* This early?"

"Yeah. No mistake about it, there's no way I would pull this thing out unless I saw him."

Taba muttered as he hugged his pillow. "So...guess Father is seriously planning for war, if he's having Zanshin scout out the place."

The Misfits sat in the room with grim expressions. Zanshin was part of Father's Family. For the most part, he was a peaceful man...which was good, considering how his ability could be used to to a do whatever he wanted if he really wanted to.

Queenie placed the bead on Taba's desk, who frowned at the small mess it left. She nodded to the questioner. "So, chief...what do we do? Do we tell these guys? Do we back up Father?"

"What do you guys feel like? Be honest: are you guys sided with Malapace or with Father?" asked Taba.

The siblings hesitated. Though it was brief, both of them faltered. They had spent their entire lives with Father and the family. Of course they would side with him: the small time they had spent in Malapace wouldn't shake their loyalty. And yet...

Queenie and Taba exchanged glances before nodding slightly. "Of course, we're with Father. Still...I don't want this war." they responded.

Taba sighed, obviously expecting this answer. Whether it was due to his blessing or his intuition, she wasn't sure. "I'm in the same boat," he said. "However...this fight *will* happen. There is nothing we can do to prevent it. In that case, how do you want to approach this? Should we fight? Should we stand back? What does your gut say?"

To her surprise, Hush spoke up. "Well...the way I see it, I don't see a world where the Family loses: even *if* their opponents knew everything."

Taba gave a soft smile. "Oddly enough? I feel the same. So, here's what we'll do..."

...

The next morning, the Misfits stood council with the Overseer. The three Gatekeepers stood by her side, each of them having concerned, yet confused, expressions.

"So, repeat what you said?" Babs asked.

Taba stepped up with strong eyes. "Father has scouted this place. War will happen in Malapace. You will lose. Please, surrender: I don't want meaningless casualties."

Their audience had differing reactions. Sana had a concerned expression, G seemed outraged, and Patchy seemed amused. However, the Overseer? She held no notable expression, with only exhaustion painted in her eyes.

The first one to step up was G, a vein pulsing in his neck. "You sure as hell got balls demanding surrender in our city. You s-"

Sana held out her arm to push the bald man back. She looked at Taba with a tilted head. "'You will lose', is that a boast? Or is that a 'fact', proven by your blessing?"

"My blessing doesn't work to such a high extent," Taba said as he shook his head. "I'm speaking my mind, based on what I know about my Family and the skills I've seen from you all. Sure, I can't say with 100% certainly that you will lose, but I do *not* see a world where you win."

"So...despite being overwhelmed by all of us, you *still* think we would lose in an all out war? *Really*?" Patchy asked.

Queenie cleared her throat. "I'm with Taba here. The fact that you guys don't even know that you were scouted yesterday proves you're all outmatched. Sure, in a fight, you guys might stand a chance...but what about the citizens? The merchants? Would they survive the crossfire?"

"If you want to fight, I won't stop you. However, *please* don't try to prevent the inevitable," Taba begged. "Just surrender, and I'll put in a word with Father to spare as many lives as possible. I swear it on my honor."

Babs said nothing, quietly sipping tea. Once her cup was drained, she stared at the trio with white irises. "Is this your conviction?"

"Yes, this is our stance." responded Hush.

"Then why tell us?" she asked.

The boys hesitated, so Queenie rolled her eyes and crossed her arms. "Doesn't matter if you know about the scouting and the war. You'll lose regardless. *That's* how outclassed you guys are right now. So, can w-"

Suddenly, a blur of flesh rushed her. On sheer instinct, Queenie pulled a chain to drag her to the ground with one arm, and with the other arm she pulled a dagger out to counterattack. She held it up to her assailant's arm, but he didn't seem to give a damn as he plunged his arm into the weapon to grab her throat, raising her into the air. Spots flickered into her vision as she began to choke. The violent Gatekeeper sneered. "*Outclassed*? You *sure* that's the word you're looking for?"

Though her windpipe was being crushed, her glare held strong. G saw her unwavering stare, scowled, and let her go, sending the girl tumbling to the floor. As she gasped for air, a bloody dagger clattered to the ground as the Gatekeeper returned to his spot, uninjured as usual. Hush knelt to his sister's feet, checking her throat out of worry. She held up a hand to let him know she was okay, making sure not to break eye-contact with the other Gatekeepers.

Taba, a bit shaken from seeing Queenie attacked, still held his chin up. "I know what you are capable of. Really. However, I also know my Family. You guys would be obliterated, and that isn't even mentioning Father himself."

"I can admire and respect you, boy," Babs said with a smile. "However, I have chosen these Gatekeepers, not to be some glorious soldiers or idols for the citizens. They are, quite literally, *Gatekeepers*. They will not fall, nor will they let the people behind them perish. I trust them with that duty."

"So...your answer is..."

She nodded. "I will take this war, not because I think we will win, but because I can't imagine my Gatekeepers failing their duty. That is all."

Queenie, though her throat was still sore, looked at her friend with worried eyes. His face was shaped into something awful, but he closed his eyes with a small nod. "Well...I...I tried, I guess."

210

"And I respect that you did, boy. Truly, thank you. You are a kind soul."

Suddenly, the Overseer twitched as she grabbed her blindfold. She immediately tied it around her face and sat motionless, seemingly observing...something. After a few seconds, she untied her blindfold with a grimace. She nodded to Sana. "Go to the third gate. You'll see the mutant."

"Is it something dang-"

Babs shook her head. "No, nothing lethal...but go nonetheless. Bring the brats, too."

Sana hesitated, but nodded. She then looked at the Misfits. "Can you guys keep up with me?"

Queenie, though still trying to stabilize her breathing, nodded. She noticed this, sighed, then turned to G. "Give her the pill, G."

"But-"

"*Now.*"

G flinched, but sulked as he walked over and handed the pill over. Queenie choked the tablet down as he rubbed her back, and to her surprise, she immediately felt better. The girl stood up and rolled her shoulders. "Yeah, we can keep up."

"Very well." Sana said with forced cheer.

She immediately bolted from the Overseer's room and the Misfits ran at full sprint in pursuit. Queenie expected Sana to be fast, but she was running at *absurd* speeds. Within a few seconds, Sana had vanished from the siblings' eyes. The only one *barely* able to keep up was Taba, who was huffing and puffing as he moved his entire body like an overclocked machine to keep her in his sightline.

In short, Hush, was barely keeping up with Queenie (who was using chains to propel herself further), who was barely following Taba, who was barely keeping up with Sana. It was a weird conga line of sorts.

After a minute of high speed pursuit, the Misfits all hunched over, wheezing as they tried to catch their breath. The boys had their hands on their knees, while Queenie hugged her stomach in an attempt to not throw up.

Sana, taking a few shallow breaths, stared at the Misfits with fascination. "Huh. Didn't *actually* expect you guys to keep up. Well done."

Taba, the first one to slowly recover, stared up with exhaustion. "Wh...what are we...looking fo-"

His words were cut off as he suddenly stared at something outside the city. Hush, recovering next, glanced up and flinched with a monotone expression. Queenie, swallowing *hard* in an attempt to push bile back down her stomach, looked up, curious to see what had captivated her friends.

What she saw was a non-lethal mutant, but one of the most ominous ones to be audience to.

It had four wings, its body coated in oil-slick feathers. It had no eyes on its face, only having a thinly curved and straw like beak. Though it did nothing but sit on a nearby tree branch, its twisted bill seemed to be cruelly grinning at inevitable destruction. Its mutation may have increased its size four-fold, yet it had a bony frame that constantly starved for its next meal. The creature had evolved solely to foresee definite mass death and arrive with eager anticipation for its next meal.

Queenie stared at the mutant vulture with dread. The omen of death, silently laughing, unfurled its wings and flew off.

CHAPTER 12

*T*he first time Hush had seen the vulture was outside the Hush clan's caves. Jin had personally come out to witness the damned thing, sweating bullets the second he saw it. The entire day was then spent chasing the bird, hoping feebly that its death would somehow "undo" its omen. The mutant vulture, in turn, flew around while easily dodging their attacks, cackling silently.

The bird ruled their skies with each waking and sleeping minute. The first few guards crumbled after three nights, refusing to stand watch any further. Jin then tried to force out a shifted schedule to force the clan to stand guard. All members of the clan, barring Queenie, took turns standing watch over the course of six weeks.

When it was Hush's turn, his eyes would inadvertently turn away from the heavens. Even when he wasn't looking at the vulture, it felt as though his skin were being pulled apart by scrambling termites. He tried everything to stop the creeping dread, yet nothing worked. If he dampened his ears, he couldn't escape the looming shadow that droned over him, a black void that was darker than his eyelids. If he blinded his eyes, the cackling of the mutant echoed through his skull. No matter what *he did, Hush suffered the judgement of the beast not just overhead...but in his soul.*

After forty-three moons, the entire Hush clan was on the collective edge. They abandoned the caves and tried to flee on foot. As the clan cowered between timid steps, the mutant vulture swooped overhead with cackles, flecks of spit raining down on the group.

It only took four days in the open for Jin to snap, screaming how if they were destined to die, they may as well live merrily and take what they will. Everyone's mentality at their limits, they all screamed wildly as they marched into the nearest town.

That was where they first met the man who would be known as Father, quietly chewing some salad in a diner with a boy who would be known as Taba. Jin saw the older man, sneered, and grabbed him by the front of his shirt with the demand of all of his belongings. As the rest of the diner fled the store, Father held up his hands stating how he didn't want trouble. The clan's leader laughed, spitting in Father's face and throwing him to the floor.

The man picked himself up, wiped the spit off his cheek, and pulled out a few coins from his coat pocket as an offering. Taba stared at them, tinges of anger in his eyes. A clan member didn't like the glare and raised his hand to strike the boy.

That clan member disintegrated within seconds into blue vapor, Father standing where the clan member once stood. While the entire clan took stance and prepared to fight, all Hush could remember was staring outside the window and watching the mutant vulture, resting on a building, leaning in with a cackle.

Within the next hour, Father single-handedly dismantled the Hush clan. The remaining survivors all fled. As Hush himself ran, he vividly

remembered looking back upon the wreckage to see the vulture picking
apart the diner's floorboards to chew on the lifeless husks that remained.

...

He grit his teeth, darting his eyes to his sister. She was pale, staring at the bird with horror. Figures. Queenie was fairly young at that time, no doubt that mutant vultures would carry some trauma for her. Seeing how shaken everyone seemed to be, Hush cleared his throat. "It's a bird. Whatever. Mutant vultures don't have immediate prophecies, so we have time to prepare."

Despite his declaration, Queenie grit her teeth and pulled out a sniper from her storage, quickly shooting a round at the bird. It effortlessly dodged the round while flying off, its beak curved upward as it continued to taunt the girl.

Before Queenie could chamber another bullet, Taba put his hand on her scope to lower the weapon. "Hush is right. There's no point in trying to kill it. We need to plan around the bird, instead. You should know this more than anyone."

"I've...also seen mutant vultures in my life," Sana said with discomfort. "Hush is right. Their effect isn't immediate, so we don't need to be worried. Let's just be wary and move on with our lives."

Everyone turned around and forced their legs to move back to the townhall. The only one who didn't budge was Queenie, her eyes locked onto the bird's oily head. Hush bit his lips, firmly grabbed his sister's shoulders, and slowly dragged her back with him.

...

"Damn it. A vulture? *Really*?" G said.

"Yeah. Though the disaster shouldn't happen anytime soon, we should take precautions." said Sana. "How's our soul scale looking?"

215

Babs nibbled on the edge of some hardtack. Though she was making no progress in moistening the dense cracker, she nodded with conviction. "It has a few more months of life left inside of it, so we should be fine on that front. Still, I would prefer to have the Gatekeepers close by on the off-chance that war does break out soon." She then nodded to the Misfits. "So...I'll use *you* guys on various missions that I see fit."

"What missions are we talking?" asked Taba. "Just errands? Or..."

"...whatever I think will minimize casualties."

"Fine," he sighed. "What do you want us to do?"

Babs finally chipped off a piece of hardtack, a small grin on her lips. Hush was slightly baffled as to why the Overseer seemed to nonchalant about such a worrying situation. As she chewed her little treat, she nodded to them. "Go rest up. I imagine we'll have an answer by...I'd imagine by noon today."

The Gatekeepers turned to face Babs with concern. "Yo. Elaborate, Babs?" asked Patchy.

She instead chuckled as she continued to nibble on her cracker. Hush noticed the worried glances of the Gatekeepers and Juliette, but stayed silent. After a minute of silence, it was evident that the elderly woman would explain nothing. So, the Misfits muttered in annoyance, got up, and left the room.

...

Hush wasn't sure what to expect when the sun hit directly overhead, but Nancy suddenly hugging them with a squeal certainly wasn't one of them.

The trio blinked as their friend quickly ambushed with joy, giving tight hugs to each of them as she did. After a few moments, the girl pulled away from the group with excitement. "Gosh, I'm *so* glad yall are just dandy! Yall doin' ok???"

"N...nancy?" Queenie said. "What are *you* doing here?"

Nancy winked as she held a finger to her lips. "We're here to bust yall out! Geralt didn't think we should rush this so he didn't tag along. Still it's me, Zanshin, Luong, Tukie, and...well, I *guess* we have Hugh, but he only just helped us sneak in. That's all."

"Wait. So it's just you four? That's it?" said Taba.

"Well...yeah. We aren't tryin' to take the city down: all we wanna do is grab you guys and leave."

"If that was your goal...you probably shouldn't have brought Luong," said Hush with concern. "That meathead is probably out to fight. He's most likely not gonna obey orders."

"Yeah, what he said."

The four of them suddenly whirled around, locking eyes with Patchy. Though the Misfits were on edge, Nancy just tilted her head with a wrinkled nose. "Huh. When's the last time you showered, sugar?"

Patchy frowned and sniffed his armpit. "Does it really smell that bad? It's only been like...a day? Two days? Somethin' like that. Anyways, is this what Babs meant by 'noon'?" Nancy opened her mouth, but Patchy waved her off. "Ah, doesn't matter. Lady, you're comin' with me."

She pouted, her septum piercing shining in the sun. "But...I'm here to pick these cuties up. Could ya turn the other way? Pleaaaaase?"

"If it were up to me, I might," said Patchy. "Sadly, it's up to Sana and Babs, and they'd kill me if I turned around."

Nancy sighed and shrugged. "If ya insist, darlin'."

Her glare turned sharp and a nearby civilian screamed, collapsing to the floor. Immediately, everyone turned to witness a man clutching his arm while writhing on the floor. Patchy, though seemingly disinterested, had a stronger stare than before.

"You let us go, and I'll spare every civilian in the city. Fa-?"

In an instant, Patchy, his eyes now glowing, suddenly appeared behind Nancy, his hand grabbing her neck. Before he could twist, she ducked, put her arms on the ground, and kicked upwards with both legs. In another flicker, the Gatekeeper vanished and appeared behind the woman, his elbow primed to strike her spine. Nancy responded by contorting her body unnaturally to avoid the blow, flipping a few feet away to safety.

Her shorts shimmered from under her skirt as she straightened out her outfit. "My my, you're everything they say you are and *then* some, aintcha?"

"People are talking about me?" Patchy frowned. "Why?"

Nancy shrugged as she pulled a scalpel strapped to her thigh. "I dunno. I guess some people think you're cute, but I don't get it."

"I don't get it, either."

Nancy quickly pricked a cut in her palm, causing Patchy to raise an eyebrow. However, blood quickly began to wrap around her hand until it formed a pressurized blade. She swung her hand around to test her weapon out. "Last chance, darlin'. Can you let a girl walk away with her Fam'?"

"Can't, sorry. Too much paperwork." said Patchy.

"I...kinda expected that this whole plan wouldn't run so smoothly. That's wh-"

An explosion rang out from across the town, causing the Misfits and Patchy to flinch. Noticing this, Nancy grinned and quickly retrieved a pebble from her pocket, tossing it to the man she had wounded.

With no hesitation, Patchy suddenly appeared next to the man, swiping him away from danger. Before the pebble landed, it glowed light blue for a split second before exploding. As Patchy vanished, Nancy took the opportunity to immediately thrust her arm into a seemingly random space in the air.

As a result, Patchy stumbled a few steps back, one arm clutching the man. His other, clutching his neck as a small trickle of blood seeped from his fingers.

"Aw, beans. I was aiming for yer head." said Nancy.

Patchy put the man down as he massaged his neck. "This...is annoying. I hate fighting smart fighters."

Taba suddenly flinched and he turned to yell to his friends. Before he could, Patchy suddenly appeared behind him, the Gatekeeper's hands threatening to snap the Misfit's neck. The siblings screamed as they bolted towards the man.

However, Patchy's hands trembled. Unlike his normal quick movements, his arms moved slowly, turning the assassination attempt into an awkward looking neck massage. He looked back at Nancy, who was sweating bullets as she raised both her arms up towards the pair. "Ah...so this is *your* blessing, huh? Surprised it's even affecting me."

The siblings dove at the Gatekeeper, who suddenly vanished...alongside Taba. Hush quickly darted his eyes around. Nancy joined them, cursing as she did as tears filled her eyes. "Sorry, sorry, I am *so* sorry. Tough bastard, ain't he? Where'd he take Taba?"

Hush closed his eyes, trying to be rational. Both the females were starting to panic, so it was up to him to stay composed. "They...probably wouldn't kill Taba. No, they'll use him as a hostage. If I were Patchy..."

'This...is annoying. I hate fighting smart fighters.'

Hush flinched as he lifted his head. "Knowing Patchy, he's probably trying to reconvene with the other Gatekeepers. We need to go to where they'd be, *now*. Nancy, who's the closest Family member to us?"

...

Harrison spat out blood, his head woozy. It was so *rare* for an opponent to injure him. How thrilling!

The man slowly got up from the ground, his teeth bloodied as he grinned. "Yer strong, aintcha? What's yer name, boy?"

The man wore a long, braided ponytail. His jaw was chiseled and he had a cocky aura around him, seemingly looking down on everyone. He wore an airy fighting garment and had no armor or jewelry. The arrogant man looked at him with a monotone face. "Trash like you? What makes you think you're worthy of *my* name? Tell you what: I'll say my name the second you land a hit on me."

Harrison took a stance and yelled to bolster his spirits. In return, the aggressor scratched his ears with a bored look. He barreled towards the man, fists clenched tightly as Harrison threw a swift punch. The man, in return, did nothing....

...and yet again, Harrison's punch suddenly...stopped. With the exception of his legs, his entire upper body had frozen. He strained desperately to reposition....and yet, his upper body remained while his legs could barely scrambled away. It was all he could do to stay conscious as the aggressor laughed with malice, brutally striking Harrison's face with harsh blows. Though they were just punches, each blow hit harder than what the girly had struck with.

Oh, how humiliating! Harrison was certain that the crowd behind him was laughing at his pathetic display. However, he still stood. As long as he stood, Harrison would be a bastion until help arrived.

THWACK.

He will not fall.

CRACK.

He will not fall.

THOCK.

He...he will not... f-

CRUNCH.

He. Will. **Not. <u>Fall.</u>**

...

Hush, Queenie, and Nancy suddenly appeared at the horrific scene. A crowd of civilians was weeping as they stood powerless upon the one-sided beatdown that was being featured. Harrison was standing upright, taking repeated blows from the bloodthirsty martial artist. Sure, Harrison's skin was impenetrable...but he could still sustain damage. It was hard to tell if the man was even conscious through all the sticky blood that was plastered upon his face.

Nancy quickly used her blessing to at least _halter_ the fighter's fists. "Hey. Luong. He's...you can stop now."

"Why? He's still standing, no?" frowned Luong.

"I'm almost certain that he's upright because of your blessing." Nancy said while rolling her eyes.

"Nah, his knees haven't gone limp yet. He can still take some more hits."

Suddenly, someone from the civilian crowd yelped in shock. Suddenly, the people began to sob in relief as a familiar, bald man slowly walked out, staring at Harrison's bloodied figure. Upon noticing his approach, Luong immediately took ten quick steps backwards in anticipation.

"Oooh," whistled Luong. "You look strong. Fight m-"

"Shut up for a second, 'k?" G said as he focused on Harrison.

G quietly rubbed Harrison's back, giving him a quick checkup. After a few moments of silence, the Gatekeeper quietly took a pill out of his pocket and gently put it in the unbreakable man's mouth.

Almost immediately, Harrison groaned as he opened his bloodshot eyes. "Hah...Master G? Wonderful. Sorry, couldn't really...*hit* him. My bad."

G looked up towards Luong, a surprisingly quiet anger radiating from the normally callous man. "No, you did good. Rest up."

"O...k."

As G approached him, Luong grinned as he held a hand up to his Family. "None of you all *dare* get in the way of this fight: he's mine."

After a few silent seconds of walking, G stood face to face with the fighter. "So...*you* did this to Harrison?"

"I was initially gonna take down everyone, but that man was insistent that he fight first," said Luong. "He rubbed me the wrong way, so I wanted to make an example of him, that's all."

"I see." G said calmly.

In a swift movement, G threw a wild haymaker to Luong's jaw. The fighter, though surprised, only grinned as the Gatekeeper's punch stopped a few inches short. Once confirming that he was locked and secure, Luong cackled as he quickly elbowed G's face. Instead of taking damage, however, the bald man simple glared back. Luong tilted his head, slightly confused, but grinned regardless as he continued to rain blows down on the Gatekeeper.

Though he was their enemy, even Hush had to wince upon witnessing the beatdown. Queenie grimaced, pulling out a dagger to fiddle with. Nancy just looked irritated, impatiently tapping her foot as she waited for Luong to finish venting out his bloodlust.

And yet...G did not falter. He did not fall. Throughout all the sticky blood that splattered against Luong's fist, the Gatekeeper did not much as react. He nodded to Luong. "You done?"

"Hm?"

Suddenly, G flipped around in the air, a sickening *crack* ringing out from his arm as he did. Luong's eyes widened in shock as a sudden kick slammed into the top of his skull, smashing him into the ground. From the cracks that appeared in the ground, it was evident that enough force was put into the blow to obliterate most men.

However, Luong was not "most men". He simply got up and leapt away with a wide grin, blood trickling from the back of his head. "You...are *splendid!*"

"I don't want to hear that from scum like you." G said.

The fighter stood tall and took a stance. "My name is Luong Xiaoli. Remember my name until the minute you die."

"I don't want to remember the name of some random swine until I die of old age, no thanks."

Luong roared in glorious delight as he sprinted to G. The fighter leapt into the air...and his hand suddenly stopped as though it were held in place by an invisible force. This stop in momentum caught the Gatekeeper slightly off-guard, his stance shifting slightly as he glanced upwards. The bald man watched his opponent suddenly "swing" through the air, using his unforeseen momentum to land squarely onto G's shoulders. Luong cackled as he suddenly twisted his body and legs, a deafening *snap* ringing from the Gatekeeper's neck.

G stumbled a bit...before planting his feet firmly onto the ground. Though Hush couldn't see his face, he could hear the Gatekeeper gnashing his teeth. The bald man raised his hands to grab the fighter from his shoulders only for his outreached arms to suddenly stop once more. Luong laughed gleefully as he sprung off of G's body, gracefully landing on the ground with one extended leg, partially bowing as he did.

"You *really* don't die?" Luong said. "Incredible! Today is the day I do the impossible and kill an immortal man!"

"You're a thorn in my ass. Piss off."

As the two men continued to exchange blows, the siblings and Nancy could only stare in mild fascination.

Queenie leaned in and muttered as she continued to fiddle with her dagger. "This...is the first time I've seen Luong struggle to kill someone."

Nancy chewed her thumb, nervously nodding as she did. "Yeah. Where...where do you think they took Taba? If that other Gatekeeper isn't here, then..."

Hush closed his eyes as he tried to get into the mindset of the Gatekeepers. They were being attacked on multiple fronts. Patchy wouldn't need to worry about G. After all: G couldn't die. If that was the case, he was probably trying to regroup with Sana so the two of them could cover for each other's weaknesses. But...if Hush were planning an attack, well...

He hesitated and looked up to Nancy. "Where's Zanshin?"

...

Patchy and Sana stood back to back in the wheat field, their eyes darting wildly. Patchy was littered in numerous wounds as he held the writhing Taba. Where was their attacker? What was happening? Why didn't Patchy remember any wound?

Sana quietly spoke in a controlled voice. "Patchy. Get out of here. Call it a gut feeling, but I think it's *you* that's in danger, not me."

Before Patchy could respond, Sana quickly darted towards her friend and shoved him to the ground, a sudden dagger attack being dodged as he did. Seeing this, Patchy's eyes widened slightly as he immediately vanished. Once confirming that he had fled, Sana's eyes slowly stopped glowing as she stared at her attacker.

It was a bony man wearing a dark cloak and hood. From the shadows of his mantle, the man had hollow eyes and sunken cheeks. Frankly, he looked quite unwell...both physically and mentally.

Sana spun her sickles as she held her gaze. "Could I have your name?"

The man sighed as he tapped his arm. "...*eight...*"

"Pardon? Is that your name?"

"...*No, that's the eighth time you asked that same question.*"

Before Sana could respond, he sunk into the wheat field behind him. The second he did, the Gatekeeper blinked with confusion. Where did...huh? What was she doing?

Suddenly, her blessing flickered and she immediately darted to her left, dodging a sudden knife attack. As she did, the Gatekeeper heard a growl of exasperation.

"*How are you **doing** that?*"

225

Sana whirled around and locked eyes with her attacker. It was a bony man wearing a dark cloak and hood. From the shadows of his mantle, the man had hollow eyes and sunken cheeks. Frankly, he looked quite unwell...both physically and mentally.

Sana spun her sickles as she held her gaze. "Could I have your name?"

The man sighed as he tapped his arm. "...*nine...*"

...

Hush, Queenie, and Nancy darted over to the town hall. Knowing Zanshin, it was better if they didn't go near him: he worked better in solo operations. Plus, he was probably targeting the only threat to his ability: Sana.

So, there were two main places that Hush could imagine Patchy had taken Taba. Either the prison in which the Misfits were initially interrogated...or the town hall.

The trio rounded the corner and suddenly stopped dead in their tracks. There was a sole guard in front of Malapace's town hall. Upon seeing their arrival, she stopped drinking from her jug and tied her drink to her waist. The woman's mask stared a void into the siblings. "So, is this your decision?"

Nancy stepped up with confidence. "Nah, sugar. It was *your* decision to take our Family. It was *my* decision to rescue them."

The Dancing Painter raised her brush. "I see." Suddenly, a crimson line splashed across Nancy's stomach. She gasped, stumbling back as she did. After taking a few steps, her left arm suddenly sprouted numerous red lines. This caused her to recoil to her right, causing a large gash to suddenly appear on her right calf.

226

And just like that, the siblings watched in horror as their foster sister crumpled to the floor in ten seconds.

Before they could even scream, Nancy suddenly stumbled back up to her feet. Her movements were wobbly, but her gaze remained as cheerful as it once had...though her mouth has taking deep breaths. "Ya...missed, darling."

"Did I?" asked Juliette. "You'll be dead shortly enough."

Suddenly, Nancy sprung forward with shocking agility from someone who had just been sliced up. Juliette took a defensive stance, parrying the invader's initial palm strike. However, the blood that ran Nancy's left arm began to form stiff lines against her skin. As the bleeding woman raised her arm, Juliette flinched instantly.

As pressurized blood sprung from Nancy's arm and began to chase the Dancing Painter down, she rolled in the air to avoid the attack. Upon landing, she struck with her paintbrush, painting another crimson line across the bleeding woman's back. The wounded woman flinched in surprise, yelping as she received another lash. Upon receiving the cut, the weaponized blood that had been chasing Juliette stopped their pursuit and quickly returned to it's host.

Juliette watched with calculating eyes as Nancy staggered to her feet with a shortened breath. The uninjured lady tilted her head. "Blood manipulation, is it? A blessing that becomes more deadly the more wounded you get...but overusing it might lead to you accidentally bleeding yourself out. Must be tricky balancing on that delicate tightrope."

The wounded woman wheezed as she stuck her tongue out at her opponent. "Bleh. I'm just fine."

She then held up her arm towards the Dancing Painter. Juliette didn't even hold a defensive position, cocking her head as she witnessed the movement. "If you do that, you'll probably die. Plus, that attack wouldn't even reach me. You sure?"

Nancy spat bloody spit on the floor, a wild grin plastered on her face. "If my death is the price needed to pay to save my Family, so be it. I'd do *anything* for them."

Hush saw his opportunity. He darted his eyes to his sister, praying that they were on the same wavelength. Seeing the worried glance flashing on her face, the older brother felt relief.

Summoned chains suddenly restrained Nancy to the ground. Their foster sister yelped as she was pinned. Once tied down, Hush amplified her sensation of pain and slammed fist into Nancy's head, his heart hurting tremendously as he knocked his wounded Family unconscious.

Juliette said nothing but simply witnessed all this unfold. Hush got up from the ground and nodded to their mentor. "Where did Patchy take Taba? Is he ok?"

The Drunken fox pursed her red lips, obviously unsure of what to think. "Whose side are you on?"

"Dad's side, obviously. Still: we didn't expect or want this invasion: it isn't fair for Taba to suffer because of it." said Queenie.

Juliette strummed her fingers on her paintbrush. "Hmm...well, how about this..."

...

Luong breathed heavily, wild ecstasy scribbled on his face. The bastard wouldn't *die*. Broken neck, broken bones, exploded arteries...nothing worked. The Gatekeeper just kept tanking every hit and responding with a stronger blow in return. Hell, it was all he could do to just *parry* the baldy's hits: even *that* caused his hands to sting.

Still, Luong was running out of ideas. What other lethal ways could he strike? What was this dumbass's blessing? Was...was it *truly* immortality? Or...or was it all one massive trick? How exciting! The fighter couldn't help but love such a cryptic mystery.

He struck the Gatekeeper's chin with a strong uppercut. The baldy, in return, gripped both of Luong's shoulders with plentiful force and suddenly moved his head with rapid force to connect a deadly head-butt. Luong immediately anchored G's head, forcing it to stop. Once frozen, he slammed his palms into the baldy's triceps, forcing him to loosen his grip. Once Luong obtained the slightest bit of momentum, he kicked outwards to push the Gatekeeper away.

Luong rubbed his shoulders. At *minimum*, they were sprained. What grip strength! The average man would surely have lost access to both arms from that grab. But...Master Xiaoli was anything but *average*.

Before he could scramble to land another hit, the fighter flinched as he saw someone slowly approach from behind the bald Gatekeeper. She held up an unconscious body before dropping it to the floor.

No way...Nancy?

...

Juliette tossed Nancy's limp, tied up body to the floor. Though this was the compromise that their mentor had proposed, Hush felt a tinge of anger seeing their foster sister treated in such a manner.

The Dancing Painter nodded to the bewildered fighter. "You have lost. Leave."

Luong said nothing, simply staring at his Family's still body. He slowly walked up to her body and placed his fingers on her neck. Once confirming a weak pulse, he tightened his lips and stood up. "What did you do to her?"

"She fought me and lost."

"No. I *know* Nancy. She wouldn't be knocked out like this. She would either return with a wide grin or in a body bag. There's not a scenario where she returns unconscious by the enemy's own hands." Luong crouched in preparation. "*What did you do to her?*"

Before Juliette could respond, Luong got up in a rage and bolted towards Juliette, rage coursing through each of his steps. As Luong reeled his fist back, the fighter was suddenly stopped by a well-suited man's grip. With his free hand, the new guest slightly lowered his shades to maintain eye contact with Luong. "Stop embarrassing yourself. You all lost, damn infants. Told you guys to wait, didn't I?"

Everyone flinched at his sudden appearance. Where had he come from? Why was he here? Could...could they defeat him?

The man pulled a cigarette and lighter from his pocket. He lit the tobacco, took a deep inhale, and exhaled with an exhausted sigh. Geralt looked over at Juliette, who had immediately taken up a defensive stance with her hand on her mask.

"What's your goal? You aren't exactly the 'mercy' type, right? So, why spare her?" he asked.

"We can fight, sure...but people will die on both sides. I'm not exactly a fan of that. So, here's the deal: we keep the Misfits, and in return, you take *her* and get the hell out of Malapace." proposed Juliette.

Geralt took a drag from his cigarette, exhaling softly while he thought about her proposal. "So...what it was before. How do we know you won't just execute them?"

Juliette's mask twitched, but she stayed emotionless. "You have our word: we will keep them alive."

"No torture or punishments?"

"No torture or punishments."

"Cool. We have a deal."

Geralt calmly grabbed Nancy and draped her over his back in a piggyback ride. As he did, he whispered something to the fighter. Luong scowled, but nodded stiffly at the smoker.

The dapper man turned to the Dancing Painter. "I told him to go grab the other members of our Family. The one who's fighting that one female Gatekeeper and another who's doing...things. You have my word that they'll be out of your hair, for now at least."

"Oh, the guy with the fuzzy hair? He's under custody too. Sorry, you aren't taking him."

Geralt silently chewed on his jaw, slightly shaking his head. "You're pushing it, don't you think sweetie?"

"He bombed a few houses," she responded coldly. "We have at least three confirmed deaths due to it. I think you can make an exception here, no?"

Using a free hand, he quietly reached towards his pocket...but stopped. He sighed, but nodded slightly. "Fine. As long as you give me your word that he'll be kept safe, I have no qualms."

"I must admit, I didn't expect you guys to be so...compliant." said Juliette.

"Yeah, well, I saw the damned vulture flying around the city. I don't want that thing's omen to happen while my Family is invading."

"Fair enough."

Geralt secured Nancy on his back, a cigarette between his lips. He nodded to the siblings. "Stay. **Put.** We'll come get you guys eventually, I promise. Understood?"

While Queenie hesitated, Hush nodded.

And just like that, the Family retreated from Malapace, numerous deaths narrowly averted.

CHAPTER 13

Patchy winced as he bandaged his own wounds. Taba, handcuffed to the prison wall, stared at the scruffy man with a confused look. First the Gatekeeper went to assassinate him, then he immediately went to...protect the teenager? Taba understood that Zanshin's ability played a huge part in that interaction, but *surely* Patchy would prioritize his own life after getting shanked for the fourth time.

Furthermore, Patchy had the most curious body. He had different skin hues, textures, and even hair patterns. It was as though his skin had different borders, like how a river might change colors when flowing into the ocean. It looked...unnatural. Monstrous. Inhuman. Dare he say, immoral.

Patchy finished slapping on the last bandage with a groan and slipped on his coat. The Gatekeeper nodded to the Misfit. "You stay here for a bit. I'm gonna go do some questioning on our friend."

Taba grit his teeth as he unconsciously rattled his handcuffs. "Don't you *dare* harm him."

"Oww,"Patchy groaned as he rubbed his wounds. "I normally wouldn't give a damn, but no way people came out of his attack unscathed, right? So, I'm gonna question him. If I like his answers, he can hold an audience with Sana. If I don't, I'll snap his neck. Cool?"

Before Taba could respond, the Gatekeeper vanished.

...

As he sat in his gray cell for what felt like hours, the Misfit couldn't help but feel anxious. He prayed that Toukie would be ok. The flashback of the raggedy boy being caught off guard right before Patchy knocked him out still shook Taba to his core.

Taba had mindlessly scanned the cracked, gray room endlessly. The only window was tiny, had bars, and was *much* out of reach. The ways the vents were slanted made it impossible for any outsider to peek inside or help out. Even if they could...Taba was handcuffed to the prison doors. He really wasn't going anywhere. All he could do was ask various questions in his mind, each one begging for the safety of his friends...both in *and* out of Malapace.

Suddenly, Patchy appeared with a mutter. Taba scrambled to his feet, concern surging through his chest. "Is...did you...?"

"He says he'll talk, but *only* to you. So, you feel like cooperating?" Patchy asked.

The teenager hesitated. Something felt off. Too many things didn't add up. Why didn't Toukie blow up his restraints? Why did Toukie want to speak? What did he want to speak about? Furthermore, if this was something that Toukie only wanted to tell Taba about...why even mention the *hint* of a plan to the Gatekeeper?

Well, the only way these questions would be answered was with an interrogation. "Sure."

Patchy shrugged, undid the boy's handcuffs, held him close, then the pair suddenly vanished. Well, saying "vanished" was incorrect. The scenery around him changed in an instant. It was the equivalent of walking out of a bathroom and into the middle of a cornfield. It made no sense and was disorienting.

Taba blinked and rattled his head. As he turned his neck, he locked eyes with his Family member.

Toukie beamed a toothy grin. "Taba!"

The boy instinctively stood up, handcuffs rattling against the table as he did. His hair was poofed up in a massive afro, with a small chunk of his hair scorched away. He donned his usual overalls with no shoes on his tanned and calloused feet. Toukie held up an arm to give a signature handshake, his face morphing into annoyance as his restraints prevented him from giving a proper greeting.

Taba sat across from the dark-skinned teenager with a nod. "I'm...honestly surprised you're still alive. You doin' alright? Did he harm you?"

"Nah. The weirdo was just asking really basic questions. Didn't even try to threaten me." said Toukie.

"That *weirdo* is still in this room." Patchy said.

He rolled his eyes, his chained hands flipping the bird to the Gatekeeper. "Cool. You're a weirdo."

Taba ignored the interaction and leaned into his chair with a whisper. "So...what did you want to tell me and how are you *actually* alive?"

"My soul is already dispersed in the city. I told the stinker that if I die, my blessing goes off and people blow up." grinned Toukie.

The Misfit frowned. *Does his blessing automatically go off upon his death?* **O**

235

Taba leaned back in his chair with mild impressment. "Huh. Didn't think you'd have the balls to just...hold the city hostage."

"Puh-*lease*," said Toukie as he rolled his eyes. "I've done worse, you know that."

"Fair. Still, why'd you let yourself stay caught? Couldn't you just escape?"

Toukie shrugged. "Well...I guess I just wanted to tell you. The Big Papa told me to stay quiet about this...but it feels weird to not let you in on one of his plans, y'know?"

"Plans?"

"Yeah. The Big P wants to use the chimera."

Patchy raised an eyebrow. "Oh? What's that?"

Toukie grinned as he raised his middle fingers higher. "Oh, you not hear me properly? I said we're gonna use the *chimera*, you dipstick."

Taba hesitated. Chimera...was Dad that desperate? Or...or was he planning something else? "Is it worth telling me this plan? You've essentially laid out your hand in front of 'the dipstick', and I can't really do anything with that info."

"Ya think so? The Taba *I* know would exploit even the smallest bit of info. Hell, the fact that you're still alive right now is proof of that, right?"

"I mean...not...really?"

"Whatever. Still, you go do your thing. I need to stick around to hold the city hostage. Till Big P decides to make a move, I'll stay here. Well, either that or until I get bored. Coolio?" said Toukie.

Taba sighed. "Touks. Stay safe, and don't be dumb, alright?"

"Safe is boring, but fine...fine."

Taba got up and returned to Patchy with a nod. The two of them suddenly reappeared next to Babs in her room. She scowled at the sudden appearance. "A warning would be nice, you damn whelp."

"Sorry Babs, but we really don't have the luxury of time. We need to move as soon as possible." said Patchy.

The Misfit's mind raced wildly. Chimera? What would...could Dad be planning...? Still, on the off chance that he fails...but...was he banking on the idea that they were being held hostage by Malapace? If so...

Taba made a decision. He looked up and locked eyes with the Overseer. "I'll make you a deal that'll work out splendidly in your favor."

The elder's eyebrow raised with amusement. "Ah? Go on."

"There's a mutant out there called the chimera. It's a unique thing, an abominable amalgamation of numerous different mutants. I have no idea how, but there is heavy evidence pointing to Da-I mean, *Father* using the mutant in taking out Malapace."

"You say there's proof. Can you tell me?" asked Babs.

"No."

"Oh my. Why is that?"

"Because then I won't have leverage here." said Taba.

"I mean...what's stopping me from just snapping your neck?" asked Patchy. "That blood girl isn't here to save your skin this time."

Taba locked eyes with the Gatekeeper. "Simple, because *you* guys don't know jack about the chimera. The only reason *I* know about it is because our Family has tangled with it a few times. The chimera wouldn't visit a place as 'safe' as Malapace, nor would it invade just any neighboring village that contains only scraps. No, there's no way you guys know about it. Plus, you can't hide your lack of knowledge from my blessing."

The scruffy man wrinkled his nose. "Ugh. Smart people." He got up and nodded to the Overseer. "But yeah. We caught a prisoner who mentioned a chimera. Do you know anything about it?"

"Eh...only a bit," said Babs. "Not enough to have a decisive victory. Well, I imagine that you Gatekeepers could win against it, but in a full scale invasion? Even for you guys, it'd be difficult to win *while* protecting our citizens." she then nodded to the teenager. "So, what's your offer, brat?"

Taba took a shaky breath, but nodded firmly. "Me, Queenie, Hush, and Juliette. Send us out and I *promise* that we'll take the thing out."

Patchy opened his mouth to protest, but the questioner cut him off. "*You* were the one who said we were on a time crunch, right? You guys can't leave the city, since you're the defenders. If not the Gatekeepers, who else is capable of taking down the chimera? Juliette might, but she doesn't know anything about it. That's why me and my friends will play support in helping her take it out. Plus, as long as she's supervising us, there's no way we can escape. There is *no* downside to this plan for you guys."

Babs tilted her head, her earrings jingling slightly as she did. "That's the most curious part though, no? Why propose a plan that seemingly is going *against* your 'Family'? Why propose it?"

He hesitated, eyes glancing at the floor slightly before locking eyes with the stern woman. "I have faith in Father. He...there's *no* way he hasn't made a 'plan b' for something like this. If anything, I'd imagine that he's planned me proposing this plan to you guys."

"Wait wait wait. If this is a trap, then why should we voluntarily step into it?" asked Patchy.

"I'm taking a pretty big gamble myself. If I'm wrong, that means I've sabotaged my Family. I could be reading into this too much, so it's up to you to decide what's the best call. However, I know for a *fact* that the chimera would be horrible to bring into any fight."

The Overseer rubbed her wrists, her white eyes staring into nothingness. "What a conundrum. Hm. I'll have an answer for you guys by night time. Till then, let me think."

...

Taba spent the rest of the day in his cell. Well, that was to be expected. He killed time by doing small workouts in his tiny cell. By the days end, the poor ventilation of the room left the small enclosure feeling humid. After a day of mindless exercise, Patchy suddenly appeared with exhaustion spread on his slightly glowing eyes. "Ugh. Let's go, Babs made her decision."

The two warped out of the musty cell and into the Overseer's chambers. By her side stood G and Sana. His friends sat on the ground with Juliette standing by their side, sipping away at her flask. Upon seeing his entrance, the siblings instinctively rose before being shoved to the ground by Juliette. She recorked her drink and tied it to her waist. "Sit. The Overseer speaks," said Juliette.

Taba gave a reassuring nod to his friends before turning to the elderly woman. She was kneeling on the floor, her eyes closed in deep concentration. After a few silent seconds, her pale eyes opened to stare at the souls of everyone in the room.

Babs cleared her throat. "Earlier, Taba's Family launched an attack on Malapace. Though the attempt failed overall, there's no doubt it

239

could have been worse. Due to some intel, we were able to discover that Taba's Family has plans to use a chimera for their next attack. So, here is my decision based on such intel." The Overseer raised a bony finger and pointed at the Misfits and their mentor. "Juliette. You will be accompanied by Taba, Queenie, and Hush to subjugate the chimera. While I understand that this is most definitely a trap of some sorts, I have confidence that you will be able to overcome any adversaries in your wake. You leave at sunrise. Any questions?"

The siblings looked confused, staring at each other with worry. Juliette simply shook her head. "None, Overseer. We leave at dawn."

"Good," Babs then clapped her hands with a grin. "Now, if you all are still hungry, let's go eat."

Tabitha entered the room pushing a tray of cart of food, waved enthusiastically, then left. There were various cuts of meat, a selection of steamed vegetables, and jugs of cold tea. The Gatekeepers, obviously used to this, plopped to the ground with a sigh and grabbed a plate. Juliette quietly knelt and daintily grabbed one as well. The Misfits, slightly unprepared for such an intrusion, awkwardly grabbed their own plates.

Taba scooted next to his friends. "You guys ok? They didn't...do anything, did they?"

"Us? Bro, are *you* alright? What happened? Where were you the entire day? What'd they do to *you*?"

"I sat in a cell and did nothing. I talked to Toukie though." said Taba.

"Wait, Toukie? The guy that can blow things up? They caught *that* guy? How?" asked Queenie.

Taba hesitated before leaning in. "I think it was voluntary. Toukie is kinda holding the city hostage with his blessing."

"That's Touks for you," muttered Hush as he stabbed a forkful of beans. "Reckless and idiotic."

"What's wrong with that? If anything. I think that just makes him cool." said Queenie as she bit into a drumstick.

The older brother smacked his younger sister in the head, causing her to yelp in surprise. In response, she scowled and wiped her greasy hand on her brother's jacket, who grit his teeth in irritation. The two continued to bicker pettily as Taba withheld a grin, grabbing some sliced potatoes.

The dinner was quiet, the only sounds echoing throughout the Overseer's chambers being the scraping of forks against soulmade china. After finishing her meal, Babs dabbed her lips with a napkin before speaking. "You brats are probably a bit confused as to why we're eating like this, right?"

Queenie spoke with a mouthful of chicken. "Whaf dof if maffer? Foof if foof."

"Chew with your mouth closed, nimrod." said G.

"She isn't wrong: it's *just* food," replied Sana. "Let them eat peacefully. Ok?"

G grumbled into his plate of pork and beans as Patchy quietly snuck a stalk of celery onto Sana's plate. When she stared back with pointed eyes, he held his arms up and retreated with his veggie. The Misfit trio quietly ate their meal as Juliette quietly sipped away at the clear vodka that was being served, barely touching her own plate. Once everyone had finished eating, Babs reached into a compartment hidden in the food cart, pulling out a small pot that looked like a teapot without a spout. She softly grabbed both handles, walked over to each person's cup, and poured each person a drink by pushing into both handles softly. The liquid that came out was a shimmering color, like oil spilled into a pond. Once all three Misfits had full cups, Babs placed the teapot down with relaxed fingers.

She smiled softly at the trio. "What I've poured out is essentially my soul. If you ingest it, my fate will be tied to yours. If you die, I'll die too. I hope this shows you my sincerity."

Queenie gagged as she pushed her cup away while Hush eyed his drink with suspicion. Taba simply blinked with a blank expression. Huh?

Is...is she telling the truth? **O**

Taba hesitantly wiped his pinky on his shirt before carefully dipping it into the teacup. The instant his finger soaked into the liquid, the world around him blinked. White carpets flickered into grass, his friends turned into burning houses, the Gatekeepers melted into flames...

...and the Overseer shrunk into a little girl, holding the hand of young boy, both children staring into the flames. The girl, despite being taller, stood behind the young boy, staring at his backside with blank, white eyes. The boy, in turn, gripped her hand tightly, a trembling grimace plastered on his face. She opened her mou-

-Taba suddenly inhaled as a strong grip swirled him back into reality. He looked down to his hand to reveal Hush gripping it tightly into the air, a slight tremble in his hands.

His friend swallowed dryly. "Hey. You...you good? What happened? You weren't responding for a solid ten seconds."

It was only after Taba tried to move his body that the stiff coldness flooded his nerves. What the hell...? Who...?

Taba pulled away softly with trembling shoulders, wiping his clammy face with his shirt. "Yeah. I'm...yeah."

He looked up to the Overseer, trying to read her expression. Her eyebrows were wrinkled into a furrowed mess, lips tightened with concern. Her clear eyes held infinite wisdom as she calmly folded her hands into her lap. What...what had Taba just witnessed? Was that...?

Taba stared at her for a few seconds before gently pushing his teacup towards the Overseer. He then pushed his friend's teacups away as well. "We'll...pass on the offer, thanks."

Babs sighed as she opened the top of the teapot, the liquid from each of the cups softly floating into the container without a single drop being wasted. Even spilled tea that had soaked into the carpet was picked up with ease, discarding any dirt it may have picked up. Once it was all securely stored, she placed the teapot behind her with a sad smile. "Very well. Go sleep, I'll see you tomorrow, child."

...

Taba didn't like night. Every time the sun went down, the boy felt chills and shudders. Honestly, he wasn't sure why. This was something that was beyond a primal fear of the dark: it was as though he were shuddering from a past memory that was no longer there. Every time he curled up under his sheets, the air suddenly became dense as his lungs squeezed, suffocating him with the guilt of...guilt? Why would he feel guilt? Did he do something?

He got out of his futon and crawled out to the winter air. As he shivered upon kissing the cold air, he saw Father quietly chopping wood with an old, yet sturdy, axe.

243

The older man heard the crunch of gravel and turned around, an odd smile tracing his lips. "Can't sleep?"

Taba shook his head with weary eyes. "I never can."

The boy grabbed another axe and began chopping his own pile of wood. Geralt was off on patrol, ensuring no mutants got close. Meanwhile, Zanshin was...well, he wasn't really sure where Zanshin was. Still, that was about to be expected: no one except Dad really knew what Zanshin was up to.

As the duo chopped wood, Dad groaned as he wiped some sweat off the brow, grinning as he did. "Whew. Nothing like sweating in winter air. It's like a little war is being waged between my body heat and the air around me."

"I...kinda get that. Still, why don't you use your soul for this? It'd make life a lot easier."

"Yeah, but sometimes..." Father grunted as he swung his axe again. "...it isn't about taking the easy route. Sometimes, there's beauty in the struggle."

"I don't think I'll ever be able to see you eye to eye on that."

Father chuckled as he continued to swing his axe. "That's fine. You don't need to see me eye-to-eye on everything. As long as you can understand where I'm coming from, that's all I can ask for. After this, lets go into town: I haven't tasted salad dressing and croutons in so long."

...

Taba woke up stiffly, groaning as he rolled his back. The bed was somehow more stiff than some caves he had slept in. He stood up, stretched with a guttural yell, then began to wash up.

He slipped on a white shirt and pants before heading out. As expected, he was the first one up. That was expected. Normally, he would

244

jog a few laps and do some calisthenics...but Taba wanted to check in on Babs...*especially* after last night.

The Overseer's room was shockingly unguarded. In fact, the entire hallways was unlit with only dim moonlight illuminating the stone floors. He quietly opened her room, and to his surprise...she sat in the middle of her room, staring back at him.

"You don't plan on sleeping?" asked Babs. "You still have two more hours till daybreak."

Taba plopped down, staring at her. "You know why I'm here. What was that tea? Hell, *how* did you turn your soul into a drinkable liquid? Why'd you choose to become Malapace's leader? What the *f-*?"

The blind woman seemed unsurprised at the questions, lifting an arm to cut him off as though she had heard it countless times. "The tea is an unwanted gift...and my biggest burden. I never asked for it and I'm not open to talking about it...for now, at least. As for becoming the Overseer for Malapace: it was never intentional. I simply did what I could to help...and people forced me into this position. They're all idiots."

Taba's nose twitched as he held back a snappy retort, slowly exhaling his frustration through his nostrils. "You don't want to talk about the tea, fine. Whatever. Still: you *do* realize that me, Queenie, and Hush are your enemies, right? Like...we plan on overthrowing Malapace."

"Mhm."

"So...why spare us? Why even give us the *option* of accessing all this information? War is going to ignite because of us being held here, you know that."

Babs sighed as she leaned back on her hands. "Don't flatter yourself: you aren't as important as you think you are: the war was inevitable."

"If you knew that taking us would mean war...why?" asked Taba.

"It was either take you or kill you, and Sana wants you brats alive. Plus, this was probably the best opportunity to actually prevent as many deaths as possible. So...I took it." said Babs.

Taba frowned as his eyebrows furrowed. "*You* took it? You sat in a room the entire time, the hell do you mean? What responsibility do you have for Sana's choices?"

The Overseer stared back with white pupils. "You would be right...if I were some random old hag. Unfortunately, I've been designated as the leader. As such, all responsibility falls on me, no matter how much involvement I've had with the initial decision."

"I don't get you. Doubt I'll ever get to see you eye-to-eye." he muttered.

"No, I think you'll understand eventually. No doubt about it. Hell, maybe you *already* understand me...but you're in denial." she chuckled.

For some odd reason, Taba found himself cracking a small smile. "I don't want to understand it though, damn it."

Babs laughed dryly, with an air of both amusement and sadness. "Sorry, kid. You're a leader: it's inevitable."

...

The Misfits and the Drunken Fox stood at the city's gates. Of all the Gatekeepers, only Sana saw them off with tight hugs and goody bags. After Sana ruffled an exasperated Juliette's hair, the group went off as the Gatekeeper waved wildly until they walked out of view. After walking for a bit, Juliette looked at Taba. "So, where we going?"

He chewed his lips as his blessing confirmed his suspicions. "Well...the chimera isn't a natural creature. It was created by a soul-bearer who was part of the Family. So, we just need to go find her and get the lady to split the chimera apart. Easy peasy."

Queenie frowned. "Bu-" Suddenly she turned to her left with annoyance as she stared at her brother. She was seemingly mouthing something to Hush, who in return shook his head softly.

Juliette obviously took note of the trio's reactions. "So...what's the tricky part?"

"I...can't tell you right now. But it'll be fine. We just need to do some preparations to kill the damn thing." responded Taba.

"But...you said that we would get the chimera's creator to sp-"

"Its contradictory, I know. Still, it'll make sense when the time comes. Until then, trust me, alright?"

"You're the enemy, and you want me to trust you?" said Juliette.

"Not like you have much of a choice, right?" Taba said.

She sighed. "Fine. Where to, you Misfit?"

He chewed the inside of his cheek. "After a while, the chimera evolved to learn how to absorbs others into its own mass without the soulbearer. So, we need to talk to a Family member first and *hope* he's in the mood to help us out. If not, well, we don't stand a chance."

He squinted at the sun, muttering some numbers as he tapped his fingers at alternating intervals. "Well...let's go have a chat with Maggle."

CHAPTER 14

Hush didn't unmute her for nearly two hours. It was irritating. She didn't get it. Why did they need Maggle's blessing? Why couldn't they just kill the damned thing? Why did Taba hide the fact that t-

Queenie's body jerked backwards as she looked back in annoyance at her stoic brother. He squinted at her with a frown. The message was obvious: "*Can I trust you to shut up if I unmute you?*"

She rolled her eyes and nodded. Hush sighed and unflexed his fingers. Once she was unmuted, Queenie coughed to confirm that her voice had returned, then elbowed her brother in the gut.

The party silently trekked through offroad paths, watching as the scenery slowly unfolded before them every hour. The first hour was a bunch of rocks, with everyone taking careful steps as to not accidentally stumble from loose footing. The setting melted into humid thicket as they took another detour into some damp woods. Tiny insects slammed into the party's clothes (Queenie *wished* she had some tool stored away for pests) and larger creatures scurried from the underbush to stalk them with glowering eyes before losing interest. Oddly enough, not a single predator ambushed them, but Taba seemed unsurprised by that revelation. He had probably chosen this exact route by following his questioning. Plus, whenever a beast began to stalk them...they immediately retreated when Juliette turned her head to face the animal.

Queenie hated to admit it. Damn it, the fabled Dancing Painter, her childhood hero, was cool as all hell.

Soon, the trees thinned out and the four of them stumbled out onto dirt road. Everyone, barring Juliette, was peppered with sweat. Queenie rolled up her sleeves with irritation.

She mopped her face with the bottom of her hoodie while glaring at their mentor. "How the hell are you not sweaty?"

Juliette dabbed her lips and tied her flask to her waist. "I'm well hydrated."

"Big words for a drunkard."

"Hydration is hydration. At least I'm not a waterfall...like *some* Misfits I know."

"The he-"

Taba cleared his throat as he nodded ahead. "Ladies. There's a bathhouse in the town ahead. Let's wash up, then continue on our way, yeah?"

Queenie rolled her eyes as she stared at the rundown shack ahead. She hated feeling vulnerable and there was no place one felt more vulnerable than a bathhouse. "I'll be fine. Let's just go ahead."

"No. I insist. Let's wash up."

Hush raised an eyebrow. "Got it. Let's wash up."

Queenie stared at the two guys in exasperation. "It...it's sweat. We're gonna sweat again. This is pointless. Let's just *go.*"

Juliette pursed her lips as she stared at the baths ahead. "Well. If you insist."

"You aren't even *sweating*, why the hell do you w-"

The trio pushed on ahead while Queenie groaned and followed reluctantly. She was gonna wear a coverup, whether the damn spa owner liked it or not.

However, the second the party entered the spa house, she immediately felt the soul that quietly lingered. It wasn't menacing or overwhelming...but it was similar to how glass fogged up during a shower. The soul that wafted through the air was solely an after effect.

The old woman behind the counter smiled warmly. Taba bowed slightly and exchanged quiet words with her. As he did, Juliette slowly walked over to Queenie and nodded to her. "Have you noticed it yet?"

"The soul? Big whup. What about it? It isn't a threat." said Queenie.

Her mentor shook her head softly. "Not what I was going for. I mean, the fact that you noticed is proof that you've grown. The past you wouldn't have even noticed this."

The Misfit felt her ears flush as she scowled, whirling around. Still...Juliette had a point. There was *no* way Queenie would've felt this level of soul in the air a few months ago. After a few moments, Taba walked back with a nod, holding up four cheap pieces of paper. "Alright, I paid for tickets. Let's go."

Queenie frowned, pulling out some swimwear from her storage. "So...did you guys need these or..."

"No. Enter the staircase in the locker room. I'll see you there."

"Huh?"

The boys entered their room while the girls stared at their backsides. Juliette took another swig of her drink, tapping her jug with slender fingers as she did. Without saying a word, the mentor walked into the changing room, forcing the remaining Misfit to chase after her with an annoyed scowl. Juliette took lazy glances around the locker room, her alcohol jug clattering against her hip as she did.

"Have you ever been here before?" asked Juliette.

Queenie wrinkled her nose. "I...I don't think so, no. This all looks new to me."

Juliette nodded slowly, quietly observing the various lockers. As she did, Queenie glanced around at the changing room. It was a one story building: where were these supposed stairs that Taba talked about? If there were tatami mats on the floor, she could assume that there was a hidden trapdoor...but the ground was covered in light blue tiles. As she stomped on each individual square, nothing gave out...so no hidden floorboard of sorts.

After a few minutes of stomping, Queenie heard a small cough behind her. "...What are you doing?"

She turned around to see Juliette having opened four locker doors to reveal a hidden closet. Oh. Yeah, that made more sense. Queenie stopped her stomping and cleared her throat. "Bugs. I was stepping on ants."

"I haven't seen a single insect in this bath house."

"Well your eyes just su-let's just go, ok?"

Juliette gave the faintest of smiles before ducking into the tiny closet, Queenie following shortly afterwards. It was a bit of an uncomfortable passage, with creaking wood slowly turning into dusty stone, each step sinking deeper and deeper. Eventually, the light of the changing room vanished and the pair became immersed in dark.

After a few minutes of slow shuffling, Queenie cleared her throat. "So...how did you know to check the lockers?"

She couldn't see two feet in front of her, but Queenie could *feel* Juliette's monotone gaze glancing back at her. "There were dusty footprints leading from the bottom shelf, but no footprints leading *to* the shelves. It's pretty straight forward."

"Oh. I knew that."

"Which is why you were stomping on imaginary ants?"

"They weren't imaginary: you can look at their squished bodies when we resurface."

"I'm sure I will."

After a few more slow shuffled steps, Queenie accidentally bumped into Juliette's wooden box. The girl frowned as she rubbed her head. "A warning, next time?"

"...There's a metal door here."

"...open it?"

"There isn't a doorknob."

Queenie frowned. "Use your brush. You're strong enough, right?"

Juliette sighed. "I don't have space to swing: only stab. Even then...you're in the way."

"You act as if I can't back up."

"I see. So back up."

"No."

After a while of this bickering, a voice coughed from behind the metal door in front of them. "Tickets?"

"They're with us. Here." replied muffled voices.

After a grunt, the metal door slid open to reveal a bulging man whose grubby hand clenched four cheap pieces of paper. Taba nodded as he held out a hand. "You guys sure are slow. Hurry up." Juliette climbed out of the tunnel without the help, but Queenie gratefully took the assistance. They stood in a forked road, with a similar metal sliding door to their left: presumably the passage from the men's changing room. The paths converged into a single walkway ahead, with the lingering soul being more dense in the air. The four of them walked through the hallway and blinked to see a massive blue...well, it would be wrong to call it a pool. It was closer to a pit of liquid soul more than anything. A few soulbearers laughed wildly as they dove in and out of the pit, while others chose to simply sink into another pit of bubbling "blue". Vendors sold food and drinks in the corner, with people eating and drinking with hearty laughs. Though the air was misty, the temperature didn't feel warm at all: in fact, it was slightly cool. It was an unimaginable paradise.

Juliette said nothing, but Queenie noticed the Fox's jaw locking. Taba looked around with tight lips. "Yep. It's all about the same. Let's go say hi to Maggle."

The party slowly pushed past small groups of people here and there, with their attire catching the eyes of many. A few seemed to recognize the party as their eyes flickered with recognition before darting away, whereas others just seemed confused as to why some young adults weren't wearing swimwear.

Some small shove later, and the party reached an office with another fat man standing in front of it. He said nothing, simply huffing at the sight of them. Taba nodded and flicked a coin to the guard, whose sausage-like fingers grabbed the coin before letting them in.

...and there he stood. A big man, wearing an open bathrobe with shorts, sipping away at a cup as he stared at some pictures on the wall. His pasty white skin was blinding to look at, seemingly having never touched the sun before. However, unlike the previous guards, this man seemed to be secretly well built, a wall of muscle hiding behind rolls of fat. As he turned, his luscious locks fluttered with his neck.

Maggle's shoulders hunched as he quickly swallowed his drink and placed his cup down on his desk. "Good heavens...that you, boy?"

Taba couldn't help but crack a small smile. "Hey, Maggle."

The big man roared with laughter as he quickly hugged the trio in one fell swoop, his tight hug choking out the party. After a deep squeeze, he let go with a twinkle in his eyes, his gaze falling to their silent mentor. "My my...an exquisite rose."

He quickly reached out to grab her hand, but Juliette pulled away with a mild grimace. "It isn't polite to touch strangers."

He chuckled as he suddenly reached out with blinding speed, his arm firmly, yet daintily, grabbing her hand. As he knelt down to plant a kiss, the Drunken Fox scowled and drew her arm back with force. Maggle got up with a sigh. "Good lady, how can I get to know you without proper introductions?"

"I never planned on getting to know you." Juliette coldly responded.

The big man held a hand over his chest, looking slightly offended. "Well, my! Who knew such a rose had thorns? You *know* that there are many who would do *anything* just to shake my hand, no?"

"Then go ahead and talk to *them*."

"Well, I always did like my steak with spice," Maggle said with a wink. He then nodded to the sofa in the corner. Have a seat, all of you."

The Misfits plopped down on the couch in his office, while Juliette chose to stand with her back to the office door. The big man collapsed into his chair, sipping away at his drink as he did. After a bit of squirming, he leaned back into his chair. "So, boy. How can I be of service?"

"We have plans to take out the chimera and need your blessing." said Taba.

Maggle raised his eyebrows as he sloshed his liquid in his mouth, swallowing slowly as he considered Taba's words. "Well...isn't *that* a loaded sentence. Why kill the chimera? Why do you need *my* blessing? What makes you even *think* that you stand a chance?"

"Well...we need your blessing because of the chimera's assimilation. Your potion should work as a kind of 'barrier', giving us temporary immunity against the thing. And uh...we're killing it because, well...it's complicated. It's this weird mix of being forced to, to prevent war, and having trust in Father."

"I guess the rumors were true, hm?" sighed Maggle. "The brilliant boy and his comrades, captured by the Gatekeepers." He nodded to the Dancing Painter. "So...is she the one keeping you guys captive? Say the word, and I'll release you guys *right* now...if you have the payment for it."

Juliette immediately took off her wooden box, her mask staring holes into an unflinching Maggle. Taba held up his arms in light surrender. "No, it's fine. We're doing what we can to prevent war, and our 'release' will only make the situation worse. Malapace is keeping

Toukie hostage as well. Plus, I don't think we have the funds for your...service."

"Boy, you *know* I don't need *funds* for my services. Why would I want something so cheap? But on that note, what makes you think you have the payment required for my potions?"

"So, what do you want? Weapons? Money?" asked Queenie.

Maggle rubbed his chin, pondering the suggestions. "Fine offers, truly. But no, my concerns drive further than that. It'll take an insane amount of soul to make your potions, and even if I *do*...there's no true guarantee that you'll kill the chimera, right? In which case, that's a poor investment."

"Ok...so what did you want?"

He grinned as he held up three fingers. "One: I refuse to make investment with my own funds on something so risky. So, if you want your potion...I'll be crafting it with your own soul."

He got up from his desk, pointing to Juliette and Queenie as he did. "Two: I need *her* word that Toukie will be released and that Malapace won't persecute my establishment. I'll also require a *heavy* down payment from the girly in the form of a natural weapon."

As Queenie opened her mouth to protest, the big man coughed as he slowly approached the couch, the room's shadow looming over his eyes. "Three: I refuse to waste my time and energy entertaining an impossibility. So, you three: prove to me that you've grown and take me down. Entertain me, eh?"

"Ok, but what do you mean?" asked Hush. "Like...*kill* you, o-"

His words were cut off as his head was suddenly grabbed, lifted, then thrown through the office door with a crash. Juliette had already unboxed her paintbrush and was poised to swing, her stance low after ducking past Hush's flung body. A flare of anger spiked up in Queenie, immediately pulling out two daggers from storage.

Maggle held up a finger to the Dancing Painter. "Now, sweetheart. I know *all* about you, and how you've decimated entire armies. However, if you strike, the deal is off: I won't *ever* make you potions." He then addressed the infuriated Queenie. "So, what do *you* think I mean when I say 'take me down'?"

"Oh, I'm gonna stab your neck."

He roared with delight. "That's the spirit, chum!"

Maggle ducked out of the office and into the main lobby, where the people were already scattering from the area after seeing Hush's body being flung. To her relief, Hush seemed to be alright, groaning in discomfort as he floated in a soul pool. Taba, Queenie, and Juliette climbed past the shattered door, staring at the big man as he stood in the middle of the blue liquid pit.

As he took a deep breath, soul slowly bubbled around his body and formed a protective layer around his flesh. He opened his eyes with a grin. "Well? What are yall waiting for? Take me out."

Queenie darted her eyes to Taba, whose eyes were flickering as he asked countless questions in his mind. After a few silent seconds, he nodded to her. "Fight without restraint. I'll back you up. Trust me in *everything*."

She nodded, and dashed forward. Once she stood a few feet from Maggle, she summoned chains to snag her ankle and drag her above the big man, who flinched at her sudden move. As she landed in the soul pool with a splash, she slammed her daggers into his neck.

...Only for her blades to be stopped at the protective layer that rest at his skin. He whirled around and grabbed her arm firmly, then threw a heavy blow with his other arm. She instinctually moved her legs, but couldn't budge due to his monstrous grip. So, she summoned a shield last second to block his strike. Though her defense worked to deflect his hit slightly, the shield still slammed into her nose, causing Queenie to yelp as blood suddenly flung into the air. With stars suddenly fluttering in her vision, she could only notice the sizable dent that Maggle had left in her discarded defense.

He laughed with excitement as he lifted his arm once more, but instead of striking at Queenie, he turned around and struck at Taba who had leapt in his blindside. Though he had blocked the strike, Taba was still set flying into the pool with shocking speeds. Maggle kept his grip on Queenie, calling out to Taba as he did. "Boy, you aren't as silent as you think you are."

Taba stood up in the shallow end, grumbling as he stared at the pale man. The questioner then ran through the soul at moderate speeds, making obvious movements to Maggle. In response, the big man laughed as he flung Queenie's dazed body in his direction.

Maggle's eyes suddenly widened as his neck was put into a headlock, his eyes tilting to see a determined Hush holding onto him firmly. Unfortunately, with soul coating his neck, Maggle seemed to breath relatively normally without restraint. So, he reached around and grabbed the older brother's small ponytail, using it to fling him with enough force to cause Hush to slam into the soul pool's floor. He rubbed his neck with impressed eyes. "Well then! You weren't *that* good at using your blessing before. I guess you *have* grown in these past few months."

Suddenly, chains wrapped round his arm and slowly began to drag him out the pool. He chuckled and pulled back, causing the chains to go taut and begin to crack slightly. As he did, Taba jumped forward and threw an elbow at his direction. Maggle took the hit directly, not even flinching as the Misfits' blow was stopped upon his body's soul layer. The pale man lifted a hand to strike downwards, but Taba seemingly dodged instinctively to the left while his right leg suddenly leapt to slam into Maggle's neck. Though the attack did nothing, Maggle grinned. "Boy! How were *you* able to grow? I thought you had peaked!"

Taba wrapped his leg around his neck, using the momentum to suddenly lift upwards and wrap around the big man's entire head. Though he was gasping for breath, the Misfit grinned wildly. "Honestly? I thought so too. Crazy how much I have left to learn, right?"

He locked eyes with Queenie, mouthing something to her. She hesitated, but pulled out a sniper from her storage, setting it up while Maggle's eyes widened. The pale man began to thrash wildly, but Taba wasn't letting go. Somehow, his fingers had pierced the soul layer and were resisting Maggle's flails. Suddenly, the pale man's eyes stared at Queenie in confusion, his gaze not really focusing on her. He then began to dart his eyes everywhere, as though he were searching for...something.

Though her head was still spinning and her nose was bleeding, Queenie quietly took aim. For others, this was an impossible shot: striking a fatal blow between two bodies flinging around in a pool. For Queenie? It was fun target practice.

She exhaled, then fired.

In an instant, the pool suddenly vanished and the pair was flung backwards. Queenie's vision flickered for a brief moment as she recuperated from the soul loss, but she got up and ran towards the duo. Taba rolled away from the big man with a groan, while Maggle's head was dazed as a small trickle of blood flowed from his forehead. Perhaps it was due to his dazed state or her attack, but his soul layer had vanished. Queenie quickly pulled out a dagger and thrust the blade down on his neck.

Taba leapt upwards and tackled the girl, who stumbled backwards with a scowl, her knife flung into the air. As she struggled to get him off of her, Maggle got up slowly with a groan. "Yeah...ow. You guys win. I concede. Well done, you all." He winced as he rubbed his minor head wound, his eyes' glow fading away. "Still, you lot sure have grown, hm? Your bullet couldn't have pierced my blessing before...and here you are. Man, you guys sure have grown. On a side note..." Maggle frowned. "Where did you go? Were you hiding on the ceiling?"

"Huh?"

"You vanished, girl. Where did you hide? Couldn't have been far, since you were setting up the sniper."

Their confusion and questions were answered as Hush rolled out of the pool with a groan. Maggle looked at the older brother with awe. "Oh my. You...are brilliant, aren't you? I didn't know that was even *possible*."

Hush coughed dryly as he stared at the ceiling. "Well, this was my first time using it in combat. It's...*really* hard. I never wanna try that again."

Queenie stared at everyone in confusion as Taba grinned, slowly walking over to offer a fistbump to the collapsed older brother. "Hell yeah. I *knew* you could do it."

"I'm sorry, what? Can someone fill me in?" asked Queenie.

Juliette stepped out from the shadows and put her wooden box down gently. "I'm just going off of content clues, but...Hush. Did you *partially* activate your blindness?"

He turned his head on the floor, his half closed eyes blinking slowly. "I...yeah. I...ugh. Man, I'm sleepy."

"What?" asked the younger sister. "How does that even work? What was it like to experience that?"

"It's disorienting, in all honesty. Like, after a certain point, your vision turns fuzzy...or the setting is 'different'. I don't even know how to explain it, but I think *that* is scarier than pure blindness, solely because it's *much* harder to tell when you've activated your blessing." said Maggle.

"It isn't feasible to do in solo combat though...not yet," Hush said as he yawned. "Still, we beat you, right? Will you make us potions?"

Maggle plopped down to the ground with a grin. "Well, standing up makes me dizzy, so you tell me." He nodded to Juliette, who tightened her lips at the gesture. "If *she* agrees Malapace will release Toukie *and* won't persecute my spa, then we have a deal."

Juliette looked down at the pale man with a disdainful look. "That all depends. For Toukie, if he agrees to release his blessing...you have my word. As for the spa...explain *why* there's so much concentrated soul here. The average soulbearer doesn't have even a fraction of the soul I see here. How is it even possible to extract soul from someone to this extent?"

He leaned back on his palms as his narrow eyes contemplated his next words. "Mmm...I can't *fully* say, no. All I'm at liberty to say is that, well, this is a gift from Father."

Immediately, the Drunken Fox unsheathed her paintbrush and pointed its bristles at the big man. "Explain, in *great* detail."

"My my. It's been a while since I've seen a woman who sparked my heart once more," chuckled Maggle. "Let's compromise: I won't be able to tell you anything about Father, but I can tell you as much as I can about this entire operation, as well as my own blessing."

"And why should I believe you?"

He chuckled and tilted his head to Queenie. "Because *she'll* explain it. If someone who can't tell a squat of a lie explains it all, you'd believe it, right?"

"Wait, what?" said Queenie.

Maggle winked at her. "I trust ya, girly. Don't say too much though, ya hear?"

Suddenly, everyone's eyes focused on her, and she immediately felt the pressure building. Even *if* she wanted to lie, it was suddenly impossible.

Queenie scowled as she stared at the ground. "Fine. Maggle's blessing allows him to coat soul around a person, forming a shell of sorts. Depending on the quality and quantity of the soul, the density and strength of the coated layer increases. So, Dad decided that it would be smart to give him a crapton of soul. Good enough for you?"

"Obviously not. There are still too many unanswered questions. Where did your 'Dad' get this soul? Why are there others here? What is the soul *really* used for?" asked Juliette.

"Piss off, I've said all I'm willing to say. I don't wanna say anything more."

Maggle chuckled as he gently pushed away Juliette's weapon. "Come with me, you Drunk Fox. I'll talk to you in my office. The rest of you, soak in the soul: it'll replenish ya faster."

...

Juliette held her brush with caution, staring down the enemy. From watching his scuffle, it was evident that he could easily close the gap between the two if he so chose.

As they entered his office, the enemy collapsed onto the chair with a groan as he rubbed his head. "Girly got me *good*. Ow. If I acted a single millisecond late, I'd be dead."

"You know ascension," Juliette said crossly. "How the hell could *you*, someone running a resort, know ab..."

Her words trailed off as she looked into his eyes. The joy in his smile, the twinkle in his pupils, the energy in his posture: all gone. He looked...so exhausted. Juliette knew it wasn't from the scuffle.

Magg...the *enemy* looked at her with wistful eyes and a soft smile. "Juliette, was it? You know about ascension. In what world do you think I've chosen this? If I could trade my blessing and all my gains for...no, that's not what we're here to talk about." He took a deep breath and slapped his cheeks, looking back up with forced energy. "Girly didn't have the heart to betray Father, so I'll explain what I can. Father plans to change the world, and to do that...he needs soul. Now, naturally, the best way to do that is to obtain it from others."

Her blue eyes narrowed behind her mask. "So, you've been killing innocents?"

"No, Father wouldn't do that...and if he *would*, our Family wouldn't be nearly as massive. No, what we've decided on is a mutual contract." said Maggle. He looked at her with the most hollow of eyes. "We provide patrons pure ecstasy. Unlimited food. Good drinks. Happy atmosphere. Hell, we even make them forget their trauma. In return, they give us *all* their soul."

Juliette's grip tightened around her paintbrush. "You...you scum. How many have-"

He suddenly slammed his hands into his desk, cracking the sturdy wood immediately. After a few deep breaths, he looked up with a twitching face. "Darling. Me and Father already know that. However, to force someone to live in their circumstances?" He rubbed his hands as he calmly closed his eyes. "Imagine you're a fourteen year old girl. You've accidentally killed your own parents due to your blessing manifesting in an atrocious way. You've come to despise your ability, and yet, subconsciously, you're afraid to die. No matter how many times you try to hang or drown yourself, you always find yourself flailing for air and crying so hard you vomit. Would *you* not want to forget everything, and end your life with joy and peace?"

Maggle looked at her tragically. "Juliette. It's true that Father needs their soul. It's undeniable that we're horrendous monsters who've killed numerous soulbearers, children and adults alike. However, our hearts ache all the same. *That* is the intent behind this spa house, and *that* is why we do what we do. I cannot force you to agree with our stance, but surely you can sympathize with it."

Juliette's paint brush tipped towards the ground. The big man before her had killed numerous people. He was an integral part in 'Taba's Family'. And...and yet...?

He was no enemy. She could not find it in her heart to hate such a miserable man. So, she packed away her weapon and quietly left the office of the silent, yet broken man.

CHAPTER 15

Hush, Taba, and Queenie sank deep into the soul pit, groaning as they lay motionless. The other patrons had slowly peeked in and rejoined the room to continue their party, living it up as much as they could. There were a few other adults who chose to bathe in the soul, sighing breaths of warmth as they did.

"Man, it's been a while since I've felt *this* sore. I gotta practice moving like that more." said Taba.

Hush turned his neck slightly, wincing as he did. "Ow. On that note, *how* did you move like that? Were you doing something with your blessing, because that was *not* normal movement for you."

"Yeah. I did the thing where I tried to make all my cells use my blessing individually...but that was too hard. So, I did the next best thing: I had my entire body act on autopilot with the questions 'How can we take Maggle down?' and 'What can I do to ensure no one dies or gets severely injured?'. From there, well...from there, you saw what happened."

"What? How does that even make sense? Your blessing only answers yes or no: how would it-"

Taba stared at his hand, opening and closing it slowly. "Yeah, but I set those questions as my 'goals', in a sense. From there, each question served to inch each cell closer to that 'goal'. So, for example, my legs would ask 'will jumping onto Maggle's back help me get closer to defeating him?' while my back would ask 'will his counterattack get me further from his defeat?'."

Queenie scowled as she rubbed her arms with some of the soul in the pool. "That barely makes sense. That means each part of your body was asking multiple questions every second while also making sure each answer didn't overlap with other body parts *and* with both of your questions. Not to mention the amount of soul that your method would take: that would drain you, right?"

"Yep. That autopiloting drained me in every aspect: soulwise, physically, and mentally," Taba said. "I don't think it's something I can do constantly in every fight." He turned to nod to Hush. "On that note...you grew too, right? How were you able to pull off using part of your blessing? I thought you could only shut off *all* of one's sense?"

Hush sunk deeper into the soulpit as his mouth blew bubbles into the pit. After a few seconds, he sat up slightly and glanced over to the other Misfits. "It isn't my first time doing it. I tried it out on Juliette earlier when you wanted to talk to us in front of her. Couldn't outright deafen her or she would catch on."

"Doesn't explain *how* you did it though, dingleberry." Queenie frowned.

"I was getting to that, stupid. Well, impacting someone's sense requires a certain amount of soul. So, I figured pushing back on the soul required would 'weaken' my blessing, right? So, I tested it out on her...and it worked? Tried it out later a few times on myself during training, and tried to replicate it today against Maggle. Honestly...*not practical in one-on-one combat.*"

"Why? Wouldn't using half your soul mean you could use more soul for other things, like soul manipulation?" asked Taba.

Hush rested his head against the pit's wall. "You'd think so, right? But...I'm using soul to push back against soul. So I'm actually using *more* soul than normal when partially activating my blessing. Adding in the fact that it requires a stupid amount of concentration, I can only use it if I'm being supported...for now, anyways."

Queenie flopped into the pit with a sigh. "Whatever. I wanna rest. Maggle hits *hard*, ugh."

The older brother slumped with a groan. "...Tell me about it."

...

The next two weeks were exhausting.

Since Maggle required the trio to use their own soul, Their days were spent waking up, having their souls seeped away with the big man's blessing, then soaking in the soul pit to hasten their recovery. Since the food reserves were saved for the other patrons, the Misfits had to settle for eating every other day. Sure, it felt weird going back to their old ways and lifestyle, but it wasn't unexpected.

After the third week, Queenie flopped onto bed with a scowl. "I'm gonna lose it. It isn't just tiring: this entire soul thingy is *boring*."

Hush rubbed his wrist with a yawn. "Deal with it. At least we're almost done with this."

Maggle knocked on their guestrooms and barged in with a grin. "Sorry, champs: we're only halfway there."

"Oh, bulls-"

He laughed and withdrew three vials from his bathrobe's pockets. "Kidding, kidding. Here."

The big man placed each vial next to their respective futons. Each bottle was seemingly made of glass containing a misty light blue. To those unfamiliar with it, Maggle's blessing made soul appear as though it were in a state between liquid and gas, the container's contents sloshing the misty liquid around without any real weight or resistance. Maggle leaned on the doorframe with a nod. "Alright, so, Taba, my boy. Your soul is in the bottle with the red dot. Queenie, girly. Your soul is in the bottle with the yellow dot. Finally, Hush. Son, your soul is in the bottle with the green dot. The key important part is to *not* drink your own soul. Otherwise...the protective layer does nothing and it'll just merge with your own body again."

Hush stared at his vial. "So...if I were to drink this, I would essentially regain my soul?"

"Mhm, so don't do it. I mean, you *could* if you needed the soul boost...but then you'd have no defensive layer against the chimera."

Taba twirled his bottle between his fingers. "Mm. Can you confirm with me how long this would last for us?"

"Boy, you know the answer."

"Yeah, but the others don't, so tell us again."

"There isn't an 'again' if I've never-ah, fine. It'll last about twenty-five minutes."

"Wait," said Hush. "Nearly three weeks of full on extraction barely provides half an hour of protection?"

The big man shrugged. "There's a few difficulties that you guys don't fully realize. First off, I'm storing my blessing when it isn't designed to be stored. Secondly, I'm extracting soul when my blessing's

268

primary function isn't to 'extract' soul: it's to utilize it. Lastly, I wasn't *just* extracting and storing soul. No, if I did that, what would stop the soul layer from just peeling off upon contact with the chimera? I had to layer it as well in a fine manner so the chimera would instead peel off individual coats, as opposed to sucking it all up in one go. Also considering the fact that I'm doing this with someone else's soul instead of my own, well, I think that what I did was pretty damn impressive." He retied his hair into a bun and nodded. "You get what I'm going at? I specifically designed these vials for fighting the chimera. If you wanted basic potions, I'd have finished two weeks ago, so you're welcome. Look at what I do for you all."

"What about Juliette?" asked Hush. "She hasn't been with us during the soul extraction, so..."

"I gave her a vial of my own soul to use. It'll last about double of what yours will last since it's easier to layer my own soul, but the effects should be the same."

"Why make an exception for her? Hell, considering the fact that she's from Malapace...shouldn't she have been the only one to *not* receive a vial?" Taba asked.

The pale man chuckled with a wrinkle in his eye. "Ah, we talked, and she convinced me with sultry words. Who could resist, eh?"

Juliette, being intentionally provocative? That didn't line up. Hush glanced at the other Misfits, who all shared the same look. Maggle wasn't one to hide something without reason...but he also wasn't the kind of person who liked making others worry. Probably best not to push the topic any further.

Queenie fiddled with a dagger. "So, was today the last day? Are we good to head out?"

As Maggle opened his mouth to answer, a thought flickered across Hush's mind. He stared at the bottle with a frown. "Wait, would Queenie be able to store this with her blessing? I mean...it has soul, so wouldn't that constantly drain her?"

The big man rolled up the sleeves of his bathrobe with a small grin. "You see, I'm a genius. So of course I thought of that. The bottles are thinly coated with Queenie's own soul, so they won't *actually* drain her soul while stored...as long as the vials are tightly shut. Apart from that, though, the bottles are plain glass...so stop playing with that dagger, girly." She rolled her eyes and stored her weapon away. He continued, nodding to her.. "And to answer your question, yes: you *could* technically leave today, but...why not rest up one more day? No point in leaving while tired."

Taba stared at his bottle while twirling the soul inside. "Yeah, we'll stay the night. The rest of you guys ok with that?"

"Yeah."

"I...ugh. Fine."

Maggle grinned and opened up his arms. The trio all subconsciously got up and walked closer. The second they got close, he wrapped them all in a massive hug. He rested his cheek on top of their heads. "You fools best stay alive, got it? I'd be quite sad if I got news of...well, let's not think about that. Dammit, I'm gonna miss you kids."

The Misfits said nothing, simply nestling deeper into the big man's stomach. It was weird: they all loved him and wanted to return to their family...so why didn't they team up with Maggle to try and take down Juliette? Might not be easy, but...

Hush rested his forehead on the big man's shoulder. No. That just didn't feel right either.

...

He got up with a groan, an echoing throb laced in his brain. The cave floor was damp, with a thin bed of straw scattered beneath him. As water dripped from a stalactite above him, Hush blinked as he noticed a faint trickle of light leak from a crack in the wall.

This wasn't the hideout. Where...?

Hush silently got up, doing his best to not make any noise. He took careful steps to the cave's mouth, risking a peek outside.

Instantly, he was met with a blast of cold air blown into his face. He blinked rapidly to avoid his eyes from suddenly drying out and squinted at some figures standing in the crisp morning air. There was a tall man wearing a tattered coat, a shivering younger teenager wearing only a white shirt and pants, and a younger girl wh-

Hush blinked and grit his teeth. That was Queenie. What was going on? Was she in danger? Why didn't she have a weapon out? The older brother carefully scooped up a stone from the floor, preparing a plan to take his sister back and bolt away. If he could distract the captors and then use his blessing to stealth away...

However, upon flexing his fingers, black spots danced in his vision as Hush collapsed with a gasp. The others turned around to the sudden noise and witnessed a sickly boy collapsing to his knees. To his woozy surprise, Queenie was the first to move, gasping wildly as she knelt to his level, quickly feeling his forehead with cold hands.

She tilted her head downwards to lock eye contact. "I...Oh...Are you...are you ok?"

Though his mind was blurred, he could tell that she was slowly panicking at the sight of his weakness. So, he clenched his fist and tilted his

271

head upwards with a grin. "I'm fine, relax. Get out of here, I'll hold 'em off and be right with you, ok?"

Queenie hesitated, blinking rapidly as she darted her eyes back at the two strangers. "Um...Hush? I think...these are good guys."

As the two guys slowly approached them, Hush pushed his sister behind his back with a scowl. His fingers gripped his rock with a firm tremble. "Back off. I've...I've killed people before, I'm not afraid to do it again."

The younger boy took a step back with hesitation, but the older man took another calm step with gentle eyes. He put his hands in his pockets and stared at the older brother with kindness. "Hush, was it? I heard a lot about you from your sister. I-"

"Who are you? Where are we? What did you do to her?"

The stranger smiled softly. "You may call me Father. We're in some random caves that we're using as a temporary home. And well...I saved your sister from death, then listened to her story."

Hush hesitated, the grip on his stone loosening slightly. "...What?"

Father removed a hand from his pocket and rubbed his fingers between some loose dirt. "There's no hidden meaning behind my words, child. I will say, however, I was the one who overthrew your clan...so if you wish to hold any grudge against that act, I understand."

The older brother's eyes spun wildly. This was all a bit too much to comprehend. This man saved Queenie but overthrew the Hush clan? Why? Plus, how could one man alone do that? He didn't seem to have a mass following of any sort...so...

Father seemed to notice the boy's confusion and chuckled. "Yeah, it's fine if you don't believe me for now. Still, you guys are technically home-

less...so until you get back on your feet, I just wanted to give you guys a place to stay. If you want to leave, I won't stop you two."

"And what's to stop me from just killing you outright?"

The younger boy who stayed quiet finally spoke up. "You wouldn't be able to."

The older brother stared at the other boy. He seemed fairly built for his age...but nothing too remarkable. And yet...the look in his eyes, the way he carried himself? This boy seemed untouchable. False confidence, maybe. Hush grit his teeth with a scowl. "You don't know what I'm capable of."

"Yes I do. If anything, it's you who isn't aware of what Dad can do."

The two of them stared at each other with scowls before Father clapped with a small chuckle. "Boys, boys. Relax. Hush, let's rest for now...since you can't really move. Once you have enough rest, you're free to challenge me or Taba here...or flat out leave. On my honor, I won't sway your decision whatsoever."

And so, the inseparable trio was born.

...

"You got the bottles?"

Queenie rolled her eyes and unstored the vials, 'sloshing' the soul around them before storing them once more. "Your fourth time asking today."

Hush tugged on his jacket as he glanced around the spa grounds one last time. It stayed just as he remembered. Small groups of adults, teenagers, and adolescents running around the pool-like scenery with no dread and regret in their eyes. It looked the same as it did a few weeks ago...and how it appeared six years ago, when he had first met Maggle.

The big man exited his office, wiping his hands on a tablecloth as he nodded to the group. "Y'all packed up?"

"No care package? No sendoff gifts?" Taba asked.

"That isn't how I roll, boy, and you know that." He tucked his rag into his shorts then looked up with a grin. "So, how 'bout it? One last hug?"

Queenie scowled as she rubbed her nose. "Got all my feels out yesterday, thank-you-very-much."

"Figured." chuckled Maggle.

He turned to Juliette and for a quick second…Hush caught the smile vanishing from the pale man's face. The two of them exchanged a small, somber nod, before Maggle turned to the others cheering in the soul pit. He clapped loudly, attracting their attention. With a grin, he boomed from his stomach: "*Boys and girls! Let's give a **grand** cheer to our departing Family!*"

In an instance, everyone roared in wild excitement, waving frantic arms at Malapace's party as they made their way to the exit. Familiar faces grinned at the Misfits, some of them even patting their backs as they walked away. Once they reached the front doors, Maggle suddenly jumped on the trio, causing them to lurch forward.

He grinned and kissed each of them on the tops of their heads. "Stay safe, fools."

Warmth spread across Hush's chest, and he said nothing as he embraced the big man's hug. After a solid minute of tight hugging, he let them go with a grand wave. As the doorman slid the front door open, everyone cheered as the boys exited the right door and the girls exited the left door.

Hush and Taba after clambering through the tunnel for a few minutes, they exited into the changing room and trotted out of the spa house, waving their goodbyes to the old woman in the front.

Upon stepping outside, the party was greeted by the warm summer heat once more. Everyone blinked rapidly as their eyes slowly adjusted to sunlight after being indoors for weeks.

As he squinted, Taba tightened his lips as his eyes softly darted about: a tell that he was using his blessing. Hush waited a bit before clearing his throat. "So, what's the next best call?"

"Well...we go to the chimera."

"I don't mind, but I imagined that you would want more preparation, especially after all the time you spent getting that soul vial from... *that* man." Juliette said with a slight frown.

"No, we've prepared all we could in regards to the chimera. However...we still need to *get* to the damned thing."

"Like, traveling to it? What's the problem?"

"No, the chimera is a mutant that's completely sealed off." said Taba.

Though her face was hidden, Hush could tell that she was blinking with mild confusion. "Pardon? If it's sealed away, why is it a threat? Do you have plans to unseal a sealed mutant?"

"Yep, precisely."

Juliette rested her hand on her gourd. "Why?"

"We don't know, either," Hush muttered. "In fact, Father played a huge part in sealing the chimera away in a foolproof way...so it's odd as to why he would suddenly boast about using the chimera in the upcoming war."

"Would it not be a bluff, then?"

275

"It *could* be a bluff," said Taba. "Just as equally, it *could* be a genuine threat. Still, let's consider both possibilities." He held up one finger. "Let's say it's a bluff, and Dad has no plans for it.. If it were, then Dad has no real advantage in the upcoming war, and has lost a valuable fighter because you guys captured Toukie. Well, no real advantage barring his overwhelming strength." He held up a second finger. "Let's say it isn't, and Dad has a way of utilizing the thing in the upcoming war. By *not* taking it out, Malapace, with no question, will suffer overwhelming casualties as they have to deal with *both* Dad and the chimera."

Taba lowered his hand. "Even if all that we're doing is 'meaningless', we still have valuable materials in the form of the vials. So, worst case scenario: Malapace has info on our Family, we have defensive vials, and have ease of mind in knowing that the Family has no real 'trump card' in the next war. Best case scenario: we drastically intercept the Family's plans, and shift the tide of war in Malapace's favor."

"Alright. If what you say is correct...why are *you* mentioning it?" she asked. "After all...aren't you still allied with your Family? Why should I believe you?"

Hush glanced at Taba's face. It was calm, his chin raised as he met the gaze of the stoic woman. "We're with the Family, yes, but we don't *want* meaningless casualties: especially not that of good people. Dad knows that, too. I'm certain he would want a peaceful surrender over a mass genocide. If a war were to break out, I would rather not have it involve the chimera: less deaths that way on *both* sides."

"Mhm...and you know this because of your blessing, I'm guessing?"

"Partially because of my blessing. Partially because it's common sense, and if you've ever *met* the damned thing, you'd understand too." Taba said. He raised up an arm and pointed down the road. "Let's start walking. It'll be a few days before we reach the zoo."

...

The road that Taba had pointed down quickly turned from crunchy dirt into mushy soil. Vegetation slowly became more abundant, and soon, the party was swallowed by the trees.

Hush didn't like the forest. Sure, partially it was due to the humidity, but it was also due in part to wildlife. It always felt like *something* was staring him down. He wasn't sure why, but he could *feel* whenever eyes glared at him. The beasts, mutant or not, would eventually dart back to their dens or holes...but the unease always lasted. After about the sixth creature, Hush stopped warning the party and decided to be tense all by himself. No point in continuously worrying his friends.

After a nerve wracking four hours, the party settled down in a somewhat spacious clearing. They plopped down, passed around drinks, and wafted their shirts in exhaustion. The sunlight flittered through the various leaves scattered above, the damp trunks staring down at them with frowns. Chitters, clacks, and screeks of the wilderness surrounded them. Despite the mating calls of creatures never sticking around, the chimes of the animals slowly melted into background noise. Tiny insects trudged about their tasks on the ground, winged bugs flew around their sweat-soaked cheeks, and suspiciously big cocoons wriggled every few seconds. Occasionally, the party would see a normal rabbit peek out from the underbrush before scampering away within seconds. The trees worked to shade them from the majority of the sunlight, yet also served to softly steam their skin with the trapped moisture.

Hush stripped off his jacket and tossed it to Queenie, who took it with a scowl before storing it away. He nodded to Taba, whose eyes were darting around ever so slightly. "What's the plan?"

Sweat dripped down his temple. "I...don't know. Something's wrong. Something's wrong. G-"

Suddenly, he yelped as roots snapped up his leg and dragged him underground. Taba quickly gripped onto a nearby branch to prevent sinking further, yet the branch gave away without *any* resistance, sinking him immediately into the dirt. Juliette and the siblings immediately scrambled to their feet, confused and alert at the sudden development. Hush immediately felt something ancient latch onto his leg, pulling downwards with horrifying force. Suddenly, the pull stopped and he crumpled to the ground. Looking at his leg, he saw tree branches-no, *roots*, wrapped around his leg, the ends of it oozing green as it was cut off with precise strike.

Juliette cursed as she readied her brush once more. "You two, *off the ground*: it's a mutant tree. I'm getting Taba."

Hush felt his body lurch upwards as Queenie summoned chains to suspend them midair. The Drunken Fox sprinted to where Taba had sunken, leaping gracefully over rupturing roots that failed to capture the nimble woman. Upon reaching his last position, she immediately gripped her brush and began slashing the ground with various strikes. Each hit dug up more dirt, yet roots seemed to halter the woman's progress, stopping her from quickly unearthing the boy. The mutant tree creaked and groaned, looking not so different from other plant life. However, when its bark split open to spew out steaming sap and its branches bent downwards to swat at the Dancing Painter, he immediately feared for his life once more.

The older brother instinctively flexed his fingers...then stopped. *That* was the unease he felt. He wasn't sure why, but he could feel enemies staring at him. However...trees? They had no senses for him to augment. So, he could *feel* threats, but since his blessing wouldn't work on a plant...why would he feel "danger"?

He swore under a damp breath and glanced at his sister. Her eyes were wide as she stared at the pit where Taba had gone under. Hush wasn't *nearly* as tactical as Taba...yet if he didn't take charge, Queenie would crumble.

He snapped his fingers at his sister, who flinched in response. "Snap out of it: this is Taba. He'll be fine for now. What *you* need to do is start slashing away at the tree's branches from a safe distance. Just by reducing the 'limbs' of the tree, you'll be able to help out Juliette."

She swallowed dryly. "...Alright. What will y-"

"Let me down to the ground. Trust me."

Queenie opened her mouth to protest, but nodded stiffly. The chains that suspended him vanished one by one, slowly lowering him to the ground. As they did, he immediately amplified his sense of feeling, becoming more aware of the things around him. Hush's toes touched the ground, immediately rolling sideways to avoid tendrils sprouting from the ground, failing to capture him. He continued to sprint forwards, slowly noticing a pattern emerging from the eruptions.

Then it hit him: of course there was a pattern. This wasn't some living creature who felt emotions. No, this was a *plant*: it moved autonomically. It would always perform actions dependent on the situation based on efficiency: *not* on instincts. Once Hush understood that fact, things became more straightforward for him.

As Queenie and Juliette weaved around branches and sap, Hush darted to the tree trunk and began climbing with notable speed. As the tree tried to spout out its sap, he could feel the trunk bubble internally in various locations, and could scramble out of the way before the syrup spewed out. Once he had climbed past the trunk, he darted around the thick, humid, tree branches, avoiding various swats and holding on tightly whenever it tried shaking him off.

After he clambered onto the top, Hush poked his head above the treetops and enhanced his eyes to scan the area. If this tree was a mutant...then there was a chance mutants were normal in this area. If that were the case, then it would be beneficial to lure one over here, as it would serve to distract the tree as they dug their friend out of the dirt.

Suddenly, his eyes locked onto a herd of massive beings. Numerous hands sprouting from its face. Big ears flopping around. Blue soul jutting from the corners of its jaws. Triple jointed legs. Oh...Hush was *incredibly* lucky. The mutants was too far away for Hush to impact their hearing, so he did the next best thing. He flexed his fingers to amplify his voice, took a deep breath, and screamed the most *human like* roar his lungs could muster. The mutant's big ears flinched, head turning towards the sound. Its three small eyes blinked independently and widened at the sight of the boy. Excellent.

He climbed down to the forest to look at the situation, the instant humidity blending his sweat with moist eyes. Queenie was strung up to a tree's trunk, cutting away at branches that tried to drag it below. Numerous other trees seemed to have noticed Juliette and were unifying their efforts to capture the woman. Her fox mask was off, sweat beaded on her brow as she rained numerous cuts down on the branches only for each branch to return twofold. Though it seemed as though she had abandoned the idea of unearthing Taba, the spot at where she had dug still showed signs of dirt flicking everywhere, indicating that he was indeed being dug up, albeit *much* more slowly. Hush scampered down the tree quickly to help their mentor out, watching in horror as her movement became more tight and focused as she began to dodge multiple roots, branches, and sap from every direction at once. Her eyes were flickering everywhere, her brush spinning wildly, her sandals kicking away at the wood from the ground. Gradually, her footing got more and more cramped as roots threatened to entangle even the slightest misstep.

The Dancing Painter was slowly being overwhelmed.

As his toes touched the ground, numerous roots sprouted up to grapple Hush. The older brother began dodging to the height of his abilities, using his heightened senses to their utmost capabilities. The pressure that was on Queenie and Juliette had gone down just slightly, but the party was slowly being conquered. That was fine. They just needed to bide their time fo-

The trees suddenly cracked open with a massive scream as the mutants from before burst into the clearing, their calloused skin shrugging off any attacks as the arms sprouting from their face instantly crumpled away any branches or roots that existed. Juliette noticed the mutants, the skepticism and bewilderment shining from her glowing eyes as the creatures began to dismantle the mutant trees around them. One of the mutants lowered its long nose to the ground where Taba was buried, sniffed, then slammed its numerous hands easily into the dirt. After a bit of rummaging, Taba was lifted up to the skies, his neck limply dangling as his chest softly moved up and down.

Queenie and Juliette were breathing heavily as they stared at this herd of mutants crowd them, patting them with their face-arms, ears flopping excitedly at their presence. Hush slumped to the ground, relieved at how well things had turned out.

Mutants, by most cases, were savage. However, there were always exceptions. Though no one knew why, *these* mutants seemed to love humans. They would always crowd around them with excitement to pet and give them attention. Thank goodness for this love, too. If it weren't for that, these pack animals with high intelligence, extraordinary senses, powerful muscles, and tough skin would be near impossible to fight or flee from.

As the creature began to use its numerous hands to pat and stroke Hush's face, the older brother could only laugh as he, in return, shook hands with the mutant elephant.

CHAPTER 16

‘ *..and yeah. I always suspected Jin was...but...'*

• *Dad stared down at the shivering girl with a small nod, showing comfort by quietly listening to her vent her worries out. He was too trusting. Even with his ability, Taba wasn't sure if housing these new orphans was a good idea...since Dad was the reason these guys had lost their families.*

The older man knelt down and rubbed her back gently, a sad look in his eyes. "I see. My sincerest apologies that you've had to go through that. W-"

Suddenly, the sound of a stone clattering against the frozen floor. Taba turned around to witness the girl's older brother hunched on the floor, his arms trembling as he tried to stabilize himself. The girl left their side and scrambled to her brother, exchanging soft words as the weakened teenager forced a comforting smile. The siblings seemed to perform their respective actions instinctively. Taba raised an eyebrow. Guess they really loved each other.

Suddenly the older boy locked eyes with Taba and scowled, his fingers snatching up the rock once more as he flexed his shoulder. From his lowered stance, it was evident: the guy was used to fighting. It wouldn't be too absurd to assume that this weakened boy could kill Taba if given the opportunity.

Father took cautious steps forward and-

...

Taba coughed up moist dirt from his lungs, his chest suddenly throbbing with agony as his consciousness stirred. His blurred eyes looked up to see the two siblings...and dozens of grey hands ruffling their hair. The sight was so bizzare that Taba tried to abruptly sit up, only for his head to spin massively as he crumpled to the floor once more. A long nose suddenly sniffed at his face, causing the woozy boy to flinch slowly.

Queenie quietly hugged herself with trembling arms as Hush let out a sigh of relief. "Man...glad you're up. We don't really have a means of healing and you weren't breathing normally, so all we could do is pump your chest and pray. How you feeling?"

Taba spat up dirt and slowly moved his eyeballs around. He followed the long grey arms and saw they were attached to big faces with curious eyes, soul protruding from their faces.

"...Mutant elephants...? What...?"

Hush slightly nodded to one with his neck, causing the herd to scream in discord. After cringing for a solid eight seconds, Hush shuddered. "Yeah, saw them from afar and managed to gather them here. They were the ones who took down the mutant tree. Well... trees. More popped up after you sunk, but Juliette stalled for an insane amount of time."

"And where *is* she?" Taba asked, slowly rotating his stiff neck. "Don't see her."

Queenie tugged her sleeves with clenched fists. "She's resting by herself, don't think she likes the elephants much. Still, she's...wow. She was protecting me, defending herself, attacking the trees, digging *you* up, and assisting Hush. I...how was she doing all that with such ease? It isn't fair."

A mutant elephant began to twirl Taba's hair with numerous fingers with different hands. Unable to muster the energy to shoo the creature away, all he could do was sigh. "Well, we knew she was strong. That was expected." He gave a small nod to Hush. "Good thinking on your end. Thanks for picking up my slack."

Hush scoffed. "I arguably did the least in terms of fighting and stalling for time. Go thank Juliette next time you see her. Can you get up?"

"No."

"...Figured. Well, not much we can do, let's crash here for the night."

"I mean...is that ok?" Queenie asked, looking around her. "These are still mutants. I don't think we should trust them."

Taba shrugged to the best of his abilities. "Well, mutant elephants don't attack humans...and not many mutants out there can take on this herd and come out unscathed. They're probably our best protection for the night."

She sighed and got up, causing many mutants to scream in protest as she did. She cupped her ears, rolled her eyes, and nodded to the trees. The intention was obvious. *'I'll go tell Juliette, then. Be right back.'*

The female Misfit trotted off, a few younger mutants following her with protest as they continued to prod at her hoodie and poke her face. Once they were alone, Hush lay down next to Taba with a sigh.

285

Taba turned his eyes to the sky. "So...how do you feel?"

He could hear a chuckle from his left. "You nearly died, and you're asking *me* how I feel?"

"Yep."

"...Honestly? My hands are still trembling. You nearly died. Queenie nearly died. Juliette was slowly getting overwhelmed. I...man. I don't even want to think about what I would've done if this herd wasn't in the area...or if they hadn't heard me."

Taba stared past the numerous arms patting their head and gazed at the clouds. He didn't even need to use his blessing to think about different possibilities. "Nah. You would've been fine. You would've saved us."

Hush didn't respond. As they stared at the drifting clouds, the only sound that came from his left was a small shaky breath.

...

A day's rest was all Taba needed to stand up with a stiff back. He stood up as the sun began to set and glanced around, seeing the herd sleeping all around them, with Hush snoozing away as he rested against a mutant's stomach. Careful not to make any noise, he got up and peeked around at the sleeping creatures, looking to see if he could catch glimpses of Queenie or Juliette. A bit away, he saw a few mutant elephants huddled under the base of a tree. Probably where the girls were resting.

He gently nudged Hush's shoulder, whose eyes darted open with caution. Taba gently nodded to the smaller herd, mouthing '*let's go*'. The older brother semed to understand, flexing a few fingers to deafen select elephants as they tiptoed out of the herd. Mutant elephants loved humans...to an extreme degree. It was to such an extremity that

286

many found it difficult to get away from a herd once surrounded. Though they would never be in danger, a few stories would circulate about how humans would be stuck in the center of such herds for weeks at a time before sneaking away.

Once a good distance away, Hush glanced up at the trees with a frown. He nodded to a branch. "There."

And there they were. Juliette was leaning against the trunk of the tree, taking shallow breaths while Queenie sat on a neighboring tree branch as she stared at the approaching boys with a nod. She gestured to their mentor and mouthed '*She's sleeping*'.

Taba raised an eyebrow. He had never seen the Dancing Painter sleep in the few months they had stuck around her. Odd. Still, he jutted a thumb to the girl and pointed down the forest path, glancing at the sun. The message was obvious: '*Wake her up and let's go before it gets too dark*'.

Queenie rolled her eyes, shaking the slumbering woman's shoulder. Whether intentionally or unintentionally, she used excessive force and the Drunken Fox tumbled out of the tree. Somehow, she landed on both of her feet, glancing up to see the stirring herd. Queenie stifled a cackle as she gracefully landed next to her, Hush quietly cursing at her.

Welp. Not much they could do. Taba locked eyes with Juliette and pointed at the forest. She understood immediately, and the party fled into the forest before the herd could fully rouse.

From there, the party navigated the rapidly darkening woods, their only guide being the *mostly* recovered Taba, occasionally halting their tracks and turning at sharp angles. Now that he knew that trees could mutate, well, it let him know what to be wary of.

Is there danger to our left? **O** *Is there danger to our right?* **X** *Are we heading in the direction of the chimera zoo?* **O** *Is there a mutant tree within fifty meters of my location?* **O** *Is the mutant tree to our right?* **X** *Is...*

He couldn't quite use his blessing with all of his cells *just* yet, but he was slowly getting more comfortable activating it with both his legs simultaneously, allowing him to essentially triple his thinking power. It felt odd, being able to 'think' with his quadriceps...but he supposed he would get used to the sensation with time.

The second the moon touched the stars, the party emerged from the woods with a a deep sigh. They stepped out onto a crumbling side-walk and stared at their destination: a relic of the the world pre World War III. Supposedly, humans would capture animals and encage them here to watch. Even *if* mutants didn't exist back then, Taba couldn't help but wonder how all that worked. Capturing the animals, bringing them here, feeding them, ensuring they didn't escape, so on. All in all, it seemed impractical and pointless. Sure, there were unmutated animals that Taba had seen around in the wild here and there...but he didn't think it was worth it to capture these creatures, much less go out of his way to simply...*stare* at them. Maybe it was a status of wealth, saying that you were *so* rich that you could afford to simply pay to watch game, instead of immediately hunting it. Oh, maybe it *was* a hunting thing! Like, maybe humans would select and choose which animals to g-

He shook his head. Focus. He was getting distracted. With the task so close at hand, he couldn't afford to get distracted. Taba needed to question how they were going to kill the chimera...but more impor-tantly, how they would convince Glen to undo his dome.

288

The party stared at the withered zoo, completely encompassed with a two massive blue bubbles. Taba hoped Glen was doing ok.

...

As they approached the zoo, they stared at the little plots growing a variety of plants. Some were empty, some had little buds, and others were in full bloom with grains and bushes. Amidst it all, they saw a man who looked simultaneously toned and malnourished, digging away at the dirt, his slimy skin coated with flecks of dirt and sweat. He wore a tattered labcoat, with ragged dress clothes under his garb.

Unfortunately, Glen seemed the same as usual. Taba cleared his throat and called out to the man. "Hey Glen!"

The man stopped digging and turned around to reveal insane eyes. They twitched as his lips curled into his mouth, looking as though he were trying to chew his face off. His trembling fingers dropped his trowel and he began to quickly shake his head back and forth.

"Nope nope nope nope nope I won't take it down nope I won't nope she's in there Father said to keep it shut I can't nope no-"

"Relax. Let's talk a bit. We're actually on an errand from Dad," said Taba. Can you come closer?"

The man's body leaned away, yet his legs marched awkwardly forward. Once he was at the edge of the bubble, he planted his butt into the moist dirt and darted his eyes all around, eyes flicking cautiously at the bugs that scampered around.

Taba, in turn, sat down and stared at the mad man, smiling softly. "Hey, Glen. You doing alright?"

He scratched rapidly at his neck, eyes flickering to the treetops as his fingertips tapped at his palm. "Yep. I'm ok. Yep. If that's all, goodbye. Yep."

289

"We need to talk, Glen. Dad wants us to...well, we need to get rid of the chimer-"

Glen stood up abruptly, his eyes staring wildly at everything *but* Taba. "Nope. Nope. Nope. She's busy with it. She's almost there. Nope. Can't let you. Nuh uh. Bye bye." With that, he turned around and ran past his fields, running into a crummy shack with no door.

Juliette, though her head was slightly swaying, glanced at Taba. "He's a curious man, isn't he?"

Taba got up with a sigh, brushing the dirt off his butt. "He's...well, he used to be a genius. I'm afraid the years haven't been kind to him."

"Is he important to killing the chimera?" she asked.

The Misfit nodded, knocking on the barrier. Though it made no noise, his fingers stopped at the bubble. "Yep, *very* important, as he's the one in charge of caging the beast...and his cage is unbreakable."

Juliette unsheathed her brush, nodding at the bubble. "May I...?"

He shrugged, backing away. "Try."

The Drunken Fox put her back into a double handed slash, her brush stopping instantly upon touching the wall. She frowned and backed up. "Oh."

Queenie nodded, pulled out a pistol, and fired a few rounds into the bubble, each bullet stopping at the barrier. "Yep. Kills all momentum. Sustains no damage. Doesn't run out of energy. In fact, it *absorbs* energy from incoming attacks, making it unbreakable. The only one who's able to take this barrier down is..."

Juliette stared blankly at the girl. Though her mask hid her expression, Taba could clearly imagine her blinking. "No...you mean...?"

Hush nodded. "Yeah. The only one able to bypass the barrier is Father. Anyone else, well...Glen will need to take the bubble down."

"Well...how do we do that? You know him best." said Juliette.

"I genuinely have no idea." Taba said. "He hasn't put this bubble down in over five years."

That was a lie: there was another way to take the barrier down. The bubble would fade if the soulbearer passed...but hopefully Taba could convince Glen to take the bubble down of his own accord.

...

'This is Glen and Linda. Say hi, you three.'

Taba stuck his hand out as Glen met it in the middle. Queenie crossed her arms while Hush rolled his eyes and forced his sister to slightly bow her head. Linda chuckled and bowed in returned.

Dad smiled. 'These are my head researchers: well, it's more like they're in charge of research due to their blessings allowing for it.'

The young Taba tilted his head. 'What are you guys researching?'

Linda puffed out her chest with pride as she stepped out in front of Glen. 'Ignore that runt of a man: he does nothing. I merge mutants to see how their traits combine while observing how their soul multiplies.' She leaned in with a twinkle in her eyes. 'Did you know that their soul multiplies on initial merge, but after that first merge...their soul slowly flattens *out??? And th-'*

Glen grabbed her labcoat and yanked her backwards, sighing as he did. 'Sorry about that, she's a bit...insane.' He looked at her with a frown. 'Seriously, they're kids. I don't think they'd understand. There's a chance that they don't even have manifested blessings.'

Linda looked at Dad. 'Hey, they have blessings, right?'

'Yep.'

Linda looked back with a grin. 'So what was the problem, again?'

'You're incorrigible.' Glen muttered.

She reached upwards and pecked him on the lips with a grin. 'Why else would you fall for me?'

He wiped his lips, face flushed. 'There are kids, Lin. Calm yourself.'

Queenie frowned as she nodded to him. 'Ok, but what do you do? Same as her?'

Glen let go of Linda with a frown. 'Well, no. I'm just as curious as she is about mutants, but only her *blessing* allows for the fusing of the mutants. My job is to protect her as she gets close to take notes.'

'Yeah but...where are you even getting mutants? They aren't exactly easy to come across.'

Glen opened his mouth to speak, but Linda shoved him aside with wild eyes. 'This zoo is a damn mutant magnet! They're attracted here, and it's your guess as to why! Maybe they were normal animals that got mutated and they have fond memories here. Maybe they're attracted here due to the resources. Maybe it's because o-'

The male scientist sighed as he squished Linda's cheeks shut. 'In short, Mutants come here. To make sure we aren't overwhelmed, I make sure to put a little dome around the zoo,'

Taba glanced around at the bubble that surrounded them. "Ok...but is this dome really that strong? What's to stop anything from breaking through?'

Linda removed Glen's hand from her mouth and blurted out with excitement. 'Check this out!' She grabbed a rock from the floor and threw it at the barrier. Though the dome had acted like a wall to the trio, they stared in surprise as the rock easily sailed through the bubble's walls.

Glen scowled and clenched his fists. 'Lin, what the h-'

She grinned an infectious grin. 'You see, the trick to his blessing is-'

...

Taba stared at Glen's shack with sorrowful eyes. The man was a genius. Calm, composed, and tactical. It was an absolute travesty what he had deteriorated to.

He peeked over his shoulder to make sure Juliette wasn't watching, then kicked a rock casually towards the bubble. As expected, it clattered inside the domain easily. Yep, as expected...the barrier had the same properties as it had all those years ago.

Taba looked upwards and noted bright, fluffy clouds littering the sky. *Will I be hit by rain in the next week? O Will I be hit by rain in the next five days? O Will I be hit by rain in the next three days? X*

He tightened his lips. The Misfits had four days to find a way to either find a way to bypass the bubble or get Glen to willingly turn his blessing off. Once the rain pierced the veil, no doubt the insightful Juliette would take notice and ask questions. As Juliette wobbled towards a tree to lean against it, he locked eyes with the siblings and they all nodded. They huddled closer and exchanged glances.

"Does he have any new weaknesses in the dome?" asked Queenie.

"No. Same weakness, nothing new to exploit."

"Damn," cursed Hush. "Does that mean we have to..."

"Well...it'll rain in four days. For now, we should use that as a deadline for when Juliette discovers the 'other' way to penetrate the bubble."

The Misfits fell silent as they searched their own thoughts. Taba quietly asked questions to think of different ways 'through' Glen's blessing. Hush stared at the trees where Juliette was rubbing her temple with one hand and sipping from his jug with the other. Queenie stared at her toes, her eyebrows furrowed as her fingers nervously peeled and unpeeled the tape off her dagger's handle.

And in silence, the first day ended.

...

'Lin, are you insane?*'*

'Science has always needed a drop of insanity, no?'

Glen's eyes were wild as he stared at the monotone woman. Though she seemed nonchalant, Taba noticed her fingers slightly trembling as they were tucked away in her elbow. He didn't need to ask his soul to know she was putting up a front. Dad most likely saw through the façade as well, his lips tightening as he considered her proposition.

He rubbed his dry hands and stared at her determined eyes. 'Linda, while I'm genuinely flattered you'd go this far for me...I'm with Glen on this. This idea sounds insane, and well, I don't know if I can in good conscious allow this.'

She rolled her eyes and grabbed a bunch of papers off her desk. 'Squids. Pufferfish. Snakes. Leopards. Millipedes. Doesn't matter what the mutant is, it will *merge seamlessly without flaw. 'Normal' with 'mutant', 'mutant' with 'mutant', both combinations result in a merged hybrid mutant. Hybrid mutants fuse seamlessly with hybrid mutants. Plus, each merge results in greater soul and abilities. So...why not throw a human into the mix? Wouldn't they be able to then wield unfathomable powers and soul?'*

Glen scowled as he grabbed a random paper from her hands and scanned it. 'Lin, this isn't funny. Each merge has always turned out more savage, cunning, and harder to control. Hell, even-', he scanned the paper he had snatched from the female scientist, '...the 'bombardier beetle and bumblebee fusion' was fatal. I remember this one specifically, because the thing nearly **killed** *you the second I put my blessing away. Your stupid idea has so many flaws. Who's getting fused? How will they approach*

294

the current version of mutant we have right now? What happens when the fusion doesn't fail? What hap-'

Linda stepped in boldly and sealed his lips with a quick peck. She stepped back and took a shaky breath, combing her hair with her left hand's fingers as her right hand's trembling fingers tapped her stomach. 'Ok, hun. Shush. I'm not an idiot, I've thought of all this. I'm not planning to ask anyone to be the test subject: I plan to take on that role myself. No one knows more about the ins-and-outs of the mutant than I do, so I'll be able to step in and fuse myself with the thing. The fusion won't fail: it never has.'

'Lin. You're mad. Why are you so certain about all this? Your sample size is nowhere large enough to be this confident.'

She nodded to Taba. 'It's why I asked for him to be in this meeting.' Linda looked at the young child. 'Hey. Will my merge with the mutant be successful? Will I obtain its abilities? Will my soul increase?'

Taba stared at her quietly as he asked her questions. '..yes. Your blessing will work. From the looks of it, the thing's abilities will be enhanced after your fusion. Your soul will increase exponentially to unfound heights. Hell, from what I'm asking, it seems like it'll be self sustaining...and you won't even need to eat or drink to sustain life anymore.'

She turned back at her fiance with a confident grin. 'Boom. See?'

'But...but it isn't how you want,' Taba said softly. 'I don't know how, but my blessing is advising against it. I don't think you should do this.'

Linda stared at him briefly before being shoved aside by Glen, his wild eyes staring holes into the child. 'What do you mean?'

'I...I asked if she would regret this. She would.'

The silence rang loudly in the room as the adults exchanged nervous looks. After a few quiet seconds, Dad cleared his throat and slapped his thighs, commanding the attention of the people. 'Linda. I...truly do care for you. Without a doubt, this will help further my goal...but I don't want this for you. Neither does Glen. Hell, from the looks of it, neither do you. Please, reconsider this Li-'

She slammed her arms on the table, the papers she held scattering and crumpling under her weight. After a few trembling breaths, she looked up with watery eyes. 'You wanna know something? I held my sister's body in my arms as she crumbled away to a freak blessing manifestation. She didn't even know what was happening, but I won't forget her confused eyes as she stared up at me. Now you're telling me the goal is within arms reach, and all I need to do is suck it up, be uncomfortable, and no one else will have to go through what I did? Do I look so selfish as to stay ignorant, turning my eyes away from endless possibilities and potential solutions? Really?'

Glen gripped her arms, swiveled her body to face him directly, opened his mouth to scream....then slumped to the ground. After a few seconds, a small, shaky breath whispered out from the floor. 'I...Lin. I could give less of a damn of the world. Please, don't do this. Don't leave me.'

She held up her quivering jaw upwards, refusing to let her overflowing eyes burst. She turned to Dad, slowly nodding. 'If you don't want me to do this, stop me yourself.'

The older man looked at her with sorrowful eyes and stood up. He walked over to her, then wrapped the scientist in a soft hug, squeezing her back as he rested his forehead on her shoulder. 'I...can't force you to do anything, you know that. If you truly want to do this...I won't stop you. Will you truly live through a new hell for your ambitions?'

Taba watched from the sidelines as the woman gave a fake, bold smile. 'Please, do I look so weak as to chicken out last second? I made

my mind up four months ago: I'm only announcing it right now because
everything is set in place.'

She pulled away from Dad and nodded to the crumpled man on the
floor. 'Can I have a few moments, Father?'

He nodded, gestured to Taba, and the two of them left the sobbing
couple to their own devices.

...

When he got up, Taba noticed that Queenie's sleeping bag was empty. Juliette was sleeping as she slumped on a tree stump, while Hush laid motionless in his own sleeping bag. The teenager got up and walked around the impromptu campsite and eventually noticed the girl crouching by the soul bubble, quietly reading a book with Glen's wild eyes staring at her as he babbled incoherently. The two of them noticed his approach and directed their attention to his groggy face.

He nodded to the pair. "Hey. It isn't like you to be awake so early."

Queenie tightened her lips as she gestured to the book. "I wanted to know more about the chim-the current specimen. I asked Glen and he handed me a list of all the fused animals."

"Many animals, yep yep. Some mutant, some normal. Ant, armadillo, bat, bear, bumblebee, bombardier beetle, hippo, leopard, the five-lined skink lizard, monkey, pufferfish, rattlesnake, squid. Many animals, many traits."

Taba knelt next to Queenie and scanned the contents of the journal notes. It seemed as though varying traits from each animal would be honed and added onto each new creation. The physical power of some animals and the defense mechanisms of others combined into something that seemed something purely phantasmal. If Taba hadn't witnessed the chimera himself all those years ago, he would probably assume that this was just based off some child's imagination.

He flipped through a few pages and then looked up at the girl. "This is good info and all...but this isn't like you. Why get up so early for this kinda info?"

Queenie chewed her cheek. "Eh." She tenderly grabbed the book from Taba and casually handed it over to Glen through the bubble. She waved her farewells to the twitching man, then nodded to the questioner towards the woods. They trotted out of the mad man's earshot before she leaned in. "I know of a way to get inside his blessing. Spent all night thinking about it, and I know it'll work. Plus, my way makes it so Glen doesn't have to...well...die."

Taba blinked. She had thought of a way that his blessing had failed to find? How? "What? How? What's the way?"

"You'll find out, but trust me when I say I can get you guys in. All we need to do is prepare for fighting the chimera. When you're ready, we can all head into the zoo."

Was she lying? He could always *ask* his blessing...but...

"Can I trust you to not be stupid?"

"Yep. Maybe. Eh, probably not."

He sighed. That meant her plan was probably stupidly reckless...but also meant that it would absolutely work. He couldn't think of a way to ask his blessing to reverse engineer her plan, but he didn't need to: if Queenie said it could be done, it could be done. "Fine. I'll spend the next day preparing, so you better be ready when I give the green light. Got it?"

She chuckled and offered a fist, to which Taba tapped with his own closed hand. "Whatever you say, boss. Now, get to making a plan to beating the crap outta the ol' chimera."

CHAPTER 17

Taba quietly wrote in the dirt with a stick, muttering as his eyes darted subtly. Queenie's brother was slowly encircling the bubble, trying to map out the zoo from what little he could see. Juliette? Well, she continued to snooze away.

Queenie was a bundle of nerves. She hadn't been lying about being able to burst through the barrier...but she wasn't sure if it was the best idea. It would drastically neuter her fighting capabilities in the fight, but well, that was for future her to worry about. She needed a path and this was the only way she could think of without killing off Glen. Taba most likely would have never considered this in his questioning, since he was too selfless...so it was up to her to be selfish.

As her tummy rumbled, she scowled and rubbed her gut. Living in Malapace had made her too soft. She had gone days without proper meals, and now going a few hours without a bite would leave her stomach rumbling for more. She had gotten too comfortable with the sensation of a full stomach. Queenie would have to skip meals when she returned to the cit-

She blinked. Returned? Why did she immediately think of returning to the city? Was she *that* conditioned to the place? Or...or by any chance, was she-

Queenie scoffed and threw her dagger in the air, staring as the blade sliced through nothingness and twirled with no ambition. Nah, that can't be it. Her mind was just too used to the place after sticking around there for months. She would've thought the same if she had stayed anywhere for months at a time: this wasn't unique to Malapace.

She suddenly heard a shrill whistle scatter across the air. Queenie turned her head and met eyes with Taba, Hush stopped his scouting and Juliette roused from her slumber, glancing at the questioner. Seeing his determined gaze, everyone slowly trotted over to his spot to see what he had to say.

Once they met up at his location, he nodded to the party. "From Glen's notes, I made a list of traits that the chimera will most likely have...and have developed a response to each one. Well, in regards to their defensive attributes, anyhow. We just need to avoid the thing's offensive traits to the best of our abilities because I don't see a world where we completely outspeed or overpower the creature."

He then began to slowly break down the chimera's innate traits in fine detail, explaining possible solutions to each and every one, using his stick to draw out positions and attack routes in the dirt. After twenty minutes, Queenie's head was spinning with tremendous detail. Ugh, she hated plans.

"...and I can see the squid's traits allowing for multiple limbs, but I really think that its inherited trait will focus o-"

Queenie coughed loudly, cutting off Taba mid-sentence. He looked at her with a quizzical eyebrow as she sighed loudly. "Look, None of

301

this will stick in my head, you of all people should know that. Can you list out the main traits we should look out for? That way, our head isn't bogged down in the middle of the fight considering possibilities that'll never come."

Hush shot her a harsh glare, but she didn't care. While overthinking worked wonders for Taba, it would only serve to hinder those who weren't on the same mental level as him. The only one who might be able to keep up with Taba's reasoning would be Juliette, and even *then*, it wasn't a good idea to fill her head with meaningless data. The questioner needed to learn how to simplify data for those not able to keep up.

Taba's eyes were mildly annoyed, but he sighed. "Yeah, fair enough. Things to look out for: the ant's ability to carry multiple times its own weight. The bat's hearing and echolocation. The cheetah's speed. The muscle mass and strength of the bear and hippo. The bombardier beetle's acid attack. Pufferfish's poison. Rattlesnake's venom. However, the things to be *most* wary of are the squid and lizard's traits."

"Why those?" Hush asked. I imagine their traits are the least scary of the listed animals, no? I'd be more afraid being being sprayed by acid than whatever a squid throws at me."

"Remember, this is a result of a *scientist's* experiment. It isn't a freak mutation, they were intentionally chosen," said Taba. "Linda most likely chose those animals due to specific traits. I think sh-"

Juliette raised her hand, to which Taba flinched and nodded to. "Uh, whatsup?"

Her void eyes stared into the boy's heart. "Why are we making plans to kill the chimera? Was the initial plan not to get the beast's creator to split the beast apart?"

302

The Misfits exchanged glances. The jig was up: no point in hiding it any more. Taba nodded. "I lied. Sorry."

In a flash, the teenager raised his arm and quickly blocked the blur of the Drunken Fox's strike, just *barely* avoiding being strangled by the stoic lady. The veins in his arm budged as he winced at her grip. She held her box with her free arm, leaning in to stare the boy down. "You...*really* thought it was a good idea to lie to me?"

Taba tightened his lips, using his free arm to wave Queenie and Hush back. The female Misfit grit her teeth, hand clenching a dagger she had subconsciously unstored. Her brother had also taken a stance, his hand flexed in anticipation for a fight.

The questioner's hand was turning slightly purple, but he stayed calm. "It wasn't with malicious intent, Juliette. The creator of the chimera is dead: assimilated into her own creation. It's impossible to split her apart from the thing, but this mission wouldn't have been approved if I told you guys that."

The Drunken Fox's grip tightened even further, causing Taba to wince. "You don't know that."

"...I do. I knew even before you knew."

"How would y-" Her mouth opened slightly, loosing her grip. "Ah. Your blessing."

Taba pulled away from her, rubbing his arm as sweat dripped from his palm. "Yeah. Still, we need to kill the chimera: not taking this mission would be an utter mistake. So many would die if it were left alive, so I did what I could."

She tightened her lips. After staying silent for twenty seconds, she slowly nodded. "Fine. Still, what makes you think we can take the mutant down? You guys nearly died against a mutant frog and tree. How do you plan to win against something like *this*?"

"If it can bleed, it can die." Queenie said.

The Dancing Painter's mouth twitched. "Do you not bleed?"

"I wouldn't know. Guess that means I'm immortal."

Taba stepped in between them, glaring at the two. "Enough. No point in squabbling amongst ourselves. I'm confident we can win...*if* we work together. Juliette, I can't force you to fight with us...but our chance of victory goes down to zero without you. Will you trust me?"

"Absolutely n-"

Hush stepped in and whispered something to the woman. She flinched, slowly turning her head to stare at the young adult. "...W hat's to stop me from killing you all, right here and right now?"

A thin ribbon appeared across Hush's neck, dripping across it's edges. He didn't as much flinch, but simply stared at the lady with bland eyes. "Do it. Go ahead. Lose your greatest bargaining chips against the Family, and watch as everyone you know and love crumbles away in the next war. If you're that confident in your own power, well, you'd losing nothing by killing us."

"You truly think those I love are still alive?"

Hush held his head up high. "Well...am I wrong, Jules?"

In a moment's flicker, Juliette threw her body's weight into a single punch, landing squarely into the young man's stomach. He crumpled to the ground with a wheeze, desperately sucking in whatever air he could. Queenie snapped, jumping at her mentor with a scream-

...Only to be knocked down by Taba. As he pinned her to the floor, she darted her eyes upwards and screamed obscenities at her friend, hand trembling with malice and fettered rage. He looked at her with restrained anger. "Hey. Stop."

"Oh, piss off you fu-"

He leaned in with a snarl. "You *promised* to me that you knew a way into the bubble, and that you'd provide a way when I asked. I know you're pissed. Seriously, I get it...but *stop*."

The glare in his eyes made her stop wriggling. It had been a while since she saw him *this* angry. What was going through his mind? Taba pinned her down for a few more seconds before standing up, calmly walking over to Hush, who lay choking on his own lungs. After massaging his friend's chest for a while, he looked up at Juliette with firm eyes. "Hush isn't wrong: you *could* kill us...but we have a mutual goal. Neither of us want meaningless deaths. You don't have to like us, that's fine. Still, killing us would eventually lead to the mass death and defeat of *both* the Family and Malapace. So, help us kill the damned thing, then you can consider killing us afterwards. Fair?" He helped his friend up off the floor and nodded to the two women. "We'll head out tomorrow. For now, we should rest to recover from today's scuffle. If you have the heart to help us tomorrow, well, come on by. Until then, you two sort things out."

The two men limped off into the impromptu campgrounds, leaving the quiet anger of Juliette and cuffed wrath of Queenie to stare amongst each other. The woman gently caressed the top of her wooden box without breaking eye contact of the infuriated girl. For some reason, their mentor's expressionless stare only served to irritate her further.

"You piss me off." Queenie said through gritted teeth, white knuckling her dagger.

"Is that so? What are you going to do about it?"

She was in range. If Queenie threw her dagger, it would land squarely into the woman's forehead: end of story. Plus, she was an enemy of the Family: getting rid of her would be of great use to them all. After a few silent seconds, Queenie swore loudly and stored her dagger away. She made a stupid promise to Taba to help him out...and unfortunately, Juliette's cooperation was absolutely needed for that.

"So. You know I hate you."

"Yeah."

Queenie felt a vein bulge in her throat as she spit out a venom-dripped request. "Cool. Can you help us?"

"Why would I help you liars?" Juliette asked.

"Because the chimera is a *wee* bit more important than my stupid pride and your stupid...well, *everything*. I would rather not have people die due to me not being able to bite back my tongue."

Juliette took a swig of her drink, twirling the alcohol around her mouth as she stared at the sky. "Do you truly think that the Gatekeepers wouldn't be able to take the chimera down without civilian casualties?"

The young girl exhaled as to calm her heartrate. After a moment, she nodded softly. "Yeah. It's impossible."

"Oh, if that's the case, what makes you think us four have a shot at killing the thing?"

"I don't know. Genuinely, I don't," Queenie said. "Still, if Taba says its possible...it's possible."

"You would place your life in the boy's word? Truly?" Juliette said with slight judgement.

"Yeah. Without a doubt."

Juliette took small steps towards her and leaned forward until her mask was only a few inches away from the girl. "Even if he told you to die for the greater good?"

Queenie stared back with irritated eyes. "Please. If Taba tells me to die, I imagine it'd be for a good reason. Taba wouldn't tell me to march towards death unless there were literally no other options left."

The woman shook her head, retreated a few steps to pick up her wooden box, then walked back into the woods silently. Well...crap. There goes Taba's main offense. Did Queenie blow it? Whatever. She did her best, not her fault if Juliette was going to be stubborn. Still, as Juliette returned to the campground, she couldn't help but feel stinging guilt and found herself actively avoiding Taba. How would she even break the news to him? Ho-

Holy *crap*, she forgot about Hush. Was he ok? He had taken a pretty harsh hit. She bit her lip, took a deep breath, and took timid strides towards the direction where she last saw the guys go. Even if she couldn't bear to confess her failures...she needed to check on her brother. She peeked around different trees, looking for the male duo before finding them crouched behind a tree, Taba massaging her brother's gut.

"Breathe slowly."

She heard a raggedy breath, followed by violent coughs. After a few seconds of this repetition, Hush scooched closer to tree to lean against it's base, taking slow breaths as he stared at the treetops. Taba then turned to where she stood, nodding to her. Caught slightly off guard, she flinched before stepping closer. "Uh...hi."

He nodded to the clearing where she entered. "You guys talk it out?"

"I...well...no. Didn't go so well. Sorry."

Taba shook his head. "It's fine. She'll come by tomorrow: just confirmed it right now."

She sighed, a weight being taken off her chest. "You have no idea how...man. I feel like I can breathe again."

Hush coughed on the floor. "Oh, *you* feel like you can breathe?"

The younger sister knelt down, her hands unsure of what to do. "Y-yeah. You, uh, you alright? Any serious damage? I mean, I don't have any proper medicine in storage...but uh...I m-"

"I'm fine. It hurts like hell, but I'm fine," Hush wheezed. "Give me a good night's rest and I'll feel swell afterwards."

She frowned as the memory of the small exchange between her brother and Juliette resurfaced. "So...what did you say to her to cause that kinda reaction, anyhow?"

"I just made a small threat along the lines of this being her last chance to take out the chimera, and how there was a vulture back at Malapace. That's all."

That answer seemed off to her, but Queenie decided it was best to not push the subject further. Her older brother then locked eyes with Taba, nodding as he did. "So. You have a plan against the chimera?"

"Well...I have a general idea of what to expect, but I won't be able to make a plan until we see the thing. That's the biggest concern I have." said Taba with a furrowed brow.

"Ok...well, do you have a way to kill it?" she asked.

"Eh. There are a few ways, not sure which one will end up being used. For now, let's rest up and we can head out tomorrow morning." he responded.

And so, the Misfits went about their ways to kill time as the sun scorched the heavens. She wasn't sure what the other two did, but Queenie spent her day sitting outside the bubble summoning and storing her dagger at seemingly random spots. Sometimes, they would be summoned two inches to her left. Other times, four feet in front of her. She wasn't sure how tomorrow would play out...but it'd be interesting, no?

...

The trio gathered in front of the bubble with groggy eyes, blinking away the sun as they stared at the misty soul that lay in front of them. Tiny birds chipped away as big fluffy clouds slowly loomed around the sun, its warm beams being blocked by cool breeze. As the wind scattered across the treetops, the smell of freshly tossed plant life filled their noses. For such a ominous day, the weather was stupidly perfect. Sure, Queenie would much prefer this over rain dripping over her eyelids or the sun beating on her neck...but wasn't it supposed to rain tomorrow? Shouldn't it be more cloudy?

Eh, whatever. Guess it wasn't bad weather to die.

She cracked her neck and stretched her back, peeking at the woods around her as she did. "So...where's the lady of the hour?"

Taba rubbed his face, bags under his eyes. "She'll be here in about two minutes. For now, mentally go over what to expect from the chimera."

Hush crossed his arms, tilting his head slightly as he frowned. "Fast. Strong. Coated in poison. Spits venom. Spits acid. Am I missing anything?"

"Yeah, the sq-"

Suddenly, everyone flinched as they heard the rustle of leaves from behind them, the soft sashay of sandals crunching under loose dirt approaching their location. The Misfits turned around and watched their mentor slowly walk over to their location...wearing no mask. The three of them flinched as her piercing blue eyes gazed into their hearts, her usual fox mask clattering against her jug against her hip. Oddly enough, as beautiful as she may be, Queenie had to actively resist the urge to flee as she locked eyes with the Dancing Painter.

Without blinking, Juliette walked up and crossed her arms. "Well. Here I am."

Taba blinked, obviously at a loss for words. "I-...yeah, yes you are. Well, everyone ready?"

"No."

"Not really."

"Eh."

Taba nodded. "Cool, me too, but we gotta get this ball rolling. Just focus on dodging. All of us will support Juliette, so just keep slashing at the thing." He then nodded to his mentor. "We'll do what we can to set up opportunities for you."

Juliette nodded to the bubble. "Well, what's the plan to get past that?"

"Queenie said she knew a way."

The girl in question flinched as she suddenly felt sharp eyes pierce her being. "Oh, did you now?" Juliette asked.

Queenie swallowed nervously as she tried not to lose her nerve, pulling out the soul vials from her storage. "Yeah. Everyone, drink up: don't know if we'll have time once inside, right?"

The two guys grabbed vials, uncorked the tops, and downed the gassy liquid. Juliette reached into her sleeve and tilted her head back, downing hers as well. Once confirming everyone had taken their drinks, Queenie grabbed her own vial and took a quick swig of the soul.

It was a weird feeling. After all, Queenie had never drunk soul. It was like breathing in heavy air, or drinking in a chewy cloud. Once it trickled down her throat, the soul seemed to dissipate into her entire being. The more she chugged, the more she felt her body pump up with energy. Her veins bulged with life, her head felt as if it were glowing, and her muscles felt loose and tightened all at once.

She shook her head, unconsciously grinning as she did. The others stared at her with blank stares. Though they were slightly hissing blue, they were not shining as brightly as Queenie was.

Hush cautiously lifted up his hand. "Uh...Queenie? You...you go-"

Without speaking a word, she quickly grabbed everyone into a tight hug, trying to spread the soul that was now bubbling from her body to the others. Once enveloping them with her soul, she closed her eyes and imagined them all breaking through reality...

...and stored herself, Taba, Hush, and Juliette into her storage.

The others flinched at the sudden change of environment, amazed at the vast wideness of clear infinity that stretched to nothingness. Though she would have loved to let them explore to their hearts content...storing herself momentarily was already taxing on her soul. Storing *four* people? Well, she didn't have much time before she collapsed entirely, damning them all to perish alongside with her.

For some reason, Juliette was *much* more taxing than the others. No...it wasn't *her*...but her equipment? The brush, along with the jug and mask was sucking up a drastic amount of soul. It almost felt as though Queenie were storing two different people.

She grit her teeth and pushed everyone forward. Now was not the time to be concerned about some minute details. It was weird, seemingly taking random steps in a blank nothingness, but Queenie was going off of her gut feeling on *where* in her space felt right. After twenty steps, the excess soul from her vial had already run out, and now her *own* soul was rapidly depleting. Cursing loudly, she shoved Juliette and her friends forward into varying spaces before it was too late and summoned them back into the world.

Just like she hoped, she reappeared in a rusty and abandoned zoo. The bad news? Everyone had been separated. She was alone, and wasn't sure if others were in the enclosure with her. On the plus side, she had summoned all of them, seeing as her soul wasn't being drained sharply as it was before.

She wiped the sweat from her brow and took her time to glance around the area. The place was full of rusted fences and empty exhibits, sure, but for a place that had been abandoned for years...the place had a shocking amount of vibrant colors. Bright green leaves, red tents, blue shop displays, and so on. The air felt still, but that made sense: everything was blocked off from the outside world. Wait. No. That didn't make sense...only soulbased objects or abilities were blocked from entering Glen's barrier. Things like rain and wind should be free to enter casually...so where was the bree-

Suddenly, she felt sweat run down her spine as her breathing increased. No, there was breeze...but her body was actively ignoring it. She thought she was feeling sick due to the exertion she had exhibited with transporting the others through her storage...but that wasn't it. This was a primal instinct.

She felt as though she were being watched. Observed. Hunted.

Queenie summoned daggers as she took a defensive stance. Maybe she was being paranoid. Hell, there was a good chance she was on edge for no reason. However, it had been a while since she felt fear of this caliber...and who was she to deny her gut instinct? She took a shaky breath and focused on listening to her environment. Though she stood in the middle of an empty pool exhibit (maybe it housed an aquatic animal?) and had no cover, that also meant that if the chimera were to jump her...the creature's location would be exposed. In that brief window, she would counterattack to kill.

A twig snapped in the underbrush to her right and she swiveled to face the noise, sweat flicking off her brow as she did. Her hand was slightly trembling, but not to the point where it was impossible to wield her weapon. When was the last time she felt such fear? The last time she felt so vulnerable? Well...that didn't change what she needed to do. She just needed to win.

As she stared at the plant life, she suddenly heard what sounded like a baby's rattle: an eerie sound that was both mesmerizing and petrifying. With the song ringing out through the trees, out of the underbrush stepped out...it...no...her? Queenie wasn't too certain what she was looking at. It looked like a lady with a shimmering outline, but for some reason it was difficult to focus on the stranger's being. Every time Queenie tried to stare at her, she found her eyes slightly glazing over as the body melted into its surroundings. The thing's body was bumpy in certain places, but very unmistakably female in others. Though it were covered in human skin, the "skin" also seemed to be layered with tiny scales that shimmered in the sunlight. The scales seemed to be adorned with spots and stripes, and dripping with small bits of liquid. From her behind was an impossibly long tail coated in coarse fur, tipped with a spike at its end. Despite all that, it was the head that was most appalling. Tiny eyes littered the thing's forehead, each one darting in varying directions. The thing had massive fur-tipped ears, each one bigger than its own head. The nose was squished into the face, and her mouth was split open vertically at the chin, each "side" of the mouth covered in square teeth with jagged flats. Drool escaped from her mouth, its forked tongue wobbling wildly in the air, flicking massive wads of yellowish venom onto the floor. The blobs of saliva hissed on the floor, melting tiny puddles as it did. Any spit that landed on the woman seemed to sizzle meaninglessly against her scales.

Various emotions scattered around Queenie's mind. Curiosity. Fascination. Excitement. Sympathy. Anxiety. Unease. Fear. Concern. Dread.

Then, all its eyes clicked into place as it stared at Queenie. As it did, all of her thoughts and emotions fled her mind. The chimera then cackled a startlingly human laugh as it tilted its head.

"*Human? Evolve.* **KILL**"

Suddenly, the woman crouched low, its body bubbling with energy...and Queenie watched as the being suddenly melted away. Honestly, Queenie's gut instinct demanded her to run...but would that really help? No, she was safest knowing she was in danger, as opposed to falling under the illusion of safety. How was the chimera able to turn invisible? The thing was based off real abilities...so what creature allowed it t-

'However, the things to be most wary of are the squid and lizard's traits.'

Queenie cursed as she held her daggers up. Could squids go invisible? She didn't know a damn about animal anatomy. Maybe she should have paid attention to Taba's rambling. Well, no point in crying over spilt milk.

She suddenly felt a pressure rushing towards her at alarming speeds. On pure instinct, she dropped to the ground and felt a burst of wind fly over her head. As the chimera zoomed by, Queenie twirled on the floor and stabbed upwards. However, while the blade made contact, it only scraped uselessly against the thing's scales, with poison dripping down onto her arm. Almost instantly she began to curse as needles trickled across her skin, her hand flaring bright red as it began to tremble. Queenie summoned chains to hook her backwards and onto her feet, keeping her eyes on her surrounding as she did. She couldn't afford to look at her injury, but her left arm was burning up, with its twitching becoming harder and harder to ignore. If this kept up, it would be impossible for her to properly hold her dagger.

She flinched as something slammed from above her, pinning her onto the floor. How did it get *above* her? As the poison from its hands slowly worked to irritate her left shoulder, the thing uncloaked and she stared down the woman as it cackled maliciously, bits of spittle burning holes into her hoodie. As the thing's acid sizzled into her skin, Queenie flinched with pain, suppressing her grunts as her mind worked overtime.

The chimera's hands began to glow light blue, left hand on its stomach as the other firmly gripped Queenie's right shoulder. Suddenly, she felt her mind feel as though it were scattering and *merging*

315

with...something. It felt as though her rationality was being overridden by pure animalistic instinct. If she had protection against assimilation, Queenie imagined she would be safe. Unfortunately, she didn't have that luxury. Before she lost her mind, she screamed, stored the dagger from her left hand away and jumped into her storage, scrambling a few feet away before hopping out into the real world once more. The burning from her left hand had vanished, but was now completely numb as it stayed unresponsive to any of her thoughts. Her hoodie had blocked the poison from spreading to her right shoulder, but she had lost access to her left hand's fingers.

Down a hand, a quarter of her original soul remaining, and alone with no protection whatsoever. Many would simply crumple and despair at inevitable demise. However, Queenie *refused* to die a meaningless death. She took a deep breath and summoned chains to hoist her up to the sky, using her good arm to fling herself higher and higher. She she rose higher and higher, she summoned a sack of sand and scattered it around to the floor. It was momentary, but she saw a few grains of sand bounce and stick of the chimera, flying upwards to her location.

Sure. Why wouldn't it have wings? Why not?

After ensuring the thing was following her, Queenie summoned numerous chains to snag onto the chimera's legs. Though it stayed cloaked, she could feel its head tilt downwards as the woman looked at what was chaining her down. Taking advantage of her divided attention, Queenie summoned one more chain to wrap tightly around the thing's neck, securing it tightly into the air. Before the creature tore through her restraints, Queenie began to freefall towards the being, summoning a claymore as she used the momentum of gravity to accelerate her swing downwards onto the invisible being.

Surely enough, the heavy weapon tore through the thing's scales with relative difficulty, slicing off what felt like the chimera's arm. She let out a blood curdling scream as the two of them tumbled towards the ground. Queenie, exhausted from using all her soul, desperately summoned weak chains to try and slow her fall with minimal success. She crashed into the floor with killed momentum, groaning with pain as she struggled to stand back up. Her entire body ached, and she was certain she had broken a bone *somewhere*...though she wasn't sure where.

Queenie looked up at her opponent with exhausted eyes...blinking as she watched the lady stand up with ease. Well, that made sense: the thing supposedly had high muscle density along with scales: both probably acted to defend itself against the fall.

What she *didn't* expect was for the chimera to sprout out a new arm, coated in yellow poison. Sure, it didn't have as many scales...but the woman was flexing her arm casually, showing that its mobility hadn't died down whatsoever. What the f-

'*However, the things to be most wary of are the squid and lizard's traits.*'

Queenie cursed, forcing herself to hold a dagger with a trembling right hand. The thing had regeneration. Was it from the lizard? Sure, lizards could grow their tails back...but it would only discard the things as a last resort. Did the mutant have the same weaknesses, or was the drawbacks mitigated with its mutation?

Unmatched physicality. Sturdy defenses. Stealth. Flight. Poison and acid. To top it all off...regeneration. The chimera had no weaknesses. Queenie had no shot of winning. Still, she wouldn't go down without a fight. The female Misfit held up a trembling dagger to her opponent, an exhausted grin plastered on her twitching face. Hopefully, the others could stop it.

Suddenly, the woman's face morphed into something of disgust as she hissed, taking cautious steps backwards. Queenie raised an eyebrow at the sudden reaction. Why wa-

Juliette suddenly jumped out of the treetops with glowing eyes, slamming her brush into the mutant's head. The chimera roared with anger, stabbing her tail towards the Dancing Painter. Her mentor leaped backwards with grace, taking a defensive stance as she stared down the enemy.

From her sides, Taba and Hush emerged from different walkways, staring at the tired girl. Hush rushed to her side, kneeling at his sister's side. "We heard the thing scream. You ok?"

Queenie chuckled softly. "I'm alive, so maybe? Well...I don't know. The chimera is stupid strong." She nodded to Taba. "Do we have a shot of winning, big guy?"

Taba stared the thing with careful eyes. After a few seconds of silence, he slowly nodded. "Yeah. Let's go."

CHAPTER 18

His sister looked awful. She was covered in scrapes, her left hand was blotched red and twitching, hunched over at a crook, entire body was trembling, and her eyes were half-closed with exhaustion. Honestly, it was as if he were looking at a walking corpse, and that scared him. Still, he took a deep breath and carefully examined her face and body. She didn't seem to be weakening and was her condition was overall stable. Good.

"You should probably run." Hush said.

"No. Like hell I'm gonna flee." she said.

Taba nodded. "Queenie has the right idea. Splitting up is a bad idea against something as strong as this thing. She's most safe around us."

Hush pursed his lips. He had a point. Speaking of the chimera...Juliette was dancing around an empty field, her eyes flickering wildly as she flicked her brush wildly. Where was the chimera? Was it...

"It's just like I was worried about," Taba said with a frown. "The chimera can camouflage due the the ability of the squid."

"Squids can go invisible?" Hush asked.

He shook his head. "No, but some can camouflage as a defensive measure. If you focus, you can see a little shimmer around the chimera's edges as it moves around: it's probably what Juliette is tracking."

Surely enough, as Hush enhanced his eyesight with his blessing, he could see the chimera's outline darting around their mentor with frightening speeds. Though she was able to dodge and deflect all the blows, none of Juliette's attacks had the power to actively harm the mutant. Her glowing eyes narrowed as the screech of metal against scales rang through the air, the mutant being under constant attack from Juliette's blessing. However, the chimera's scales simply regenerated any chips and scuffs with no effort, locking them into a stalemate. No...the chimera was speeding up its attacks and was getting used to Juliette's movements. If this continued...

Hush flexed his fingers as he hunched to the ground. "We need to help her before she's overwhelmed."

Queenie grabbed his jacket with weakened fingers, wheezing as she did. "Wait. You should know what the thing is capable of, first." She then broke down all of the chimera's abilities. The more she spoke, the more bewildered Hush became. How was Queenie able to stall out such a creature for even a moment?

Taba, keeping his slightly darting eyes on the battlefield, nodded. "That's about what I expected. Good on you for staying alive for this long."

She chuckled softly, taking a knee as her head slightly swayed. "I would've done better, had I gotten protection. Oh well."

Hush tilted his head at his sister's odd comment. "Protected?"

Queenie tightened her lips, seemingly cursing a slipup. Hush noticed that Queenie's body did not have the light blue glow from the vial she had drunken earlier. "Hey. Where's your soul protection?"

She stared at the ground. Taba finally stopped staring at the fight and looked at Queenie with disbelief. "No. You didn't."

Hush felt his heartbeat rising in anticipation. There was only one answer that could explain the reactions from both Taba and Queenie. "Did...you *did* drink one of our soul vials...right?"

Queenie stared at him with an apologetic look. "Look. I-"

Taba cleared his throat loudly. "We'll talk later, *after* we all get out of this alive. For now, stick to taking Li-the *chimera* down." He nodded to Hush. "Enhance Juliette's sight. We're gonna dive in and do what we can to hinder it's movements."

"What about the poison?" Hush asked. "It'll get on us if it touches us."

Taba gestured to Hush with a reassuring nod. "You can use soul manipulation to protect yourself on top of the soul protection you already have. It isn't a foolproof defense, but it'll slow down the spread of the irritation."

"You want me to use my blessing on Juliette while also using soul manipulation on myself?" asked Hush. "I don't ha-"

"You can. I promise you."

Without elaborating further, Taba bolted towards the Dancing Painter with staggering speeds. Hush cursed and gave a hesitant glance to his sister. Queenie gave a soft nod, her half-closed eyes shining with fierce determination. With a heavy heart, he turned his head away from her and ran after his friend, flexing his fingers as he did.

Juliette was raining numerous invisible slashes on her opponent. However, the slashes only amounted to stalling out the chimera's endless onslaught. It was swooping around the sky, swinging off fences, and scampering across the floor in a translucent shimmer. Hush enhanced Juliette's sight, and instantly, the woman's strikes and counterattacks honed in with stronger accuracy. While invisible, the chimera hissed and spat out blobs of acid as a response. However, the attack amounted to nothing as the attack was minced into fine mist before it reached Juliette, fizzling out in the air.

Hush and Taba both circled the battlefield, unsure of how to truly step in between the two monsters. The wrong misstep would result in being turned into a red splatter or being dismantled with a single blow. Taba was the first to see an opening, diving in low to leg sweep one of the chimera's scampers. Though it barely amounted to causing the mutant to stumble for one second, Juliette took that opportunity to grip her brush with both arms and slash fiercely into the air. Though it appeared as if she had missed, the Misfits knew instantly that she had set up a devastating blow in that singular spot. Taba's move had provided them a win condition.

Now...if only they could trick the chimera into crossing that spot.

It noticed Juliette's move, and reemerged with a scowl plastered onto its misshapen face. The creature raised her arms and the party stared in bafflement as the chimera's arms began to expand to a cartoonish size. It was as though it-

Pufferfish. Gorilla and bear. Rattlesnake. Bombardier beetle.

Hush's eyes widened as he realized what was about to happen just a moment too late. Before he could yell out a warning to his allies, the thing slammed her fists into the ground, shattering the floor around them with shocking ease. As her arms collided with the pavement, spurts of venom and poison gushed out of its arm's pores, splattering indiscriminately throughout the air. As the party struggled to keep their footing while dodging the acidic venom flung everywhere, no one could afford to keep their eyes on the chimera.

Hush heightened his hearing to make up for where his eyes had failed. The older brother heard the subtle flutter of wings fly up to the sky across the sound of chaos. Ducking behind a crumbling building, he peeked up through a cracked window with fear gripping his heart.

The chimera hovered over them all, looking down with its numerous superior eyes. It unhinged her jaw and Hush watched with horror as it slowly began to grow a sticky ball within it's cracked jaw. He wasn't sure what the material was, but judging from the bright color, the bubbling texture, and the hissing sounds...it most likely wasn't good.

He turned to his friends to scream out a warning...and froze. Juliette was hunched over a stunned immobile Queenie. The Dancing Painter's kimono's back melted away to reveal her exposed muscles and spine. She struggled to stand up properly, using her brush as a impromptu cane, but with each step she took, blood spurted out of the Drunken Fox's back, forcing droplets of sweat to dribble down her neck. Taba lay on the floor, his leg bloodied and heavily wounded from the sudden strike. He was biting his left arm with enough force to pierce skin to muffle his screams, and held a dagger with his right arm with trembling determination.

Hush was the only one who had dodged the attack unscathed...but what could he do? The only one who could consistently keep up with the mutant's movements and attacks was now fatally injured. The

Misfit with the means to reach the chimera was wounded and drained. The Misfit who could create the most efficient plans was caught off guard and immobilized. How could a guy like him-

'Nah. You would've been fine. You would've saved us.'

Hush grit his teeth. They needed him more than ever. Who was he to turn down their expectations? The older brother would meet their trust...even if it killed him.

He darted out of his cover and used his blessing to partially blind the chimera. Surely enough, the only thing it could see was the darting man across the crumbling zoo. She turned away from his wounded friends and flew after him while continuing to form her attack.

Once he was a good enough distance away from the others, he turned back and tilted his head up to the sky. The thing was part bat, right?

Hush enhanced the creature's hearing, used soul manipulation to enhance his vocal cords, took a deep breath, and roared with murderous intent. Instantly, the chimera flinched, relaxed her jaw, and clutched her ears with a wail, stumbling slightly in the air as she did. In her moment of weakening, the mutant's attack fell to the ground, losing its shape as it did. With the ball's size...no doubt Hush would be caught in its splash radius. However, the others would be fine. He had no regrets.

And yet...as the yellowish-orange ball fell from the heavens, a boom range out and the chimera's attack exploded into a grand splatter midair, intercepted by...something. Hush turned his head to the direction of the sound and saw his sister, half conscious on the floor, having opened a window to her storage with her free hand to summon a cannon to launch a cannonball in the thing's direction. Even on death's door, his sister never missed her shots. What an idiot, he would have to yell at her later for doing something so risky.

While the tiny blobs of poison rained from the sky, Hush quickly used soul manipulation to guard his body. Despite it all, he winced as numerous acid pellets dripped on his skin, burning him with each patter. Right after the last bit of toxin fell from the sky, the chimera thumped onto the ground with a screeching groan. As she lifted her head with rage, Hush's heart stopped as he locked eyes with all sixteen of her eyeballs. This was how he di-

Suddenly, with shocking speed, Taba roared as he jumped onto the chimera's back, using both his hands to slam his dagger into one of her left eyes. She screamed in agony, flailing wildly to buck the teenager off. Despite being down one leg, Taba hung on for dear life as he locked eyes with Hush. The older brother had no idea what Taba wanted...but his friend needed help. So, with a heavily wounded body, Hush hastily limped over to the beast.

The thing yelled in defiance, flexed its tail and stabbed towards Hush. He stumbled sideways in a pathetic attempt to dodge, turning a fatal heart stab into one that pierced his lung. Using her tail as a rope, he pulled himself closer and closer to the beast, while gripping tightly to ensure she couldn't escape. Hush could feel a burning liquid fill up his lungs: he didn't have much time before he collapsed.

Once he got up close to the chimera, he used his blessing to scream loudly once more into the creature's ears, causing her to instinctively cry and clasp the sides of her head with both her arms. Using that moment of weakness, he forcefully plucked its tail from his chest, grabbed the thing's slimy tongue, and used his entire body weight to fling her as far as he could before the poison in his body completely paralyzed him.

As he collapsed onto the floor, he fixed his twitching eyes towards the tumbling duo. They were flung a few meters away, stumbling around as the chimera both tried to upright itself and remove the dagger from its eyeball. As Hush's throw began to lose momentum, Taba saw an opportunity, using his good leg and both his arms to push upwards from the ground, flinging the creature a few more meters down the road.

As it tumbled down the pavement, she quickly got up, faced the two guys with dripping malice-

...And Linda's rage turned into shock as her head suddenly separated from her shoulders, the sound of a metallic slash ringing through the air as Juliette's previous decisive slash hit its target true.

The body trembled as it tried to stand back up once more, but hundreds of powerful slashes suddenly obliterated the chimera's body. While whole, the creature could have easily regenerated from such blows...but without a head? The mutant's regeneration struggled to keep up, and eventually, chunks of lifeless meat slapped onto the floor.

Linda's misshapen head lay on the floor, her numerous eyes watering...and that was all Hush could remember before blacking out.

...

Her firm hands gripped the brush with ferocity, taking quick breaths as she did. Juliette wobbled slightly as she leaned against her weapon, her simmering back stinging against the cool breeze. She pushed her makeshift cane forwards slightly to take another step, pulses and spurts of agony splashing out her back as she did.

Queenie, that damned idiot, decided it would be a good idea to use her blessing while having nothing in her well. Taba, though completely covered in rashes and splotches, was conscious. Though he seemed unable to move from his position, his eyes were slowly looking around as to see the aftermath of the fight.

Juliette's biggest worry was Hush. The guy had taken a direct hit from the chimera's stinger, and judging from how the boy's shirt was slowly staining red...he was being either poisoned or burned as she stood around...doing nothing. So, she dragged her legs forward, grit her teeth, and endured the agony that followed with each twitch.

The chimera's head lay behind her...but Juliette couldn't afford to give the thing attention. It was obviously on its last legs, crying in frustration. How a beast could understand emotions any extent was beyond her, but soon the thing would bleed out and die.

A whisper suddenly rained around the broken zoo as a soft drizzle suddenly sprinkled the area. Though the Dancing Painter was over-all indifferent about rain, this timing couldn't have come at a worse time. Each droplet stung her back, exposed nerves crashing against the unforgiving chill of the rain. Juliette by no means had weak pain tolerance, yet even she couldn't help but wince and crumble to her knees after only a few splashes of water.

As pain continued to ring throughout her body, she desperately wished to pass out. However, doing so would nearly guarantee that each of the Misfits would die. Sure, she owed them nothing. Sure, they were enemies. Sure, they even *threatened* her at times. Despite it all, she couldn't willingly abandon the brats: she saw too much of herself in them. Hell, she saw too much of *Sana* in them...and Juliette felt as though failing these kids would be the same as betraying her friend's trust. So, she white-knuckled her brush and widened her drooping eyes, forcing adrenaline to pump through her exhausted body.

It was a good thing that she forced herself to stay awake. Had she passed out, she would have missed *his* entrance.

The first sign of *him* was the entire soul bubble surrounding them...popping. No, it didn't pop: it was as though the entire barrier converged into a single point. The second sign was the sudden tailwind that appeared as *he* stepped down onto the zoo. This wasn't teleportation or superhuman speed, no. It was as though *he* had flung himself and caught himself with his own soul.

The last sign? The chill that ran through her exposed spine. She had clashed with mutants and soulbearers alike. Hell, she had fought *wars*. And yet...none of these events made her shudder as *his* presence did.

The man knelt down at Hush's level, putting his hand on the Misfit's chest. Suddenly, a wave of light blue coursed through the unconscious man, the sudden energy causing Hush's body to jerk and jolt with vigor and his skin slowly turned back to a normal hue. The man stood up, not even addressing Juliette, and then...he *appeared* at where Queenie lay. He did the same to her, and just like with her older brother, she too began to regain color and stabilize her breathing.

The man turned to the last Misfit member-and stopped. He sighed, smiling softly as he did.

"Taba. You're pushing yourself. Lay down."

Juliette turned her neck and stared in dumbfounded awe at the heavily injured boy standing upwards with an unnatural twist in his posture. Taba was wheezing with what sounded like a collapsed lung, doing what he could to...show respect?

Taba tried to raise his arm, but the effort proved to be too much, causing him to groan and fall to a knee. The boy spat up crimson saliva and looked back up at the man with determined eyes.

"Hey, Dad."

Upon hearing those words, Juliette's eyes glowed blue once more. She didn't give a *damn* if she had ascended already or that she was heavily injured. If the man standing in front of her was the head of Taba's Family...then she had a duty to see him dead.

The Dancing Painter leap into the air, her eyes twitching as her heart thumped at dangerous speeds. She slammed the brush down at where the man stood, aiming to split his skull vertically. The Father, in turn, ducked out of the way and counterattacked with a palm strike to her side. The blow caused a surge of agony throughout her body, yet she bit her lip hard enough to sprout blood, landed on both her feet, dashing forwards once more.

She swung her brush in rapid motions, mixing up a combination of front slashes, thrusts, and sweeps. Each blow was promptly side-stepped with frustrating ease. Furthermore, the Father wasn't crossing over onto her memories, making her echoes useless. Juliette grit her teeth, pushing past her pain to fling her brush's bristles onto the man's waist. He simply stopped it with his hand and stared at her with a familiar, yet rare, expression.

Juliette's eyes widened. It was the *same* expression Sana wore when fighting someone tremendously inferior to her. However, it wasn't an expression of mockery or arrogance. No, his eyes were kind, sympathetic. As he casually swatted away all of her lethal blows, the Father's eyes remained compassionate with his mouth tightened into a sad frown. It was as though he were simply trying to see things from her perspective, or withstanding the flailing of a toddler.

Suddenly, she let go of her brush and slammed into his chest with both her arms. The Father stumbled back a few steps into one of her memories. Once he crossed her blessing, Juliette replayed the memory and echoed it endlessly, determined to cut him in half.

The sound of metal screeching cried against the rainy atmosphere. The Father stumbled out from the attack, grabbing his bleeding abdomen with a gasp. She wasn't sure *how* he wasn't dead after that attack...but he bled. He could die. Juliette put pressure on her legs, determined to use soul manipulation to close their gap to end the fight in one swift strike-

...and her eyes fizzled out as she slammed facedown into the floor.

No. Once more. I can...do...

She lifted her head, yet her body and soul refused to ascend any more. Her body was undergoing autonomic body shutdown, her senses shutting off one after the other in a desperate attempt to survive. First was her ability to feel, then her hearing, then her sight. Even her lungs threatened to stop breathing in an attempt to save energy to stay alive for just *one* more second.

As her consciousness drifted away, all the Drunken Fox could think was how comfortable death felt.

CHAPTER 19

T aba stared blankly at the fight that unfolded before him. Dad was still a superior fighter, yet he was astonished at how fluidly Juliette moved despite being so heavily wounded. His shock grew even further when she was able to land a blow against Dad with her blessing. Sure, he wasn't trying too hard...but all factors considered, his mentor was putting up a shockingly good fight.

But of course...she was wounded and drained. Shortly after injuring Dad, Juliette collapsed, her body quickly growing still on the wet floor. Witnessing this, Dad turned to him while clutching his stomach.

Though his entire body stung with poison and exhaustion, he winced at the sight of the cut. "You...should heal up."

Dad opted to reach inside of his pockets to pull out a roll of gauze, opting to hastily cover the wound with a sloppy roll of bandages. "It's fine. I'll hold out till I get home and see if Nancy can patch me up."

"She's alive?"

"Yeah. Refused my help though and chose to stubbornly heal herself. She's...well, we knew she isn't the type to willingly lean on someone."

Dad stepped next to him, kneeling so they were at eye level. He put his hand on Taba's head and a wave of soul suddenly flooded into the teenager, causing him to twitch unpredictably as his well slowly began filling up. Slowly, his body began to repair itself in response to this surge of energy. After a few seconds, he shoved Dad away with a concerned glance to Juliette's lifeless body.

"Can you do the same to her?"

Dad hesitated but nodded. He closed the gap in one step and slowly began to fill her well. Her body didn't twitch and convulse as the Misfit's bodies did, but seeing her slowly breath once more filled him with relief. Sure, it seemed as though she took *very* shallow breaths...but better than being still on the floor.

He stood up from her cold body with concern in his eyes. "She's alive...but barely. If she decides to give up on staying alive, she's gone."

Taba struggled up to his feet, wincing as he did. He hadn't fully healed, but he could stand up with enough effort. "You can't give her more soul?"

"I'm only giving her soul and sparing her as appreciation for shielding Queenie," Dad said with a frown. "Whether or not she chooses to live is on her."

"Harsh, but fair...I guess."

Suddenly, the two of them heard the shuffle of feet against puddles behind them. They turned around to see a disgruntled man stare at Linda's crying head on the floor.

"...Linda."

Glen held her head in his arms, softly cradling it in his body, ignoring the poison that slowly spread through his hands. She cried into his chest while instinctively trying to bite his stomach at the same time with minor effect. Dad said nothing as he slowly approached the two, kneeling in front of him. He exchanged a few whispers to the broken scientist, who hesitated and responded by hugging her head more tightly. After a few minutes, Glen sobbed as he gave the chimera's head up with trembling hands. Dad stared at her crying eyes with sorrowful sympathy, placing his hand over her forehead's eyes.

"I'm sorry it took so long, Linda. Thank you."

The chimera closed her eyes, trickles of crimson tears escaping each eyeball as the head glowed faintly blue. After a few moments, the head fizzled away into pure soul along with the chunks of her body that lay scattered across the abandoned zoo. The spray of soul seeped into Dad, his body glowing slightly as he did.

As Dad stood up, Glen grabbed the older man's sleeves. "Please. Me too."

Dad stared at the broken scientist with sorrowful eyes, shaking his head. "Not now, no. Let time pass. If you still feel the same after a few weeks, I'll do it...but not while you're distraught."

Glen balled up his fists, screaming into the pouring rain as he stood up, punching Dad squarely in the jaw. The older man stumbled back into the pavement as Glen awkwardly tackled into him, flailing wildly as he did. Dad did nothing to block the hits, simply allowing the wailing scientist to let out his sorrows. Despite Dad's stomach wound slowly getting more and more irritated, he did nothing but took the beating with no resistance.

After a minute of the pathetic display, Dad simply sat up and hugged the scientist quietly. "Let's go home. People miss you, Glen."

Dad stood up, leaving Glen on the floor, and stared at Taba with a firm stare. "What will you do, son?"

Taba hesitated, waving him closer. Dad raised an eyebrow, but walked closer while wiping his bloodied nose. Once within earshot, Taba leaned in slightly and spoke with a raised whisper. "Was the whole point of the chimera to absorb its soul?"

Dad sighed but softly nodded. "Yeah, kind of...but it was something that was in the works for a while. I needed a way to relieve Linda without using too much soul and take down Glen's barriers. Figured using Malapace was the best solution for all this, since it would minimize the risk for the Family."

"But...that implies that we would be able to take down the thing, and we all nearly died," said Taba. "No, we *would've* died if you hadn't shown up. Why were you so certain we could pull this off?"

Dad smiled and ruffled his hair. "Because I trust you. I know what you're capable of. That's all."

"Well, we weren't strong enough to take the Gatekeepers down though."

"...and I told you that. Who was the idiot to try anyways?"

"My blessing said we could win."

Dad grabbed Taba's shoulders firmly, frowning as he did. "Son. What your blessing defines as victory is *not* what *you* define as victory. Would you truly feel satisfied if you could win, if it meant sacrificing both Queenie and Hush?"

"...no."

"Exactly. That's why I said to not engage. Yes, you would win...but those two would die. I wanted to wait a few years to plan out a full scale war...but not much we can do about this. The question now is...what will you do? Will you come back home with Queenie and Hush? Or do you wish to stay at Malapace?" asked Dad.

334

Taba hesitated. He was absolutely still loyal to his Family...but if that were the case, why did he hesitate? His gut wanted to know more about Malapace and its people. The Gatekeepers, Juliette, the Overseer...everyone. Had they been mindlessly selfish villains, he would return home. However, his few months of stay had proven that they were simply humans living their own lives. Taba couldn't turn his back on that fact.

"Let me stay at Malapace...for a little while longer, anyways." Taba said.

Dad's eyes wrinkled softly, a look of understanding washing over his face. "I see. The reason?"

He released a shaky breath. "I...don't really have a good one. It's just a gut instinct telling me I would regret going home now. I think it's the same with Queenie and Hush."

Dad lifted his arm...and ruffled the teenager's hair some more. "Figured you would say that. Keep the siblings safe, alright? They can get reckless without your guidance: especially Queenie. Hush tends to overexert himself, so keep an eye out for that too. Oh, also, don't stay up too late. Make sure you sleep in from time to time, ok? You don't need to work out *every* morning." He wrapped Taba up in a tight hug, the older man's stomach wound slowly dripping blood onto Taba's chest. "Proud of you, son. Stay safe."

Taba blinked moist eyes away. "Love you, Dad."

"Love you too, son. Stay put, help will come."

He stepped away and went back to Glen as he wiped his face, picking the scientist up. He waved a farewell to Taba, and the two men faded away into the woods.

...

Taba stayed put for approximately eight hours, but it felt as though weeks had passed as he glanced at his team with concern. Queenie and Hush seemed to be in a much more stable condition as they dozed off, but Juliette seemed to have gotten a virus, her face turned feverish as her breaths became even more shallow than they were. Well, it was likely she had been infected: a lack of skin on her back would do that. During his wait, he walked around the abandoned zoo to see if he could salvage anything to help his friends rest up more comfortably. However, all he was able to find was a slightly deflated rubber wheel inside one of the enclosures, as well as a raggedy blanket in a gift shop. He carried Hush and placed him next to his sister, then rested their heads on each side of the wheel. Taba then draped the blanket over Juliette's exposed back and winced as her unconscious face morphed into one of discomfort.

Once he had done all he could, he rested on a tree stump and stared at the rain droplets that poured from the sky. He had already dragged his party under some tents so they would be sheltered from the rain. Taba stared at his exposed leg, flinching as he tried to flex it back and forth. During the fight, he had made a massive miscalculation with his blessing. He was subconsciously thinking with multiple parts of his body, but had foolishly ignored his soulwell since he figured the soul used wouldn't be an issue. That led to him suddenly running out of soul, causing him to stumble at a wrong time. Why did automatically using his blessing drain his soul much more than when he manually used it? It was something he needed t-

Boy.

Taba flinched. There was no mistaking that he had "heard" something...and it was under the same tone as his normal questioning. However...wha-

Nineteen years, and you finally understand how to use your blessing. Be better, boy.

"What the hell? Who...?"

However, he was met with silence. Taba wasn't sure what the hell had just happened. All he knew was that something regarding his blessing had reached out to him for the first time in his life. If he had the soul, Taba would be rapidly asking questions about the sudden event. Shame his well was tapped out at the moment. Oh well, this would just have to be a fun sideproject on his own time.

He stared as raindrops dripped of the browning leaves above him and simply waited. After a while, he heard the pitter of footsteps in the pavement down the road. He peeked his head out and saw a familiar bald man run towards him.

Taba got up with a wince and waved at the Gatekeeper. "Hey G. Over here."

The bald man stopped in front of the Misfit, taking deep breaths as he did. He took a deep breath to slow his heartrate down before nodding. "Cool. Where's Julie?"

"In there with Queenie and Hush."

G turned on his heel and ran into the tent, with Taba following with a slight trot. Pushing aside the tent flaps, he saw the Gatekeeper kneeling in front of Juliette, muttering something as he clasped his hands together with his back turned to the questioner. Taba frowned: he didn't take G as a religious man, and yet the man continued to speak in hushed mumbles. After a few minutes of whispers, Taba stared in awe as the natural complexion returned to Juliette's face.

She still looked weary and hadn't yet roused, so G simply scooped her up onto his back, nodding to Taba. "Can you grab your friends?"

"No. I'm pretty weak right now." said Taba.

"Damn right you're weak" G grumbled. "Whatever." He put the weakened mentor down and stretched his neck. "Well, nothing we can do but wait for the cart. Now, tell me...what the hell happened? Was the chimera that strong?"

"Well...yeah, but...no, yeah. The chimera was that strong."

Taba considered telling G about Dad, but there was no point. It didn't benefit the Family. G shrugged silently and the two of them sat under the muffled patter of rain. Surely enough, after some time had passed they heard the rattle of a wooden cart outside their tent. G hopped to his feet while also scooping up Juliette, peeking outside and waving someone over. Taba got up and limped over to the entrance to see a worried Sana dash over to the Misfit.

She grabbed his face and sharply turned in around as concern flooded her eyes. "Oh. Oh no. Are you ok? How are you feeling? Are yo-"

G patted Sana's shoulder, causing her to glance over at her fellow Gatekeeper with annoyance. However, upon seeing who he was carrying, the blood drained from her face.

"The kid's ok. Julie, however..."

Sana poked the unconscious woman's cheek with trembling fingertips. "She...she's burning up. Is she...?"

G pushed past her and strolled over to the cart. "She's not good, but she's stable at least. We need to have her rest up in Malapace. Go grab the other brats."

She looked at the bald man with mild confusion before her eyes widened, darting into the tent to look at the other Misfits sleeping soundly on the floor. She quickly put her cool hand on both of their foreheads, her lips pursing slightly as she did. "Not...*as* hot, but still warm."

She scooped the two of them up with each of her arms and nodded to Taba. "I'm glad you're all ok...but what happened? Was the chimera that strong?"

"Yeah."

She raised an eyebrow and Taba cursed. She could probably tell he was lying, or at least that he was omitting information. Still, the Gatekeeper didn't push the subject further and simply pushed out of the tent and climbed onto the wagon, gently placing the siblings on cotton coated bench. Taba climbed in after her and glanced around the wagon bed with confusion. "Where's G?"

Sana nodded to the front, revealing that the bald man was pulling the wagon with his own strength. With a deep breath, the Gatekeeper pushed at the wagon and slowly broke out into a light sprint, pulling the reins with shocking speeds. It was slightly more bumpy than if a horse were pulling them along, yet *much* more faster.

Taba gripped his seat and tried to resist the motion sickness for as long as he could as Sana cradled Juliette's head while stroking the backs of the siblings. She gave a tight smile to the wobbling boy. "Try to get comfortable. It's a long trip back to Malapace."

...

339

While lugging them along like nothing, G ran for six hours straight. Occasionally a mutant would be lurking in the underbrush, but Sana would hop out of the cart, quickly dispatch the creature out of sight, then chase after the cart to hop back in without too much concern or worry. As Taba's brain rattled the entire ride, he couldn't help but feel a bit frustrated at her lack of concern. The three Misfits struggled against one mutant frog while the female Gatekeeper was casually swatting numerous mutants away with not so much as an afterthought. Was the gap between them that massive?

G only slowed his pace down once the grand view of the city's walls loomed over the trees. After a few more minutes of trotting, he let go of the reins with a groan, stretching his shoulders widely as he did. Taba took wobbly steps off the wooden wagon, stumbling slightly as his feet touched stable ground for the first time in hours. Sana hopped off the ride carrying each sibling under each arm, being careful as to not disturb their slumber. She gestured to G, who rolled his eyes to grab the feverish Juliette from the wagon bed.

Before they could enter Malapace, the third Gatekeeper met them, giving a nod to the others. "Yo."

Patchy raised an eyebrow at the unconscious Juliette. "Oh damn. Babs wasn't lying?"

"No, but why are you here?"

He shrugged. "Can't a guy welcome his friends home?"

G and Sana stared at him blankly, causing an awkward air of silence between them all. After a few seconds, he sighed and waved his hand. "Fine, it's because theres a crowd of people behind the gates waiting for your return and I figured it wouldn't look good if the fabled 'Dancing Painter' returned unconscious and covered in wounds."

Sana smiled. "There we go. Now, was that so hard?"

Patchy...pouted? "Hey, you act like I wasn't worried about you guys."

"Piss off," snapped G. "Now, how are we getting inside? Julie needs to be looked at."

The scraggly man smiled, his eyes slowly glowing as he held out his arms. The other Gatekeepers walked over to grab onto him, and an unsure Taba followed suit. The second he latched on, the scene around them changed as they appeared in what appeared to be a bedroom. G set down Juliette down on the bed with her back facing upwards and nodded to the others. "Alright, you guys get out: I need to give her medicine and treatment."

"The pill won't work?" asked Taba. "It's worked before."

The bald man stared at him silently, his eyes twitching as he did. "Well, Ima give her the pill, but its gotta be injected you nimrod. I don't think Julie would want an audience for that, right? So...scram."

Sana put down the siblings gently in different cots, smiling warmly to G as she did. "Look over these guys too, ok?"

He scowled but turned back to them with a dismissive wave. Patchy, Sana, and Taba exited the room quietly and looked around. Taba took note of the scenery with a frown. "Shouldn't I be resting up too? I'm not exactly fully recovered."

"If you were conscious for the entire cart ride, I think you're recovered enough," Sana said. "Babs wants to talk to you, lets go."

The three of them trekked through the city, with cheers and chattering whenever a citizen recognized the Gatekeepers. Sana would politely acknowledge them with warm smiles and waves while Patchy ignored them dismissively. A few merchants and soulbearers seemed to recognize Taba with hushed whispers and pointing. He wasn't sure *where* they knew him from: maybe it was from the bracket tournament. Whatever, he didn't really care: let them spread rumors.

After a while of cheers and jeers, they eventually reached the town hall. Tabitha looked up from her paperwork and greeted them with a big wave and smile. "Hey guys! The Overseer is wai-"

Patchy walked down the hallway without as much as an acknowledgement. Tabitha's brow wrinkled in slight frustration as Sana gave slight apologetic bows. Patchy kicked down Babs's door and revealed a table set up with three teacups, the fourth teacup being sipped by the Overseer herself. Upon their entrance, she nodded while daintily holding her cup. "Welcome back, child. Tea?"

The three of them took their spots and slowly began to take cautious sips of their drink. For Taba, the tea tasted closer to warm water, but he took small sips to show respect. After a few silent sips, Babs nodded to Taba. "So, boy. How was it?"

"You're...uh...are you talking about the tea?"

The blind woman tilted her head with a small grin. "Sure, why not?"

"It's...nice. Thank you."

She chuckled as she placed her teacup down. "Lying isn't your strong suit, is it? But no, how did you feel about the chimera? Any...developments?"

For some reason, it felt like the elderly woman's white pupils stared through his entire existence, as though she knew everything. Still, he didn't feel like sharing their encounter with Dad in front of the Gatekeepers. "Well, the thing was tough. We barely scraped by, and most of that was because Juliette was doing the heavy lifting."

"I know, I saw her fight. The 'connection' was a bit fuzzy, but I'm proud of what she was able to do." Babs said with a pained smile.

"Wait...did y-"

Sana took one more sip of tea, cleared her throat, and got up. "Me and Patchy should check in on G. Later, Babs."

The elderly woman scowled. "My name isn't Babs, you dam-"

Patchy grabbed Sana and the two of them vanished before Babs could finish her statement. She sighed and leaned back on her hands. "Those two take years off my life, I swear. Anyways..." She stretched and leaned on the table with a crooked smile. "Yes, boy. I saw it all. I saw 'Dad'. Well, at least until Juliette went unconscious."

For some reason, Taba felt a bit relieved but he wasn't sure why. "Well, he didn't really do anything to help against the chimera. He was just there-"

"...to absorb Linda's soul?"

He stared at her, stunned. "How...how do y-"

Babs downed the rest of her tea before dabbing at her mouth with a napkin. "I had a hunch when you began talking about your 'Father'. The two of us go *back*."

He hesitated, his skin suddenly feeling uncomfortable. How much did she know? "If you're trying to interrogate me, I don't plan on saying anything."

Babs shook her head as she poured another cup of tea. "Nah, I have an idea of what he wants, anyways. I won't ask meaningless questions." She took a small sip, her blind eyes staring aimlessly at her teacup, hesitating slightly as she did. "Is...is he doing ok? Is he eating well? Did it look as though he were getting enough sleep?"

343

The following questions caught the stunned Taba even further off-guard, so much so that he couldn't help but answer with blank honesty. "...Dad's always skimped out on food and sleep. He keeps prioritizing the Family over his own wellbeing. Everyone keeps trying to feed him or doing his tasks so he has time to sleep, but Dad keeps finding other things to keep him busy. He seemed more stressed and tired when he showed up at the zoo."

The Overseer sighed softly. "Yeah, that sounds like him. Damn idiot."

Normally, Taba would dislike others badmouthing Dad, yet coming from Babs? He was fine with it...hell, it almost felt like a weird level of respect. The two of them sipped the bland tea for twenty minutes in silence. Taba was curious on their relationship, but he had no soul. Hell, even if he *had* the soul to ask, it didn't feel right to intrude onto the Overseer's business...as odd as that seemed. Objectively, it was smarter to know more about Babs...but his gut told him to not peer into her history.

What...was "right"? Taba found the line between "right" and "wrong" blending more and more with passing day in Malapace. Could two opposing sides be correct? Was one side "more" right than the other? What should he do? All Taba could do was sip tea and pray war never came. It would come...it was inevitable.

And yet, Taba prayed regardless.

About the Author

S eon Jung has *always* loved fantasy. He's adored diving into different stories, exploring their worlds, and theorycrafting numerous
"what if"s for different abilities, lores, and so on. It's this admiration
that's nurtured his curiosity and imagination from a young age. One
day...he decided to share his world with earnest hopes to spark that
excitement of fantasy in others. He truly thanks you, the reader, for
the time you've spent indulging him!

Seon spends his time writing, worrying about his car's 'check-en-
gine' light, playing games of all kinds, and loving God. He believes that
there is a fine balance of formality and goofiness that humans should
strive to balance, and that everyone should "know when to lock in,
and when to be a goober".